FLEABAG

FLEABAG

– BOOK 1 –

SOMEONETOFORGET

Podium

Published in 2023 by Podium Publishing, ULC
www.podiumaudio.com

FLEABAG

In the lower reaches of the Bone Pits, under a hundred different bridges, pulleys, pipes, and walkways of steel, a solitary form lay limp on its side, breathing slow and heavy.

Its fur, once remembered in fading memories as a light shade of gray, was now a sickly sheen of green and black, matted and glued together in squishy clumps by the toxic sludge it'd trudged through to find something to eat.

Its eyes, a beautiful shade of hazel gold, were hazy and unfocused like faded glass. One of its ears was stuck flat to the top of its head by dried waste, and the other was twitching around, trying futilely to listen out for predators. Pus and brown-green chemical sludge would occasionally drip out of said ear, down its neck, and puddle on the floor one viscous drop at a time.

Its muzzle was marred by thin lined scars, infected and trying to scab over. Its nose was dry, unusable, unable to smell anything but the burning stench of waste and acid. Its lungs burned with every breath as if scrubbed with sandpaper. Fleas and ticks marred its numb body, draining it of life one day at a time.

An adventurous rat about the size of the canine's leg wandered closer, curiously sniffing at a hind paw. It opened its maw, ready to try and chew through skin—

And then a siren blared out from above, red light flooding the small corner, and the rats gathering around the canine's limp form scattered, squeaking as they dived in rusty pipes or squeezed between shifting pulleys.

The red light shone down, illuminating the canine's slowly shifting ribs and angular, starved frame. The animal moved a little, struggling to lift its head. Slowly, sluggishly, it rolled onto its belly, legs still limp under its body. Despite the incoming danger, it could barely muster enough strength in its cannibalized muscles to position its legs under its torso.

The thunderous booming of machinery and gears grew closer, and the canine slowly managed to lift itself up, legs shaking like twigs about to snap under pressure.

Slow, jerky steps carried it up the stone steps one at a time as the sounds of rushing liquid and shifting gears echoed down the tunnel. Mere moments after it dragged itself up the steps, a big portion of the metal walls in the back and front of the room slid upward, a veritable tide of factory and two-legger waste rushing past, a river of filth.

The canine didn't turn, stumbling forth as pipes, latticework steel walkways over sheer drops hundreds of meters deep, and cobbled alleys flitted past in a fugue.

It was dying. It knew.

Too weak to hunt for food. Too weak to take it from others.

So it stumbled forth, a dragging specter of fur, skin, and bone. One paw after another, eyes blurry with tears. It was too weak to hold its neck up, snout almost touching the ground.

Green-gray smog covered everything around it as it walked, the factories above all venting their fumes into the pits, the smell forever etched into its sensitive nose. It might have been stumbling toward the unknown for minutes. Might have been days. It couldn't tell. Eventually, the smog was left behind, and the orange-red artificial lights of the pits were exchanged for the soft yellow of light crystals.

It simply followed the sound of life, not wanting to die alone.

It walked until its shaking legs could take no more, and it stumbled before collapsing on its side.

Sounds filled its ear and movement filled its eyes, incomprehensible, directionless. It was too exhausted and lost to process anything.

As a two-legger walked through the alley, he paused and moved his foot to slowly wedge under the canine's frame, lifting its body effortlessly and quickly shoving it aside to lie against the alley wall. The two-legger shook his foot in disgust, then turned away.

"Fuckin' fleabags everywhere . . ."

His footsteps faded.

Time passed.

People walked past it by the dozens, sparing it nothing more than a pitying glance at best; a disgusted grimace at worst.

Unconsciousness consumed it.

When it woke up, the streets were emptier, shady figures in cloaks and metal face masks being the only occasional passersby.

It didn't move. It barely even breathed, uncomprehending eyes staring at the gray, squeaking creature sniffing at its snout.

A pang of pain shot through it as the tiny mouse decided to start its feast from its nose, and its malnourished jaws reflexively snapped open and shut with strength and speed borne of desperation, rage, and fear.

For a few moments, the canine sat in silence as it kept its jaws clenched with whatever meager power it could muster, its taste buds too burned through to recognize the taste of copper as the mouse squirmed and twitched between its canines one last time.

Slowly, lethargically, the canine struggled to its feet, leaning liberally on the cobbled wall to its side. With great effort, it tilted its head back and swallowed its first ever kill like a snake, not bothering to chew.

No sooner had gravity adequately assisted its weak muscles in moving its prey into its stomach did it let its legs fold out from under it, sliding back down on its side against the wall.

Its eyes fluttered shut, ready to fall into another exhausted nap.

Without warning, it felt something shift and unlock inside its mind with an almost physical sensation. Startled, its eyes shot open as it tried to get up, legs flailing and sliding across the ground for a moment as they buckled under its own weight, its body only rising an inch or two.

It stopped quickly and sat on the ground, swerving its head back and forth, eyes darting around the abandoned alleyway. After several moments of nothing, it relaxed.

Somewhere in the back of its mind, like a task put on hold or an errant thought saved for later, something waited. Yet, as much as the canine focused, it could not grasp the thought nor understand where it'd come from.

The short burst of adrenaline faded, and with it, most of its energy. A wave of dizziness turned its mind to fuzz, and as it placed its head on the ground, its eyes slid shut once more, hoping it wouldn't be the last time they did so.

-System Access Requirement Reached.
\\ Minimum Intelligence Threshold Reached.
\\ Secondary System Communication Method Activated.
\\ Language: Carmeran
\\ Initializing . . .

-Species: Wolf
-Name: None

-Racial Skills: [Pack Hunter], [Quick Learner], [Devourer]
-Acquired Skills:
You have gained the Skill [Pain Resistance – Level 1]
You have gained the Skill [Infection Resistance – Level 1]
You have gained the Skill [Poison Resistance – Level 1]
You have gained the Skill [Corrosion Resistance – Level 1]
You have gained the Skill [Disease Resistance – Level 1]
You have gained the Skill [Restful Awareness – Level 1]
You have gained the Skill [Tough Skin – Level 1]
You have gained the Skill [Iron Stomach – Level 1]
You have gained the Skill [Magic Resistance – Level 1]
[Pain Resistance] has Leveled Up. Level 1 → Level 17
[Infection Resistance] has Leveled Up. Level 1 → Level 7
[Poison Resistance] has Leveled Up. Level 1 → Level 12
[Corrosion Resistance] has Leveled Up. Level 1 → Level 4
[Disease Resistance] has Leveled Up. Level 1 → Level 4
[Restful Awareness] has Leveled Up. Level 1 → Level 2
[Tough Skin] has Leveled Up. Level 1 → Level 2
[Iron Stomach] has Leveled Up. Level 1 → Level 3
[Magic Resistance] has Leveled Up. Level 1 → Level 4

-Acquired Traits:
Enduring (1/5): You have felt the chill of death multiple times and sur-
vived. You are slightly tougher.

CHAPTER 1

The Great Tower rang once, the deep sound reverberating downward through miles and miles of haphazard iron architecture, reaching even the deepest reaches of the Bone Pits.

The wolf's crusted eyes slowly opened at the sound after a moment of straining, much to its own surprise, and for a moment, it simply lay there, unsure of what to do. Its imminent death was something it had seen as a fact, yet now, it felt better than it had in months. Pain still wracked its body, but it was faded, distant. Rather than each breath sapping its willpower with the searing agony of all its wounds, it was just . . . a mild ache.

Its breaths came easier, its thoughts were clearer, and the countless fleas and ticks that had attached themselves to it seemed to be having a harder time than usual tormenting it.

Out of curiosity, it shuffled its paws under its chest as best as it could—and pushed.

Besides a tremor running through its weak legs, they surprisingly obeyed. Moving them still felt more like commanding straining tendons rather than even a single shred of muscle, but it walked on regardless, confused yet cautiously optimistic at the sudden improvements it felt.

For a while, it simply followed the sound of nightlife with its single functioning ear, hoping it would run into some half-rotten garbage that no two-legger would eat. Odd barks, strangled grumbles, and melodious howls littered the more open and lively areas, dozens of two-leggers packed tight in buildings reeking of both poison and food at once.

Then, out of the corner of its eye, it spotted a flicker of movement in the shadows of an alley to its right, barely wide enough for a two-legger to walk through comfortably, with looming metal walls on both sides and about as long as two two-leggers were tall. It seemed to be little more than an architectural mistake, in the corner of which was a tiny dark spot on the ground that moved and twitched with movements so small it was nigh imperceptible.

It stopped, its ear straightening as it tilted its head.

Deciding that something that was so much smaller than even itself might be a good prey, it cautiously stalked forward, lowering its head and going even slower than it already had. The shadow of the sphere lights outside receded as the darkness embraced its gaunt form.

Only a couple meters away now from the small dark mass on the ground, the wolf recognized a familiar scene; one that it'd had many scraps with other strays over when it had woken up in the pits for the first time, having no memories of anything but basic concepts and definitions in its head.

A mouse lay dead against the wall, the front half of its body half eaten by a small group of armored six-leggers, each roughly one-fifth the size of the mouse itself.

Perhaps due to its extremely cautious approach, or perhaps because the mouse was in a corner, none of the armored six-leggers had noticed it approaching, too busy with their meal.

After a few seconds of judging distance and risk, the wolf experimentally opened its jaws, stretching them as wide as it could. It tilted its head a bit to judge how difficult it would be to down the mouse and the six-leggers in one chomp.

Maybe risky, but definitely possible.

The appearance of the six-leggers tickled at the back of its mind, and a word for them begged to be drawn out of the abyss.

The wolf ignored it, crouching low on shaky legs and prowling closer and closer, until a single lunge would be enough. It cared not for the minutes that passed or the rapidly decreasing mass of the mouse being speedily devoured by the six-leggers. Coiling its abused tendons and ordering its lethargic muscles to life, it lunged with an audible snap.

Teeth scraped against stone for a moment before they closed around its prey. An instinct in the back of its mind told it to shake its head—one which it suppressed, fairly certain its fuzzy mind would be unable to handle it and make it disoriented like last time.

So, it simply clamped its jaws as tight as it could, observing the singular six-legger which managed to escape scuttle away into a hole in the stone, the rest squished into a blob of gore along with the mouse in its teeth.

Then its eyes rose and gazed upon the dead end in front of it. Fear coiled low in its gut as it realized that there would be no escape if something cornered it.

With as speedy steps as it could manage—which weren't speedy whatsoever—it retreated back to the street as it snapped its head back and ate, keeping its head tilted sideways to have a single eye on the entrance of the cramped alley.

Thankfully, nothing blocked its exit, and after a few moments of cautiously walking away from the scene, its tail hesitantly wagged just a bit.

It was utterly exhausted, both mentally and physically, and it was still horribly hungry.

But it felt like it had a chance. One of those giant rats might be too dangerous a prey to be worth the fight, but if it could move, it could scrape together enough food to keep going.

Instinctually, it knew that even its meager recent snacks should have filled its tiny stomach, but for some reason, it felt ravenous. It was a strange hunger, neither purely physical nor purely mental; some odd mix of the two.

Yet, the wolf was familiar with hunger, refusing the odd, risky urges its empty stomach pushed toward it.

Attacking a two-legger—staggering and stumbling or not—was a terrible idea.

As it wandered around, looking for a half-decent place to sleep, it had to stop and retreat increasingly often from incoming two-leggers, or squish against a wall as they passed, ready to bolt if they shifted their stance toward it. While some of those creatures had tossed scraps of edible food before, most two-leggers either stared it down with a strange, contorted expression that couldn't be anything good, or a few outright tried to chase it out of their territory. Yet when the entire world was their nest, there wasn't really anywhere safe it could go without any two-leggers around.

All the places devoid of two-leggers were full of brown-green toxic waste and the equally dangerous animals that gathered around such places. So it took the route of least danger, trying to seem as small as possible as two-leggers made noises at each other and mostly ignored it.

Many times over its short life, it had heard certain sounds be uttered by the two-leggers as they looked at either itself or some other kin. "Mutt," "fleabag," "stray" were the most frequently repeated words, yet try as it might, it couldn't recreate them nor understand why they used such complex and differing noises to alert each other to the presence of canines.

All of a sudden, a realization struck the wolf.

It was ever since it had seen—or more accurately, *felt* that odd dream of ideas, thoughts, and concepts yesterday, that it knew what it was. That it was different. The others of its kin were by all accounts very similar in build beyond some small differences, but somehow, it knew that it was a wolf now, while the others were . . . something close, but not the same.

Somehow, they knew as well, or so it would seem as it looked back on their interactions. It would explain many things the little wolf had sat and wondered about when it was resting but unable to sleep, either due to a cacophony of machinery or due to pain.

Many times had it tried to ingrain itself into a pack, only to be chased out without a reason. One sniff was all it took for a curious kin to turn flighty and avoid it entirely, if not outright snarl and snap at it while retreating, as if the wolf was about to try and eat it whole despite the obvious size difference between the teenage pup and full-grown canines.

Yet try as it might, it couldn't detect whatever it was the other canines had smelled on it, besides the usual filth.

Now, it finally had an idea as to why all its look-alikes recoiled at its presence.

It simply did not belong. It was alone. It always had been, its few understandings of social interactions and the world observed from afar, learned or remembered through unknown avenues, or inferred from base instincts. But the realization that it wasn't just unaccompanied but well and truly *alone*, the only one of its kind in the small world it knew . . . that realization made its steps slow until it was simply standing in place, dazed.

A deep sense of loneliness made its chest tight, and hazy memories of sleeping in a pile with other wolf cubs were brought to the forefront of its mind. The feeling of warm kin against its fur, their breath tickling its ears, the rise and fall of their chests syncing up as if they were all one single entity, the warm feeling of contentment.

It never knew where those dreams came from, as all it had ever known were these streets, bridges, alleys, and sewers. But they felt real, and many times they'd comforted it when its mind was trying to soothe its worries over the encroaching clutches of death.

Its tail drooped low, and it resumed its wandering with low spirits, keeping an eye out for a decent place to sleep or any lucky scraps of food. Many alcoves, corners, and safe-seeming spots were mentally noted, yet most were too close to barrels of chemicals, pulleys, or various bits of moving metal—all things it had learned not to trust after it had almost lost its tail when it fell asleep on a gargantuan gear that started moving.

Much time passed, two-legger figures clothed in brown and various shades of gray hurriedly moving past and around it, their body language tense and weary. The wolf didn't react to them too much, simply making sure to keep its eyes on errant pipes just in case the two-leggers were being cautious because something was about to break. Two-leggers were usually only scared of other two-leggers, and rarely ever bothered with the wolf, so it simply trudged past them. As long as they weren't looking at it, two-leggers were more concerned with . . . whatever two-leggers did.

Its steps slowed, and its parched mouth begged for water, but it continued, ducking into smaller alleys in the hopes of finding a safe spot to sleep, where rats and mice couldn't find it and try to nibble on it. Even if it wasn't that sleepy at the moment, walking while digesting food felt oddly uncomfortable.

An idea popped into its head and was almost immediately discarded. It could try to bait the rodents by pretending to be asleep for another quick snack, but it simply didn't have the energy to *pretend.* The moment it closed its eyes for more than a minute, it would probably fall asleep and wake up with another giant rat trying to chew through its fur like last time, and that just wasn't a fight it wanted to take.

Although . . . maybe it could just . . . sleep in the open? Two-leggers hated rats and mice, and actively went out of their way to kill them. While the feeling of being exposed was—

The wolf's train of thought faded away as it walked out of the alleyway, noticed the sudden lack of walls around it from the corner of its eyes, and froze with its paw midair as soon as it raised its head, eyes wide open.

In front of it was the largest open space it had ever seen, stretching on for hundreds of meters in every direction. Hundreds upon hundreds of two-leggers were flecked throughout the massive crescent-shaped open area, somehow looking like a small number in comparison to the sheer amount of space on display, little more than moving dots from its position. The wolf craned its neck upward, for the first time feeling its eyes actually strain to make out the details of the countless black lines, towers, latticework bridges, and elevation platforms covering the open area like an unintentional dome of mind-boggling complexity and scale.

Giant sphere lights were connected to thin metal towers which punched through the crescent metal platform and reached up to the bridges and walkways above, seemingly created for the sole purpose of lighting and connecting various hanging wires from one place to the next. A metal rail framed the platform's edge to prevent two-leggers from falling into whatever was below, and dozens of small structures were dotted throughout the gargantuan area, with bright signs covered in odd shapes. Two-leggers would walk to those odd structures with a half-open front, gibber at each other for a bit, then be given things to carry away, either in bags or directly placed on their back pouches.

The things they were given varied wildly, from odd, glowy things made of tiny bits of metal somehow stuck together, long, sharp metal claws, oval-shaped glass bulbs with glowing liquids inside, metal containers with caps on the top, incomprehensible tiny bits of metal, and there was one especially large and sturdy-looking building which seemed to give out nothing but dried . . . green . . . somethings. They looked oddly organic and familiar, but it had never seen anything quite like them before.

Its first thought was that the two-leggers might be making a new nest as it finally let its paw hit the metal underneath, tail involuntarily wagging in excitement as it gazed around an entirely different world in wonder.

The streets and alleys it knew were all so . . . small, all of a sudden. All the miles and miles of snaking tunnels, toxic waste pits, alleys and bridges and factories—all of them now seemed like only a tiny part of a bigger whole. One so big it was almost scary to imagine.

To the wolf's right, the metal crescent abruptly stopped at a certain point, cobbled stone replacing it with giant streets twice to thrice as wide and multiple times as long as those it was used to traversing through. In a daze, it walked forth, eyes drinking in every detail it could.

Even something as simple as the streets that led to the platform were so foreign. Whereas below they were uneven, cobblestoned lines—like snakes that changed width with every few steps, moving in dizzying spirals and the occasional rare straight line in between—the roads here were perfectly straight between the buildings framing them on either side, smooth and flat and completely linear; almost blocky.

The two-leggers were more varied as well. More colors adorned their odd coverings. Their gait was more certain, less wary than it was used to.

Without even realizing, its tail had started to wag like crazy as it moved skeletal legs fueled by nothing but excitement, staring in complete disbelief at the colossal tower that the crescent platform was framing.

Its eyes felt like they were burning just trying to open wide enough to see the whole thing from one end to the other, even from more than a hundred meters away.

It watched through the iron framing and glass as its innards shifted, lowering a giant platform to the level above them before a bridge extended outward to connect to the level above. Even further above, another platform performed a similar action, barely visible through the smog.

Some kind of . . . transportation structure? Or maybe it was building stuff?

As if the world was reprimanding it for admiring something made by its betters, a two-legger chose that exact moment to let its eyes wander to the wolf from where he was talking to one of the shopkeepers, an expression of disgust taking up his face. It raised a finger toward the wolf, whose eyes were still nailed to the tower in wonder.

"[Spark Bolt]."

If it weren't for the sound of continuous, deafening *pops* that accompanied the spell, the wolf wouldn't have had enough warning to instinctually dart forward and to the side away from the loud noise, its weak legs buckling the second it tried to lower its stance and stop its momentum, making it yelp as it tumbled to the ground in a heap of tangled limbs.

After a moment of panicked flailing, the wolf scrambled to its feet and dashed back to the alley it'd come from with a hurried glance back at the man who'd shot the spell, leaving behind a surprised pyromancer and an irate shopkeeper.

"Are you stupid, kid?! No fuckin' magic in the market!" a voice barked behind it.

Familiar alleys welcomed it, and after fifteen or so seconds of running, it turned its head to see if it was safe. Seeing nothing following it, it wheezed and coughed through still-burnt lungs before stumbling to a dented iron crate sitting discarded in a corner. No sooner had its shoulder touched it did its limbs crumple like wet paper, falling asleep before it even hit the cobblestones.

CHAPTER 2

The wolf dreamt.

Images, concepts, names, functions, and definitions flashed rapidly before its eyes. The gray mice from before floated and flashed across its sight, and like an unraveling tapestry, split. Its fur, soft and insulative, was broken down, a combination of oily guard hair on top and a thick underfur beneath. The guard hair kept moisture from reaching the skin, and the underfur acted as an insulating blanket to keep the little creature warm.

Then in a dizzying flash, it split again. Its nails separated, and he saw the strands of biological material which created them. It split again, its organs, their purposes, even some names like *liver* and *heart* being embedded into its mind, knowledge so smoothly placed it felt like remembering something it had forgotten rather than something it had just learned.

It split again, its muscles breaking apart, its bones splintering to reveal they were made of some sort of hardened connective tissue, its ligaments, joints, and eventually, its brain, all being shredded apart and understood on an intrinsic level.

A vague notion of choice hung over its half-aware mind, and for a moment, the dream turned lucid. Its mind scoured through the options presented, yet none but one felt like it would be even remotely useful. Much like in a dream where it had no notion of questioning what was happening, it simply moved on, the consciousness retreating back to dormancy.

The six-leggers.

Cockroaches.

The information was far, far more vivid this time, the names flashing in its mind along with every function and placement in a giant burst of information which nearly woke it from its slumber as it lodged into its mind.

The compound eye, the antenna, the metathorax, mesothorax, the abdomen, stylus, cercus, walking legs, wings, hind legs, mid legs, forelegs, cerci, maxillary palp, tibia, tarsus, femur, coxa, the abdominal segments, and the trochanter, all the knowledge of their functions and their placement on the cockroach was absorbed. And then the cockroach split, its insides unraveling, its complexity almost painful to its mind to comprehend.

The ventral cephalic trunk in its head, interwoven around the dorsal cephalic trunk, the thoracic and abdominal spiracles, the lateral, dorsal, and ventral longitudinal trunks that ran down its sides, the atrium, and a few dozen more organs flashed by in its mind, all fitting in such an incredibly small being with the utmost efficiency.

The choice hovered once more, and the dream turned lucid.

The amount of things this creature had at its disposal were numerous, and for a moment, the wolf simply thought of them all in awe.

Yet, the unspoken question it was brought there to answer still hovered. And the wolf hesitated, looking through all the organs which worked like bricks, one supporting the other, all useless without each other.

All but two. The cerci, thin hairs connected to an internal organ that could sense even the slightest of changes in wind speed and direction. These hairs could not only easily blend into its own fur—the cost of the new organ was low. Of course, by what metric or how any of this was happening, it didn't know, but seeing as it was a dream, it was not particularly questioning of its circumstances.

Then, it turned its focus on the antennae, organs which would connect to the brain and sense vibrations. They would probably look strange on its head, unless it used the much more effective antennae to replace the whiskers on its snout. With but an errant thought, it also removed the pain receptors from them.

The choice solidified in its mind, and its consciousness sank back into sleep.

Yet at the same time, it didn't. Sleep was once a complete darkness, coming and going in the blink of an eye, yet now the wolf was in an odd limbo between being awake and asleep, able to feel the sensations of its body, able to hear the sounds around it. Like a flitting, momentary dream, sounds and sensations were combed through and discarded if they were not alarming, and despite the tiny amount of mental capacity such a thing required, the wolf felt safer than it ever had in its sleep.

In what felt like little more than a moment, footsteps neared, and the wolf's subconscious jolted it, its eyes snapping open. Despite the usual drowsiness that usually followed its sleep, no such thing was felt, its mind and body instantly awake and aware. It turned, seeing two small humans staring at it, and it jumped to its feet with far less pain and effort than what such a motion should have required. Not to say it was negligible, but quick movements were but a far-off dream just two naps ago. Even its burnt lungs seemed to be healing, slowly but surely.

The two two-leggers seemed to be paying a lot of attention to it, their eyes wide open and focused on it, so it bent its legs into a half crouch, ready to bolt. The humans were small, but the wolf still barely reached their chests. The half-crouched stance made them stiffen instantly, the small male reaching for a blunt pipe that it had tucked into its skin layers.

"Holy shit, it's still alive," one of the humans breathed out.

The wolf didn't know what the sounds meant, but the soft tone was sometimes used by the nicer humans who'd throw some edible waste at it, so it tilted its head as it tried to understand their intentions through the contradictory sounds and body language. Which was something two-leggers did sometimes, it had come to find out.

"I mean, we could still kill it. It's got a lotta energy compared to how it looks, but it doesn't seem tough. And it will be a good meal, at least for us. Just um . . . distract it, and I'll hit it on the head real hard, okay? Don't get bit; it looks sick," the male human whispered, touching the quivering, smaller human female on the shoulder.

The wolf didn't like their body language, from the way their muscles were tensed to the nervous way they observed it. While keeping its eyes on them and an ear behind its form, it quickly backtracked, keeping its body diagonal to the pair. The humans hesitated for a moment, then the thin male stepped forward aggressively, only for the smaller female to grab his arm and shake her head, saying something the wolf couldn't catch with its single functioning ear pointing in the other direction.

The humans backed away as well, and the wolf's muscles relaxed ever so slightly as their forms fled around the corner of the alley. Looking around, it realized that it was, once again, completely lost. Two-legger nests were too large and too complicated for it to have the mental capacity to map out anything more than a few spots, but simply by finding downward-tilting roads and alleys, it could at least figure out how to go to the only place that had any food for it, which were the lower, dirtier bits of the human nest.

Part of it hesitated to return, remembering the rivers of thick burning sludge that separated the lower parts, yet it was too weak to go anywhere but there. Two-leggers were oddly wasteful, and while rare, it wasn't entirely uncommon to come across dead bodies that had been flushed down from the upper parts of the iron nest. The variety was fairly large, ranging from winged creatures to two-leggers to canines or scaled creatures. The small, squirming ones eating them were even a decent snack, if a bit repulsive to its instincts for some reason.

Maybe once it grew a little, it could hunt rats. Or an isolated two-legger, though it wasn't sure if two-leggers were protective enough of their nest-mates to hunt it for doing so, so until it knew, it would probably continue avoiding them.

With slow, careful steps, it slowly stalked through green-and-yellow-tinted streets, under hanging signs and barking and howling two-leggers, squeezed through metal fences both bent and cut through, crawled under tightly pressed pipes several times larger than itself, lapped up some dripping water from one of the leaking pipes for a few minutes and rested, then continued until it found what it was looking for: one of the giant pipes that led directly down to the green-brown rivers, diagonal, huge, and hanging over a complicated network of abandoned automatic factories, walkways, bridges, and cables.

After a bit of climbing and a small jump, it got on the pipe, tail tucked between its legs. It began to slowly, *slowly* inch its way forward on the downward-sloping pipe, the eroded nature of the metal the only thing giving its paws any friction and preventing it from slipping off into the increasingly lifeless darkness underneath, lined with cold, dead metal.

Its instincts screamed at it, turning its limbs stiff with the fear of the giant stretch of air and cables separating it from the walkways underneath. Yet, it still inched forward, knowing it had to use whatever meager energy reserves it had to get to the only feeding ground it had proven at least a little successful in.

Eventually, the pipe connected to a giant metal rectangle drafted onto a cylindrical pillar of steel that reached up and down beyond where its eyes could see, and the wolf had to jump to the metal walkway underneath to continue. If only it could grip the metal bars the two-leggers used to descend to the burning rivers or use one of their hanging boxes that went up and down on one of the iron cables, its journey would be little more than a field trip. But it couldn't.

Bracing itself on legs quivering with fear, it powered through the instinctive fear of the massive height underneath the walkway, reasoning to itself that it had taken such drops a dozen times before. Yet, the temptation to walk back up the pipe and take the long, long way down through the snaking alleys and stairways was still there.

But it knew that was the wrong choice. Its legs hurt, its deaf ear was slowly becoming itchy and attracting more and more tiny flying insects, its limbs felt weak and wobbly, its throat felt so dry it was worried it would start cracking like dried dirt, and its functioning ear was so swamped by the constant clanging, humming, and shrieking of the shifting metal in its infinitely vast surroundings that it was starting to feel a little dizzy.

The thought of getting dizzy when it was sitting over a death drop was the straw that broke the camel's back.

With a timid shuffle that made its fur crack and split from where the sludge had solidified on its back, it moved to the corner of the pipe, and with a yelp of fear, allowed itself to slide off onto the walkway underneath.

Its legs crumpled like wet paper, and the walkway *moved* for a moment with the familiar rattle of failing metal, filling it with cold terror.

But even as the metal railing kept wobbling in its loose casing, the walkway stabilized. With a mild pant to its breaths, the wolf slowly got up from its bruised rib cage and walked down the winding staircase that curled around the metal tower like a jagged centipede, bits of broken and bent railing the only thing stopping it from falling off to its death from a single misstep.

Small, flat metal platforms were placed in front of heavy iron doors every few feet down, allowing it a moment of relatively safe rest on its journey downward. The metal towers usually reached around some sort of two-legger gathering spot, and from there, it was only a short walk to the burning rivers.

An entire hour of cautiously walking down the stairs, resting, and repeating later, it finally reached the bottom.

A few two-leggers were drifting around the giant open area around the base of the tower, all covered head to toe in extra skins, with glass and metal coverings over their faces. Some of them were checking up on some of the two-leggers made of rock, waving their hands around and touching their glowing bits, repairing the erosion and cracks, before ordering them around to continue whatever it was those things did.

The wolf really disliked those things. They were shaped like two-leggers, but narrower and shorter, their limbs able to shift and extend with a sound like grinding gravel, and despite moving, cleaning drains, and hauling waste into the burning rivers like living beings following their instincts and orders, they weren't alive.

They were just moving rock. It made no sense, and it was just unnatural.

But they weren't dangerous. The few times it had seen some living things in the area attack them, they'd just ignored the animal until it gave up. So the wolf stalked around the edges of the square, avoiding the scant few two-leggers hanging around and repairing their deformed stone duplicates, and sought to find a place to rest for a while.

In less than a minute of slow walking, the sounds of life and activity were drowned out under the cacophony of shrieks, groans, and rumbles of the surrounding machinery. Bent pipes leaked foul-smelling liquids into the cobbles. Exhaust pipes snaked toward the walls of the pits and shot upward, hidden behind a mess of scaffolding and wires from which the humans repaired and maintained them.

Barrels of dangerous green liquids were thrown haphazardly around every corner with space, waiting for a stone two-legger to come pick them up and empty them into the metal boxes that emptied their contents into the burning rivers. Some pipes would expel a fine, odd-smelling mist with a menacing hiss, which the wolf avoided out of sheer caution. The humidity of the environment was staggering to get used to, but after a few minutes, it grew accustomed to it.

It found a spot relatively free of danger, hidden behind some sort of segmented cylinder surrounded by spiraling wires, and crawled under the half-hanging mass of cables which ran into it, appreciating the warmth of the odd machine. It fell asleep almost instantly despite the dirty water soaking into its paws and chin.

In what felt like little more than a few seconds, a crackling sound woke it from its sleep, and a menacing sound somewhere between a hum and a buzz made it panic, scrambling out from under its cover to run away. After it moved away a few meters, it turned and stared at the cylinder where the sound was coming from, the volume getting higher and higher.

And then, with a deafening crackle that made it yelp, arcs of white shot out from the top, flashing to the water with speed it couldn't fathom.

And straight to its paws, still partially submerged in dirty water.

A pained sound like a high-pitched yowl ripped itself out of its throat as its muscles seized, feeling like a thousand needles stabbed themselves into its hide and dug into its bones. Despite its seizing muscles contracting and tightening without a goal, it managed to jerkily stumble and fall away from the puddles of water—partially due to how little meat it had on its bones— and it half crawled, half stumbled away from the scene with its tail tucked between its legs, which were barely responding to its orders, still twitching and buckling.

After sitting panicked for a few moments as the shocks faded, it snarled, its head turning wildly to see what had hurt it. After several moments of nothing, it relaxed a bit, its senses not picking up anything dangerous nearby besides the still oddly buzzing machine.

The wolf was about to continue, to go and find something to eat or just find some spot to *finally* sleep uninterrupted for just a few hours, when a certain sound pierced through the now faint buzzing in the background of its grimy path.

The squeaking of a rat.

It turned around, ready to bolt, but after a moment of confusion, its eyes wandered back to the machine.

In one of the puddles, a small rat was suffering in much the same way the wolf had, trying to walk yet twitching and rolling instead, the white arcs ravaging its soaked, tiny body much more than they did the wolf.

Despite the adrenaline in its veins directing it to run away, it slowly stumbled back to sit next to the puddles, its movements a little more even and controlled by now, and sat on its haunches, watching the rat, waiting for it to either stop moving or grow so exhausted it could eat it. After a minute or two, the rodent barely twitched, its chest pumping up and down as it hyperventilated.

After five minutes, shallow breaths and weak twitches were all which signified the rat was still alive. The wolf crept forward, wary and uncertain of if it would get shocked again, and slowly put a paw in one of the puddles. A minor shock burned through its nerves as it yelped and jerked back a bit.

Its curiosity overcame its hunger for now, and it moved back to the puddle, very slowly putting its paw next to the water.

Nothing.

It then slowly put its paw in the water, and despite being ready for it, the wolf was still startled by the shock, retreating a couple steps back as its mind struggled to understand why this water looked normal but momentarily took over its limbs and made them hurt. It stomped its paw on the ground a bit to get rid of the numbness, and it was fine again.

It moved to another puddle, putting its paw in it.

Nothing.

Puzzled, it tilted its head, trying to find some pattern to what was going on.

It took more than a few attempts as it ran around the area, shoving its paws into water with increasing fervor to try and understand what was going on, until eventually, the machine crackled again, this time much quieter, and white lines visibly flashed down from its top down to its base, spreading throughout the water that touched the metallic base bolted into the cobblestones.

The smell of charred rat confirmed the rodent was definitely dead, and after a moment of staring, the wolf moved to a puddle that was isolated, carefully putting its paw into it.

Nothing.

Then, with extreme hesitation, it put its paw on a small puddle connected to the water that had the white lines running through it a moment ago.

Pain shot through its front leg, and the pup snarled in response as it jerked back, experimentally moving the limb back and forth in the air to gain back the feeling. As its eyes settled on the rat, it couldn't help but linger on the mystery of the sparky water.

After a couple seconds of thought, it realized what was happening.

Or rather, a rough approximation of it.

After bracing itself on its bad paw, which had been shocked a bunch, it leaned forward over the puddle and quickly put all of its strength into a swipe with its good paw, managing to batter the semifried rat out of the water with only a few minor shocks to its leg.

After another minute of waiting to make sure no more sparky water was on the rodent, which was about as large as its entire head, it poked it with its paw, and judging it safe, quickly chomped down.

In little more than a few bites that felt amazingly easy, it devoured the rat, fur and all, and started licking the blood off the floor. Smacking its jaws shut with a meaty clack of satisfaction, it turned and walked off into the dimly lit undersides of the mechanical behemoths above, wondering why its teeth had felt almost as much resistance when biting through the rodent as they did when biting through air.

CHAPTER 3

With a jaw-popping yawn, the wolf settled to sleep, tucked next to a small series of heating pipes that kept it blissfully warm. A few moments later, its consciousness faded.

You have gained the Skill [Electricity Resistance - Level 1]
[Electricity Resistance] has Leveled Up. Level 1 → Level 2

The wolf dreamt once more, seeing the rat it had devoured be deconstructed piece by piece in its mind.

Yet, there was no real difference between a mouse and a rat besides size and tail structure, so there was little to see, and its choice in the dream was that the rat had nothing it wanted.

The odd lucid dream faded, and for the first time in the last couple days, nothing appeared to disturb its sleep besides the usual annoyance of the flying little things. Hours and hours passed, and eventually, it opened its eyes, feeling well rested for what must have been the first time ever. It had no frame of reference to know how much time had passed, no sun to indicate, but it felt like it had spent the better part of an entire day sleeping, based on its internal clock.

Wasting no time, it got up and walked toward the faint sound of rushing liquid, a strained sound that barely slithered out from under the all-encroaching cacophony of pounding metal. Its paws pounded against humid, grimy stone at a steady trot, feeling solidified waste tickle against the underside of its paws from where it had fused into the mossy stone and tainted it brown green. The noxious scent of fumes invaded its nose, which was probably both good and bad, as it meant its nose was healing from the burn, but it also meant it could smell the foul scents of the rivers again.

Meaningless shapes of uncountable varieties and dizzying complexity surrounded it, but besides a cursory glance to ensure nothing was about to break and hurt it, it continued through them, the sound of rushing liquids getting closer and closer. It ducked under a pipe so hot it released faint white wisps of steam as the surrounding moisture settled on it, and a forty-five-degree-angle incline met its eyes, which turned into a far less steep angle a few feet down and met in the center with another identical one on the other side. Right where the two met, a canal lined with lead directed the vast majority of the river, with bits that overflowed usually sliding back into the canal from the downward-trending walls.

How it knew what a canal—or lead—was, it didn't know, but questioning things had never given it anything but a mild headache, so it left it alone.

Dead and rotting bits of blackened meat were strewn all around the edges of the canal, interspersed with dissolving, unidentifiable materials of less organic origin. Some parts of the river frothed and churned as if alive, the liquids interacting and reacting with each other in a cacophony of sizzling, boiling, and light screeching when the most volatile met the lead. Glowing green insects buzzed all around the rotting corpses, undulating and covering them from top to bottom, carrying with them the pungent miasma of decay.

Bits of slowly evaporating green-gray foam were strewn about on the edges of the canal, and brown slugs the size of the wolf's front legs were gathered around the foam, hooked tentacles slithering out of their under-sides and prodding at their surroundings as they walked, occasionally finding some organic material and dragging it under themselves to dissolve it in mere moments.

Some slithering vines twisted, their needled leaves piercing into slugs that wandered too close by before the vines contracted and wrapped around the squirming creatures, after which too much glowing plant matter was cover-ing the slug to see what was going on.

The wolf tilted its head as it stared at the plants, finding them oddly familiar, and after a few moments, it remembered the organic, dry-looking green stuff that one of the metal buildings above was giving out to the two-leggers, back when some human had thrown orange sparks at it.

It continued observing the river as it turned its body and walked up toward the source, hoping that the droppings near the top would be less dissolved, rotten, and less dangerous to eat. It wasn't exactly sure why, but the closer one was to the top, the less dangerous the river's liquids were. Maybe the liquids simply didn't have enough time to grow and become stronger; it wasn't sure.

That also presented the problem of less scavengers and more predators lurking about.

In an area like this, the only things that could be around the more dangerous rivers and survive were either scavengers, like the things it saw below, or stronger creatures that had adapted to the environment, like those brightly glowing chubby things that jumped around everywhere, the eight-tentacled things that stuck to the bottom and waited for things above to come so they could drag them under and consume them, or the utterly terrifying behemoths that were those scaled quadrupeds with maws twice as large and long as the wolf's entire body.

It couldn't even hope to compete, so it was simply going to see what kind of things were around the river, and if they were dangerous, it would return to one of the bridges that went over the canals and go look for a less risky choice. There were many burning rivers in the nest, and it didn't have any desire to risk its life in a futile fight against the river dwellers.

After a couple hundred steps more, it confirmed its suspicions and backtracked in disappointment, hoping the next river was less scary.

It eventually found one of the arching bridges and crossed over the canal safely, only having to avoid a single stone two-legger on its trip to the next canal. Unfortunately, from just a glance, it could tell that this river was only a tiny bit less dangerous than the last one, so it moved on to the next canal, its legs screaming for rest, its tendons feeling *sore* somehow.

Thankfully, it was rewarded for its efforts, the next canal being about as safe as it could reasonably hope for. Besides a couple of those dangerous plant things in the corners that it knew how to avoid and a couple slugs, it was fairly safe. The flies would burst into green burning liquid if the wolf hit them too hard, so it had to approach some of the dissolving organic bits with caution and slow steps, lest it jostled the things too much and they burned another hole through its fur.

With cautious steps and a single upright ear, it crept forward, checking the washed-up bits of scrap food it could find. A couple brave rats, dissolved down to their hind legs and covered in flies, some strange black winged thing that was half eaten by the—

The wolf stopped as it realized it suddenly had a name for the flying things, out of nowhere, so naturally that it barely noticed as it used the word inwardly.

Flies.

Deciding not to dwell on it, as per usual, it resumed walking. Not wanting to waste the food while it was still there, it slowly moved its snout to prod one of the half-eaten rats, making the green glowing flies scatter, some of them trying to settle on top of it and its foul-smelling ear.

As soon as it was sure little to no flies were still attached to the rat, it gripped it between its teeth, barely feeling the pressure on them, and briskly turned around, slowly increasing its speed until it was trotting and then lightly running away, making sure no flies impacted it. After a couple moments, it turned, watching the scattered flies go off to eat the winged thing.

It didn't particularly mind the loss. It had eaten more bits of rats than anything else, and it knew they were at least *somewhat* safe to eat. It had never eaten one of the flying things.

Although now, it suddenly wanted to. Both its mind and body wanted nothing more than to turn around and charge through the flies, grab the odd black winged thing, and eat it whole.

Instead, the wolf chomped down on the half-eaten rat, flinching slightly as the familiar burning settled in its mouth and throat. It had lessened significantly, but it still hurt.

The first time it had chomped down on a rat from around here, it had been covered in so much burning stuff from the flies that its entire mouth and throat had been rubbed raw and bleeding, and it had almost choked on its own blood when it'd gone to sleep, barely able to breathe through the pain.

Lessons in the two-legger's nest were often as dangerous to its life as they were helpful.

It repeated this process a few times, but besides the tiniest of scraps, most things were too rotted, too dangerous, or too unknown for it to try and eat, despite the angry snarling of its stomach.

Still, with the total amount of about an entire half of a rat in its stomach, this had been a great day when it came to food.

It decided not to stick around too much in the area, both because some of its worst memories had been created down there, and because it was far more dangerous than the places where two-leggers were, despite more food being available.

It trotted up, backtracking to where the giant metal tower met the ground, and after about half an hour, it was safely nestled underneath the staircase it had descended with.

For some reason, the two-leggers rarely if ever used it, preferring their moving metal boxes on the inside of the tower, but it wasn't about to question why two-leggers were so insane they'd ride a moving box of metal rather than walk down like normal beings. Especially when it gave it such convenient shelter.

It closed its eyes, fully ready and willing to sleep away its digestion and go back to find a few more scraps of food soon.

[Restful Awareness] has Leveled Up. Level 2 → Level 3

A short while later, it woke up from its nap and headed straight for the canals, taking a slightly different route that used the two-leggers' streets, hoping it would help it circumvent or entirely avoid things like the sparky water from before. Its left ear had started to hurt enough for it to be noticeable, but there was nothing it could do about it, as any attempts to scratch it only made it hurt more.

It got a little lost much sooner than it expected, the sound of rushing liquid too drowned out to be distinguishable, much less with a direction that the wolf could infer with any accuracy.

With a low grumble of annoyance, it turned the corner and instantly stopped moving, tilting its head. A two-legger lay collapsed on the ground on its side, the glass mask the two-leggers wore cracked open, most of the glass missing entirely. The two-legger was groaning weakly, turning over on its stomach with slow, lethargic movements, its breathing ragged as it tried to curl its limbs inward.

The movements and motions of something dying were more than familiar to the wolf.

It had gone through them itself multiple times.

So it moved to the side, eyes nailed to the two-legger as it tried to find the best spot to wait for the two-legger to die, its limbs and heart basically vibrating with excitement at the potential of a huge meal.

The two-legger managed to curl its bottom legs under it and extended its upper legs to touch the ground, paws flat as it coughed—a wet, sickly sound. It put its bottom leg's knee against its own chest, supported it with its upper paws, and staggered upright, much to the wolf's dismay. It leaned on the wall for a few steps, each one slower and more unstable than the last, until its knees buckled, its grip on a pipe turning its body to drop on its back.

The wolf stilled its tail, which begged to wag, and slunk forward, as still as it possibly could be. The two-legger's motions were oddly reminiscent of the rat, it thought, watching its rib cage expand and contract with heaving breaths, shallow coughs shaking its entire body.

The wolf moved up against a wall and sat on its haunches, slowly becoming more confident in the two-legger's inability to harm it—so much so that it sat on its butt just a mere couple feet away, silently watching, its eyes boring a hole through the two-legger, and its right ear pointed up.

Two minutes passed without much change, and the wolf started feeling nervous as time passed and the human refused to die, wondering if one of its kin would come and take away its meal. Not only that; the more it waited, the higher the chance some stone two-legger would come and save the human. It didn't know the capabilities of those things nor if they would even bother helping the two-legger, but it definitely didn't want to find out.

After a shuddering breath accompanied by a dry-sounding cough, the two-legger's head lolled to the side, its eyes settling on the wolf, who simply stiffened and went even more statue still than before.

A halting series of tiny coughs came out of the human, something humans did when conversing happily with each other, yet the sound was oddly bitter. The wolf didn't know what the two-legger was trying to say, nor did it care too much, just hoping it would die already without it having to risk its safety by getting close and biting it.

"Haaagh. My mother . . . always said that . . . the Keeper of Oblivion sends a different . . . vision . . . for everyone. Oddly fit—" A violent cough stopped the two-legger's sounds, but it continued after a series of small con-vulsions. "Oddly fitting that he sent . . . a dirty fleabag . . . like myself." A shuddering series of sounds like the tiny coughs from earlier came from the two-legger, the sound more like a series of bastardized yelps, and the wolf tilted its head, curious as to what the sound meant.

Despite its curiosity, however, it felt a heavy sensation in its gut, an unpleasant emotion like sadness as it watched the two-legger die. It was still just a lucky meal to the wolf, but the two-legger's eyes portrayed so much emotion, so much despair, that it transcended any and all barriers that stood between them, be they barriers of intelligence or linguistic ability.

If the wolf just closed its eyes, it could easily imagine itself in the exact same position; one it had been in many times before, its breath choked by poison and fumes, certain it would die in a moment that never came, inwardly begging for one of its kin to sit next to it just so it would not die empty and alone. So a part of it was tempted to just make it quicker, jab its head into the human's neck and try to do the job itself.

Caution prevented it from following through.

"Just . . . give me a moment . . . oh, Honored Guide. Let me . . . regret just . . . a bit more." The two-legger yelped again, tears visible through its shat-tered glass mask pooling around its cheekbone.

Another two minutes passed in relative silence, the wolf's concerns fading as it stood straight, staring into the two-legger's eyes without so much as a twitch.

The two-legger's breathing grew slower and shallower breath by breath, and that relatable, heavy emotion in its chest faded entirely at the prospect of a large, fresh meal, anticipation and joy taking their place.

Renfred breathed out slowly, the motion still almost causing him to burst into a coughing fit. An odd sense of peace washed over him, tainted by despair. His lungs churned and burned and convulsed in his chest, the mana-infused poisonous fumes of the Bone Pits ravaging his insides.

His broken gas mask obstructed his view of the Guide, and for that, he cursed it more than he cursed it for causing his death in the first place. Never was a religious man; had never been a real man in general. Yet, how could he deny what was in front of him; how could he not curse his mask for not allowing him the final wish of a clear look at the servant of a *god*?

Another sob threatened to escape him as he felt death come ever closer, his legs growing numb and cold, yet burning at the same time. His vision swam, the colors changing and the shadows lengthening, darkening. It was a natural response, yet he still felt ashamed to be crying when he had already accepted what was going to happen to him the moment the glass cracked and shattered alongside his heart.

Through teary eyes, he tried to focus on the Guide.

It was beautiful, in the way few things could ever be. Wondrous in the way something could only be when one knew their time was running out and every millisecond was precious and beautiful; when every image could be the last they'd ever see.

The Guide stood above him, towering over him despite its small stature. Its form was gaunt beyond belief, little more than a skeleton draped with a hide of matted fur darker than darkness itself; like a hole torn in reality. The utter stillness of its form was that of a tree standing tall in howling gales that tore the earth around it asunder, an eternal presence that could never be displaced. Its youthful eyes gazed into his own, the deepest, most wonderful shade of gold he'd ever laid eyes upon, like liquid churning honey, like the golden glint of lost wealth, like the warmth of a campfire in a frigid winter storm, like forgotten summer sunshine and the bottom of a glass of shared beer, like the scent of midday harvest and the bittersweet sound of Eline's laugh.

The Guide gazed down upon him with a faint, cold sense of compassion.

No, not just compassion.

Of understanding.

Like a kindred soul who had felt what he was feeling now. Like it knew what he was going through. Like if only by the tiniest pluck of the strings of fate, their positions could have been reversed, and he would have been the only one in the entire world to sit by its forgotten, fading soul and guide it into the embrace of Oblivion.

"What was . . . the prayer?" he whispered, his mind fuzzy and his senses fading, the wondrous sight of the Guide growing murky.

"Ah." He remembered whispered words spoken before a flaming pyre, his mother's warbling voice the only thing to keep him grounded. "It's . . ."

No, that prayer was for those who couldn't pray for their own souls. One that was spoken if you wanted to be sure of the fate of your loved ones. Yet, he knew that nobody would speak the prayer for him. There were none left. The one he was looking for while he still drew breath was another; something half forgotten, written in a book he'd placed on his mother's pyre with a bitter glare.

"As I was lowered to . . . the cradle . . . take me to . . . my grave. Thank . . . you, oh Leader of the . . . Broken. Guide to our . . . fading souls . . . may I pay . . . the toll? . . . Oh, Revered . . ."

His mind grew fuzzy once more, trying to remember the rules. Yet, an outside force nudged him, ever so slightly, and he remembered. Sincerity was all that mattered.

"Hound of Oblivion," he breathed out, so low he feared the Hound didn't hear him. Yet, its eyes widened, its pupils growing smaller as beautiful gold spread across his vision, its fur standing on end in reaction. He twitched the smallest of smiles, happy at the acknowledgement.

With his next breath, his heart stopped.

"Hound of Oblivion," it whispered, its tone strange and full of an odd sense of awe.

A familiar sensation washed over the wolf, whose eyes widened, its fur standing on end in a wave as a shiver washed over every inch of its skin.

The abstract notion of a choice clawed at its mind as the world froze.

It lacked the complexity of its dreams. It lacked the flexibility, the understanding of what exactly it was being asked. It was a simple idea of acceptance or refusal.

It found that it could not move. The two-legger's eyes remained glued to its own, and while no breath left its lips—not the faintest twitch of movement could be seen out of the corner of its vision—they were both frozen in time, the light of life frozen in the process of receding from the two-legger's eyes.

The freezing grasp of death slithered up its spine, its gauntlet slowly closing around the scruff of its terrified neck, the tips gently scraping against its spine. It considered each option for only the most minute of moments and found that both had dire consequences it couldn't fathom nor understand.

So it accepted, and the world vanished.

It did not fade; it did not dim.

It simply vanished. There one moment and gone the next.

There was no light, no sound, no scent, not even the faintest brush of moving wind against its fur.

The all-encompassing darkness receded like ink retreating back into its fallen pot, condensing into a tiny pinprick of black in the distance, alone in a vast, endless expanse of pure white.

As if the strings bounding it had snapped all at once, the wolf could suddenly move, which it did by jerking out of its frozen position into a terrified ball on the ground, its tail tucked so deep between its legs that it brushed against its ribs as it stared wide eyed at its incomprehensible surroundings. Had it any water in its bladder or any waste in its guts, it would have expelled them both out of pure terror.

Despite the void of white all around it, there was ground under its feet, marble smooth and perfectly flat. Some corner of its mind wondered, "What if there wasn't?" and then suddenly, there was nothing below it.

It yelped in terror, legs kicking wildly as it desperately wished there was ground just under its feet, and suddenly, there was, its body slamming into it without an ounce of pain.

For many, many minutes, it simply curled into a ball and hid its face under its paws, beyond terrified and uncaring of the faint sensation of something being tethered to its very being and floating above it.

Yet, after what could have been a second or a century, nothing happened.

It slowly unfurled itself, phantom nerves making it vibrate in place. Because something called it forth, the small point of black in the endless white filled it with understanding.

It was a Guide. And it had to take the two-legger's soul to the darkness.

With just a thought that it wished to complete its goal, a single step suddenly placed it in front of the sphere of pure darkness, a gargantuan sphere millions, *billions* of times larger than the wolf, towering so high it was difficult to even *tell* it was a sphere rather than a curving mantle that passed above it to become one with the sky.

It simply knew that it was.

And out of the sphere, a two-legger's foot stepped out, followed by its shin, its knee, a second foot, and in one incomprehensibly long stride, a pitch-black titan towered over the wolf, its head so impossibly far away that were it looking, its eyes would never be able to catch even the faintest glimpse of it.

But it wasn't looking. The moment the giant's chest stepped out of the sphere, it nailed its eyes and snout to the ground in a show of submission, trembling from tail to snout in terror.

Silence. Silence like the world itself had ceased to exist. And then—

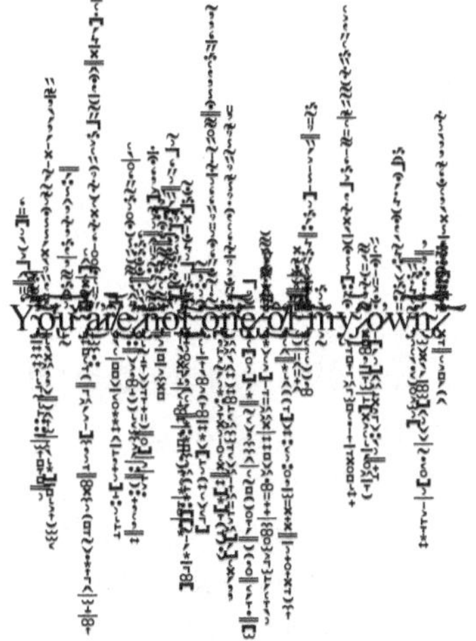

CHAPTER 4

The titan blinked out of existence, and in its place stood a giant wolf, ten times taller than itself and made of pure darkness, nothing more than a vaguely canine silhouette against a stark white background.

"This form, this voice. It should be less agonizing to comprehend," it spoke, its tone intrigued, its voice drilling into *both* its ears like the scrape of screeching metal, low and rumbling like a landslide, like grinding boulders tempered by a snarl, like gnashing teeth, yet paradoxically, like complete and utter silence.

If the previous sound was an incomprehensible cacophony of thunder, this was a comprehensive noise under layers and layers of conflicting elements that made its stomach churn.

A migraine started to pound in its temple as voice and words finally registered, and it whimpered, flattening its body as much as possible.

"Words are so meaningless when spoken to the weak," the titanic wolf rumbled, and a tendril of shadow extended out of the side of its neck before whipping toward the trembling wolf at a speed that was completely invisible to its naked eyes, both of which refused to leave the titan's paws, each bigger than its entire body.

Yet instead of the tendril annihilating the wolf, it simply passed through its chest and connected to its soul, prodding around like a needle. A vague feeling of violation, of terrible, terrible discomfort swept through the core of its very being, and the wolf shuffled, trying to make itself even smaller, hoping that it could just escape the odd nightmare it was stuck in.

Not a nightmare. The simple thought invaded its mind as if it were its own, like a reply, and it stopped thinking, every ounce of its attention focused on the visual aspect of emptiness in front of it, clearing its mind. Yet, the thoughts continued to come.

Impressive, to empty your mind like that while so terribly frightened. You could have been a monk, were you a human like your charge.

Human. The two-leggers were called humans?

Yes, but that doesn't matter. You do not understand the gravity of what just happened. Child of Fenrir, Devourer of the Maw, it has been a long time since I last saw one of you.

The tone was . . . soft, laced with history and feelings it had never felt, wondrous and expressive in ways mere thoughts and sounds couldn't be.

The being tried to further invade its mind and try to plant something, and the wolf's meager mental resistances rose as it tried to force the being out of its mind and soul, yet the battle inside its mind might as well have been an ant trying to hold back a dragon.

But the being *did* stop.

Hm. Have it your way. I'll just speak. Its thoughts, whether they were its own right now or not, rang with amusement. *Now, allow me to give you another choice. You did the work of one of my Guides by accident, without being able to understand what you were agreeing to. That odd rune in your skull prevented me from putting the information of what each choice presented into you, at least not without killing you on the spot.*

What those choices was, was to become one of my own. Or to reject the responsibility and opportunity that man gave you and forever be barred from entering Oblivion, doomed for your soul to continue reincarnating throughout the cosmos, unaware of your past lives until the very moment your soul detaches from your vessel, only to forget once more the moment you begin again. The curse of life, discarded.

The wolf squirmed but remained in its submissive pose, its mind swimming with questions the being saw but left unanswered, almost amused at the wolf still uselessly trying to force it out of its head.

You are too small-minded to even understand most of the words and concepts I'm saying, and I can only shove so much knowledge into your skull without breaking you when there's another influence already in there. Normally, this wouldn't matter. But I will admit to bias. I miss Fenrir's children. They brought me so many . . .

I will give you a choice. A clear one.

For bringing me this man's soul, saving my Guides the tedium of doing this themselves, for being one of, and the last of Fenrir's pure-blooded children, for involuntarily giving me something new to see, you can take this man's toll, a fraction of his soul, and grow your own with it. Additionally, I will give you a little gift of my own and send you back to the corporeal realm where you belong.

Or you can commit to the choice you've already made and become one of my Guides.

A vague notion of eternal servitude, the endless march of time, and the power it could gain from becoming a Guide, all briefly flashed before its eyes.

A thrum of disappointment passed through the being and directly into the wolf.

I can see your answer before you even think of it. But you are young, and I'll give you another chance when your time runs out. For now, so be it. Simply think of me when you die, and I shall welcome you. Consider all this as close to an apology as you will ever get out of a deity. Goodbye, little pup. May you be as great as your origin, should the world allow it.

The faint, near imperceptible tether connected to its soul was severed, and the intrusive presence in its mind and soul faded.

And just like that, the world returned as if nothing had ever happened, in less time than it took to blink, and the wolf stood frozen in place, barely breathing. For a few minutes, it stood still, terrified, wondering if the titan was still watching, waiting for its reaction, for an excuse to squash it like a bug. Experimentally, it got up on trembling legs and looked around.

There was something small and squirming in its chest, like a new limb suddenly grown overnight, but beyond that, everything was . . . alright.

Nothing had changed, the being from before vanished like a particularly vivid nightmare.

Even if it wasn't.

The wolf swallowed, and after only one more moment of hesitation, it got to work on cutting through the human's clothes, hooking its canines into the straps of the mask, and ripping through them with shocking ease. A few tugs later, the human's bulky skin-cover was removed and ripped apart, and with one last nervous glance at its surroundings, it bit down on the human's neck.

Like its fangs weren't even there, its gums very suddenly impacted rapidly cooling skin, and for a moment, it panicked, thinking it had somehow lost its teeth and didn't notice. It recoiled and watched the red gashes where its canines had ripped the human's neck to ribbons from the motion. Just to be sure, it ran its tongue over its teeth, and with its worries assuaged, bit down once more, ripping chunks of meat out of the human's neck and into its gullet. In less than a minute, it snapped its spine like a twig, dragging the head to hold it down between its two front paws.

Five minutes of crunching bone later, it threw its head back and gulped down the last spinal disk attached to the head, and got to work on the body.

Realistically, it knew it should be beyond full, puking its guts out from overeating. Instinctually, it knew it shouldn't be gorging itself so much after starving for its entire life. Yet, even as its teeth tore apart the human's rib cage as if it was barely there and started ripping out organs, it simply couldn't be sated. A shiver of primal pleasure ran through its body, and something in its mind stirred, churning and bubbling and hissing in its ringing ears.

Its mind and body both howled for more, so the wolf continued, uncaring of how utterly impossible it was for it to single-handedly consume a human whole. Its biology was closer to the rat than it would have expected, with the lungs, heart, and intestines being roughly in the same area.

Yet, it gave that thought nothing but a passing consideration before it rammed its snout into the human's chest and started devouring every organ of its upper body, intoxicating crimson bathing its tongue, soothing its parched throat, filling it with energy. After it had consumed the heart, the flesh, and collarbones, it turned down and shoved its snout into its intestines. Gripping them between its teeth, it began to pull them out.

In and out, over and over until its neck started getting sore from the motion, until finally, a pile of bloody intestines was laid out next to the human's hips. With one final sharp tug, the intestine pulled on the stomach, and the human's organs collapsed as any semblance of structure and order was abandoned after losing their base. Livers, flesh, small and big intestine, it all blurred together into a euphoric ecstasy as it binged on the flesh of a man alive mere moments ago.

For another ten minutes, it simply devoured everything mildly squishy looking laid before it, only barely remembering to hurriedly glance around for any prying eyes.

Twenty minutes later, it was halfway down the human's spine, licking and devouring every tiny chunk of bone and meat the human had, its tiny snout and even smaller teeth struggling with the bigger bones and muscles of a human large enough that it could have curled up into its chest cavity and taken a nap in it.

Its stomach churned, so full it should have burst ten times over, yet its belly had barely moved, an odd sensation of discomfort and exertion being the only thing that changed about its insides.

The scent of tangy iron and death hung thick in the air around the chem-scorched cobbles of the alley.

Another fifteen minutes later, it finally got to the legs, struggling to pull them out of their odd extra skin, which was disgusting and made its stomach hurt. Its ears were ringing, a faint, repeating whistle, rhythmic to the drumming of its heart slamming into its ribs. As its mind screamed to eat, eat, devour, and consume without a care in the world, its frustration grew, until it eventually decided to just tear the extra skin off with its teeth like before.

The bulky, lead-lined boots and shin guards were caked in burning river fluids, but it didn't care, clamping its small jaws around the shin and raking its teeth through the metal with only a mild feeling of strain, like cutting through half-melted meat.

But its canines were too small to pierce through the thick metal, and the more it raked its canines through it, the more jagged it became, the sharper pieces piercing and cutting its gums when its teeth nearly effortlessly sank to the base.

With a snarl of frustration, it moved up to the thigh, gripped one of the exposed leg bones, and started violently thrashing side to side, hoping to dislodge the leg from its confines. Its razor-sharp front teeth only managed to cut off its bulbous tip.

It stomped a paw, licking its chops after hastily swallowing as it tried to figure something out. After staring at the other end of the legs, it dashed to the human's ankles and tried to indulge the howling lust for food.

As its canines sank and hooked into the metal where some moving bits allowed the human to move its paws properly, a sound suddenly cut through its surroundings, and as if a burst pipe had covered it in cooling fluid, it went cold, freezing with its jaws stretched apart almost to the point of its bones snapping out of their place around an incredibly bulky, and *incredibly heavy* foot that it was somehow lifting as it raised its head.

"Renfred! You stupid, bumbling fucking gambler shitpit cunt! Where the fuck are you?!" a gruff human voice screamed from just around the corner. The wolf stood in place dumbly as it turned to look in the direction of the deafening roar, its fur standing on end with such intensity that it almost hurt its skin.

It had to run, to hide. The human sounded furious.

The small, squirming limb inside its chest bubbled and writhed, responding to the wolf's overwhelming fear, and in the split second between the human's shoulder coming into sight and the wolf's internal panicked screaming to hide in a place without a hiding spot, something *clicked* deep in its mind, body, and the limb it suddenly knew was its very soul.

A sensation like when it got shocked by the sparky water spread throughout its body; yet, instead of pain, it brought satisfaction, like the sensation of an unused muscle finally making the neural connections necessary for the wolf to use.

How the wolf used the new "limb" was less than useless. With nothing but the panicked thought to *hide*, it spread out of its chest in an instant, sputtering, dissipating, and breaking, some parts of the feeling washing over its fur while others lost contact and dissipated in the air.

As if in slow motion, the two-legger turned the corner—and froze.

Across a short, L-shaped alley whose cobblestones were utterly soaked in blood and tiny bits of viscera, only about as wide as two men were tall, a small, blood-soaked creature with wide, gleaming pools of hazel stood. A limb covered in lead almost as large as its own body hung out of overstretched jaws that had clamped onto the metal, covered in flickering, chaotic spurs and bursts of pure darkness, looking at an equally frozen human who stared back in muted horror.

The wolf broke first, hastily putting a paw on the leg in its mouth and kicking it out of jaws that couldn't stretch further with a shriek of rent metal. Then, without even a snarl, it turned tail and ran so fast it had trouble not slamming into the walls of the alleys around it with every turn.

It didn't know for how long it ran; it simply kept going until the shouts of the human in the alley faded, and then the sudden burst of strength it had obtained during its feeding frenzy started draining out of its body, until its limbs started buckling, barely managing to correct itself before it went off tumbling into a wall as a ball of thrashing legs. Yet, it continued running, albeit slower and clumsier.

Eventually, it saw a square-shaped hole in one of the metal walls, where some sort of patchwork repair had taken place and promptly failed again, and it dived in without a second thought.

A giant mass of cables covered in some bendy material embraced it like a mattress, and despite its previously terrible experience with wires and sparking stuff, it couldn't help but appreciate the warmth of the pipes above its head, the cooling blood covering the entirety of its upper body rapidly crusting on its fur and freezing its skin.

With a mild shiver, it licked its bleeding gums, and after several lengthy minutes of no danger coming, it relaxed, its panting tongue lolled out and dripping blood onto the crimson-painted cables.

It shuffled its body deeper into the mass of soft cords until it wasn't visible from the outside, emotionally and physically exhausted beyond what it thought possible. The moment its eyes closed, it rested, [Restful Awareness] rapidly bringing it back to some semblance of consciousness.

You have opened the Unique Path: [Hound of the Keeper]
Do you wish to follow it?

The wolf's lucid dream presented a choice, and the wolf focused on the symbols, trying to better understand it with all the caution and fear of an animal not wishing to confront something as dangerous as the being of darkness again.

Visions flashed and swirled before the wolf's eyes. The rough concept of the Keeper sitting in its incomprehensible realm as it contained Oblivion, countless little threads connecting its soul to puppets who flashed across the wolf's world and traveled through their chains to present souls to be cast into the rift of nonexistence, taking their toll. And one of those threads extended down to the wolf; yet, it was not a tether nor a restraint like the others, but rather, a connection. And through that connection, the Keeper would accept a trade. The wolf could expend some soul to channel the essence of Oblivion through its own soul, and expel a weaker, diluted, and finite version of it.

The visions flashed, and the wolf saw itself hurling a small sphere of pure nothingness through the chest of a human with nothing but its mind, leaving behind a round, cone-shaped hole as the sphere rapidly diminished until it exited through the human's back, barely the size of a tooth, and shot off into the distance.

Another scene depicted a spear rushing through the air, the air around it whizzing by so quickly that splinters of wood split off and disappeared. And just before it slammed through the wolf's head and skewered it, a large, roughly circular film of undulating darkness quickly formed in front of the wolf—the dark blanket diminishing into a paw-size hole of nothingness as the spear disappeared into it in the blink of an eye—before fading away to nothing, a tiny bit of soul returning to the wolf.

And finally, it saw itself use the odd thing from before, when the human had surprised it, but *flawlessly*.

It took the essence of nonexistence, and like tearing its fur off, took away its echo, a harmless darkness covering the wolf like a second coat of fur, turning it into a being whose footsteps brought no sound as it stomped on thin pipes without even a whisper of banging metal. And then, with fine control the wolf could never manage right now, it saw itself dashing around the lower canals as nothing but a vague shadow, barely visible only by the fact that it was moving at all.

Just as it thought that, the vision changed, showing how it looked when it stood stock-still.

Or rather, it *felt* like that was what was being shown, because even the wolf couldn't figure out where its body was supposed to be in the vision, until a black bump on top of a nearby pipe several feet off the ground suddenly got up on its legs and walked off into the darkness.

The instant the vision ended, the wolf accepted with a sense of giddiness and awe it had never felt before, its tail wagging in its sleep.

You have obtained the Unique Path: [Hound of the Keeper]
You have Leveled Up. Level 0 → Level 1

You have unlocked Attributes.
-Available Attribute Points: 1
-Base Attributes:
Strength (+0)
Speed (+0)
Dexterity (+0)
Endurance (+0)
Perception (+0)
Resolve (+0)
Intelligence (+0)
Soul (+0)

The wolf focused on each word to parse their meaning, but the moment it understood that Endurance meant something like a combination of physical toughness and stamina, it instantly chose it.

Endurance (+1)

The symbols continued moving across its dream-sight.

- Acquired Skills:
You have gained the Skill [Mental Resistance - Level 1]
You have gained the Skill [Soul Perception - Level 1]
You have gained the Skill [Mana Perception - Level 1]
You have gained the Skill [Mana Manipulation - Level 1]

You have gained the Skill [Echoes of Oblivion - Level 1]
You have gained the Skill [Bloodrush - Level 1]
[Mental Resistance] has Leveled Up. Level 1 → Level 28
[Corrosion Resistance] has Leveled Up. Level 4 → Level 5
[Restful Awareness] has Leveled Up. Level 3 → Level 5
[Iron Stomach] has Leveled Up. Level 3 → Level 4

-Acquired Titles:
Witness of Divinity: You have seen a being of divine nature in their own realm. Your illuminated gaze shatters all illusions and pierces through any and all falsehoods.

-Acquired Traits:
Timid (1/5): You have fled from danger equal or lesser to yourself multiple times. You are slightly faster when fleeing and are slightly slower when attacking.
Scavenger (1/1): You eat the unwanted remnants you can find rather than what you can hunt, trade, forage, cultivate, or steal. You are harder to notice when intending to scavenge.

The wolf mentally went through all the changes and roughly understood what had occurred as it swept through them, its mind unable to read the text but deriving meaning and information from them regardless.

[Bloodrush] was essentially that sudden boost of strength, endurance, and speed it had gained when it started trying to eat the human's legs, something that could be activated with a thought, lasted for maybe half a minute, and the wolf had to wait for a while to be able to use it again.

[Mental Resistance] was . . . some type of mental wall that would block things like "The Keeper" from delving into its head, assuming they were a couple million times weaker than it.

The skills with *Mana* or *Soul* in them only provided it with definitions and ideas so abstract and strange, it couldn't make heads or tails of them; only that they were about seeing and moving whatever *Mana* and *Soul* were.

It kept "reading" and paused when it finally understood what Timid was describing, after a few moments of focusing on it.

Was the human who was roaring and screaming equal to it? Or lesser? The idea was ridiculous, simply by dint of size. The human had towered over it, twice to thrice as wide and four to five times as tall, covered in thick extra skins and plates of lead. But the odd symbols in its mind were what had given it its newfound vigor, the very reason it was even alive right now.

If something had the power to help the wolf like that, not only was it friendly but it probably knew better than it did by a long shot. Additionally, the way the creature of darkness had planted information in its mind was oddly reminiscent of how the wolf kept getting definitions and random tiny bits of knowledge in its mind, and even more reminiscent of the way the odd symbols of its mind kept seemingly pulling information out of the aether and into its brain.

So, maybe . . . maybe it *could* kill a human in a fight?

But why would it risk such a thing? There were more than enough creatures in the nest for it to eat if it could even entertain the idea of attacking a human. It felt like it could definitely defeat one of the giant rats now, at the very least, so it would start there.

Its thoughts drifted back to the words, wishing to refresh its memory, and the information spread itself before him at the mere hint of its intentions.

-Species: Wolf
-Name: None
-Path: [Hound of the Keeper] Level 1

-Available Attribute Points: 0
-Base Attributes:
Strength (+0)
Speed (+0)
Dexterity (+0)
Endurance (+1)
Perception (+0)
Resolve (+0)
Intelligence (+0)
Soul (+0)

-Racial Skills: [Pack Hunter], [Quick Learner], [Devourer]
-Acquired Skills:
[Pain Resistance - Level 17]
[Infection Resistance - Level 7]
[Poison Resistance - Level 12]
[Corrosion Resistance - Level 5]
[Disease Resistance - Level 4]

[Magic Resistance – Level 4]
[Mental Resistance – Level 28]
[Electricity Resistance – Level 2]
[Restful Awareness – Level 5]
[Tough Skin – Level 2]
[Iron Stomach – Level 4]
[Mana Perception – Level 1]
[Mana Manipulation – Level 1]
[Soul Perception – Level 1]
[Echoes of Oblivion – Level 1]
[Bloodrush – Level 1]

–Acquired Titles:
Witness of Divinity: You have seen a being of divine nature in their own realm. Your illuminated gaze shatters all illusions and pierces through any and all falsehoods.

–Acquired Traits:
Enduring (1/5): You have felt the chill of death multiple times and survived. You are slightly tougher.
Timid (1/5): You have fled from danger equal or lesser to yourself multiple times. You are slightly faster when fleeing and are slightly slower when attacking.
Scavenger (1/1): You eat the unwanted remnants you can find rather than hat you can hunt, trade, forage, cultivate, or steal. You are harder to notice when intending to scavenge.

Many of the things listed were small improvements it wouldn't have even noticed or paid attention to had it not checked using the odd symbols and the info they gave.

It still had no idea what *soul, mana,* and *divinity* were, and trying to focus on *Echoes of Oblivion* provided nothing but hazy images of moving darkness rather than the detailed visions of before, but it was enough for it to feel at least a *little* aware of what was going on with itself.

The second it had finished seeing what had changed, the process of deconstruction started, the human it had eaten being picked apart in its stomach and mind both.

Information flashed, embedded, and collected, full of holes yet more than enough to understand to some minor degree of depth how a human body worked. Where to strike, what the weak points were. Their olfactory senses, the range of vibrations their ears could pick up.

Dozens upon dozens of names flashed past and into its mind, interlocking functions unwrapping and stretching for it to better see how they worked.

And it was in awe.

The human brain's mental acuity was over three times better than its own. Their sight was roughly three times better, their range longer and with the ability to perceive *new* colors the wolf had never even seen before. It had some vague notion of green, light yellow, and light blue, but that was all it could really see beyond varying shades of shadow. Humans could see *so much more.*

That wasn't all. Their joints allowed for so much flexibility. They could twist their arms around in ways the wolf couldn't even dream of without something important snapping and breaking. The way their chest was structured allowed their arms to spread, and if the wolf could replicate that or find some way to make its own paws do the same, its sideways maneuverability would be *incredible.* Its own body was built for rapid forward movement, but if it could incorporate their pectoral muscles and arm joint structure into its frame somehow, it could have amazing mobility in all four directions. The secret was in the shoulders, but it didn't quite know how to replicate that on itself without sacrificing forward speed.

But if it combined the best aspects of its paws and the hands of a human, it could climb and manipulate things so much easier. It could even use *their* devices, like ladders and the metal grips they used to drop down to the canals without it having to risk its life or waste half a day to descend. Not to mention it could use its claws to actually *attack* rather than just using them to gain traction on the ground when it ran.

Yet, when it entertained the idea of adding any of those useful features, it became aware of what it would be adding them *to.*

Its own body.

It could examine itself now. It could see all the badly healed fractures, the infection that had rendered its left ear useless permanently. It could see the utterly indestructible material its teeth and claws were made out of, yet not its composition or how to recreate them. It could see some of the things that made its body so incredible, yet at the same time, so horribly vulnerable. Even compared to a human.

A single layer in its rib cage? Why do that if its body could have another set of flexibly movable bones underneath the gaps just to ensure its organs were safe from small, stabby things? Why was its stomach so important yet so exposed? Why was its spine so . . . *fragile?* Why was its tail so useless? Why was its natural lifespan so horribly small compared to humans?

The questions piled on and on as it mentally checked itself from top to bottom, and eventually, it noticed something, a new growth running down the insides of its snout, slowly but surely. The antennae it had wished for. It was just starting, the nerves being constructed by its body, inert and only foundational until the proper receptors in its brain were constructed.

But the visible confirmation that all the bits of this process had a true point, a real impact on its form, chased away the bitter anxiety of a body whose imperfections were all laid bare and criticized. However, as it mentally stepped back from viewing the fine details, it noticed something else.

Another bit of floating information in its mind. A jumbled mess of flesh, fat, organs, and crushed bones floating in nothingness waiting for the wolf to tap into.

And tap into, it did.

With as much caution as possible, it looked to the "hormones" its body produced and found the thing that caused it to grow, aptly named *growth hormone*, along with another more complicated name it couldn't quite grasp yet. It used the human's bones to make its own better. Stronger and heavier, if only by a little bit. It assigned the human's flesh and organs to be quickly digested, and gently nudged its body to produce a *little* bit more growth hormone, enough to grow bigger just a bit faster, but not enough to cause complications in its body, one that it wasn't entirely knowledgeable about right now.

Caution above all else.

It used some bits of cartilage to reinforce weak joints, some bits of flesh and blood to replenish that which it had lost from its bleeding mouth, and after some serious deliberation, tried to do something a little more complicated.

Adding more tendons.

If it was understanding the information before it correctly, tendons lead to increased muscle mass, *vastly* increased strength, and it was something its body could do naturally, completely on its own, rather than something the wolf would have to irrationally worry about crippling itself with if it did something wrong.

It took a long, *long* time, even in its dreamspace, but it eventually managed to mold a functional shape in its leg bones and joints for the new extra tendons to run through, with heavy, *heavy* assistance from the odd presence in its mind that made the text symbols appear. Of course, it was just a sort of direction more than anything else, and the physical changes would take a while to appear, but it was a great start.

Those changes complete, it returned to its previous grafting procedure and quickly chose to have its eyes be more humanoid in structure but not appearance, enough to be able to see more colors, see farther and sharper but still maintain its superior night vision by keeping the reflective lining behind the retina. It thinned the nictitating membrane around its eyes and made it denser instead, both to reduce the blur in its vision and to not lose the extra protection the membrane provided.

It thought long and hard about the human brain, yet it was just too complex to feel safe picking it for itself with such little information. That, and *something* warned that it would have to change both its size and current skull structure to accommodate a brain of such complexity and size.

Besides, what if it ended up feeling, thinking, and acting like a human while stuck in the form of a wolf?

Even if it *wasn't* stuck in the form of a wolf, it *liked* being a wolf, for all the good its species did it. It didn't want to be a human, neither in its brain nor in its body. So, as tempting as it was, it felt like it just didn't know enough about the structure to apply it to itself without breaking or making something terribly wrong.

The eyes were surprisingly simple, but that was about all it could really use right now, besides their excretion system for cooling themselves off. Excreting fluid to cool themselves off using air currents was an interesting design, but unless the wolf could figure out a way to be able to turn it on and off at will so it wouldn't accidentally boil or freeze itself to death by messing around with its body's poorly understood heating and cooling mechanisms, there wasn't enough information for it to work off. And its mind was already heavily struggling to understand everything it was being jammed full of, even with the odd floating symbols helping it so much. If it were awake, it got the feeling that not even a *fraction* of this would have been possible.

But why did it perfectly understand how cockroaches worked after having only one bite of them, despite the comparable complexity of their forms, yet the human body that had taken almost an hour to consume was . . . vaguely interpreted, but not yet understood?

Despite eating the insects, the amount of material on them was barely equivalent to the human's fist. Six whole cockroaches were barely big enough . . . to . . .

Six.

It was the number.

It understood cockroaches perfectly because it had eaten six of them, or so it thought. The exact number was half forgotten, and it did not particularly care about the specifics, but it understood what it needed if it wanted to survive, and maybe even thrive.

It had to get smarter, stronger, and bigger. It had to eat more humans, which it could only feel comfortable doing if it could at least double its current size. Maybe triple it?

But then, it would be too large to pass off as just another canine, and the bigger it was, the more attention humans would pay to it, making it harder to hide, blend in with the other canines, and maybe even make them recognize it on sight if they caught it eating one of their own.

So . . . why even fight?

The human had succumbed to the poison and died without the wolf even having to do anything.

If it could somehow make its own poison or . . . No, *venom*. But the only way to make it would be to *eat* extremely dangerous, venomous creatures, wait for its body to create the venom glands, and find . . . *some* way to put that poison into the humans, then wait for them to die.

Too . . . unrealistic. And scary, and risky. And lots of other things it didn't quite have the words for.

An ambush . . . it could work. Jump out of nowhere, bite a hole into their glass-mask thing, and wait for the human to die again. An ambush would be its best chance . . . but still dangerous if it screwed up.

Its only *safe* course of action was to keep running from danger using the Timid and Scavenger traits until it could find another lucky break and grow big enough to start fighting and hunting humans.

It had to be smarter. If humans could make such incredible things with only three times the intelligence it had, the wolf could only dream of how much more fluid and effortless it would be to use its [Devourer] ability when it understood the human brain structure enough to mimic it. Among . . . well, everything else. It had no illusions about its intelligence, and the floating symbols definitely helped it understand its place.

It was much smarter than any animal should be, but not smarter than any human.

For the remaining time of its rest, the wolf posed countless questions and clarifications to the floating symbols, most of which were ignored.

CHAPTER 5

When the wolf woke up, it was to the sound of approaching humans. Its eyes shot open, more than well rested, and it quickly sank low on its legs, crouched and ready to bolt out of its hiding spot.

Its single ear strained to listen, and it quickly deliberated whether it should flee instantly or try and hide first. Then its eyes lowered to the small but noticeable trail of blood that led directly into the hole of metal it'd dashed into, and it decided.

With but a thought, it activated [Bloodrush], planting its front paws on the lip of the vent it had entered through, and kicked with its back legs to leap out onto the alley.

Behind it, in the distance, it heard the faint sound of humans conversing, but their volume was muted, their growls subdued and sounding . . . irritated, more than scared or threatening. It didn't dwell on it much and simply rushed away, its eyes gradually widening as it realized just how *good* it felt.

Rushing through the metal maze with all its might, it let out a happy bark as its tongue hung out the side of its mouth, slowly but surely turning its sprint into a trot as [Bloodrush] faded, until it decided to stop completely and examine itself.

Although it could see very little with its eyes compared to what it could see when dreaming, it did notice that its bones and joints were a little less defined than yesterday, no longer like sharp angles that jutted out of its sides but . . .

Well, more like *blunted* angles that jutted out of its sides.

It did have to resist the urge to chase its own tail, though. It didn't feel bendy enough to reach it, anyway.

Still, it was ecstatic, and despite the ravenous hunger, it felt more than satisfied. It could barely feel any ticks on its fur anymore, its skin seemingly growing too tough for the insects by a combination of [Tough Skin] and the Endurance attribute. There were still a couple of those large ones, but once it found a rough enough spot to scratch them out of itself, it would be free of the pests, finally.

There was also a sense of long-lost safety in the fact that it actually had the strength to run away now. It did reprimand itself for running for longer than necessary, but it was a fairly mild self-criticism, as it had no idea how good those humans would be at tracking. They had a terrible sense of smell, but their eyes were great.

It resumed its walking, looking up at the towering structures of iron above itself, stretching on and on until the smog rendered it unable to see the ceiling of the cavern, giving them the illusion of reaching into a smoke-drowned sky.

Pipes and masses of wires ran between the structures and through them, giving its surroundings the sense of a maze in the truest sense of the word. One stretch of cobbles was a tunnel with a roof of pipes that opened into a multilayered series of hammocks made of cables that went up endlessly, then a sudden drop into an open coal chute, and a pathway on the side that led to sparking cylinders, and it continued with no sense of direction or logic but number plates that the wolf could find no pattern or direction in.

The only sign of organic life was the rare human, covered completely in their extra skins and glass masks as they checked wires, carried things into the buildings, or ran around with some kind of humming, glowing device, moving it up and down the exposed bits of machinery they could find.

Interspersed through all this were the even rarer humans who climbed up and down the structures without such a suit and just a mask, banging and clanging and fiddling away at every bit of their nest structure they could find, hanging hundreds of feet in the air and climbing about like insects, dots of moving black in the incomprehensible and seemingly useless maze of machinery.

There were still a lot of humans down here, but in comparison to the nest above them, they might as well not even be there. Even in the slow half-hour walk it took to get back to the canals—mainly using the glowing marks in the distant cave walls and months of experience—it barely saw two dozen humans altogether.

It was a welcome change in pace, even if the air there hurt. It hurt a lot less after the symbols helped it, but it still burned, and even though it knew that being around this place would keep leveling its Poison and Magic Resistance skills, it wasn't particularly keen on staying more than necessary. It would hunt around for a few scraps, then start making the journey to get to the level above, where rats could withstand the far milder levels of poison in the air, and it might even find a dead human again, with any luck.

Its level of success was not exactly staggering, but the difference was more than obvious.

The Scavenger trait had severely understated the effect it would have. The dumber creatures, like the glowing flies, barely even noticed it, even if it shoved its snout into their prey and suddenly dragged it away. Stronger things like the predators near the tops of the rivers still easily saw it, but as long as it was simply moving about with the "intent to scavenge," creatures of a lesser nature barely saw it.

In one particularly risky experiment, it tried to see how close it could get to one of the glowing predator vines before it noticed the wolf, and quickly realized that checking how its trait worked definitely didn't count as scavenging. It would have lost at least an entire toe had it not activated [Bloodrush] in a panic to jump back.

Still, the amount of actual food it could find without having to worry about every tiny little squirming or frothing thing? It had doubled. And feeling a bit more confident than before, it even found some of the melted blobs of skin and flesh that were those black winged creatures it saw and heard squeaking around up high on the pipes, and ate them, only mildly regretting all the burning liquid in its throat. It would probably not get anything useful out of them besides filling its stomach, so ruined they were by the fluids, but any food was good.

It hurt, and its throat felt raw from the liquids on the fliers, but it had a feeling all the excess flesh waiting in storage could heal that minor injury overnight. Maybe it could restore its ear, too, but it was so close to its brain, and the structure was so small and complicated that—

The wolf paused.

There was no real difference between one ear and the other, besides the side of its body they were on. It could just . . . copy what was on the right and use the human's meat to create it.

But how would it get rid of what was already there? The injury itself was healing, the infection done and receding, but now it had an ear that was on the border of being dead flesh taking up space on its precious head when it could fit something better there.

After a few minutes of deliberation with no answer but wild, unintelligent theorizing, it gave up and spent a few moments trying to reorientate itself as it hopped up on the edge of the canal, its feet thanking it for finally being on semiflat ground once more. Managing to find a spot to peek at the walls of the cave and the blurry glowing things on them, it compared the distance and realized it was closer than it had thought to the spiraling stretch of chaos that led to the upper levels.

After an exhausting three hours of walking uphill at a snail's pace, it found a fallen gear covered in rust leaning against a dented wall, and slept underneath it.

The process of deconstructing the flier began, but it provided it with nothing but a vague notion of where its organs *might* be, and a name.

A bat.

When the wolf awoke, it was to the faint scent of copper. Its nose seemed to have healed enough for it to at least be able to smell itself, and its fur absolutely reeked of blood. And despite the abundance of blood it had ingested from the human, it was extremely thirsty, its throat dry and its body begging for some actual *water* rather than the thin slime that blood was.

There weren't many places for someone or something that wasn't a human to drink water from. In fact, its best chance was to find some leaking pipes and lap up the water that formed underneath them.

After another hour of slowly trotting up a very vaguely defined path through the iron jungle, presumably made by the humans, it began slowly recognizing its surroundings and took a dip into a little crevice that was so tight even its thin body could barely squeeze through, finding what it was looking for: a perpetually leaking pipe that it had stumbled upon when looking for a safe place to sleep.

It had to stop and stare for a moment at the tiny green things flanking the puddle of water. Curiously sniffing and pawing at them, it deemed them safe, and after licking up every drop of water it could with its unfortunately still numb tongue, it pushed its snout against the iron, trying to get one of its eyes as close to the odd green thing as possible.

Small as it may have been, it was definitely strong, because it seemed to have snaked up and *pushed* the iron plates out of the way to grow . . . out of where?

After observing it for another five minutes without any sort of sudden revelation to its origins and nature coming to its mind, it simply got up and walked in circles in the little alcove where the pipe ran through, alternating its stare from the humans' strange nest to its own legs, still skeletal but no longer to the point of it looking absolutely grotesque, where it could see its tendons poking out through its thin fur. It felt great, but that was only by comparison. It had no delusion that compared to most of the other kin in the humans' nest, it was weak and still entirely too thin.

It was going to fix that.

Moving was a chore, however, even if it moved in small circles. Its fur was so matted by filth, blood, and melted together by the times it'd had to rush through the burning river on the few occasions it had drawn the attention of the more dangerous beings of the canals that it was simply too . . . inflexible, pulling at its skin with every motion like the plating of a cockroach but without any of the defensive capability, just heavy and annoying.

Thankfully, its sense of taste was still numb at best, which it wasn't planning on fixing anytime soon, deliberately directing the human's flesh to become its own and turn to better tasks. After a self-cleaning session that left its tongue feeling raw, however, it realized that it would probably have an easier time just . . . cutting through its fur.

It was really hot in the canal area anyway, and the only time the wolf ever got cold was if it was wet or simply too starved to produce its own body heat efficiently. So, using its front teeth with the utmost caution, it got to raking through its fur like a human would a razor, mentally noting to prod around the [Devourer] skill with the symbols' odd visions to see if it could make itself more flexible.

It could probably figure it out on its own given time, but frankly, it had only a vague idea of what it was doing, and it feared that making itself *too* flexible would end up making it less . . . solid. Like its joints and bones could snap out of place when it didn't want them to, making any impact suddenly dislocate important bits of itself outside of where they should be.

It sounded a little odd in its head, but its logic didn't *feel* wrong, so added flexibility was something to be looked into but not *jumped* into.

Its thoughts were interrupted by its front teeth accidentally shaving off a thin layer of skin as well, and it yelped in pain as the injury registered, jumping back to its feet.

Confusion overcame the wolf, having thought its teeth's newfound sharpness couldn't be used on itself for some reason. Its bleeding leg was only a mild concern at the moment, only giving it a couple licks to clean the wound and get it to start healing.

Experimentally, and extremely slowly, it prodded one of its canines with its tongue . . .

And nothing happened. Oh, it was pointy—extremely so—feeling like the tip of a needle more than the teeth it was used to, yet it refused to puncture its tongue, no matter how hard it pressed down on it, even when trapping the very tip between its razor-sharp front teeth and squeezing. It hurt, but that was it. It didn't make any sense.

Bewildered, it turned to the pipe of water, having only now remembered its teeth could cut through metal since the symbols appeared. But the pipe was far too large for the wolf to sink its teeth into, so it turned to a simple corner covered in swirling bits of metal which seemed to serve no purpose, turned its head, and bit.

Without even the slightest hint of pushback, its teeth sank into the metal and raked through it with a similar amount of effort. Spitting out the remnants of broken iron bits out of its mouth, it returned to focusing on its tongue, pressing it into its canine with the intent to pierce it a bit and draw blood.

Two things happened at once.

Its canine went into its tongue, just a bit, then stopped, resistance registering suddenly. And something about the puzzle of the situation clicked into place through the haze of pain as the wolf hung its bleeding tongue out of its mouth.

It could control how its teeth worked with its mind.

Rolling its tongue back into its mouth, it turned to a support rod nearby, about as thick as its waist, and tilted its head with open jaws, focusing on having its canines not pierce or cut through the metal. As it closed its jaws, the metal remained unaffected, its teeth raking against it uselessly.

It tried again, now with the idea to pierce but not to cut, and its teeth sank in as if through air. Experimentally, it tugged. It didn't move even the slightest bit, its teeth firmly stuck in the iron.

It then focused on having its teeth cut through a *little*, and with a mighty pull, it slowly began to cut through the metal. Satisfied, it focused on its teeth cutting through completely and yanked back, feeling not the tiniest shred of resistance as its teeth just phased through the metal, leaving deep wounds into the support rod.

Then, with as much caution as it could muster, it focused on its teeth cutting through anything *except* its skin, and found that it could cleanly shave its fur off with no issue. After a few more minutes of experimentation, the wolf got back to its grooming, mentally pushing some extra bits of the stored flesh to heal its tongue and foreleg.

Half an hour later, and with over half its body feeling like it could finally breathe, it trotted out of its little metal alcove, occasionally stopping to lap at its leg wound. Shaving its fur had definitely done it no favors in the sense of appearance, it noted, as without the extra bulk, it looked even more like a thin layer of leather stretched tight over a skeleton. The extra bulk it was slowly getting from the human helped, but it was still slightly disturbing when every movement was clearly seen through its own skin, like its leg tendons tensing and relaxing with every step.

The majority of its backside was still unshaven, and its head and shoulders were too, for obvious reasons, but it couldn't deny that it had been a great idea. Without all that extra baggage, it felt a couple stones lighter, which certainly helped with its stamina.

Eight more hours of walking, interspersed with many short naps, and it came across a small pipe full with the sound of rushing liquid. Trying to see if it could wet its head and back enough for the crusty fur to soften or get cleaned, it approached the thin pipe, only about as large as its muzzle, and hooked a canine into it.

Smelling the foul scent of the canals, it quickly removed its tooth from the metal and retreated as the pressurized water exploded out of the hole. Yet, it was still just water, if extremely foul smelling.

Deciding to risk it, it walked to the rapidly growing puddle on the floor and dipped a toe in.

Absolutely nothing.

Half an hour of rolling around on the ground and rubbing its face against everything it could find, it shook itself free of all the liquid, taking the opportunity to get rid of the few remaining ticks and other things on its back by rubbing against some metal wire fence.

And finally, after another hour of walking, it was finally out of the maze area, the path before it quickly simplifying into an extremely wide rectangle that led to the floor above, around which were . . .

A startling amount of humans.

Its steps slowed as it watched them curiously.

Humans tended to go into the giant towers to descend to the lower levels, so there were rarely any people hanging around the entrance to what might have been the most toxic place in the nest. And if it wasn't the tower, they'd use some boxes being pulled up and down along some thick wire to make shorter trips that didn't land them straight to the bottom.

It couldn't help but worry that maybe they were there to hunt it for eating one of their own.

Humans were odd creatures. Some had horns, some had soft, peachy skin, some had tails and scales, some were smaller and had green skin, usually being led around by some bigger humans, some even had a mixture of all of the above from what it had seen, but the one thing they always seemed to carry with them when they got ready to hurt something, was an inanimate object. Some long, pointy stick, some sharp piece of metal, maybe some of those glowing devices, or some long, oddly glowing sticks with crystals on top.

And almost every single one of these humans was absolutely covered in extra metal coverings and had some sort of weapon hanging on them or in their hand as they conversed.

With mildly trembling legs, it stalked forward, but besides a few odd looks, nobody seemed to be actively looking for it. A little more confident, with hesitant but quick steps, it moved forth, swerving its head around as much as possible to ensure no sneak attacks, [Bloodrush] hovering around the forefront of its mind to be used at a moment's notice.

Besides some curious looks, however, few paid it attention.

Until someone who was in that group of *few* loosely raised her hand in its direction.

"[Control Beast]," the woman said, her tone oddly curious as she tilted her head of light-blue hair, wearing some formfitting extra skins and carrying some sort of curved wooden shield on her other hand.

The wolf stopped in its tracks instantly, its eyes bulging as it felt a strong, foreign compulsion to follow the woman. It turned a little, its mind pushing [Bloodrush] to the forefront as it tried its best to resist the insistent desire— no, the *need* to follow the human's orders.

"C'mere, little guy," the woman—presumably; the wolf wasn't close enough to smell her scent and confirm—cooed, quirking her lips upward from more than two dozen feet away. Yet the wolf heard her nonsensical human speech and understood what she meant regardless.

As if bewitched, its legs carried it forward, and after a moment, it struggled to find a reason to resist the human's influence in the first place. This . . . this felt *right*, somehow. Perhaps out of sheer stubbornness, however, it kept doing its best to fight it, until it remembered it had [Mental Resistance]. With a conscious order for the skill to rise to its full power, the human's hold broke like cut strings, and the wolf turned, activating [Bloodrush] as it fled at full speed.

The woman let out a surprised gasp, as did some of the humans it dashed between, and just barely, it heard her parting words.

"That dog was Awakened!" the woman excitedly barked out, and the wolf saw out of the corner of its eyes as almost a dozen humans all armed to the teeth simultaneously turned around to look at it, their eyes wide, another dozen looking around curiously for where the wolf was.

Not looking back, it dashed through the streets with all its might, sending its claws the intent to pierce through the stone *just a tiny bit* to add more traction to its gallops. Some humans barked at it as it dashed through, under, and between their legs and coats, but besides a single dodged kick, none tried to stop it.

Five minutes later, it ducked into a tiny set of stairs that wrapped around someone's home, rushed up the thin pathway that led up to a place of yellow light, and found itself in one of those open, circular areas surrounded by buildings where humans gave each other things.

It turned around to look for any angry human pursuers as it panted. Finding no danger at its heels, it relaxed, discovering a relatively untouched and unseen corner behind a cart to sleep in.

It didn't like to sleep around humans, but with its [Restful Awareness] skill and their *general* apathy toward beings like itself, it could at least take a short nap to let its limbs rest up from the abuse they'd endured during its escape. As long as it didn't make more humans mad by breaking their skills with [Mental Resistance], it should be fine.

It slept in peace, surprisingly, despite the constant clamor of its surroundings.

CHAPTER 6

"Silthen, I am one *hundred percent* positive that dog was Awakened," Aitra insisted with a huff, gesturing to the entrance of the Bone Pits to their right with her kite shield. "It literally just walked out of the *Bone Pits* while looking like something an [Animator] raised from the grave, then proceeded to *break through* my level sixteen [Control Beast] spell like it was tissue paper, then clearly activated *something* and ran! Also, its eyes were *glowing*. If you had looked at it, you would know. It's either a doppelgänger or a decently leveled Awakened!" she reasoned, feeling like she was a moment's away from just walking away to find the damn dog herself.

Silthen groaned as he ran a hand through his brown hair, his eyes half lidded from annoyance, then he spoke, gesturing with his hands.

"Aitra, okay. Even if it *is*, what do you expect us to do? Chase after some small dog in a goddamn labyrinth Dungeon city? We're more likely to get lost trying to get the damn thing for you; we don't have a tracker, and the Factory teleporters open soon, so we might lose our chance to be among the first batch going in.

"And even if we *did* get it, what the hell would you do with it? You're a [Spirit Summoner], not a [Corporeal Summoner], and you won't be for likely another couple years. You want us to just lock the thing in our inn rooms until it's able to have enough intelligence not to hinder or outright get us killed in the Dungeon?"

Curse him and his reasonableness!

"We could at least sell it to some fat fuck noble for a couple hundred gold crowns! That's multiple times more than we'd make by killing some weak-ass golems and digging their cores out!" she protested, inwardly drooling over finally having a little bit more change in her pockets.

For a moment, her teammates' eyes lit up a bit, appearing skeptical for the first time, only to be shot down by Silthen again.

"*If* we catch it. *If* we don't get lost, then there's the fact that we're not going to get any levels on our paths or progress for our skills by chasing some starving mutt around like idiots. We're not chasing it. That's final."

Ankhan, the feather-headed Corfid, nodded. "Yeaaaaaaaaaaah, I'm with Silthen on this one. I can barely find my way back to our inn even after a week, and every time I leave, I feel like I'll turn a corner and turn around to find a wall behind me. This place is a goddamn maze. Also . . . the locals are fucking scary. Have you *seen* how they glare at us?"

Nakim snorted from atop her crate, where she was swinging her legs back and forth, her innumerable needles, darts, and daggers so well concealed even Aitra couldn't tell where she'd shoved them into this time.

"No, they glare at *you* because you look like a rich boy peacock. Nobody gives a shit about you down here unless you look or act rich or annoying, and you act and look like *both*."

"It's not my fault I'm dashing. I'd look like a king wearing a potato sack." Ankhan shrugged, and Aitra watched Nakim's teeth grit, her fingers tensing with the desire to throw a dart into his forehead.

While she didn't share the animosity Nakim had for Ankhan, she could agree that he was, if nothing else, making them look bad in the eyes of the locals. Wearing a gaudy bright red brigandine in the dirty slums was already stretching it. Layering on a *cape* for no reason was just making him look like a prick, especially considering that the only reason they were down here was because the teleport distance was shortest here, and thus the cheapest, only being one silver per person to enter.

Maybe if he were a high-level adventurer it wouldn't seem as pretentious, but he definitely couldn't back up his wealth with power. He had no notion of "saving," and it seemed like that extended to more than just conserving his mana.

Being the youngest member of the team however, and already feeling a bit chastised after being denied the chance to find that Awakened dog, she said nothing.

She just couldn't get over how quickly they discarded the idea of capturing that little stray. As an aspiring [Corporeal Summoner], a dog was the *perfect* thing to bind as a first summon.

When the old Academy found a way to breed the [Devourer] skill out of wolves, followed by the systematic annihilation of said wolves, things had been smooth sailing between the newly made creatures called dogs and humans. Until a couple centuries later, when through the selective breeding—or perhaps some other factor—it was theorized they were too far from their origins in the eyes of the system, and that changed their Awakening requirements so much and so drastically that nobody could figure out what they even were anymore, or if most dogs were just locked out of the system by default.

Humanoids roughly tended to have to reach a certain level of intelligence, which everyone but the most mentally disabled could pass by the time they were six or seven years old.

Dragons were just *born* with access to the system, seen as animals, people, *and* monsters, because the world was unfair.

Dogs?

Nobody knew, and that was part of what made an Awakened dog so valuable. There were plenty of other tamed creatures for people to bond with or create summons out of, but none were ever so compatible and easy as dogs. They were literally made to be companions to humanoids, unlike a raptirid, any one of the various species of elemental salamanders, or the tiny thraklings that people were hankering after just for the pride of having something that was *sort of* like a wyvern or a drake on their shoulder, if about the size of a small dog.

They were all fine and all, but they were difficult, and paths that dealt with summons, familiars, or *god forbid,* soulbonds, all had the common issue of the bond between the human and the animal they were with.

Raptirids were smart little bastards, but they were greedy as hell, had a nasty temper, and were more than a little difficult to control. You couldn't chastise them too much without building resentment, and they felt entitled to rewards even if they knew they didn't do the command right. They were also overactive, every minute of sleep being paired with twenty minutes of constant yelling and flying about. You had to have a damn leash on them at all times or risk losing them the first couple years. And despite their intelligence, it was extremely rare for a raptirid to genuinely bond with their owners, limiting the communication and teamwork of the summon severely despite their natural predatory abilities.

Salamanders had the opposite issue. They were extremely easy to bond with, but they were stupid, and barely did anything. Getting a fire salamander to spew a bout of flammable liquid at something hostile was an exercise in futility if it wasn't feeling directly threatened. You had to have a low power control spell on them *constantly,* or else they wouldn't feel the tiniest bit motivated to move. They were pretty cute, though.

And thraklings were like raptirids, if you made them twice as big and gave them the attitude of a psychotic pyromaniac.

A standard dog was *perfect*. It was weak on the spectrum of available summons, especially when technically there were *thousands* of different animals one could get, but they were by far the most stable and reliable. They absolutely adored their owners if they were treated well, and that bond let them flawlessly communicate and understand the summoner without even a word being spoken, almost like a permanent telepathy spell. Paired with some skills like [Elemental Summon Infusion], they could be a surprisingly diverse companion, able to act as artillery, infantry, or a shock troop, rushing in and out of battle with [Haste] buffs and shields.

She was still far away from becoming a [Conjurative Summoner], but she still felt like she'd just lost an amazing opportunity. For a stray to either have learned [Peace of Mind] or [Mental Resistance] at a level where it could break her spell so easily, it must have been absurdly strong for its age and size.

Maybe if she hadn't relied on her skills so much and approached the little thing with some meat in her hands, that whole fiasco could have been avoided.

She sighed as she leaned back against a metal wall, wondering when the doors would open and they'd get to step through the teleporters so she could let out some of her frustration by throwing spirits at the golems.

Thinking about the Factory definitely didn't help her mood, unlike what she'd expected. She had been to other Dungeons before on the opposite end of the world, but comparing them to the Factory was downright insulting, in both size and complexity. This place was the size of several small countries, *without* factoring in the actual country sitting on top of it.

And they were going to go straight inside very soon.

It was a little terrifying, the fact that the Bone Pits were so lethally toxic that they had to build warded military facilities around all the entrances to the active floors of the Dungeon below, with the only way in or out being a bunch of teleport platforms and portals. The possibility of something breaking the teleportation magic and the purification wards would all lead to a scenario where they would either be stranded in a dead, city-sized labyrinth of metal covered in poison fumes from top to bottom, or at best, stuck in a warded facility, waiting for rescue as food supplies dwindled.

Not that any unfortunate fate awaiting in the Dungeon would be much better, but thankfully, few were psychotic enough to go lower than the topmost active floor of the Factory, and her team wasn't a part of that small percentage.

* * *

When the wolf awoke, it was around the time the light crystals would dim in what it assumed was a way for humans to tell the time by counting light cycles.

It stretched its forelegs and dipped low to the ground with a jaw-popping yawn. During its nap, it had confirmed that roughly three-fourths of the human still remained as a blob of gore stored . . . *somewhere*, and had tried to prod around its body to better understand how it worked, to varying success. It had tried to toughen up the insides of its throat, but even during the process, it somehow knew that it wouldn't be much of a change and would just increase the chances of inflammation, making it choke, so it'd dropped the idea quickly.

It turned and walked through the open area, most of the humans congregating around the wooden carts and going in and out of the glass-covered buildings as they gave things to each other allowing it a surprising amount of ease in its navigation.

Yet, as it went to curve around some female human's legs, the woman crouched low on her ankles, her coat pooling around her feet, and extended an open hand toward it, palm up. The wolf stopped in its tracks, curious yet cautious. As it examined the woman, she reached into the basket she was holding under her other arm, and with a bit of fiddling, pulled out something vaguely white and . . .

Smelling like food. *Good,* human food.

Then she held it out to the wolf, making some odd sort of cooing noise.

The wolf eyed the taller human female standing behind the woman as she looked around, wary but not nervous or aggressive, and it decided to go for the food. Extending its neck out as far as possible, and with its legs in a half crouch, it slowly sniffed the delicious scent of the fluffy yellow-white food, the human's hand, and even proactively set [Bloodrush] in a corner of its mind to be used if the female tried something.

As its teeth closed around the edge, it made them not cut, only pierce a little, and quickly dragged the piece of food out of her hands, chomping it down in a single bite before licking its chops. The woman moved the corner of her lips up and cut out another piece, which the wolf ate with increasingly less suspicion until it barely sniffed them before throwing them down its gullet, and until it was eating out of the human's hands.

The taller female glanced at them, and her expression tightened.

"My lady, please do not debase yourself by letting mangy, dying mutts *lick* your *hands*."

The woman moved her shoulders up and down once as she reached for an entire loaf of the white stuff and laid it down just below her knees, extending an empty hand toward the wolf, which licked it once, twice, and then nosed it in gratitude before quickly moving forward to take the food away from the woman by stabbing a canine through the corner and dragging its body back. With its eyes on the women, it pinned the food with its paws and started tearing it apart with gusto.

"Katherine," the woman started softly. "Can you not see that its eyes are glowing? *Don't alarm it,*" she added on quickly as the wolf continued staring at them, biting chunks out of the rapidly diminishing food in front of it.

The woman in the back suddenly nailed her gaze on it, and it stiffened slightly, its lightly wagging tail going rigid.

"Awakened," the woman in the back breathed out. "*Or* something an [Animator], [Infuser], or some type of summoner lost."

The woman in front bobbed her head then extended the basket behind toward the tall woman, who quickly took it. She muttered something, and a thin film of white covered the hand the wolf had been eating off. Then, just after the wolf finished the odd rectangle of food, she extended an open hand toward it, and the wolf tilted its head as it licked its chops. After staring at the hand for a moment, it moved forward, gently nosed it, and started wagging its tail as the human got closer, rubbing its snout, head, and under its chin.

Humans were dangerous and scary, but if they were nice, the wolf loved nothing more than to let one pet it. After getting progressively filthier and bigger, that quickly happened less and less frequently, so even if it kept its eyes open and [Bloodrush] in its mind, it luxuriated in the hands of the human quite easily.

"What do you wish to do? Do you want me to capture it?" the woman in the back questioned the one on the front, who shook her head side to side.

"No, we will do precisely *nothing*. You know that even if I brought this little guy home, they'd take him from me and give him to my father or brother. Can't have the bastard child running around with an Awakened guard dog by her side. I'm just going to heal it a little and leave it alone. Someone who actually lives down here could use its companionship more. And, we still have to visit the red-light district and the orphanages."

She spoke softly as she scratched, an oddly pleased air about her, and the woman behind her bobbed her head mutely.

After a couple moments of the wolf enjoying a pleasant head massage by the odd human, she put her fingers onto its infected ear, and before it could even flinch, an odd tingling sensation washed over both its surface and its insides. A moment later, the pain vanished as the dog jumped back, startled. Neither of the two humans moved as it shifted, one of its paws gently poking its ear, finding that it still hurt, but less than before, and all the itchiness had disappeared.

Hesitantly, it approached the crouching human, who still hadn't moved, and nosed her hand. She touched its foreleg this time, and the wolf watched in fascination as the scabbed wound healed a thousand times faster than normal, its skin visibly growing to cover and consume the scabs until all that was left was the faint marks of a scar.

Although still guarded, the wolf let the human poke its ear a couple more times, each time making it less painful and itchy, until eventually, it was barely able to feel anything. Relative tingles of numbness, sure, but that was all.

"Alright, let's go," the woman in front of it said and regretfully retracted her hands, the odd white film over them disappearing into thin air as she brushed her paws down the extra coat of skin that hung loose down to her ankles. "Used up a *lot* more mana than I expected, so let's take our time for me to recover a bit."

The woman in the back bobbed her head, and they turned around to leave.

The wolf followed for a bit, both curious and hoping that if it bumped its nose into the food basket enough, the human would give it more food, but eventually, the woman turned and barked out a "No!" and the wolf cowered back, knowing it had pushed the human's patience.

Adding that round, open area into its mental map of the human's nest, it stalked through the streets, for some reason drawing a *lot* more stares and double takes than it was used to. It sped up, moving as far away from human noises as possible, and made its way to the trash area of the human's nest, where humans would throw unwanted stuff into a large pit which periodically made everything disappear. The rats with their small bodies could stuff themselves in and out of bags quickly, allowing them to easily traverse the human's waste, something the wolf could not do.

But the rats tended to mostly steer clear of the large, turning gears that crushed the waste bags, staying on the more stable ground *around* the base of the hole, where the occasional human would go and check up on the machinery down there.

Of course, the only way to get to the bottom was by walking down a giant spiraling staircase, at least for itself, so that was where it headed.

Following the more foul-smelling pipes for human waste tended to lead to the waste pits, or at least relatively close to them, as humans separated their bodily waste and other waste for some reason.

As long as it gave the wolf a vague sense of direction, it didn't particularly think about it too much.

The usual sights flit by its eyes as it wandered around. Humans mating in alleys, some fighting and killing each other in very similar alleys. Rowdy giant groups of humans howling with each other and knocking together some metal liquid holders, gathered around some odd boxes and machines that spewed distorted sounds and melodies. The occasional spot where humans would give each other things stuffed between living blocks. Until eventually, its eyes turned to an alley much like any other, recognizing by smell that it had found its mark.

The fact that the alley led into a small, protruding walkway of metal without a railing but with some strange hooks framing a gargantuan cube-shaped hole definitely helped.

It moved out of the way of some human as he pushed a foul-smelling cart toward the hole, watching curiously as it put the hooks around one of the two pipes on the bottom of the wheeled cart, and then pushed the cart over the edge, the trash spewing into the hole while the cart stayed upside down just under the walkway.

A very sturdy one, thankfully.

The human yanked a lever on the side the wolf hadn't noticed, and the hook curled into the platform, placing the cart back on its spot, and the owner simply grabbed it and moved past it once more.

Well, it had definitely found the trash pits.

CHAPTER 7

A rat as big as a human's head was sitting with its back turned to the wolf as it nibbled on a piece of bone scavenged from the garbage bags, but the moment the wolf got close, the rat turned around, its beady eyes zeroing in on the wolf in an instant.

The wolf wasn't even sure what had made its ambush fail, but it didn't get much time to think on it.

The rodent rushed forward, its meager meal forgotten. Knowing it was just a false charge for intimidation, the canine forced itself to freeze, [Bloodrush] ready to activate in case it got too close.

Unfortunately, it *wasn't* a false charge, the insane vermin rushing at something two-and-a-half times as tall and thrice as long as itself, as if it were nothing more than a cockroach-size meal. The wolf activated [Bloodrush] just as the rat's absurdly large frontal teeth went to clamp down on its paw, pulling said paw back and trying to swipe the rat away as the wolf jumped back with its three other limbs.

Its legs weren't built for much sideways movement, however, so all it ended up doing was knocking the rat over on its stomach with three short but deep gashes on the top half of its body from where its nails tore straight through its fur like mist.

The wolf reminded itself to check if its nails had changed like its canines later.

As the vermin twitched and writhed in pain and disorientation for a short moment, the wolf jumped forward with a snarl, clamping its jaws shut around its back legs and hips, and proceeded to tilt its head at an angle as it hurriedly lifted its head.

Not wanting to allow the rat the leverage or time to curl its abdomen and claw its eyes out, it threw its head toward the ground diagonally, slamming the top half of the rat into the cold stone below with a muted, *satisfying* thud.

Then it simply carried over the momentum of its first swing to drag the rat off the ground in the same direction, swung its head in a half circle, and slammed the rodent into the ground with another diagonal swing of its head. It repeated the process of swinging its head around in figure eights for almost the full duration of [Bloodrush], snarling all the while as best as it could, a thin sense of rage and bloodlust welling up inside it. Then, just a couple seconds before [Bloodrush] faded, it allowed its teeth to cut rather than only pierce as it swung its head sideways, tossing the rat away as its canines tore four giant rends into a third of its body.

It jumped back for a moment and crouched down, its fur spiked and bristling as it growled at the unmoving rodent. After multiple seconds of nothing happening, its lips relaxed, and they covered its teeth again. It observed the splatters of blood painting the spots it had slammed the rat into before observing the utterly unmoving rodent, and after an almost disbelieving poke of its paw, it confirmed the rat was, indeed, dead.

That . . . had been scary for a moment, but *easy* compared to what it had been expecting. Sure, it was *bigger*, but the rats were so incredibly aggressive, it had simply assumed there was a reason for it—that they were strong enough for it—and it had simply panicked or ran away every time it was attacked. Mice were relatively tame. Rats were just . . . illogical.

Even as its teeth tore its prey apart and quickly devoured it, it almost couldn't believe how well that had gone. It knew better than to rush things and get hurt, but it couldn't deny that its confidence in its ability to hunt had considerably risen after that encounter.

After licking the blood off the walls and floor, it eyed the dimly lit stone walkway surrounding the giant expanse of gears on the bottom of the hole. The walkway was only about two-thirds of the way down into the hole, just high enough for the rats to clamber in and out using the machinery on the sides and the trash itself, but nowhere near low enough for the wolf to head down itself.

But since every rat it had met was absurdly aggressive at the first sign of life, it was betting on them rushing at it the moment they saw it. Mentally deciding to scavenge for scraps around the hole until it could find an isolated rat or two to bait into attacking it like the first one, it got to enjoying passively watching the shifting bumps of darkness as they wormed their way in and out of the bags, at least two dozen rats just among the first few meters of the hole.

It kept a healthy distance, and eventually, it saw a rat excitedly clamber out and separate to find a private place to eat its haul before the bigger rats stole it.

The wolf moved back several meters, then decided it was ready to kill another rodent.

Just to make sure the rat saw it, the wolf stood up straight, then chuffed through its front teeth quietly, but not quietly enough for the rat not to hear it. It turned, and predictably, it dropped its food and rushed forward with an odd-sounding squeak.

The wolf didn't understand their behavior at all, but as long as it got free, fresh food out of it, it didn't really care.

The fight with the smaller rat went almost exactly the same way as the first. It simply rushed blindly at the canine, and when it got close enough, the wolf jumped back and battered it onto its side with a paw, then instantly dug its back legs in and leapt forward to grab the most available part of its body, the front half. Its canines dug in, and the wolf did only two figure-eight slams with the rat before it threw it onto the floor and backed away.

The rat was alive, but unable to move from the four gigantic gashes across its body, each spanning almost a fourth of its form. It barely took five seconds for the twitching, shredded prey to finally die.

It continued like this for hours, constantly hungry despite its sated stomach. Because while it wasn't *physically* hungry, now that it could stockpile flesh and food for its needs . . . why stop? It could technically eat endlessly. The human's blob of gore was almost imperceptibly reduced as it was digested, and its flesh was slowly added to the wolf's own without showing any signs of decay. It had free food-and-flesh storage, so the wolf was going to use it.

The process was rather delicate, and it ran out of patience with wasting its spit by licking blood off the ground, so it simply sat in a corner near the spiraling metal staircase, waiting for a rat to come close, as it either *very* gently scraped a nail against the rock and cobble to draw the rats to itself, or waited for the fresh blood scent to draw the attention of the other rodents, who came to eat their deceased brethren.

There'd been one intense fight when two rats rushed it at the same time, and it had to juggle between battering one of them to the ground then biting and throwing it onto the floor once, before repeating the same with the other. It was only due to using the [Bloodrush] it had saved up that it didn't get bitten, allowing the rats' injuries to kill them from blood loss as the wolf moved back from the crippled vermin.

Its fear slowly but surely evaporated, routine replacing it as hours passed by with the thrill of the hunt to embrace and indulge in.

It started counting the rats it had consumed, and when it counted around two dozen, it decided to retreat and find a place to sleep, starting to feel exhausted.

As it went up the staircase, however, its paws felt a vibration ring through the metal, and it focused on its hearing as it looked up.

Humans were descending.

The staircase was *really* wide, but it was terrible ground for the wolf to fight or run, so it simply descended again, going to the opposite corner of where it had been lurking and fighting, and after a brief encounter with another rat that it eviscerated with hurried fury borne out of fear, it rushed to the dark corner and got to eating, watching the staircase for a chance to ascend.

Eventually, a band of four humans occupied the rectangular area around the staircase, and after a couple minutes of them doing some weird movements and making their weird grumbles to each other, they moved toward the hole, obviously intending to attack the rats.

Judging by the humans' rather blandly colored coverings, they were most likely nothing like the crowd of humans waiting outside the place of burning rivers in terms of pack status. Maybe they were just some sort of servant, or just too young and weak to be given good stuff; the wolf didn't particularly understand humans.

And it had no desire to, at least right now. Right now, it just wanted to sleep and tune itself a little. It *really* wanted to hurry its body along in the process of making its antennae, especially considering just a moment ago, it was vibrations which made it realize something was coming down the stairs.

The wolf licked the blood off its snout as best as it could as the humans formed their weird battle formation of three up front and one in the back, and sensing the tension in the air, it got up with quickened steps toward the staircase.

Just as it turned to climb upward, an orange light burst from behind. It instinctively dashed up a couple steps and turned its head around, limbs ready to rush up and away if it was under attack.

It relaxed and straightened its legs once it realized the human in the back had done one of the strange mystical things humans did by making a ball of light float above her head, likely to draw the rats toward herself like the wolf had done.

Or . . . no. Rather, it was probably so her group could see better. It kept forgetting how terrible humans were at seeing in the dark.

Relieved, it turned back to keep rising up the steps.

And stopped once more, the creaking gears of its mind starting to spin.

It didn't know *why* exactly, but humans rarely ate the rats, only the most sickly and starved daring to do so. Which meant that if the humans killed the possibly *hundreds* of rats in and around the pit, they would do . . . what? They wouldn't eat them. Maybe burn them? Humans did burn a lot of good meat, including their own dead sometimes for some insane reasons the wolf couldn't figure out. Or they might just leave the rats lying around for someone to push into the trash pit, where they would most likely *somehow* end up in the burning rivers down below.

All that flesh, going to waste.

It turned around again, watching pensively as hordes of frenzied rats dashed at the humans, cleaved apart by spears, some strange weapon the wolf didn't have a name for, and the strange mystical energy the female in the back was using.

Its ears perked up as it realized something again, the odd, nonsensical descriptions it had gotten about [Mana Perception] flashing in its mind.

It was mana. The human was doing something with mana.

And the humans were not having as easy a time as the wolf had expected. They probably hadn't realized just how many rats were in the trash bags and open pipes with their horrendous hearing and even more worthless sense of smell. They were still tiny things compared to the humans, and rats couldn't chew through leg armor, the only part of the humans covered by metal, but they outnumbered each human by almost thirty to one, with even more constantly getting drawn out of the trash pit by the loud sounds of battle.

Oh, they wear metal only on their legs on purpose. They came prepared.

Still, they were constantly having to backtrack, yelling at each other, and only managing to attract more rats with their idiotic barking.

The issue was *where* they were retreating toward. They were slowly backing up to the staircase, the only way of escape. Toward itself.

The wolf didn't really know what to do.

It was feeling greedy, and it wanted nothing more than to find some way to help the humans kill the rats, if for no other reason than the fact it could get such immense amounts of mass out of the steadily increasing horde if they were all somehow killed.

If the humans killed only half of them, the other half would eat their brethren in no time, and the wolf would get nothing out of it, so the situation was out of its control, truthfully.

Additionally, it was exhausted. It had been down there for multiple hours, and even if the majority of that time had been spent waiting and resting between bouts of short battles, it was still weak and malnourished. If it weren't for that +1 in Endurance, it felt like it would be dragging its feet right now.

Its mind recalled the vision it had gotten when deciding to accept or reject that choice of a path, and it narrowed its eyes, trying to focus on the limb in its chest as it watched the human's increasingly messy battle as the seconds rolled by.

It could . . . sort of feel it; not anywhere near as intense as that time in the alley, but it could feel it. The more it fiddled with the limb and tried to make it shoot a ball of darkness like it had seen in the vision, however, the more it realized how terribly difficult it was to use the limb. It felt like trying to operate a human device with its paws; it just couldn't catch onto the *mana* thing and properly push it out of its extra limb.

Growing frustrated and anxious as the battle with the humans drew nearer and more frenzied, it gave up with a mental side note to try and figure out how to throw the balls of darkness later.

The humans were *definitely* losing. It looked like a slaughter if one went by sheer numbers, but their movements were getting messier and sluggish, the two males and single female at the front constantly retreating, the female in the back using her mana more and more sparingly.

Seeing how the battle was going, it inwardly wallowed in disappointment and turned around to resume its climb. The humans would retreat or die, and the horde of rats would consume everything that was edible afterward. There was nothing to be gained from sitting there so near to danger.

The climb up the massive spiraling staircase was comparatively short to other distances it sometimes had to cover—thankfully—despite being tiring, the structure no more than perhaps ninety or a hundred feet deep. The vast majority of the depth of the pit was unavailable to two-leggers and itself with said staircase, or it would have been double or maybe triple that length.

No, not two-leggers. Humans.

It had gotten used to calling them as such in its mind. It also sounded better, but it was wrong, because the big dark thing had called them humans. Besides, it didn't want to piss off the dark thing by thinking of them as two-leggers after getting corrected. Just in case it was still watching.

As the entrance to the trash pit slowly revealed itself around the cylinder of metal that was in the center of the staircase, the wolf stopped in its tracks, confused.

The problem was that where the staircase *should* open up to freedom, it was instead transformed into a tight wedge, a thick piece of iron blocking the escape near the top where there was no railing.

Was that something the humans did? Why would they deny themselves an escape route? It had never seen or been down in the waste pits with humans down there before, but that action made no sense. Why were humans so *insane*? Rats were aggressive; humans just seemed straight-up *suicidal*. What was the point of blocking their escape?!

The wolf stood there, bewildered for a moment, and then turned and pushed its head between the thin pipes of the railing on the side of the stairs to look below. Sure enough, slowly but surely, it could tell by the light of the human female that the group was ascending, the horde of rats clambering up the steps after them in a mass of dirty fur and shrill-sounding squeaks.

They were only at about the first of the ten levels the stairs had, but that didn't change the fact that the wolf was *stuck* with humans and a horde of frenzied rats slowly climbing their way up. And if the humans' formation broke and they ran up, it would no longer be a slow climb. They'd reach the wolf in no time.

It moved itself as far up as it could, wedging its head between the last step and the iron plate, but despite looking as closely as it could, found no weak points it could exploit. It tried to tilt its head and bite through the metal, but it was too flat, and all its teeth managed to do were some shallow rends into the metal and some light cuts on its gums as it tried to cut it open.

It turned around in mild panic, cursing the stupid humans and their stupid, useless senses for not knowing how many rats there were, wondering what it could do to escape its predicament. It could . . . it could cut off a portion of the stairs, maybe about half a level's worth, and wait for another human from outside to come over to lift the iron plate, or it could move down to help . . . them . . .

Help them what? Fight a horde of rats? It would stick its snout in to bite something and get its eyes ripped out before it could even close its jaws. Even if the humans below were the ones who could open the way to safety, it wasn't like they would have any room whatsoever to lift the heavy, thick iron plate while fighting for their lives. Just from experimentally hitting its head on the iron, it could tell it was *really* thick. They'd get overrun, and the wolf would get swarmed and eaten alive.

With that horrifying mental image in mind, it activated [Bloodrush] and dashed one level down. The staircase was far too large, around ten loops high, but all it needed to do was cut off a sizeable enough part of it to isolate itself from the humans and the rats, and it would survive.

So, it hurriedly got to work. The structure was secure and sturdy, but it was also simple. Meaning that it was actually fairly easy to cut. The problem was just how *wide* it was. It seemed as if it had been made for at least four humans to walk side by side, for some reason.

It hooked its canines over the railing, cut through the thin pipes, and then used its nails to cut through the film of steel just below, leaned back . . .

And froze with indecision, frantically looking for the best and fastest way to cut through the metal and get the horde stuck far away from itself. The build of the staircase was just planks of metal extending out of a thick tower in the middle into a spiral, with a thin sheet of iron on the outside of the planks connecting to each and every one of them, upon which was the railing. For added support, or so it seemed, there was the occasional bar that connected all of the stairs together on the outside, going through the railing from the top of the structure all the way to the bottom. The wolf looked at the support pipe for less than a moment, then clamped down with every sharp tooth it had, moving its head around in a semicircle to weaken it as much as possible.

Despite the hollow metal being a bit too wide for it to cut through on the outside of the rail without falling to its death, the weight of the staircase disconnecting *should* easily snap that little bit of iron. It practically flew up the stairs again as soon as its mentally marked cut-off area was dealt with, its teeth gnawing through every support pipe on its way back up to the last loop of iron planks.

It was simple, yet the wolf wasn't the smartest, and thus found it very mentally taxing to theorize and visualize all this. Regardless, it rushed to finish before the thirty seconds of [Bloodrush] faded.

Using its nails, it dug its right paw's tip into the inner edge of each plank and cut through by dragging down, then went up a step and repeated it all in a frustratingly slow but thankfully easy and simple process.

After a couple repetitions, it learned how to just shuffle backward on its legs rather than wasting time turning around, doubling its speed. It broke the routine quickly to chew another pipe to bits, uncaring of its blood dripping out of its mouth as the sounds of shrill squeaks and human grunts, jabbering, and battle cries grew nearer.

Then the skill faded, leaving the wolf feeling completely and utterly exhausted, its legs growing weak and jittery, but it pushed itself to continue, the combined weight of the iron planks slowly making a creaking, groaning sound as they strained the thin film of metal on the outside, slowly tilting on the inside as more and more were disconnected, the spot where it first cut slowly sagging inch by inch.

The only thing keeping the planks in place at all was the relatively thin metal on the outside, and groaning, damaged pipes.

Judging from the sound, the humans were getting frightfully close, their fighting retreat seemingly having turned into an outright retreat as the clamor got closer and closer with increasing speed. The wolf felt panic claw at its insides as it pushed its overworked, trembling body to continue just a little more, just enough to ensure that neither rat nor enraged human could possibly leap over the gap it would create in the stairs.

It chewed through another support pipe, then out of the corner of its eye, saw movement through the gaps between the planks as it turned around.

It'd severely underestimated how quickly humans could rush upstairs when in a panic, it seemed, because it felt like just a second or two ago, they'd been at *least* a full loop below. It watched in frozen surprise as the band of humans abandoned their stable footing to continue to race up the planks it was planning to cut off, which bobbed and groaned and tilted, one of the males losing his footing and getting covered by the horde almost instantly with an anguished scream, his companions letting out exclamations of what might have been sadness or frustration as they fought to keep their balance on the unstable platforms under their feet.

Something the rats had much less issue with, considering how often they rode on bits of machinery to move in and around the human nest.

The female with leather shoulder coverings—*oh, that's what the brown stuff is*—dashed up even faster, leaving the other female and male behind in a mad dash for freedom.

The weight of the rats on the lower end of the half loop the wolf had weakened caused something to snap, presumably a support pipe, and the entire staircase, including the spot the wolf was sitting on, jerked and groaned suddenly. Only the wolf and the human female with leather coverings on her shoulders even managed to stay upright, heart-wrenching screams of agony and terror shrieking out from behind the female as her two companions were covered in mangy, sickly fur, the resulting blob writhing in panic as the rats started to chew through anything they could get their teeth on.

No doubt to be a slow, horrific death, as the rats started chewing off little pieces of them at a time.

The footing of the stairs would only improve as the human got closer, and the upright female looked at it with an accusatory glare full of murderous rage and grief, now only about fifteen stairs away from the wolf itself. The wolf snapped itself out of its frozen state and jumped to the film of iron on the outside. With a trembling paw, it hooked its middle nail on the top, pushing down on the slowly bending metal, cleanly severing it, before hurriedly jumping up the steps, away from the sagging stairs.

The damaged support pipes snapped and bent with clangs and groans, weighed down by four humans and hundreds of rats, and the human female's face contorted in a mix of fury, despair, and horror as something below snapped, the stairs dropping out from under her with a loud shriek that mixed in with the screams of herself and her packmates, just a few steps away from the wolf.

The wolf watched with trembling legs as the portion of the spiral it'd cut off slammed into the level of stairs directly under it, which bent sideways toward the outside from the sudden weight, and with another *literally* deafening series of metallic bangs and metal shrieks, the cut loop slid and scraped off to dive into the darkness below.

It turned over midair and slammed into the stone ten levels down with an impact the wolf could feel in its bones, rats being flung around in every direction during the flip or crushed beneath the deformed metal, hopefully along with the humans.

It didn't particularly *like* humans, but they were usually apathetic at the very least, or nice like the lady from before, so it could find no joy in having their death be a painful one. Better to be crushed than eaten alive.

With about half a level of stairway being the only thing keeping it from sliding off to the bent level of stairs underneath, it felt anything but secure, even as it backpedaled up and pressed its back into the iron plate.

Eventually, however, after what might have been hours or minutes, it calmed down, and a mixture of exhaustion and trust in its [Restful Awareness] skill allowed it to finally rest until someone came to lift the iron covering, either to repair the staircase or to check on their fellow packmates.

The symbols quickly came to notify it of new changes.

You have progressed on your Path.
[Hound of the Keeper] Level 1 → Level 8

-Available Attribute Points: 7
-Base Attributes:

Strength (+0)
Speed (+0)
Dexterity (+0)
Endurance (+1)
Perception (+0)
Resolve (+0)
Intelligence (+0)
Soul (+0)

The wolf was *extremely* tempted to just dump all seven points into Endurance, but decided to at the very least check every attribute and what it meant. Everything until Endurance was easy to understand from a glance.

Perception was one that immensely interested the wolf. The symbols didn't explain *how*, but putting points into Perception would essentially heighten its senses, from scent to hearing to how quickly commands traveled throughout its body, how quickly its eyes sent signals to its brain, and how quickly the brain processed them. Something that was . . . very interesting, but the wolf was fairly certain that, given some time, it could do most of that on its own.

Its body was already in the process of making its eyes see better, and while it didn't know how its ears worked well enough to tune them yet, that [Devourer] racial skill was still changing. Just a day or two ago, it didn't seem to be able to let it see or change its own body, and then suddenly, it could.

It didn't know if it was tied to age, level, or whatever else, but it decided to put just one point in Endurance and Perception for now and keep the other five points.

Endurance (+2)
Perception (+1)

The next was Resolve, a very strange and seemingly unimpactful attribute. It was essentially one's mental resolve, or willpower. It could make the wolf less weak to temptation and shield its mind, soul, and mana from outside interference, as well as assist during magic use when someone had to put their willpower into a mana skill. And that was it.

It was basically a weaker version of its [Mental Resistance], but included shielding its "soul," with the added bonus of making it easier to tell a mana skill what to do. Which might help with [Echoes of Oblivion], but the wolf really wasn't sure if it wanted to put points into something it already had half covered on the off chance it could help with casting the weird shadow skill.

After a moment, it decided it was worth it.

Resolve (+1)

That done, it continued to Intelligence, and barely contained itself from dumping all four attribute points into it without a second thought.

It was just a shortcut to being smarter. It could allow the wolf to process information better, recognize patterns better, visualize, theorize, *understand,* and even *remember* more—and better. It could help it identify how other beings felt in the moment, and even in hypothetical scenarios by running simulations in its mind, the latter of which it couldn't do right now if it tried. That, and it had a strong feeling putting more points into Intelligence would allow it to better understand itself and its prey using the [Devourer] racial skill.

It turned to the final one, Soul, and after staring at it for a while, finally realized what the weird limb in its chest was. It was Soul. Putting attribute points into it would strengthen it, allowing the wolf to feel and use it with more ease. Strengthening it would also allow it to secrete more of the odd thing that mana was, which was the thing that [Echoes of Oblivion] used.

Thinking of which, it really had to figure out how that skill worked. Every time the wolf would activate it, it would feel the limb in its chest deflate a bit with an odd sensation of something rushing out of its body, like a gas through its flesh—likely the skill expending mana to channel the darkness. But no matter how hard it focused during its tests, all it could manage were odd, flickering puffs of dark mist which held in place randomly over its body, nothing like the liquid, solid, and gassy darkness it had seen in the vision of its path.

It remembered now that it'd accepted the path *before* it had even gotten the skill, and grew puzzled at how that worked, but then returned to the matter at hand, making it a question for later.

After a lengthy session of thinking, it realized that it didn't know what to do. It *wanted* to dump three points into Intelligence and one into Soul, but it wasn't sure if that was a good choice when *one* swing of a human's sharp metal rod could easily kill it.

Yet, putting anything into speed and strength was useless, as it already had plans to naturally attain those. And when every day could be its last, as today had proven, it wasn't particularly keen on keeping its points for later when it could only access the odd numbers while it slept.

With mild hesitation, it succumbed to temptation.

Intelligence (+3)
Soul (+1)

The change was instant, its mind feeling clearer than ever before, every battle with words in order to get information no longer a slow, taxing process but a smooth mental question and answer. It felt much like how its body had felt more *solid* when it put points into Endurance, but about thrice as noticeable. Before it could do anything to test it, though, letters covered its dream-sight once more.

[Mana Perception] has Leveled Up. Level 1 → Level 2
[Mana Manipulation] has Leveled Up. Level 1 → Level 2
[Soul Perception] has Leveled Up. Level 1 → Level 2
[Bloodrush] has Leveled Up. Level 1 → Level 2

-Removed Traits:
Scavenger (1/1): You eat the unwanted remnants you can find rather than what you can hunt, trade, forage, cultivate, or steal. You are harder to notice when intending to scavenge.

-Acquired Traits:
Hunter (1/2): You hunt living creatures, whether it is for survival, sport, or personal gain of one manner or another. You are slightly harder to notice when intending to hunt.

The symbols faded, and the wolf's dream turned toward the most detailed deconstruction it had seen so far.

It wasn't even like with the cockroaches. It saw what bones were made out of—thin, hardened hairs of connective tissue. It saw what white and red blood cells were, how the brain interacted with the body by receiving and giving signals via chemicals and pulses of electrical signals. How its digestive tract melted and broke down the things going through it, how its muscles would behave before and after stress. How microscopic things would trigger the olfactory neurons and use the odor receptor to identify the smell by sending a signal to its brain, and a thousand other tidbits of information.

Every single minute thing was laid bare in utterly astonishing detail.

Then, parasites. Insectoids. How they used their hosts to feed and how their reproduction worked; how a being without a brain operated. Interesting, but useless to the wolf.

As the vision faded, its deeper understanding of how creatures functioned on the inside giving it a strange sense of creativity, it turned to see its own body. With two extra points in endurance, it felt fairly confident its body could handle rapid changes, so for once, it threw caution to the wind.

Well, not exactly, but it did take some risk.

Its left ear was no longer necrotic and infected, and there was some sub-dued blood flow in it, but it was still deaf, which was something it quickly got to fixing by observing its functioning one for a few moments and copying the structure to its left ear, somehow knowing it would take about one rat's worth of material to fix it. Which was an astonishingly cheap cost.

Moving on, its skull was marked by some odd mana-made symbol, but it couldn't figure out what that did, if it was natural, or if it was even harmful, so it let it be for now. Its tendons on the back of its legs were forming with adequate speed, about one-fourth the width of its natural ones and still inert and stretchy so as not to snap from pressure before they were fully formed and thick enough to handle strain, so it decided to speed things up.

A *lot*.

Another near-death experience had made it realize it was doing great by its old standards, but still kept getting into situations where it was in too much danger to be comfortable with.

So it spent what felt like literal *days* doing nothing but using its new-found intelligence boost to assist it into adding more tendons in every part of its body that used them. It was complicated to see the connection of how this little rope contracting would impact everything connected to it, but with [Devourer] being *so* accurate and easy to use, the wolf eventually managed to reinforce itself with more tendons—from back legs to front, to spine, and tail.

And it felt instinctively that soon, it would be able to mess around with its teeth and claws, which was something it was heavily interested in. It also felt that the racial skill would be changing soon . . . somehow. It was just a vague sensation of incoming change without any more information, so it didn't wonder too long on that.

For now, though, it looked at the stored flesh, joints, ligaments, mem-branes, and anything besides bones that it had gained from the rats, and invested about half of them—ten or so rats—into speeding up its tendon growth. Another four rats' worth of material went into *significantly* increas-ing how fast its antennae and cerci hairs would grow, and kept about ten rodents to be quickly absorbed nutrients to support its quick transformations without massive fatigue. All the ways it was changing itself were beyond the scope of its poor understanding of reality, but it knew that massive, rapid growth needed equally large amounts of energy.

Seeing how the human's materials were of slightly . . . higher quality—as it knew by some instinctual knowledge—it decided to use half of its remaining flesh to add to its own bulk, at a pace that was far faster than before, and finished it off by using every bit of rat bone it had available to slightly condense and harden its own bones even further.

The actual process of that was broken into three smaller ones, but that was thankfully handled by [Devourer], and all it had to do was make the choice.

Then it looked at itself for any improvements it could make, and found a couple. [Devourer]'s way of digesting biological material, it instinctively knew, was perfect. There was no waste; there was nothing lost. It was the peak of efficiency.

So . . . what was the use of having its abdomen clogged with intestines? All it felt it needed was its stomach, as it seemed to be where [Devourer] originated from and where it took the material for its later use from, but all that the excessively long tubes of intestines were doing was taking up space, since nothing really went past its stomach.

It had been about three days since it last had to poop, so having a useless orifice and the majority of its abdomen clogged up by intestines just seemed wasteful. It considered dissolving the intestines for nutrients and removing the hole on the back of its body, which was something its body could do in a manner of a couple of days according to [Devourer], so it went through with the decision.

Not having anything to fill the extra space with after it was done, it simply chose a couple thin and jointed bones to keep its abdomen from appearing far too thin and drawing attention to its odd body shape. And extra stopping power from sharp things was always good.

It couldn't help but wonder how it was that the [Devourer] skill worked. It felt like its mind could simply switch from observation to modification, and the end result would be like a drawing or a symbol saved for later use.

Experimentally, it mentally added another set of ears on its neck and tried to solidify it as a different painting to choose from later, if it wished.

And it worked.

It wasn't going to use the remembered painting, because it was impractical, but it was nice to know it could test things and have the skill remember them for later use, should the wolf need them done quickly.

With that done, the lucidity and awareness of its dream faded, and it returned to the limbo of half-aware sleep.

CHAPTER 8

Eventually, the wolf was stirred out of its rest by a surprising amount of pain, and regretfully, it neither felt nor heard any humans approaching to let it out of its prison, suspended over a . . .

Well, not quite a death drop, but the level below was bent and damaged, so if it slipped off its perch once, it could easily slide off and drop to its death if it wasn't careful and ready.

Thankfully, it was a little too pleased to care. As it moved down a few steps to catch one of the wall lights the humans had put around the lip of the entrance, it observed its limb as if it was something it had never seen before, watching it with wonder and excitement.

No matter how it moved its leg, it couldn't see its bones nor the tendons, hidden under a coating of newly formed flesh and fat. It turned its head to look at its hind legs, and its hips were no longer an angular mess, its ribs no longer giving off the impression they were trying to break through its skin and escape. It was still rather skinny, but it looked twice as healthy as before its sleep. In fact, its skin was starting to feel a bit tight, likely from the overnight bulk added to its form.

After hopping around a bit and walking up and down the stairs, it noted just how incredibly full of vigor and energy it felt. The Endurance stat was definitely not something to take lightly. It felt like it could take a hit from a boulder and survive.

Of course, it wasn't stupid enough to try such a thing, but the feeling was reassuring all the same. It yawned and turned to look at the points where it felt pain, which were . . . everywhere.

Its snout was in pain, a rather constant sensation not unlike a headache; one which traveled from behind its eyes and straight down until it was next to its nostrils. Painful, but also reassuring to know the antennae were growing so quickly.

The less reassuring part was the pain it felt in every single bone of its body. It didn't know if it was simple pain from its bones rapidly changing and growing, or because there was something wrong with them. Generally, pain meant something was wrong, and the pulsing, intense waves certainly didn't *feel* good, but at the same time, it couldn't really come up with any other reason for its bones to suddenly hurt. Not even microfractures, as it hadn't really gotten into a genuine fight since it had eaten the rats.

Having nothing else to do, it moved up to the iron plate and sat down, ready to try and learn how to use the mana.

The limb it felt in its chest was a bit more responsive, and so it spent every ounce of energy it had in learning how to manipulate it, feeling like a pup learning how to walk all over again. Sometimes, it slipped through its mental guidance; sometimes, it simply refused to be used. Yet, despite the wolf's growing frustration, an hour later, it had wrung its soul dry of every drop of mana, and it couldn't say that it was displeased at all with its progress.

Sure, it wasn't *useful* yet, but it could at least force the mana out in the way it wanted to. A puff of black mist appearing over its snout where it was *supposed* to was a vast improvement over the flickering, dissolving bits of smoke it could conjure before.

Out of curiosity, it decided to go to the railing and find out what had happened down below, its footsteps surprisingly heavy as they hit the metal underneath. With a bit of head turning, it shoved its head under the railing pipes and looked down, expecting to see nothing but a horde of rats cleaning up their brethren and the humans.

Much to its surprise, however, it was dead silent, the blinking dark-yellow lights of the trash pit illuminating countless unmoving silhouettes as they lay dead and broken down below, the smoke and copper scent of their blood flitting into its nostrils and invading its mind and stomach with the need to feast.

The rats had seemingly been scared away by the earth-shaking impact and had most likely retreated to feast somewhere safer. They were surprisingly logical beings when there were no other living things involved.

And that gave it an idea. A very greedy, perhaps dangerous idea.

It yanked its head back and shortly checked its nails, which it had forgotten to do during its sleep. It found them much the same as before, if a bit thinner and longer, likely a combination of growth hormone and the [Devourer] skill.

It quickly but carefully moved down the loop, its sides rubbing against the metal cylinder in the center, until it came to the spot where the loop stopped. With trepidation, it looked down at the full loop of bent stairs underneath and found that it wasn't so much scared of the *drop*, which was a distance it had taken many times before, but of the possibility of hitting the metal and sliding off to its death.

For a minute or two, it practiced with the mental control it had over its nails, just to feel a bit more reassured, and after realizing it was just wasting valuable time, hesitantly went to the last step, its right side basically scraping off its fur with how hard it was pressing into the metal center of the stairs.

It crouched low and used its newfound intelligence to visualize the drop and the actions it would take over and over, and finally, it turned its body so its snout was facing the cylinder and jumped off sideways to the best of its ability, tucking in its legs to its torso.

Despite its best efforts, a yelp of fear choked out of its throat as it dropped. The second its body slammed into the tipping stairs with a deafening clang, it tilted its paws downward as its elbows curled, and stabbed its nails into the metal, immediately halting its slide.

For a moment, it simply panted from the adrenaline rush, then with as hurried but careful steps as it could manage, it continued digging its nails into the metal and slowly made its way out of the tilted section step by step in an awkward, sideways shuffle down the stairs.

As soon as it felt no pull of its body weight against its nails, it realized it was walking on straight planks by now, and quickly glanced behind itself to confirm.

Not perfectly straight, but straight enough to not be an issue.

It was also mildly embarrassed to note that it had been so focused on *not* looking at the drop, that it had forgotten most of the bent section still had the safety railing attached, if a bit more *compact* than before.

Those thoughts were all rather easily swept away by another breeze upon which rode the bittersweet miasma of death, blood, and decay.

Something about a breeze even existing down in a pit felt a bit strange, but it didn't ruminate too much on such thoughts as it quickly trotted down the stairs.

As it made its way to the final loop, it quickly got to work on eating all the rat carcasses it could find, a task which was surprisingly annoying to fulfill when its mouth and canines were still so small. It had to carve out slabs of meat with its front teeth a lot of the time with the larger rats, which were as lengthy as its head and nearly twice as tall, and the amount of fur it digested was frankly appalling, yet slowly but surely, with excitement and hunger slowly buzzing in its veins, it made its way down.

At the last couple steps, the familiar sound of squeaking caught its attention, and it slowly curled its legs into a crouch as it stalked around the corner. The dim light reflecting off the metal plates of the rectangular tunnel illuminated nothing but a small rat nibbling on one of its bisected siblings, so the wolf decided to test out its Hunter trait.

The results were that even as it towered over the rat just a footstep or two away, it didn't notice it one bit, simply digging its snout deeper into its kin's putrid innards.

Having completed its experiment, the wolf dashed forward, and using the strategy that had proven most effective versus the rats, simply bit into its hips, reared its head up, and then snapped it down, letting its teeth cut the flesh open before the rat could even realize what had happened.

Its skull cracked against the stone with an oddly hollow-sounding *thunk*, and after a single twitch, it stopped moving. The wolf quickly chomped its prey down before focusing back on its feast, its tail slowly starting to wag as it realized just *how much* meat there was available nearby.

Hours went by in a fugue as it devoured burnt, crushed, stabbed, and cut-apart rats strewn all about the tunnel. Its jaws and tongue muscles started cramping before it had even made its way out into the pit area. Eventually, a shuffling sound to its left made it freeze with a rat hanging out of its mouth. It snapped its head to the sound, fur bristling and [Bloodrush] ready to activate. But it didn't growl. Not yet.

Nothing happened for multiple seconds, then it caught movement to its left and observed in silence as something behind a mound of rats shifted, the twisted form of the staircase having squished them into a glob of gore. Then a sharp gasp sounded off, and the movement stopped.

Cautiously, it backed off toward the wall as it started to circle the mound of metal under which was the struggling creature, simply to have some distance between whatever was moving and itself, and its eyes caught a dainty, furless paw extending out from under a rat's mangy corpse.

No, a hand.

One of the humans was alive.

Unsure of what to do with this new revelation—and remembering the hateful glare of the leather-clad human from before—it simply stood stock-still and watched silently as the human struggled to dig themselves out from under the weight of metal planks and rat corpses.

It didn't need its newfound intelligence to know the human was likely severely injured, every shift accompanied with a strangled gurgle or a gasp or some sort of half-hitched yip. Even as the minutes rolled by, the human's efforts were only rewarded with a single finger's width of progress at a time, and the wolf . . .

The wolf was torn.

Humans weren't bad. Suicidal to some extent, but most simply allowed it to live and do its own thing without particularly caring of its existence. Some had shown it kindness, which was something no other creature ever had. It wasn't exactly *grateful,* but it could recognize that the humans, in all their illogical, suicidal glory, were the strangest, most suicidal, and kindest creatures to be found in their own nest, shown evidently by the fact that they even allowed other creatures to exist in their home.

And watching one die like this was just . . . uncomfortable. It made its chest feel weird, a sensation similar to when the first human it ate had died, but less visceral; more resigned. It could kill the human with one bite through the back of their neck. The human could survive its injuries with the help of some of her kin, maybe, although that presented the danger of her telling the other humans what it had done. Which was . . . a frightening thought.

Also, even if it didn't want to *kill* the human, it definitely wanted to eat her, even though its jaws were cramping and its snout was so covered in blood and guts that it couldn't even smell or taste anything but copper; it simply wanted to use its meat-storing abilities to their fullest extent.

It dropped the rat in its mouth and moved closer, [Bloodrush] ready to activate at the first sign of danger. Using its nails to dig into the gore and drag the corpses off the human, who was covered up to her forearm, it started from the top, dragging off one, then two rats. The human gasped, her hand reaching out to the wolf, prompting it to stop and lean back for a second.

"P-Please . . . he . . . lp," the woman croaked out quietly.

Deciding it was being too timid again, it redoubled its efforts to dig the human out, who was pinned under four iron planks and a small assortment of gore and rats, as she continued making her human sounds.

"S-Say some . . . thing," she breathed out, and was ignored by the wolf, who wondered once more how difficult it would be to learn human speak.

Each bit of fur and flesh removed further uncovered the human's wretched state, entire chunks of her flesh completely ripped off and the skin covered in holes where the rats had chewed through her coverings. The fingers were the worst, the bone actually visible in some parts, the wounds growing less severe as they traveled up her forearm.

Before long, it managed to catch a glimpse of her head-fur, however coated in crimson it was, and quickly focused on snagging its teeth on corpses covering her head and dragging them off.

"H-He . . . llo?" she breathed out weakly, her fingers twitching.

The wolf only spared her a glance, noticing that she had been so completely covered in rats that they'd shielded her from both the fall as they got squished under her, and the impact of the iron slamming into her back as they got squished above her.

A particularly large rat on top of her nape panted and twitched, not dead, and the wolf wasted no time in snatching it up and repeatedly slamming it into the floor as it squeaked its shrill sounds and struggled to fight for its life. Growing annoyed at the constant, almost shrieking sounds of the rodent, it snarled and got up on its hind legs as it raised its head to the sky and put its whole body weight into a particularly vicious downward throw.

The rat slammed into the stone with a meaty, wet thud, and didn't move again.

The wolf shoved it aside with a paw and got back to work on unraveling the human, who had gone completely and utterly still as she struggled to control her breathing.

Likely trying to play dead, something she hopefully wouldn't have to pretend about soon.

Another couple of wrenched-off corpses later, and her nape and shoulders were revealed, showing no leather coverings of any sort, meaning that this was the woman making the light sphere when the attack started.

The woman made some sort of strained and poorly muffled yelp sound, her shredded free arm curling back to cover her head with sluggish, jerky movements.

Which was annoying, for more than one reason. One of which was that this woman reminded it too much of the woman who had fed it the yellow-white stuff above in the square. They were different humans, it assumed, but every time it thought about snapping her hand off and just biting through her neck, it hesitated.

The second reason was said hand, which would make killing her needlessly painful and annoying.

It didn't particularly *want* to kill her, though.

There was a chance this human could tell the others about it, which meant she was a risk. She was also dying anyway, so killing her quickly would be a mercy, considering the other humans above seemed to be in absolutely no hurry whatsoever to come save her and her companions, or unlock the iron gate above.

But even though she could tell the humans about it, the wolf didn't particularly stand out in any way from other canines. It could hide about as well as it always did, in plain sight and the humans being none the wiser to its presence. What would she tell them? Some black dog cut off the staircase?

Would the humans even believe her if she told them?

Was it worth taking that chance, however, just because the human female reminded it of a kinder woman from above?

It didn't know.

So it simply stood there silently, unsure of what to do as the human female tried to play dead.

CHAPTER 9

Five minutes passed, then ten, and the wolf still didn't know what to do.

It didn't *want* to kill the human, but it was going to die anyway. Slowly and painfully.

After another five minutes of its thoughts running in circles, it decided to ignore the woman. If she lived, she lived. If she died, she died. There were three other valuable humans it could be eating rather than wasting its time trying to figure out what to do with the one who still lived.

So it trotted away, and instead of eating everything in its path, decided to start by the important bits. Humans first, small rats that would be easy to eat second, and if its jaws could hold up after all that, it would eat whatever remained.

It found one of the males first, who had thankfully smashed its skull open on the stone with its fall, bits of its brain and blood seeping out of its head like a cracked egg.

After hooking its canines into the human's neck, it pulled with all its weight and strength, just enough to move the man out of the pile of rats he was in and closer to a cleaner area near the still-living female, before it started its feast.

Humans were *so* much tastier than rats; it couldn't believe it had wasted hours on eating the rodents rather than hunting for their corpses first. No dirty fur sticking to the insides of its throat, either.

It *hated* that.

The head was cracked open, so licking up its brains, chewing up its skull, and eating its neck proved to be a task of no more than five or ten minutes. After raking its canines up and down the human's body to cut through its coverings, it clumsily scratched at the corpse, watching sliced plates of leather, some tinkling bits of metal, and various straps of cloth and leather fall off the man, one of them covered in cracked or outright broken glass bottles full of glowing liquid.

It sniffed at them curiously, then reeled back from the utterly *bizarre* stench coming off them, clumsily trying to wipe at its snout with its leg to get the sweet, bitter, foul, and wonderful smell out of its nostrils. After sneezing once, then twice, it shook itself and got closer to the little bottles of glowing liquids.

They were almost like the burning liquids of the flaming rivers down below, if probably a different color. Its eyes were still slowly being adjusted to be able to see more hues like the humans could, so it wasn't quite *certain* they were all different colors, but their shades of yellow and blue were far enough from the green of the rivers for it to be sure they were at least different.

It had actually forgotten it had started the process of changing its eyes, so it was going to speed that up quite a bit when it went to sleep again.

At the moment, though, it was mostly curious about the bottles. The first two were cracked open, their contents mixed and tainted with blood and guts, but one of them was miraculously intact, so with the utmost care, it hooked its teeth on the small bottle's neck and pulled it out of its fabric sheath. There was some sort of weird wooden thing on the top, and after stabilizing the bottle on the ground with its paws, it grabbed onto it and pulled it off with an odd popping sound.

The stench was still horrible. And amazing.

Which meant it was just *extremely* confusing, so it mostly shut out its sense of smell as it gripped the base of the bottle's neck between its front teeth, and very slowly tilted its head back.

The liquid, thick and almost like slime, hit its tongue, but besides a small amount of numbness, nothing happened, so it tilted its head a tiny bit more and allowed a bit of it to trickle down into its throat, swallowing before carefully putting the bottle back between its paws.

It really needed to get some more dexterous paws; these things were *infuriating* to use when trying to work with human trinkets.

For a moment, nothing happened as it swallowed. Then a warm, soothing numbness suddenly overtook the pulsing waves of pain coming off every bone in its body before it wormed its way up to its cramping jaw muscles.

For a few heartbeats, its body was blissfully unattended by its longtime companion, the pain seemingly gone, and then slowly, the numbness receded, and it crept back into the wolf's body. *Slightly* lessened, but still there.

It looked curiously at the bottle, then decided that while that was *useful,* it didn't really have much need for it. It had a high-level [Pain Resistance] skill, and lessening the pain would only reduce how quickly that skill further leveled up.

In fact . . .

The wolf turned its head to look at the living human, who was trying to discreetly shuffle out of its prison of iron and gore.

There was enough rat meat for the wolf to eat nonstop for *days.* And three humans who were all about twice to thrice its size still, so it might not even have time to eat the girl if it killed her. That, as well as the reminder of the woman who had fed and healed it, and an honest desire just to see what would happen, was what made it decide.

It picked up the bottle with its front teeth and trotted over to the human, who went limp as she heard its footsteps approach.

Deciding the female was no real threat, it chose to alert her to the fact that it wasn't genuinely blind and stupid, and thus prodded her mauled hand with the pain-remover bottle. She flinched, but refused to move or take it.

Growing annoyed, the wolf put it down on the ground, lamenting how much of it spilled out of the open top, before clamping its teeth around her wrist, an action which made the girl's breath catch as she started to tremble. The wolf moved her arm so her hand landed on the bottle before letting go with a short chuffing sound.

After a short moment of indecision, her hand slowly started patting at the bottle, and after she realized it was a pain-remover bottle, she gasped. For the first time, some life seemed to enter the female, and she raised her head, revealing a mangled, eyeless mess of blood and flesh, chunks missing from her lips, nose, and brows as she turned toward the wolf before her neck went limp in exhaustion once more.

"Tha-thank you," it breathed out, and with weak fingers that could barely hold on to the bottle, she drew her arm back before placing the dirtied bottle neck to her lips, turning her head sideways to drink up the pain remover with greedy gulps.

Not wanting to waste time, it chewed up a small rat as she continued drinking the liquid, disliking how the corpse felt like an overfilled balloon as its guts and blood dripped and ran down its jaws and chest—

. . . Wait, what even *was* a balloon?

After a moment of thinking and only getting some images of fabric filled with air, it stopped caring and tilted its head back to hastily swallow the small rodent.

"Thank y-you. T-Thank you," the human gasped out repeatedly as soon as she finished the bottle, and the wolf watched her for only a moment before growing rigid in surprise.

Her flesh was knitting back together, the wounds closing and her bleeding ceasing at a speed that was unimaginable to the wolf. No flesh was restored, and she was still blind, but it watched in fascination as her wounds scabbed then turned to skin in a sped-up process that took only a dozen or so seconds, her mangled fingers twitching.

That liquid could *heal injuries.* It was still useless to the wolf, as it couldn't carry it around with itself until it got hurt, but the revelation was still surprising.

Deciding to help the human a bit more, it let its bottom jaw hang loose and hooked its top canines onto increasingly more difficult to remove rats the closer it got to the main parts of her body. They would either break apart or just be too deeply wedged between the human and the iron planks above to remove, so after some annoying digging, it decided to just drag the human itself out.

"Can you . . . understand me?" the girl asked quietly, then sharply inhaled in surprise as she felt its canines carefully dig into her shoulder garment.

It planted its paws down in a wide stance with its neck extended over the human's head, unaware of the bits of blood dripping onto the back of her head and making her flinch, and slowly started using its meager legs and muscles to walk backward.

After a moment of strain, the human started assisting it as she feebly grasped at the ground and tried to pull herself out. It was . . . somewhat effective. One finger's width at a time, it dragged her out, having to adjust its grip on the tearing fabric the girl wore several times.

The wolf was unsure as to why it was so impatient lately, but it was quickly growing annoyed at how much energy it was expending on the human, so it decided to activate [Bloodrush] and heaved backward with a low growl of effort.

A distant, foggy recollection of it doing something similar with a small stick and another kin on the other end surfaced for a fraction of a second before it faded, and it redoubled its efforts from anger at having its mind denied of that memory.

The female gasped and groaned in pain, but helped as much as her useless arm could allow her to, and finally, the resistance snapped away, and the wolf managed to yank the girl out of her prison of gore, whatever was keeping her trapped likely broken or removed as it hastily used the last few seconds of [Bloodrush] to drag her for a couple feet through grimy, crimson-wetted stone.

"Thank you," the girl gasped as she tried to turn over on her back, grunting in pain. "A-Are you . . . a summon?" the human continued muttering.

The wolf ignored her, considering its self-appointed duty to be complete, and it quickly trotted away to continue eating the human it had started on a couple feet away.

It still kept an eye on the human, though. Just in case.

Everything hurt, but nothing was more intense than the feeling of helplessness she felt.

The healing potion was only designed for surface wounds, so she couldn't see anything, but she could hear the sound of ripping flesh, the tearing of fabric, could smell the miasma of blood and death hanging in the air so thick it felt like inhaling water from the foulest swamps with every shaky breath.

Before today, she didn't know the sound of flesh being ripped apart, but as the minutes rolled by in relative silence, she was forced to become familiar with it as the beast devoured what she assumed were her former teammates, and she felt tears build up in her mangled eyes, the salt springing a fresh wave of pain through her.

She didn't like them. Hell, she was basically the team's property, too indebted to them to deny them anything, even when they would push her down and force themselves on her. If anything, she was glad they were gone. Evil and reckless, every single one of them. So she wasn't crying for them.

No, she was crying because she was scared she would be next to enter the monster's jaws.

Any monster was terrifying, doubly so after having had to endure the agony of being eaten alive before the world dropped out from under her as she was crushed inside a frenzied blender of teeth and snouts.

Yet, there was nothing more terrifying than a monster with intelligence. And although she'd only caught a glimpse of the canine before she fell, two wide, golden-gleaming eyes framed in darkness were engraved into her mind.

She didn't know *what* it did, but she knew it had somehow broken the staircase. She knew it could *recognize* a healing potion, and that for one reason or another, it had given it to her. The problem was that she didn't know if she was given the potion out of some sort of mercy, or because the beast wanted its food fresh and alive.

It was presumably not intelligent enough to understand speech, however, judging by the complete and utter lack of any response.

Never had she cursed her choice of a path more than now.

She'd been so naive. So optimistic and bright eyed as she looked down the innards of the sprawling Dungeon below and thought to herself that she just wanted to help people; a stupid, misguided notion borne out of guilt from her noble birth.

So when she, like any good elf, had started practicing magic and the [Infuser] path opened up for her, she'd taken it immediately, thinking she could finally escape her insane parents to make a life for herself. She had a wonderful support path that increased the potency and efficiency of her buffing spells, which would only grow stronger with time and more specialization, and all she had to do was level up. People would be clamoring to get her at their side in their Dungeon dives, allowing her to live a life free of guilt and court.

And now, look where she'd ended up. Level seven, crippled in a trash pit, covered in blood and guts, blind, helpless, and most likely about to be devoured.

With just three useless spells in her repertoire, she might as well just tilt her head away and hope the dog, or monster, or whatever the thing was, made it quick. Even if she wanted to cast [Sparkburst], it was unlikely to do anything unless she got her hand cupped around its eyeball or something.

It wasn't even a real spell. She'd just been trying to learn pyromancy from watching a street performer and learned how to throw sparks, which the system registered as a spell for some reason. Its use was more of an intimidation trick against stupid animals than anything useful in a fight.

So . . . she could do nothing but wait and hope.

It was common protocol to lock the entrance to aboveground when someone took a rat extermination quest put up by one Dungeon Baron or another, simply so in case of the mercenaries *failing*, the streets above wouldn't be flooded by bloodthirsty rodents the size of a large cat.

And their minder waiting above *should* have noted the large crash and lack of people trying to get out of the pits, which meant he was probably already back at the guild to report on their deaths and get another party to clean up the rats so the workers could fix the staircase.

That process could take anywhere from a day and a half to *a week* . . .

Could she even survive this long in a hole with an intelligent monster that was most likely chewing up her teammates a couple feet away?

A particularly loud snap of crunching bone made her flinch, and she decided to at least try to crawl and shuffle *away* from the source of those horrendous sounds.

Gods above, just crawling made shards of agony spear into her very soul.

She didn't need a medic Pather to tell her that her hip bones and legs were probably little more than bony splinters. Wearing metal greaves like the rest of her party had only made the rats concentrate on her upper body, and she vividly remembered the almost cushy crunch of the vermin below her a split second before her legs slammed into the stone.

That and her right arm being broken made crawling backward a near impossible task. And the fact her fingers kept sinking into blood or gore or mangy fur, making bile crawl up her throat with every push, didn't help either.

She gave up on moving fairly quickly.

Okay, Embreeil. Think. What spells do you have to deal with this?

[Sparkburst] was most likely useless, even if it was her highest-level spell. Mostly because her half teammates, half creditors thought it was useful since it was flashy, even if it didn't do anything, and told her to use it all the time.

[Illumina] was similarly useless, but only because she didn't have the mana reserves to use it offensively. If she were higher level, with more natural mana reserves and with more points in Soul, she could summon an orb of light in front of someone's face and permanently blind them by burning their retinas in an instant, but the most she could do with what she had was make someone rub their eyes and blink for a few seconds. She could use it to buy time, maybe?

Her final spell was simply [Haste], which would give her a bonus to Speed and Perception, and would be useful, *if she could walk.*

She had no option but to wait and hope for rescue.

And then . . .

Then what? Her life was as good as over. She could never gather the coin necessary to restore her sight with a healer. They had grown more common since the Church of the Six-Winged Dove settled in on the city out of the Dungeon, but restorative healers were still far, far beyond her budget. Maybe she could get one of the golem specialists to give her a golem's eye if she worked for a few years.

And where would she even work? She was probably too scarred to even be accepted at the most filthy brothel. She could do little more than beg.

The realization that no matter what happened, she was already as good as dead, weighed heavier on her chest than any heap of corpses and metal ever could.

As the minutes rolled by and her exhaustion overtook her senses, she fell asleep to the morbid lullaby of snapping bones and tearing flesh, her body soaked in freezing crimson from the tips of her toes to the roots of her hair.

CHAPTER 10

The wolf took a deep inhale, its snout pointed to the cable lines above.

It didn't know *what* exactly, but it could feel something changing about the [Devourer] skill.

As its feast continued, a buzzing of adrenaline, of excitement, of *hunger* beyond the depth of its own flesh ravaged its sense of patience, and before long, it was taking a couple minute-long rests in between feedings. As soon as its jaw stopped feeling like it was about to fall off, it continued to devour the countless rats. It *could* sleep, but with every minute wasted, the flesh grew less nurturing and more and more unusable for anything but subpar nutrition.

A factor about flesh that it had not considered before was simply its state of decomposition. Decomposing flesh was much less effective for nutrients, and it honestly wasn't entirely sure of how [Devourer] would be able to put rotting flesh to use.

It could take the normal flesh in storage and use it for keeping itself fed for prolonged periods of time, using the water content of the blood to keep it hydrated, with the rest of the bits being used as nutrition, among various other possibilities. But the instinctual knowledge that came with the skill was that rotting flesh, depending on *how* rotten, gave much less to work with. Less of *what* or *how*, it wasn't sure.

So even though it had devoured almost a third of the damn rodents and two of the humans, there was just too much stuff to eat and not enough time, especially with the humid heat inviting an utterly infuriating amount of insects to help the process of decomposition along. For the first dozen or so hours, it was fine, but then, it was as if they materialized out of thin air to settle on everything in sight.

The buzzing wasn't even the worst part. The worst part was that it was so absolutely drenched in blood that it had a near constant cloud of the damn things nibbling at its fur and trying to get into its ears. Anger was a rather rare thing for the wolf.

Until now.

It hated insects, it decided.

They were even more frustrating than the realization that the other human female had unfortunately landed in the trash pits, which meant it only had two humans to devour, as going into the trash pits was a rather swift guarantee it would get stuck and crushed by the gears at the bottom when they started spinning. Well, not a *complete* guarantee, as it knew there was a gap between the gears that the rats used to clamber up, but close enough to not even consider risking it.

It didn't regret helping the human female, as she hadn't been any trouble to it as the hours passed, but that *greed* in its mind insisted it just go back and kill her. She was defenseless, blind. It would just take one careful snip at the back of her neck to sever her spine.

But it refrained, [Mental Resistance] pulling its weight once more to push the greed and bloodlust back.

If only that would work on its damn *temper*, because those stupid flying little things were buzzing and humming and constantly ruffling the fur on the inside of its ears as if they were trying to look for a place to burrow, and it was driving it insane.

Eventually, it stopped in the middle of chowing down a half-rotted rat and snarled in frustration as it shook itself free of the flies.

For about all of one second, before the damn things returned.

If only it could . . . breathe fire, or electricity, or spew those toxic discolored bits of air, or *anything* to kill these pests—

A sound like countless tiny bits of shuffling paper to the side made its head snap up with a dry crackle as the solidified bits of blood on its neck and chest broke apart into chunks. It saw the human with her hand up, a bright burst of orange sparks spewing out of her hand in a cone at the large horde of insects trying to settle on her, before tugging her coverings over her head with the same hand as soon she was finished.

A good idea, actually. It should do the same.

The important part was that the insects died by the hundreds, and for about five whole seconds, the human was free of the annoying flies.

Perhaps she wasn't as little of a threat as it thought she was. She was still blind, though, and her hearing and sense of smell was likely as useless as any other human's, so she was still relatively harmless as long as the wolf didn't let its nails scrape the ground and reveal its location if it moved close to her.

It could only look on with jealously as the girl blasted the insects again, so after a few moments of doing exactly that, it turned back to the rodent at its feet, the motion being accompanied by a bout of sudden dizziness.

It stumbled in place for a moment, and after the floor stopped moving under its feet, it realized that it hadn't slept in . . . more than a full light cycle. More than a day. Not a great choice on its part.

With a yawn full of annoyance and slowly encroaching exhaustion, it trotted over to the scraped-off remnants of fabric from the human male it had just finished eating an hour ago, hooking a canine into the biggest piece of fabric it could find—the back portion of the man's covering—and prepared itself for a bout of dizziness.

It was just heavy and stiff enough from being soaked in blood that it could easily drape it over its head and ears like one of those weird head coverings humans used, so the wolf tilted its head and moved it side to side to start building momentum as the fabric swung back and forth, and then swung its head in a semicircle to make the fabric drape over its head. It was a bit awkward, and it had to unhook its canine from the fabric using its tongue, but it worked.

It really needed to figure out how to make its paws able to switch to "human mode." Its own "fingers" were basically immovable, never mind being useful when trying to handle anything with any sort of dexterity.

For a few long moments, it stood rigid as the world spun, until the feeling of disorientation faded.

Its hearing wasn't terribly dampened by the fabric, and it kept the flies away from its ears, so it used what little it could see under the covering to find a decent, dry corner to tuck itself into for a decent sleep, laying its head chin down on the floor with its paws keeping the fabric tight over its ears to keep the flies from waking it up.

Its body had been so overworked that it was having trouble snapping itself out of perseverance mode, but after five or ten minutes, it finally fell back to the familiar lucid dream as the symbols welcomed it back.

[Infection Resistance] has Leveled Up. Level 7 → Level 8
[Iron Stomach] has Leveled Up. Level 4 → Level 6
[Mana Perception] has Leveled Up. Level 2 → Level 3

[Mana Manipulation] has Leveled Up. Level 2 → Level 3

-Acquired Titles:
Glutton Beyond Compare: You have eaten multiple times your body weight over a single uninterrupted period of consumption. You gain +1 to Strength and Speed while your stomach is adequately filled. Bonus is doubled when your stomach is filled to the brim.

That . . . was unfortunate. Its stomach was *literally* never filled. It all went into the [Devourer] skill's storage. Maybe it could . . . find something solid its skill couldn't eat and just have it inside its stomach permanently? That sounded possible, but at the same time, it sounded not only dangerous but also very difficult to undo.

So that wasn't happening; at least for now.

A bit disappointed with its new title, it watched the symbols leave, and the [Devourer] skill activated.

The rats it had devoured still had plenty to show, surprisingly, and the information wasn't exclusive to them only. They shared a downright ridiculous amount of similarities to humans, which was absolutely insane to the wolf, as the two creatures couldn't be further apart from the other. But if the symbols said it was true, then it was true. It was still bizarre, however.

The process of information rushing to its mind was so much smoother than before, so much easier, that understanding of said knowledge came like a brick sliding into its place in a wall. Seamless. Down to the cellular level and even deeper into the insides of the cells, it learned all there was to know, the difficulty no larger than remembering an odd mental image it had forgotten.

The humans were next, and it noted that part of the reason they were so smart was due to the folds in their brains, not the size of them. But it still had no idea how to recreate that intelligence without the possibility of breaking itself, so it left it as something to be thought about later.

It looked at the odd way the humans used their tongues and vocal cords, and had an idea.

The human girl knew how to use mana to summon that cone of sparks, or that orb of light. Which meant that not only did she know how to use and manipulate the mana—she also knew how to actually turn it into different things.

And if it could learn how to communicate with her through their weird way of yipping and barking and grumbling, it could get the girl to show it how to do it as well. Humans had a far larger variety of ways and sounds to communicate, most of which were probably very specific, so it wasn't *too* far-fetched of an idea. Its vocal cords were already very similar in structure to the human's, if a lot lower in their pitch and baritone, so it wouldn't even need to do any changes there.

It had never tried to speak like a human, but if it could get the girl to start blabbering again, it could sit nearby and try to mimic her.

Frankly, it had no idea whatsoever of how to learn another species' method of communication. It believed it was smart enough to do so, especially if it kept putting points in Intelligence—which it *absolutely* planned to do—so the only barrier was . . . what? Time?

The other humans didn't seem to be in a rush to grab her. It might have time. Alternatively, it could just drag her into one of the less toxic areas of the last floor with the burning rivers and keep her there. It would be like keeping and feeding a pup, except it would be larger, needier, and a human.

. . . Which was unlikely to work, and the human could easily die from the poisons, not to mention the logistical mess that getting her down there would be.

So it had to hurry and try to learn how to speak human while it still had access to a stuck, defenseless one who couldn't see it. It knew that humans used a combination of their tongue placement, teeth, and vocal cords, using the air to make said cords vibrate to create their speech.

The problem was that its tongue severely lacked the dexterity that theirs had, as well as its mouth structure being much different.

One of those issues was something it could fix.

Its tongue was an essential heat regulator, so it couldn't just pick a human tongue to replace its own, meaning that it would have to do some manual work.

The humans' biological components flitted away, and it was left in the void, not focused enough for the skill to bring forth its own body while lost in thought.

The [Devourer] skill had changed somehow. The mental space was not unlike the series of floating knowledge and matter it was before, but the wolf had the vague idea that it could do much *more* all of a sudden.

It just didn't know what that *more* entailed.

It prodded around, trying to figure out what had changed, until eventually, something clicked, the symbols that strengthened it suddenly giving it information.

One of the things that had changed was the speed. The energy of the skill could change the wolf faster now, as if a pinprick-size hole had expanded to allow more of the energy to flow between itself and its ability. The other things that had changed were control and understanding. It could control much more finely what it wanted its resources to be allocated to.

And its newfound understanding of how the skill worked was quite enlightening. When it had first gained access to the symbols—*letters*—it had thought that it was taking flesh from that odd storage and just placing it on itself; that it was using the bones of the rats to strengthen its own. But that didn't seem to be how the skill actually worked.

It simply transported the flesh to a void, somehow, then turned it into an unseen, unfelt energy, according to whatever the wolf told the skill to do with it, before using that energy to change its body. It couldn't peer into said energy, its structure, nor what its conversion rates of flesh to energy were; neither did it get the feeling that it would be able to in the future. But it knew it wasn't mana. It was something entirely unique.

Its curiosity of how the skill worked being sated for the moment, it thought of its body, and with but a thought, its structure appeared, hazy and sharp, invisible and glowing, a shapeless shape.

That . . . was new. And it was giving it a headache the more it focused on the *visual* aspects of it.

It used to see itself as it was in its sleeping position, with the ability to float around like some detached, airborne eye that could see through layers of solid flesh.

Its ability to perceive itself was . . . not visual anymore. It could just feel and become every tiny bit of itself. It was, frankly, extremely annoying and disorienting, at least for now, but it was somehow easier and smoother to use the skill like this, so it tried not to feel disgruntled at the change, focusing on its body instead.

By the time it woke up, its antennae would be complete, all its whiskers fallen out to be replaced by long, chitinous organs it could move, covered in microscopic hairs. Just sticking its snout to the ground would allow it to feel every walking human for multiple *dozens* of feet through the vibrations on the stone, and even just flaring the antennae out would allow it to feel the vibrations on the air. It could use that, along with its ears, to precisely pinpoint the source of most, if not all, sounds.

The cerci hairs would be complete as well—just a few extra long hairs among its coat—and it would be able to tell any and all changes in wind direction, allowing it to sneak up on prey better without the wind carrying its scent to said prey. Or allowing it to dodge noxious fumes before the breeze blew them into its face.

It would also be much less starved in appearance, and the thin layer of fat under its skin would probably double by the time it woke up. Its flesh was slowly but surely growing, and although it was tempted to add more, it could tell that it was already going to be a little oversized to pass as a dog when it grew into an adult, so it didn't wish to accentuate that problem. Wolves were naturally bigger than dogs, it seemed.

Then it remembered that all the extra tendons would give it a *lot* of extra muscle mass anyway, and so decided to pump a bit more growth hormone into its body. Hopefully, by the time it grew into an adult, it would already be too strong to be bothered about humans wondering why it was so much larger than the other dogs.

If it decided to even stick around where humans were, for whatever reason.

That done, it looked into its storage . . .

And mentally gawked at just *how much* flesh it had to mess around with. It was a mound of flesh so large it could be used as a small dwelling by a human.

It looked to its extra tendons and prodded around to see how quickly it could have them grow, adding and removing the skill's essence as its mind seamlessly swapped its form for a copy it could experiment with.

It could have all the tendon work finished within just five days, and although it was skeptical about such fast-paced changes, it had a small mountain's worth of essence, and leaving it sitting there felt like a waste. Up until now, it'd always lived day to day, hour to hour, and now that it had leeway to save up and think of what would happen later, it had to control itself to not just throw all of the skill's essence on its body and hope it worked out.

A quick but careful check of its previous work made it notice a few of its new tendons would snag on its spine and various other bones when doing specific movements, and thus discarded them.

In just *five* days it would be almost *twice* as physically strong—assuming its rather amateurish attempts at adding more tendons worked as it had envisioned.

The mere thought made it giddy, its tail wagging against ground sticky with half-dried blood in the real world.

It peered into its body more closely, noting the things that were beneficial and those that weren't. It noticed it had a rather puny amount of those things called "vitamins," and thus dedicated about twenty rats' worth of essence to generate more and pump it into its bloodstream slowly over time.

Its bones were hardening quickly, and the process would be finished in a couple days. While hardening them further was tempting, it also wanted to keep itself *sort of* light, just because of the unsafe, rickety grounds it sometimes had to cross, and to conserve more energy as it moved around.

Its changes, for some reason, sped up significantly when it slept, so it realized that if it wanted to change faster, it could just sleep constantly, something the wolf mentally noted to do more from now on.

It could get rid of some of the fat it'd decided to put on to shed more weight, but the fat had been added for the purpose of insulation from both the electricity thing and to keep its body warm, so it let it be for now.

It looked for any other improvements it could make, and after a moment, realized it had a problem.

There was a lot of flesh in storage and little to spend its essence on.

Its intestines were also currently in the process of being dissolved, and after a bit of nudging, it realized that it could have that part finished by the time it woke up, leaving it with a lot of empty space in its body. The jointed miniature rib cage of bone it had placed under its abdominal muscles would be ready in perhaps seven to eight days—or light cycles—so its abdomen would hopefully not be so grimly thin it would draw attention.

The lack of intestines would actually make it much lighter, but still, it felt like a waste for its abdomen to just be a film of muscle over a few shoddy bones.

But what could it put in there? Maybe an additional lung? But it had no idea how that would go in a fight. If it had to clench its abdomen, its lung would get squeezed, so that wasn't quite viable. A . . . liver?

Oh. Wait. It didn't *need* a liver, did it? A liver helped with production of bile, which it did not need, production of certain proteins for blood plasma, which some essence could easily take care of instead, and it helped with producing something called cholesterol and some specific proteins that would help it carry fats through its body. Which was *another* thing the [Devourer] skill could take care of, and at about the same energy efficiency.

After much deliberation, it decided to keep its liver, as it assisted in its internal structural integrity, and it had nothing to fill that space with for the moment.

In general, it let its insides remain much the same, and then focused on its muscles. It considered making them harder or more resilient, but that would also *probably* make its movements stiffer and its muscles less stretchy, so after dedicating some essence to fully repair every single small injury on its body as it slept—including the regeneration of the tiny hairs on the inside of its cochlea which gave it the ability to hear—and fully restoring its sense of smell and taste, it turned to inspecting its body a bit more for anything else it could fix or improve.

After some deliberation and mental fumbling, it managed to make its body cut most of the hairs on its upper body in half, just to get rid of all that extra weight from the crusted filth it couldn't reach before with its teeth. Filth that had densified significantly from its feast, at least on the underside of its neck and chest. It was mildly embarrassed it hadn't thought of doing that before.

Still, it was incredible how much fine control the skill allowed the wolf to have over its body, to the point it could pinpoint specific hairs and cut them to specific lengths just by dissolving the unwanted or overly long bits into the skill's storage.

It then checked its eyes for progress and tried to see how much it could rush the process along. It wanted better sight—was absolutely intrigued at the idea of *more* colors—and pushed that process as much as it reasonably could. It was ready to dump half the mountain of rats into the process, but after a certain point, it just refused to be further sped up, some sort of bottleneck in place preventing it. So it carefully tuned the maximum amount of flesh it could, and in about ten days, it would be able to see *new colors* for the cost of about only ten rats.

It tried to imagine how that would even look, but much in the same way it could not imagine the sky when all it had known were pipes and darkness—despite knowing what it conceptually was—it could not imagine the colors the humans saw.

Finally, he reached its tongue. The reason that human tongues were so dexterous was that they were purely muscle and taste buds, while its own tongue had substantially less of both in exchange for much higher blood flow to the organ, which was used to regulate its heat.

So, after much, *much* fiddling, it figured out a way to put more muscle fibers into the organ without restricting the blood flow too much, thus making its tongue a bit more dexterous in exchange for slightly less efficiency in its body-cooling abilities, forcing the change to happen in mere hours thanks to the low volume of flesh produced. It didn't even have to rush the process along.

Then it looked at its reserve of roughly one-and-a-half human bodies and assigned them as nutrients. They had no real difference from the rat meat besides their higher-quality flesh being equivalent to more essence, but it preferred eating humans over the furry rats, so for the sake of mental organization, it would put humans as food.

As soon as the wolf thought that it had nothing more to see or change, its consciousness faded entirely, and it peacefully slept, hours passing by in moments.

Until a shrill scream startled it awake.

CHAPTER 11

The crunching, the buzzing. They never stopped, even long after she'd covered her head and ears with a torn piece of her robe; even long after the beast had gone silent. The hours passed by like nails raking down her back—long, painful. Slow.

She focused on the letters floating in her mind, clinging to them.

Not because of the skills she'd gained, nor the singular level she'd gotten from being dragged on the quest to kill the rats.

But because it was all she *could* see.

She'd heard that blind people and animals with no concept of language would see the System as a series of concepts and ideas, and part of her had wondered what it would be like now that she no longer had sight.

And to her great relief, that hadn't happened. She could still see the System's information, faint white letters floating in place in her mind, as if she could still see. So she stared at the window with eyes that weren't there, just to indulge in what she could no longer have outside her own head.

-Species: Humanoid
-Race: Elf
-Name: Emhreeil
-Path: [Infuser] Level 7

-Available Attribute Points: 0
-Base Attributes:

Strength (+0)
Speed (+0)
Dexterity (+0)
Endurance (+0)
Perception (+0)
Resolve (+1)
Intelligence (+4)
Soul (+2)

-Racial Skills: [Attuned], [Quick Learner]
-Acquired Skills:
[Magic Resistance - Level 5]
[Mental Resistance - Level 6]
[Poison Resistance - Level 4]
[Pain Resistance - Level 8]
[Illumina - Level 6]
[Sparkburst - Level 12]
[Haste - Level 9]
[Mana Perception - Level 15]
[Mana Manipulation - Level 9]

-Acquired Traits:
Kindhearted (1/3): You have shown yourself capable of both sympathy and empathy, and have backed up your emotions with actions that you believe were moral. Gain +1 in Soul and Resolve when helping sentient beings as long as you do not assist them with committing actions you find immoral.

She focused on her one and only gained trait with the acidic, bitter taste of resentment. Were she not "kind," would she have some other path that would save her? Something, some spell that could kill the monster prowling around her? That could help her regain her sight?

Focusing on the past, she'd learned, was among the most meaningless things anyone could do.

But so was everything else right now.

So she continued, her mind rolling down a well-walked spiral until she was so deep that everything faded under a thin veil of despair.

How long until she was rescued? Did she even want to be rescued? Without her eyes, she couldn't even tell how much time had passed. It might have been two days, or it might have been six. She was so dehydrated. She was so *hungry*.

Maybe she should just . . . anger the monster on purpose. Bare her throat, make it quick.

Because she couldn't find any other way to escape her predicament. She had nothing, nobody. Even her fumbling attempts to attract the monster to her, to see how amicable it was in the vain hope of it being some bound creature or some summon she could befriend, had done nothing to attract its attention.

How much longer could she last without water? She had no idea, but the headache pounding in her skull didn't give her much confidence. Yet she could do nothing but stay rooted in place, withering away like a poisoned plant.

Or she could just . . . stick her palm against the holes where her eyes used to be and activate [Sparkburst].

Minutes passed in silence, her mind slowly growing foggy. She thought of a warm bed, a cool glass of water. Pain suddenly registered as tears came out of her tear ducts to pool inside the sensitive holes of her sockets, and she hissed, hurriedly trying to tilt her head to let them drip down the side of her face. Unable to do anything, she let the minutes pass her by as she sat there, her mind slowly emptying of all thought, slipping into a fugue.

Then, in an instant forged out of a piece of her consciousness, her sight returned.

The staircase wobbled under her feet as she watched Kisae speed past them with the [Haste] spell she'd demanded, leaving them behind, the horde at her heels.

Something snapped, a scream tore at her throat as she lost her footing, and then her world was nothing but fur and teeth and agony, blunt teeth yanking bits of her flesh off as the world began spinning, the [Sparkburst] spell on her right hand burning her own skin, eyes ripped out of their sockets, teeth snagged on tendons, fingers tearing, the clicking of teeth, the **shrieking—**

She woke up with a terrified scream, attempting to bolt upright and open eyes that weren't there anymore and only managing to raise her torso a couple inches off the ground before gasping and lying back down. She panted in pain and panic from the sudden jerk of wakefulness jostling her broken limbs, and for a moment, she simply breathed in the miasma of rot in the air, until her brain remembered her predicament and she relaxed back onto the stone as best as she could.

The scrape of nails on stone neared, and she took in a shaky breath as she tried to muffle her whimpers of pain.

Despite the fact that she just wanted to give up, she was scared. She didn't want to die, so she tightened her throat, gritted her teeth. Yet, much to her dismay, the clicking nails kept getting closer. Logic told her that if it wanted to kill her, it would have done so ages ago, but her mind kept conjuring the stomach-churning sounds of the thing battling the rats, the horrid, endless sound of crunching bone and tearing flesh.

She didn't need eyes to hear its pacing, to know it was right next to her, circling around her form as if deciding what to do with her now that all its food had rotted away. She could be next—a realization both comforting and horrifying in equal measure.

Her heartbeat hammered away in her chest. Minutes passed in relative silence, and then a singular bark, *far, far* too loud to be coming from a canine of the size she remembered, broke the silence, and she flinched.

And then, silence, once more. Yet slowly but surely, shrill squeaking came closer and closer, and she could only tremble in fear while hoping the monster would protect her.

The wolf could only guess what had made the human scream. Maybe a dream. Maybe it'd tried to move, only to feel whatever injury it had. But despite circling around her thrice, it could find no new wound or threat besides a single rat in the opposite end of the pit.

The vermin would slowly come back now that they thought the danger was away, so it would probably be best to move the human far away from the lip of the hole and somewhere the wolf could keep her close. If she died, that would be unfortunate, but it was going to make damn sure the human didn't die before it learned how to move the mana or at least how to communicate a bit.

Now that it was certain there was little danger, it sat on its haunches and accessed its body.

Not only did it *feel* amazing but it *looked* amazing compared to before. The excess fur covered in filth had mostly disappeared from its body, making it feel just a bit lighter after shaking off the chunks of blood and dirt. That lightness was somewhat offset by its additional fat and a bit more muscle, which the wolf was more than grateful for, but with its intestines gone, it was still about as light as when the symbols came to its mind for the first time, despite all its added bulk.

It almost couldn't see the outline of its ribs anymore, and the rest of its body was similarly filled out. Just a couple days more, and it wouldn't even look or *be* malnourished.

It spun in a quick circle just to feel the air on its new cerci hairs, pleased with how easy it was to know how the wind moved around its body. A mild advantage, but a welcome one.

The cerci hairs were . . . *strange*. There was little to no airflow down here, so it had to spin a couple more times to figure out how each sensation of displaced air felt, from pushing it out of the way to the air retreating around its form on the other side, but it got a grasp of it fairly quickly.

The thing it was most excited about, however, were the antennae.

It was like having a dozen extra tiny, flexible tentacles on the end of its snout. Moving each one individually felt as natural as twitching an ear. A bit of experimentation in individually moving more than two of them in opposing directions proved *difficult,* as if strings had them tied together and it simply couldn't extend an antenna too far in the opposite direction. But it was definitely possible. It wasn't a biological restriction but more one having to do with coordination.

Experimentally, it pressed them flat on its snout to hide them, immediately disliking how intense the sensation of the antennae burrowing into its fur was. The miniature hairs on the antennae were a bit more sensitive than it had expected, and the sensation of hiding them into its fur felt much like having an overly sensitive area rub against rough fabric. Not painful, but overloading to the point of it *almost* being so.

It suspected that was largely due to the fact it had removed pain sensors from the organs rather than the sensation *actually* not being painful.

Then it decided to flare them all out at once, all fourteen twitching antennae, and the world . . . deepened. Or rather, its perception of the world did. Even from the simple vibrations in the air, it could very, *very* faintly feel distant impacts and hums, mechanical and not.

It lowered its snout to the ground, its flexible antennae moving erratically, brushing against each other and the ground. There was just *so much* information in an instant that, for a moment, it felt overwhelmed, prompting it to yank its head up. After a few seconds of preparation, it shook itself and bent down once more.

It was like getting a tactile sensation of everything in contact with the stone below its feet, the sensation peaking with vibrations of varying strength. It felt that the gears of the hole were arranged in a sort of grid made of lines and levels, the lines of gears at the top row further apart than the ones below, repeating for five levels until anything that made it out of the bottom would be smashed together.

It felt places where the stone's vibrations magnified and condensed—into pipes and stairways buried into the sides of the pit, into rooms full of moving . . . metal? It felt like the gears, which were metal.

The pit was already gigantic, but knowing just how much *more* there was to its sides and underneath made it feel completely dwarfed.

But it didn't matter.

Because it could *feel* almost all of it.

Its tail wagged with so much strength that its hips were forced to move side to side in a sort of overly excited wiggle, and it sniffed at the ground once more before stomping a paw, its eyes closed.

It couldn't see, but it could *feel*.

There were pipes of metal running through the stone, rooms embedded in the sides, accessible through other tunnels it couldn't feel the entirety of—cubes of stone full of inert machinery waiting to start spinning the gears. There were tiny impacts following a pattern and unstable path, which it quickly realized were actually *rodents* as they scurried out of the pipes. There was some complicated mechanism connected by pipes running up the walls to the wolf's sides and toward the top of the pit, connected to four metal boxes inside of which were complicated bits of wires and metals.

The human behind it shifted, just a tad, but the light thud of her head hitting the stone told it *exactly* where she was, even if the impact was muffled by her hair.

It slowly peeled back more and more of its antennae as it continued reading the vibrations around itself, noticing that it could feel and sense less and less with every peeled-back organ. It was like having a dozen ears all working in harmony to send it clear signals.

It was amazing.

It was so happy that it honestly didn't know what to do with itself, so it nailed its eyes on the singular rat on the other side of the pit, gathered as much air as it could into its lungs, and let all of it out at once with a booming bark that made its throat hurt a bit, the sound easily carrying to the other side of the massive pit.

The rat turned at the sound, spotting it, and started its long, frenzied journey around the edge of the pit toward the wolf, who genuinely started feeling its tail growing sore from its wagging.

A celebration with a snack. What more could it want?

It lowered its snout to the ground just to confirm that the mounds of trash had muffled the sound of its bark enough to not attract more rats than it could handle. Besides a low buzz of activity from a couple that were already near the top, it was "silent."

It hopped back and forth in place just a bit before directing its gaze to a plate of metal on the wall behind it and trying to visualize if it could accurately toss the rat onto its center, just as a test of accuracy—or rather, a game.

And froze in place as it saw another wolf, ears shooting straight up.

Wait, no, that wasn't right.

It tilted its head, and the other wolf did the exact same. It thought back to how light interacted with the human and wolven retinas and pupils, and realized what was happening. A reflection.

A reflection that was *wrong*.

It moved its head, flaring its antennae in specific patterns as it approached. The reflection was a perfect mimicry of its actions, but not its form. It mimicked exactly how the wolf moved and acted, if mildly distorted from detritus and a thin layer of moss growing on the shiny plate.

But its eyes were glowing in the reflection.

It hadn't done anything to its eyes that would do that. There was no light entering and reflecting the lining in its eyes right now. They were just . . . glowing. Two yellow circles of gold with the background of a mangy-looking canine on a dirty plate of metal.

Why were its eyes glowing?

No other canine it had ever seen had glowing eyes.

Even as the furious squeaks slowly got closer, it couldn't look away, confused and worried.

If its eyes were glowing, why hadn't it noticed? Why did its eyes not *see* the light that seemingly radiated out of its irises? It made no sense. Was the light only visible from a certain angle, allowing it not to be bothered by the golden luminescence?

From simple logic, all it should be able to see should be a bright yellow light, even if it closed its eyes. So this probably had to do with the thing that *broke* logic, which were the symbols.

After it spent a minute thinking, it couldn't really remember anything eye-related in the symbols besides the title *Witness of Divinity*.

Could it turn that *off* somehow?

Because the more it looked at its own glowing eyes, the more it started to realize that blending in with the other canines was going to be much harder than it thought. It made sense now why humans kept giving it second looks, and why it was suddenly drawing so much more attention than it was used to. The humans probably kept pausing to see if its eyes were reflecting light from some strange angle, or if they were actually glowing.

The shrill squeaks came closer and closer as the human started breathing faster, whimpering short words at the sound that the wolf didn't care to register, instead turning to rush at the rat, no longer in a good mood.

One swipe, bite, and thrash of the vermin later, it wrenched its head to the side and accurately slammed it onto the plate of metal with a rattling bang before getting back to thinking, only idly checking for any more rodents that would disturb it.

Hunting with its eyes giving away its position like that was going to be *really* difficult, at least against anything with any semblance of self-preservation and wariness. There had to be a way it could turn it off, because otherwise, it would be nothing but a detriment to its survival. It knew that traits couldn't be turned off because it had asked the symbols, mostly due to the fact that it hadn't liked the Timid trait slowing it down when it began hunting. But it hadn't considered asking if titles could be turned off.

Skills like its resistances could be mentally dialed up and down, even if it was awake, with little more than a thought, but trying to focus on the title and asking the symbols to disable it did nothing. Maybe it could just make new eyes. Or would those be affected too?

The symbols sometimes answered its questions, so when it slept again, it was going to have a *lot* of them.

For the moment, it couldn't do anything about the glow, so it simply turned to the human, who was still breathing harshly, and tried to consult its internal clock. It had been . . . two days since it broke the staircase? The human must be starving, and she would definitely need some liquid to survive.

It glanced at the shredded rat lying limp under the metal plate, tilting its head as it tried to remember what human stomachs were designed for.

Yeah, that would work. Not the safest, because human stomachs were weak to raw meat, but it didn't have many options to feed her.

Plus, if she cared that much, she could just burn the thing with her mana fire thingy and eat it after drinking the blood. Blood was about . . . nine-tenths water content, so all it had to do was grab some rats, bleed them into her mouth, and then let her do whatever she wanted with the meat, and she should theoretically survive.

As it gripped the rat in its jaws and trotted back to the human, it began to wonder if the girl was really worth all the trouble, trying not to think how suspiciously long it was taking for the humans to come pick her up.

At this rate, it was starting to come up with escape plans of its own just in case the humans never showed up.

CHAPTER 12

The wolf paused for a moment and put the rodent on the floor.

The human couldn't digest the hair on the rodent, and the guts of the rat were a thing so vile that it was only thanks to the [Devourer] skill that the wolf itself could nonchalantly eat them. Not to mention, it was highly likely the human would get sick from ingesting rat blood, which could result in puking. Which would only dehydrate her *further* and could potentially make keeping her alive harder.

Of course, that wasn't a guarantee, as every human it had devoured had slightly different strengths and biological capabilities, but it was likely.

There were also other problems that would build up were it to feed her rat's blood. For example, humans had trouble getting rid of the iron in their foods and bodies, so feeding her rat blood would give her an iron overload. That would lead to various annoying and potentially dangerous issues, but only in the long-term.

Another more obvious issue, and one that would occur with near certainty, was disease. That, the rats carried *plenty* of. It didn't know what diseases exactly, nor how they worked, but the microorganisms inside the rats and the substances *on* the rats could seriously mess up a weak human, especially since it probably didn't have any skills and natural resistances to such things like the wolf did.

That actually explained a long-time question it held about why humans rarely ate rats. Although burning the meat would probably solve most of those issues, there was also the problem of *hunting* the rats. One bite from them could be seriously difficult to deal with for things with weaker immune systems than itself, like humans. The amount of filth and bacteria in their mouths could easily kill someone if a bite was left untreated.

As it raked its teeth through the rodent's corpse, slowly peeling off its fur and yanking out its intestines, which it quickly ate, it thought of alternative solutions to keep the human alive. It could create a sack of skin on its leg and direct a bunch of blood to be formed inside it from the [Devourer] skill, before making a small hole and letting the human drink the blood.

It was a bit of a bastardization of the design of human mammaries, but it didn't particularly care about how sanitary or uncomfortable something like a skin sac full of excess blood would be when it could easily hook a canine on it and just cut it off. It would be painless, and not terribly difficult to form, design, or get rid of.

So long as it kept the human alive, it was an option worth considering. The wolf wouldn't even become anemic, as the blood would be provided by the [Devourer] skill's essence.

So while that triggered a bit of an . . . *offensive* feeling, to do such a thing to itself, it *could* do it, and its blood was undeniably far better quality than rodent blood. It could also tweak it to be higher in water content, as well as pump more vitamins and minerals into it so it would be even closer to water, and thus keep the human healthier.

Actually . . . couldn't it just *create* water?

Biological understanding was based on several dozen concepts and ideas that the wolf shouldn't understand, like chemicals, electrical signals, energy and heat generation, and various other small tidbits that were necessary but otherwise unrelated to biology and more related to how the world itself worked.

It was a curious thing, that the wolf had learned of them anyway.

Yet it didn't *feel* like those extra bits were being taught by the skill. It felt like information pulled out of nowhere on the spot and shoved into its mind to fit whatever it was curious or focused on at the moment, rather than information so well placed it was like remembering something previously forgotten, which was how information taught by the symbols felt like. And that odd learning process had started long before the symbols appeared.

It felt like something *other*, something different the wolf didn't know about working *with* the skill to teach it.

Something to be considered and explored later.

As it focused back on its task ahead, it believed that it *technically* could reduce the plasma content of its blood until it would essentially just be slightly slimier water. The question was if it cared enough to change its body like that by applying that skin sac idea onto itself, even if temporarily, just to avoid getting the human sick.

The answer to which, for the moment, was a firm no.

It likely didn't have that long with her, anyway, before her kin would arrive and help her, so it was going to stick to its original plan.

The *bigger* problem would be communicating and getting close to the human without scaring her into throwing mana things at it, like those sparks.

After biting off the rat's head, forcing its hide down its throat, and carefully chewing through its organs, all that was left was a husk of bloody flesh, which it hooked onto its canines before carefully trotting to the side where the human's unusable arm lay. If the human tried to do something with mana from its hands or something else, the wolf would have more time to react from the injured side, or so it hoped. It raised a paw with a short chuff through the meat in its maw to alert the human to its presence and poked it in the side, prompting her to jerk in surprise.

"H-H-Hello?" the girl squeaked out in acknowledgement. The wolf grumbled lightly back in a sort of greeting. Not that it was at all sure if the human would understand its meaning, but hopefully, that would eventually be resolved.

It walked around her shoulders to position itself above her head, its mind just as focused on the blood being wasted with every moment it wasn't dripping into her mouth as it was focused on the human for any sudden movements.

It clumsily raised a paw and prodded her cloth-covered head this time, making sure to have its nails unable to cut. They had no way of communicating, but it had to find a way to tell her what it was doing, so physical touch would have to work.

"You don't understand me . . . r-right?" it whispered, shying away from the wolf's touch by tilting its head away, and the wolf sensed her fear slowly evaporating as the seconds passed by while it clumsily tried to tug the head covering off her mouth.

The head covering had been a great idea, considering the open wounds that were her eyes, so while it was tempted to just yank it off, it refrained, largely due to the presence of the flies. If they were anything like cockroaches, they wouldn't hesitate to plant their eggs in her eye sockets, which would be . . .

Just the thought made it shudder. Getting rid of something like that would be *horrible.*

While it was good that the human was suddenly less scared, it didn't care all that much, carefully balancing the act of moving its paw to drag the fabric off her mouth with the act of paying attention to her mana and constantly twitching its ears to be rid of all the flies still buzzing around.

Most of said flies were focused on the rotting corpses, thankfully, but that still left a ton of them to bother itself and the human.

As soon as it got the bloodied fabric bunched up under her nose, it tilted its head to see better and aligned the rodent's neck stump with her lips, watching the drops of crimson gather before slowly dripping downward.

The process of skinning and eating its organs had significantly drained the rodent of blood, which was a bit annoying. There were probably little more than a handful or so that it could drip into her mouth before all the blood trapped in the veins and muscles would stop moving. The first drop met her chapped lips and trickled down to the side of her mouth, her head already turned away from the wolf. The human stiffened, but the wolf sensed no mana being involved with the way it clenched its working fist, so the wolf remained in place.

Another drop, and another, and her tongue curiously flitted out between her lips to taste the liquid.

And she stiffened even further, bunching her shoulders up near her neck despite her injured arm being jostled by the movement.

It gave a short grumble, partly to comfort the skittish human and partly to rush her along, because it'd just watched a drop trickle down her cheek, utterly wasted.

It was just blood. Fairly vile blood, sure, but would she rather die of dehydration than eat something gross?

Humans were not only built extremely strangely from a biological standpoint—they were also utterly illogical. Another drop trickled down her lips, and the wolf grumbled again, more forcefully, putting a paw on her mouth and pulling her bottom lip down just enough for a couple drops to enter her mouth.

She would only survive three to four days without water, and it'd already been around two and a half days since she'd come into the pit with her team. So the fact that she wrenched her head to the side and out from under its paw was highly frustrating to the wolf.

Another couple drops were wasted.

Just as it was about to give up and eat the rodent by itself, the human turned her head up toward the wolf and hesitantly opened her mouth, with her nose scrunched up into a sort of . . . grimace?

Finally, they were getting somewhere.

For a couple minutes, the wolf stood in place, weathering the discomfort of the annoying insects to let the human drink. Sometimes, it had to pause and rake its nails through the flesh to make the corpse bleed a bit more, and sometimes, the flies would try and enter the human's mouth, and she had to twitch her facial muscles and blow out air to make them go away. But regardless of those interruptions, around a small cupful of liquid was extracted in the fifteen or so minutes it took to hydrate the human.

It chuffed through its teeth once it decided it was done standing in place and put the rat's mutilated remains on the floor, quickly devouring it. The human would survive for a while without food, not to mention that digestion needed water, which would further dehydrate the human. So it wouldn't even say it was being greedy for eating the rodent without trying to get her to eat first. Even if it was mostly *motivated* by greed.

It could, after all, put the food into much better use than the human could.

The girl made some gagging noises shortly after swallowing the final small mouthful, but settled down quickly as the wolf chomped down the rat in a few final bites. Raking its nails through the flesh had made it exceptionally easy to tear apart and swallow.

As soon as it clacked its teeth shut for the final time, licking bits of gore and blood off its chops, the human took a deep breath and softly spoke.

"Thank you."

The wolf didn't understand, but it chuffed again and moved to the human's injured side before settling down on its haunches as the human pulled the bloodied fabric down to her chin again. Now, to try and speak. The sound of *thank you* that the girl had made was relatively simple compared to the frenzied gibberish they used with each other sometimes, so it was a good base for it to start.

It just didn't know *how* to start.

That, and it remembered it had to get the human up the stairs before more rodents started showing up. Trying to communicate with her while surrounded by rats was just *asking* to die. The rodents didn't exactly investigate every sound, but they would at least turn toward it just to check, like any animal. And if they thought that something was alive, they'd rush at it.

Making sure to make as much noise as it could reasonably make as it walked back up toward the human's head, simply to not make it panic, it mentally prepared itself for hard labor. With one last searching look for any nearby rodents, it chuffed again and bent down to the human's left shoulder.

It slowly bit down, making its teeth only partially cut through, and as soon as its canines bit through the tough covering and pricked the human's skin, made them not cut at all.

With [Bloodrush] at the ready for the merest hint of mana or movement of the human's uninjured hand, it leaned its body weight back and started pulling. Even with its natural strength, far greater than any normal canine of its size, it instantly realized just how difficult it would be to drag her up an entire loop of stairs.

Its body weight was too light to give it any great assistance in dragging the female. Even if it leaned all the way back and pushed with its paws, it was still far too small to easily drag humans around. It could only hazard a guess that it had been some sort of feeding frenzy which had allowed it to drag the even heavier male earlier. Still, it heaved back, and the human started slowly moving, one tiny bit at a time.

And with that movement came pain, the human's breath hitching as she sucked in air through her teeth in a sort of warning hiss, a sound which made the wolf tense, ready to snap its jaws open and turn its head to tear her throat out in an instant if she tried anything.

That, or at least use the human's fear to make it rethink any notion of attacking.

After a moment, the human relaxed a bit, its breathing strained from pain.

"Sorry," it said, and the wolf took it as a signal to continue.

Which it did, sometimes having to separate from her to kick some rotting rodents out of their path before darting back and slowly dragging the human to safety through her grunts and groans and harsh breaths.

Just to experiment, it tried to *invite* that strange bloodlust that came from its skill again, even starting to think of random things which might trigger it. Imaginations of battle and danger seemed to do nothing, so it began imagining that at the top of the stairs was a huge mound of meat—nurturing that image—and just the tiniest trickle of power entered its limbs at the mere prospect of feeding.

That was so . . . strange. It explained much, but it was also a highly restrictive power. That, and it wasn't terribly potent. Dragging the human got a bit easier, but that was about it. Still, it could trick the skill into empowering itself with the power of imagination, so that was an important discovery.

A rat eventually noticed them, one of the very few that made their way back up to the pit's lip, and it instantly rushed forth.

The excitement of battle was somewhat muted by now, especially due to how every fight with a rat went the same way, as they just stupidly rushed at the wolf. Batter it onto its side, grab, disorient, and slam into the floor, and that was that. It let the rat's corpse be for now, judging the human to temporarily be more important.

The staircase was a circular thing which jutted out of the sizable sides of the pit, all easily more than fifty feet wide, and despite having cut off a part of it and having walked up and down its entire length, it still felt daunting to tread up, especially when it had to drag a human along. A human who, despite being in *very* obvious pain, judging by her constant whines and groans, was being thankfully compliant with the wolf, even as it began to lift her torso up the first few steps.

Or she was, until a hand shakily raised to touch its neck.

A hand that, in the last millisecond, it noticed had a faint sense of mana coating it, like an invisible mist it felt more than saw. The wolf made its teeth cut through the cloth and instantly leapt back a step, raising a throaty warning snarl, ready to activate [Bloodrush] and kill the human. One bite in almost *any* spot in her body, and she would bleed out while the wolf danced away from her mana constructs.

The human froze solid, her hand trembling, and the faint scent of fear entered its nostrils, something it felt like it wouldn't even be able to detect without that singular point in Perception.

"I-I'm sorry. I'm sorry. I was . . . I-It's a [Haste] spell. I'm sorry," it whimpered, laying its quivering hand back onto the floor, her chest moving up and down with her uneven breaths as the faint sense of mana around her hand dissipated.

Accepting her swift submission, it stopped the rumbling growl in its chest and relaxed its lips to cover its teeth again.

It was expecting the human to try and hurt it, yet it still felt a faint sense of betrayal all the same. A coil of anger formed at the bottom of its stomach, aimed at the girl for attempting to hurt it, especially after all the help it had given her when it could have easily bit through her nape and gotten itself a delicious meal.

It sped up in its quest to put her somewhere safer, no longer caring about how much pain she was in, simply wanting to be done with its task. It hooked its teeth back into another spot on her garment intact enough to support its pull without tearing, activated [Bloodrush], and quickly dragged her gurgling, sobbing form up, step by shaky step, the sounds of the human accompanied by the scrape of metal as her iron-clad feet were dragged up the metal planks.

Three loops up, and they wouldn't even be bothered by the flies, so that was where it decided to put her.

The human kept whimpering and groaning shakily, showing every sign possible that it was in pain. After the first loop, the wolf's anger dissipated, along with [Bloodrush], and thus, with a hint of hesitation, it slowed. The human panted, and the wolf *really* wanted to join her in that particular activity, because as soon as the little boost it'd gained from imagining a pile of meat on the top of the stairs left, combined with its anger and [Bloodrush], it felt half as strong as it did mere moments ago.

It could drag her up later, it decided, and after moving her toward the railing in a position that wouldn't tug or put pressure on her injuries, as a sort of reward for not being too difficult besides that little sneak-attack incident, it finally unhooked its teeth from the torn garment.

Oh.

Its gums and jaws felt absolutely *wrecked*. It didn't even know its gums *could* feel sore. Which made it wonder what would happen if a tooth were to fall out. Would it be able to regrow the tooth? And if so, would it still have the properties of its current teeth? It most definitely did *not* want to find out, so it tried its best to remember to *severely* reinforce its gums when it got to sleep.

That done, it quickly walked back down the stairs to go pick up the rat it had killed earlier. The human could probably use a bit more fluid, assuming the rodent hadn't already bled it all out on the stone. It made a mental note to cut less with its teeth when dealing with rats it could afford to kill by just slamming them into the floor.

Quickly walking around the railing on the final step, its paws met stone once more, and it headed to the rat's corpse just two dozen feet away. It bit into the holes it had already made when it killed it just to not waste more of its blood, then turned around and trotted back up the stairs.

CHAPTER 13

The last few drops of blood dripped into the human's mouth. The wolf turned its head and dropped the rodent on the stairs, pinning it in place with one paw so it wouldn't slide out from the gap under each step, and started tearing out chunks of it at a time.

It quickly ate the rat and then moved to lie down just a step above the human, toward its injured side. Right now, it just wanted to try speaking like humans did.

After a few moments of playing around with its tongue to test its dexterity more properly, it decided to try.

"Aaaannhhhuuuu," it started, the sound coming off more like a low howl than anything resembling human speech, much less the *thankyou* sound.

The human didn't react to its howl besides slightly turning her head, likely more out of curiosity than anything else.

It tilted its head, racking its brain.

That didn't work at *all*.

Deciding to take the sound and break it into three different parts, like *tha*, *nk*, and *you*, it started practicing.

The results were less than stellar, even as hours passed by, with nothing but broken, strange howls and growls coming out of its mouth while the dim lights from above illuminated the shifting clouds of flies around them.

Speaking in human required three components. Their larynx, which was essentially long, smooth bands of muscle on the front of their throat that helped shape their voice, in a structure almost identical to the wolf's; their vocal cords, which added inflection, depth, and complexity to the sound; and their tongue and mouth, which shaped the more precise, intricate sounds they couldn't make purely with their throat.

The main problem the wolf had was with that last component. The length of its mouth was one difference. If it wanted to blow out air while positioning its tongue the right way to make the hissing sound of *th*, it would have to exhale a bit harder, because its throat and the front of its snout were much further apart than they were in humans.

Another difference, a bigger one, was its tongue.

The *nk* sound wasn't much easier. It had a snappiness to it. The wolf had to hum while trapping air in its throat by spreading out its tongue to form a seal, thus making the *n* part, then stop humming and exhale while suddenly pulling its tongue flat on the bottom of its mouth, releasing the pent-up air to form the *k* in a *sort of* clicking sound. And that was *really* hard. There was barely enough muscle in its tongue to properly do it, and it required a lot more effort than the wolf would have expected.

The *you* part was relatively easy to do, thankfully.

So while it believed it *could* communicate simple sounds like *than-kyou* once it learned how to make and cobble those various smaller sounds together, it had realized that speaking in complex sounds like a human would be harder than it had anticipated.

But far from impossible. It would have to expand its throat, make its tongue bigger by adding more musculature for finer control, and practice a bunch, but then, it would be able to speak exactly like a human, if with a bit more growl in its sounds.

With that thought acting as the closing note to its efforts for the moment, it decided it was done for the day and could really use some sleep.

It really wanted to speed up its body's progress, even if the sensation of new things suddenly being put inside it was mildly uncomfortable. The changes were so fast that its body wasn't able to entirely ignore them, so it could feel several inert tendons stretching ever so slightly with every move-ment of its torso.

After a session that was several hours long, its head felt like someone had cracked its skull open to stuff it full of hay. Mental exhaustion was no new feeling, but it was still highly unpleasant. In contrast, its body was well rested, so it got up and cautiously leaned its head down to bite into the human's garment again.

Despite the headache that her sounds were whenever anything disturbed her, it wasn't going to leave the human down here, simply for safety's sake.

Two loops of stairs left to go.

With its eyes nailed onto the human's left hand for the merest twitch, it activated [Bloodrush] and heaved back.

"*Fuck . . .*" the human groaned out in pain, a rather simple sound which the wolf decided to learn how to say later.

The task and its completion were rather mundane. It had to stop multiple times to wait for [Bloodrush] to return before resuming, and besides feeling like its teeth were about to fall out of its gums, and its legs feeling like they were made of slime, nothing of note happened. It left the human resting on the steps and trotted a little further up the staircase, went to the edge where the slabs of iron were the widest, and laid down on its side to sleep. It was out like a light within moments, the symbols quickly forming in its mind.

[Restful Awareness] has Leveled Up. Level 5 → Level 6
[Iron Stomach] has Leveled Up. Level 6 → Level 7
[Bloodrush] has Leveled Up. Level 2 → Level 3

-Removed Traits:
Timid (1/5): You have fled from danger equal or lesser to yourself multiple times. You are slightly faster when running away.

It thought about the removed trait with a sense of dissatisfaction. That added speed when defending itself or running away was far more valuable than removing the penalty it took when attacking. Because realistically, it wouldn't be attacking things all that often, and self-preservation was more important than killing.

Its rather haphazard plan was to either go to the place with the toxic rivers and ambush humans to eat, or simply go around visiting the various trash pits full of rodents around the city. That was all it really needed to do. If anything, Timid was more helpful than it was detrimental, so its loss was rather grating to the wolf.

The [Devourer] skill activated, but rather than showing it a deconstruction of what it had consumed, the wolf was taken straight to the portion where it observed its body.

It had, assumedly, nothing more to learn from rats, which was understandable.

It looked around for something to improve but could find no reasonable alterations it hadn't thought of, so besides quickly toughening up its gums and healing them a little bit from the strain it'd put them through, it simply settled for checking its progress. Then, it decided to give itself a bit of a reminder on the progress of the symbols, bringing up all of its achievements with a thought.

-Species: Wolf
-Name: None
-Path: [Hound of the Keeper] Level 8

-Available Attribute Points: 0
-Base Attributes:
Strength (+0)
Speed (+0)
Dexterity (+0)
Endurance (+2)
Perception (+1)
Resolve (+1)
Intelligence (+3)
Soul (+1)

-Racial Skills: [Pack Hunter], [Quick Learner], [Devourer]
-Acquired Skills:
[Pain Resistance - Level 17]
[Infection Resistance - Level 8]
[Poison Resistance - Level 12]
[Corrosion Resistance - Level 5]
[Disease Resistance - Level 4]
[Magic Resistance - Level 4]
[Mental Resistance - Level 28]
[Electricity Resistance - Level 2]
[Restful Awareness - Level 6]
[Tough Skin - Level 2]
[Iron Stomach - Level 7]
[Mana Perception - Level 3]
[Mana Manipulation - Level 3]
[Soul Perception - Level 2]
[Echoes of Oblivion - Level 1]
[Bloodrush - Level 3]

-Acquired Titles:
Witness of Divinity: You have seen a being of divine nature in their own

realm. Your illuminated gaze shatters all illusions and pierces through any and all falsehoods.

Glutton Beyond Compare: You have eaten multiple times your body weight over a single uninterrupted period of consumption. You gain +1 to Strength and Speed while your stomach is adequately filled. Bonus is doubled when your stomach is filled to the brim.

-Acquired Traits:
Enduring (1/5): You have felt the chill of death multiple times and survived. You are slightly tougher.
Hunter (1/2): You hunt living creatures, whether it is for survival, sport, or personal gain of one manner or another. You are slightly harder to notice when intending to hunt.

Its memory refreshed, it started prodding *Witness of Divinity* to try and find a way to turn it off or get rid of it entirely before eventually giving up at the lack of response it was getting. Its glowing eyes would just keep being a problem that the wolf would have to work around, whether it liked it or not.

Its consciousness slipped back into limbo, and it rested soundly.

The canine was gone, and so she was left to her own devices for the moment.

If one could call sitting perfectly still in silent agony "devices," that is. The dizziness, constant sensation of her intestines squirming in protest inside her, weakness, and severe need to pee were just the cherry on top.

She wasn't exactly sure of *why* the monster—or perhaps just an Awakened dog—was helping her, but she couldn't deny that, at the very least, a heavy weight had been lifted off her chest. Immediate death wasn't hanging over her head anymore, and she was almost certain the beast would have eaten her by now if it was planning to do so.

After a bit of struggling and maneuvering—and a fair amount of pain—she had managed to tie the bloody cloth around her head, like an oversized bandanna, with a knot on the back of her head, covering all the important places she wanted covered like her ears, nostrils, and mouth.

And so, she was left alone with her thoughts, which eventually turned to her oldest and best friend.

Gods, she missed Katherine. Not for the servitude and convenience she brought forth as a dutiful maid, but as a friend. As an unflinching pillar of support and strength, covered in whip marks that Emhreeil would spend long, sleepless nights treating. She wondered how she was doing now. She'd spent the majority of her personal wealth to buy Katherine her freedom after she'd disowned her family, so she wondered if she was at least living free and happy.

She really hoped so.

But as despair slowly flitted away with her musings of easier times, and acceptance snuck to the forefront of her mind, she was left with the choice of continuing to hate herself and the world, inwardly rage at her dead teammates for being so irredeemably *stupid,* or at least try and struggle through her wrecked state and *do* something.

And seeing as physical actions were out of the table, she was left with an old friend, a tool that was the object of frustration and wonder in equal measures throughout her relatively short life thus far.

Mana.

She inhaled deeply through the blood-covered cloth on her face, used to the smell by now, and started circulating the energy through her mana circuits, feeling the phantom veins running through her body flare to life.

The mana responded willingly to her commands, as easy to direct as a limb, albeit a weak one that she barely felt.

From her navel and out toward her legs.

The connection between one's mana circuits and the body was not entirely a physical one. One couldn't cut open another humanoid and extract their circuits, as they were not a tangible thing without high-level magic being involved. But there was a connection regardless, and that academic statement only solidified in her mind as a fact when she felt her mana enter her broken legs.

The circuits were . . . malformed, shrunken. Off, in a sense.

Usable, but in a way that would no doubt be more akin to *forcing* mana out rather than excreting it with just a thought, which was what she was used to doing as an elf. Forcing mana out was more in the realm of humans, or any other races who didn't have [Attuned]. Yet, there was little she could do about the state of her legs, so she focused on guiding and circling her mana, focusing entirely on the amount rather than the technique.

Sometimes, she'd secrete just a little bit of mana out of her palm, feeling it conform to the shape of the metal just an inch away from her skin—like a phantom sense of touch—but generally, she focused on simply forcing large quantities out of the core in her navel and up to her usable hand, keeping it there, and then forcing it back down.

If it weren't for [Attuned], the process would no doubt be multiple times as difficult and painful, but for the first time, that didn't bother her. She used to feel insecure all the time about her racial skill, wondering if every magical advancement she managed without a single resource was due to her own talent or because of the skill that made all elves like herself attuned to the world by nature. But when faced with her survival, that line of thought simply didn't register.

Still, the harrowing experience of getting covered in rats and tossed down from a nine-story staircase did make her realize that up until she left her home, she was . . . almost *pampered,* despite all the psychological torment her parents put her through.

She may have never been allowed to touch a spellbook or read even basic magical theory before her parents were certain they had brainwashed her to be the perfect noble elf, something that had never come to pass, but never had she felt true pain before.

Not quite like this.

Maybe that line of thinking was productive, but it felt like it wasn't, and thus she discarded it, focusing on the flow of mana. The life force of the world. That little piece of starfire that ran through everyone's veins.

It was a mindless task, but that was alright. She didn't particularly *want* to think, so she just continued. Mana circuits—or *arcane* circuits, as academic snobs referred to them as—were remarkably similar to a muscle. The more she strained them, the bigger they became—so long as she didn't strain them too much too quickly and tore them apart. Even so, simply to feel less helpless, she focused on power, on the amount dancing on the thin line between just enough and too much.

Maybe it was because she was already lying with one foot in the grave, or maybe it was because she just couldn't give a crap anymore, but she didn't follow her usual exercises and patterns. She wasn't calm nor rational enough to meditate and slowly work on her control, her efficiency.

She was simply looking for power.

Even if she only had three useless spells, she could at least force enough mana into them so each cast would be enough to defend herself with, if only for a second or two.

Despite how uncomfortable the sensation was, she continued scrounging up bits of her mana and forcing it from her navel, up to the exit point in her palm, before splitting the stream into the five smaller exit points of her fingers, the pressure mounting with each beat of her heart. She pushed it away with all her strength, yet kept the exit points firmly shut, even when the sensation became just shy of painful.

Like clenching her lips shut while blowing with all her strength.

And then she forced the mana back, and down.

Her fingers suffered from the same issue that her legs had. Most creatures used mana circuits for their magic, which were connected to their physical self to some degree, and thus, the circuits of her fingers felt like moving mana through a pipe that was gnawed on, jagged, and full of bumps. Yet, that did little besides interrupt the smoothness of the flow, and she was not focusing on the flow whatsoever.

In fact, she decided to push harder, grabbing trickles and drops of her mana and moving them out of her core to pool at her fingertips. Then she let her core generate more mana, until she was nearly full again, and she repeated the process, over and over and over and over and over and over again until her hand, from the tips of her fingers to her wrist, felt like it was about to explode.

The mana no longer felt like the nigh-imperceptible caress of a ghost phasing through her limbs. It felt like a physical force—like her blood was trying to force itself into the open air, her flesh an overstuffed balloon begging to pop—despite there being no tangible effect on her hand.

The thought of casting [Sparkburst] with all the mana trapped in her hand tickled at her mind, but the gloriousness of that sight would be entirely lost on someone without eyes. Plus, the dog would probably not appreciate the racket.

She added more, and she felt her circuits strain painfully, so she was forced to relax her mental blockade of the exit points, letting just a bit of mana bleed out of her palm and dissipate into the air.

She felt the Eye's gifts gather in the back of her mind like an errant thought she had stored to be turned over in her mind at a later date, likely some level-ups in [Mana Manipulation] or whatnot, so she ignored them, keeping the exercise going, feeling her heart ease with every passing minute.

If all she could do in terms of offense was to throw [Sparkburst], then she would make sure to pour enough mana into the spell to rend flesh from bone. Not that she was planning on attacking the canine; not unless it suddenly decided to eat her. But when blind and crippled, that added sense of safety was something she dearly craved.

She let a bit more mana slowly drain out of her palm, making sure to keep the amount of mana trapped inside her hand at a constant, not increasing it nor lowering it.

She didn't know if what she was doing was even a good thing. It might strain her circuits too much. It might give her mana fever. It might be doing next to nothing, or crushing her veins.

The mana might even explode in her hand and make her an amputee, like the horror stories she had been told of early mages trying to form magical theory.

But if all she had left was her magic, she might as well sacrifice a hand to experiment. Worst-case scenario, she blew her hand up and died of blood loss.

Not the worst way to go. Not by a long shot.

The temptation to release all that mana concentrated into a [Haste] spell, just to see how it would feel like, was immense. And with impulsiveness borne of having recently felt death's hand around her throat, she did exactly that.

And her world *exploded*.

She might have gotten a plus five in Perception or a plus twenty—she had no idea.

What she did know was that she felt *everything*. Every individual hair on her body, every fold of skin, every single one of the dozens and dozens of different, faint scents she couldn't discern the names of. She felt the brush of the humid air on her skin like the caress of a hand, the air moving down her throat and into her lungs as she gasped, the faintest of vibrations in the metal underneath her body. She heard the muted, distorted whispers of *conversation* from gods knew how far away.

But most importantly, she *felt* the immaterial little light in her chest that fed her core with mana; she felt said mana saturate itself in the essence of her soul and fill her circuits. She scrounged up as much of it as she could out of her abused core, and simply expelled it from her palm, directionless and meaningless.

And she *saw* it, not with something as restrictive as her eyes, but with her mind. A colorless energy, more of a tactile sensation, washing over the iron planks to her left as they descended. It felt as if she was reaching forth with a thousand and one half-numbed hands, caressing every inch of the things her mana washed over, the sensation growing fainter and fainter by the millisecond, until it disappeared entirely just two seconds later.

She could only revel in the amazing sensation of feeling everything through a surge of mana, even if she had no more left to experiment with what high Perception could do. But as all good things tend to do, [Haste] eventually ended, the sensations abruptly fading, and she sighed in wistfulness, deciding to revisit her magical theory while her abused core recovered.

The gestures for casting magic were made by excreting stable lines of mana in the air out of one's fingertips and drawing three-dimensional magic runes. And once someone knew or figured out how to cast a spell, the Eye recognized it and simplified the process, turning it into nothing but a thought that formed the spell and manifested it with mana.

After spending most of her money to buy a book about the basics of magical theory, and then spending the rest and going a bit into debt so she could buy the [Illumina] and [Haste] spellbooks, she'd thought she understood magic enough to at least *try* and emulate what others did, with enough knowledge in cancellation gestures to not blow herself up.

Yet, after watching a street performer for three hours straight, she'd only managed a tiny burst of sparks, even with her natural magical talent.

That had been both a sobering experience and a hard-learned lesson.

So she had decided to practice. And it hadn't been enough.

Now, she had to work harder or die. Those were the only options she had.

She formed the rune that gave her [Sparkburst], then charged it with just the tiniest hint of mana before using the cancellation runes to dissipate the spell. If she ever got good enough at mana control, she might be able to just manually drag the mana out of the runes, but for now, she used the traditional way, like all regular mages did.

The sound of steps nearing registered far too late in her overfocused mind, and she stiffened, feeling the light vibrations of the dog's paws hitting the metal just a couple steps above. Yet, it said nothing, did nothing, and thus she continued her exercise, trying not to be too sudden with her movements. Just reaching to its neck had made it extremely upset, and she had no idea if the beast had [Mana Perception], so she made sure to move her mana slowly.

The canine silently stood to her right, its calm, even breathing somehow soothing to her battered mind. As pathetic as it sounded, she couldn't help but latch on to its presence, an unbearable sense of loneliness leaving her starved for *something* or *someone*, anyone, to just be there.

At least if the dog betrayed her measly, misplaced trust, it wouldn't do so with a friendly smile and honeyed lies. Animals and monsters were honest that way.

Eventually, after an hour or two, the beast yawned and retreated back up the steps, though not as far away from her as before, and with a scrape of its nails against the metal, settled down to sleep once more.

She continued, uncaring of the headache pounding in her temple, the mindless task consuming her thoughts.

At some point, she fell asleep from exhaustion without even noticing—another disadvantage of her mind associating darkness with sleep. When she woke up, it was to the strange sounds of low howls and yips, odd hisses and chuffs, half the time sounding like the dog was trying to howl at the lowest volume possible, and the other half sounding as if it had something stuck in its throat.

Her mind eventually filtered out the noise, and she fell asleep again. The next time she woke up, it was to a paw tugging at the fabric on her face. She brought her hand up to pull the fabric off her mouth, noting that the paw retreated the instant her hand moved.

The dog remained as cautious as ever.

With a feeling of utter dread of what was to come, she opened her mouth, her features contorted in disgust.

A sickening ichor of copper poured into her mouth, a thin stream of the vile fluid coating her tongue and tonsils before quickly petering out into trickle, then a slow drip.

How did this look to an imaginary bystander? A canine of unknown proportions holding a bleeding rodent corpse over an injured woman's open mouth. Were she in a philosophical mood, she might have imagined such a scene painted in a frame, some profound message hidden in its sprawls of paint.

But all she could think about was the imagery of a baby bird being fed by its mother from one of her old childhood books, and a sudden bout of hysterical laughter rushed forth from some dormant corner of her mind. It strained and bubbled in her chest, barely managing to restrain it thanks to the liquid in her mouth, struggling not to move too much or choke.

Her chest shook in silent laughter for almost the entire duration of her drink, and as soon as she swallowed and gagged down the horrendous slimy blood, she tugged the fabric back over her mouth and clamped her hand over it, tears running down her face and pooling in her sockets as she snickered, the pain barely registering.

What was her [Pain Resistance] at now?

A quick peek revealed it to have gone up to level twelve.

Why was that so *funny?*

Maybe her body was just forcing her to relieve stress, or maybe she was just going insane. Either way, she couldn't help but find her predicament utterly hilarious.

Truly the height of decadence, to be spoon-fed the lifeblood of our lessers without having to lift a single finger! Ohohohoho! she thought in the pompous voice of her mother, imagining herself doing that *stupid* fake laughter while dramatically fanning herself with that crystal-encrusted fan as the sounds of tearing flesh played in the background of her ridiculous imagination.

"T-Thanks," she forced out between choked snickers, more because of a sense of wanting to delude herself into some kind of twisted sense of normalcy rather than anything else, struggling not to burst out laughing.

Maybe a chuckle would do her some good, but she felt sick and as if she was about to puke her guts out, so she tried to contain it. This also did *not* feel like a situation where she should be laughing. At all.

The sound of the dog eating the rodent next to her head suddenly went silent.

"Thuuuaaaankkkkhhhhhssss," the canine howled after a moment of silence, the sound transitioning into a creepy hiss toward the end, and her laughter stopped cold.

That—That wasn't . . .

Was she hallucinating?

"T-T-Thank you?" she tried again, her voice wavering.

"Thhhhuaaankkhhhhheeuuuuu," it howl-hissed in reply after a moment of silence, and she felt herself going rigid, any sense of humor completely vanishing as she felt a shiver of fear run down her spine.

Was *that* what it had been doing for all those hours? Trying to *speak?* It repeated its bastardized, spine-chilling mockery of the words *thank you* once more, and she felt her teeth clatter and gnash together, her jaw trembling.

It just sounded so *wrong.* Like something she'd hear whispered from the darkness in a horrid nightmare, and her overactive imagination did her no favors. Was this thing even a dog? What the *fuck* was she stuck with? Just because she saw some vaguely canine outline before she lost her footing back then didn't mean it was a dog. Maybe some hyperintelligent monster? A demon?

Maybe a shape-shifter who took it too far and lost themselves?

After a few seconds of shocked silence, a paw poked her in the side, and she flinched.

"Y-Yes?" she eked out, her mind reeling.

Was the beast so intelligent that it *could* understand her this entire time? Or was it just mimicking her as a way to mess around, pass its time? Or, *god forbid,* was it trying to learn how to speak? Why?

"Eeee . . . esssssss?" it hissed out like a snake, as if replying to her thoughts. She tried to grit her teeth, only for them to slide all around each other, her jaw refusing to sit still.

What the *fuck* was she supposed to do? She'd never even *heard* of a dog speaking with actual words, not even when some shady merchant was explaining to her mother why the little dog he was offering them was worth six hundred gold crowns, along with a dozen different ridiculous, unrealistic promises.

Any notion of this thing being a summon or animal of any kind was discarded.

No, she was dealing with an intelligent, merciful beast. But what the hell was she supposed to do with that information? It didn't *seem* violent or angry with her, so that let her keep her wits and not outright panic, but she didn't feel that far off from doing just that.

As stupid as the idea was, she decided to introduce herself, just like she'd been taught to do as a little nervous child scared of all the tall, well-dressed adults in the ballroom.

With an unbearable slowness to the motion, she raised her shaking hand to point at herself.

"I . . . am E-Emhreeil."

"Aaaiiiee. Ahhhhhmmm. Emmrrrr . . ." It growled, the first natural sound so far, then continued after a short pause. " . . . iiieeeellll," it finished, the sound more of a whine than anything resembling speech, and she gulped, feeling like someone had dumped a stone to sit low in her stomach. After a few seconds where she mutely gathered her thoughts, a paw poked her again, and she jumped, pressing her lips together.

"Yes?" she squeaked out, and the dog chuffed before poking her in the side with its paw again. "W-What?"

" . . . Uuuuu . . . aaaa . . . kuh," the monster replied before growling seemingly in frustration.

Oh, it's looking for new words to mimic. That realization did absolutely nothing to reduce the churning of discomfort in her gut. The monster repeated its previous noise, struggling with the *T*, and tried again.

And again, and again, and again.

All the while, she just tried to wrap her head around what kind of insane situation she'd found herself in.

"Uuuuaaaa*tt*," it finally said, popping the *T*, and then, seemingly satisfied, chuffed and poked her side again.

She was never religious, but as she tried to come up with a complicated word to keep it occupied, she started praying to any and all the deities she could remember to just send a rescue team already and get her out of this bizarre hellscape she'd been dropped into.

CHAPTER 14

It couldn't say that its decision to learn about mana and human speech was all that thought out, but it was working fairly well.

Its original plan was to learn human speech and then use it to ask questions to the human about how she used the mana, but it realized quickly that such a thing was not going to be happening any time soon. The human was also stunted because of her blindness, so even if she wanted to, it would be hard to ascribe meaning to the sounds she was teaching it. She couldn't exactly point at things she couldn't see.

It was still good practice for when it found another human, or if it could find her again in the future so they could continue after her kin came. She had a unique scent, like all humans did, and despite it being buried under a couple layers of filth, after being around her for so long, it was difficult *not* to become familiar with it.

It was an oddly fresh scent. Like air—cleaner than it had ever breathed—mixed with a myriad of sprinkles of different smells it had no description for. So, if she was nearby, it could probably track her down.

Additionally, while it had thought that the language barrier would stump any and all progress with its understanding of mana, that had been far from the case. Simply watching her moving mana around was an interesting sight.

It was difficult—extremely difficult—but after giving her another helping of rodent blood at around the fourth day's mark, it managed to sense her mana before it went outside of her body. And the way she moved it was extremely odd.

It was very . . . physical. The mana moved up and down her body, as if following the path of her bones, with the exception of the times it would just leak out of her palm.

Its attempt to do the same was a complete failure. It simply couldn't grasp onto it. It was like air. It could *direct it,* push it out, but it couldn't grasp and move it with precision whatsoever. When the wolf activated [Echoes of Oblivion], it was a *little* easier to direct the mana, and as soon as it exited its body, it automatically turned into the puffs of darkness. But when it turned off the skill, the mana became both harder to move and direct, and seemed to do absolutely nothing, simply vanishing from its perception into the open air.

At some point, the wolf had decided to close its eyes, its head resting on its paws as it sat by the girl's side, messing around with its mana to the best of its ability. Which meant it was struggling to do anything besides meaninglessly expel it.

It just felt like it was missing something, but it didn't know what.

Having grown both tired and annoyed at its lack of progress after another half hour of doing this, it simply relaxed, emptying its mind of thoughts. It still kept a mild amount of attention aimed in the human's direction, though, just in case she did something suspicious, as it hadn't forgotten about her attempt to sneak attack it.

Resting on purpose felt strange. Whenever it'd rested before, it was either because of need or because it couldn't do anything else. So the experience of just resting because it *could* and *wanted* to . . . it was extremely satisfying; fulfilling. It felt like a quantifiable improvement.

Minutes passed, and eventually, it fell into a short nap, noting that [Mana Perception] had gone up to level *nine,* while [Mana Manipulation] had remained stuck at level three. Which made sense, but that stagnation rather soured the taste of progression it had gained in its other skill.

To its surprise, [Echoes of Oblivion] had gone up to level two, which was nice, but with only a tiny improvement in how easy it was to use. It did note something interesting, however. It could see through the inky mist, like looking through a glass with dark churning waters on the other side. It was a bit difficult to see *properly,* but it was more than possible.

Which was a very convenient fix to the still-present problem of its glowing eyes. It couldn't cover itself with the darkness, nor properly keep it in place, but it could make the mist float above its snout and hide its eyes for a couple seconds at a time. Of course, the amount of mana it had inside itself was utterly pathetic, so it could only do so for a couple seconds before taking a break of another couple seconds to recuperate, a process which became increasingly slower the more the wolf did it within a short span of time.

It peeked an eye open to stare at the human, feeling all the mana in her hand and comparing it to its own.

It felt like comparing a pebble to a boulder.

Frustrating. Mana was just frustrating.

It'd had no particular issue with patience up until now, but after spending another hour trying and failing to get a proper grasp of its mana, it growled in agitation and stomped its way down the stairs to release some frustration into a hapless rodent or two.

She let out a guttural groan of relief once the beast walked out of hearing range.

For a moment, she thought it was angry at *her*. But now that it was gone, this was as good a time as any to try.

All the mana she had painstakingly gathered in her hand over the course of hours—forcefully extracting it from her core until it was barren and dry before repeating the process whenever it filled back up—was ready to be poured into a spell.

She was nearly certain that she was hurting herself with what she was doing. If the searing agony in her hand wasn't enough of a clue, the feeling of her mana circuits straining and stretching like a thread about to snap absolutely was. But she would take that risk because she didn't want to spend a minute more in this loop of maddening absurdity she was stuck in.

What came after she was outside of the pit was a towering problem she was going to ignore until the time came when she could no longer do so.

Stretching her hand above her head to feel for the railing, she trailed her fingers up the grimy iron to the top and mentally tried to reconstruct the pit and the staircase's positioning, aiming her hand accordingly to send the spell in a direction where it wouldn't impact a wall. And with a mental thought and a strain of the mind where she shoved a veritable ocean of mana into the spell, a supercharged [Illumina] shot out of her hand like a white-colored flare.

The feeling of her overstretched, abused circuits emptying themselves made her bite her lip until she tasted copper with a choked-out groan, simultaneously feeling like someone was punching needles through her flesh and bones and like someone was holding her hand over an open fire.

After flexing her fingers a few times and realizing that no amount of physical stretching would get that pain to go away, she resigned herself to waiting for the sensation to pass, dropping her hand to lay limp by her side.

Without having a connection to her, the [Illumina] spell would quickly burn out, but its blinding brightness should, at the very least, draw some attention. A bit of an empty hope, but it was all she had. Even if nobody cared enough to rescue her, which she expected, they should have come to fix the staircase by now.

After having to endure the humiliating experience of having to piss herself, coupled with a pounding headache, hunger pangs, her squirming guts, what she assumed was a fever, and a feeling akin to someone having stuffed her head full of dry cotton, she felt like she was on the verge between sobbing and laughing; between choosing to struggle and just giving up on the notion of help and frying her brains out with an overcharged [Sparkburst] to just be done with it.

It felt odd to admit, but the abomination's presence was something she craved at this point. She was still a bit scared of the beast, but it was the only form of life she'd been around for weeks that hadn't abused or hurt her in one way or another, her teammates included.

Sure, the beast was the reason she'd lost her footing in the first place, but it'd been her teammates who'd sentenced her to death, something she inwardly knew from the moment the job had gone awry but was too panicked to properly recognize. The iron safety door was too heavy to be quickly lifted, and that was *if* their minder allowed them to open it in the first place, which was unlikely.

Some bitter part of her wished that the beast hadn't granted her teammates the mercy of a quick death and had let them get torn to shreds by the rodents like they deserved, but that wish felt like the entrance to a rabbit hole she didn't want to go down.

What she really wanted was a warm, soft bed, and a hot bowl of soup.

How many days had it been by now? Where the hell was everyone? Had they written her off as dead in the guild records? Such questions plagued her mind constantly whenever she wasn't practicing, but now that she was completely dry of mana, she had nothing to distract herself with.

A dreadful doubt that maybe nobody would come to help kept creeping into her mind, and she struggled to keep the thought away from the forefront of her brain. An effort which was proving to be in vain, and thus, she decided to open her System screen to distract herself.

And she almost choked on her own spit when the System opened, and a tide of words flooded her mind.

You have progressed on your Path.
[Infuser] Level 7 → Level 8

-Available Attribute Points: 1
-Base Attributes:
Strength (+0)
Speed (+0)
Dexterity (+0)
Endurance (+0)
Perception (+0)
Resolve (+1)
Intelligence (+4)
Soul (+2)

-Acquired Skills:
You have gained the Skill [Mana Tank - Level 1]
You have gained the Skill [Mana Conduit - Level 1]
You have gained the Skill [Iron Stomach - Level 1]
You have gained the Skill [Soul Perception - Level 1]
[Poison Resistance] has Leveled Up. Level 4 → Level 7
[Pain Resistance] has Leveled Up. Level 12 → Level 14
[Illumina] has Leveled Up. Level 6 → Level 8
[Sparkburst] has Leveled Up. Level 12 → Level 13
[Haste] has Leveled Up. Level 9 → Level 10
[Mana Perception] has Leveled Up. Level 15 → Level 16
[Mana Manipulation] has Leveled Up. Level 9 → Level 11

-Acquired Traits:
Blood Drinker (1/2): You have sustained yourself on nothing but blood for multiple days and have taken your first step toward the path of vampirism. Drinking the blood of others is more palatable and nutritious, and gives you a temporary boost to all Attributes. Duration and Attribute boost strength depends on the amount of blood you have consumed and its quality.

She could only sit in stunned silence as she watched the System's updates scroll past her mind's eye.

After an entire twenty years of living, she'd only gained a few skills she genuinely wanted. The moment she'd turned her back on her family, she'd discarded all the ones she didn't want. To see such progress so quickly was not something she'd been expecting.

Additionally, the skills were all things she'd never even heard of before.

The System sometimes gave more or less information on skills for no apparent reason, and as she mentally questioned what each of them did, she only got any concrete information about [Iron Stomach] and [Soul Perception], which were already rather self-explanatory names.

She activated [Mana Tank] and . . .

Nothing happened.

"What . . . ?" she murmured to herself, furrowing her eyebrows in confusion.

Just to be sure, she deactivated and activated it again, noting it was a sort of passive skill which could be toggled on and off rather than a skill that was used once and had a cooldown.

Even after waiting a couple minutes, she noticed absolutely zero difference in anything, so she left the skill on and instead focused on her mana in preparation of checking her other new ability. [Mana Conduit] activated with a thought, and she gasped in delighted surprise as she felt her soul pulse with power, feeding her core with mana at almost triple its normal speed.

She started counting the seconds as they passed by, noting how it stopped working after thirty. Then she started counting to see what its cooldown was, and after exactly two minutes, she felt it become available again.

She activated it once more to replenish her mana, even if she had absolutely no plans of abusing her circuits any more than she already had for the day, and decided to hold on to the attribute point she had for later, since she couldn't decide on where to put it.

With that out of the way, she read the Blood Drinker trait once more, and felt her breath stop. Not catch nor hitch; she simply stopped breathing.

Vampirism.

Of course.

How did I not think of that?! she inwardly screamed as she reminded herself to keep breathing, feeling the nascent flutters of hope pick up in her chest while a tiny, hopeful smile curled her lips.

Vampires could basically heal anything by drinking blood! Of course, there were severe drawbacks—moral *and* technical ones—as well as the path to becoming a vampire being a rather vague and secretive one, but the trait had given her both a clue and an idea.

The Church of the Six-Eyed Crow.

If any place in the Dungeon hid a vampire within its halls, it would be that! Her recollections of her religious studies were a vague, blurry mess, but she remembered there was a strong connection with the church and vampirism, even if she didn't quite remember the reason.

Vampires were extremely rare, extremely secretive, and extremely withdrawn, so finding one to help her change would be really difficult, but if . . . if she just begged, offered whatever she had to the church and pleaded, did anything they asked of her, it wasn't too far-fetched a hope that they could put her in contact with a vampire who could turn her.

And she would be able to fix herself. She knew the drawbacks to becoming a vampire were as immense as the advantages, even if she didn't know *what* they were, but anything would be better than shambling from place to place, hoping that someone would be kind enough to give her their unwanted scraps to eat until she died of disease and exposure.

With that crushing weight of uncertainty no longer sitting on her chest, she felt like she could breathe the putrid air just a bit easier. She had a plan, a concrete course of action to take when she got out of this godforsaken pit.

If, a corner of her consciousness corrected, and the smile wilted away as quickly as it came.

Right.

Suddenly, she was wishing the beast would come back up already.

There was just something so cathartic about violence.

The amount of rats hovering and clambering up from the mounds of trash were even more numerous than they were before the incident with the staircase, so it had no shortage of food and entertainment, even if it continued being relatively cautious about the process.

One tiny chuff, one scrape of a nail, and it would quickly bait whatever rodent had seen it into the shadow of the staircase, where it would promptly shred it apart, then stalk back toward the feasting vermin and repeat.

It even decided to get a little more confident and creative, and managed to make rat hunting an even easier task than it already was. Why would it exhaust itself by slamming the rodent around the floor when it could simply throw the rat onto its side, rake its canines through basically *any* part of its body, and then walk back and watch it die without lifting a paw?

Whether it was through the spine or the abdomen, it was all equally effective. Sure, it took a bit longer for a rodent to die when it was shuffling and dragging itself toward the wolf with its intestines trailing behind, or twitching on the floor unable to get its limbs to work rather than having its skull smashed into the floor once or twice, but the wolf didn't particularly care about how quick a kill was, only that it died.

At least when it came to things other than humans.

It wasn't like rats gave it pets and food every once in a while, so they could suffer; it didn't really care.

Overall, it was a relaxing hunt, with a good haul of seven whole rodents to consume and add to its stockpile, and one saved for the human.

The blinding burst of white light which shot out of the pit, however, straight from where the wolf had left the human, was a less welcome sight than its pile of game, and it could only stare at it with a sense of indecision as it quickly faded out of existence.

It wasn't going to *stop* the human from signaling for help, but it was tempted to. It felt like it was just on the *cusp* of understanding how the mana thing worked, and it doubted it could stumble onto an opportunity like this again.

The wolf decided it was done pouring out its frustrations on the rats, so it quickly dragged the bodies up onto the first floor of the staircase one at a time, just to be out of sight from the hordes of squeaking vermin.

It *could* eat while in sight of a threat, but it didn't particularly want to.

After eating seven of the rodents, it trotted back up the stairs to feed the human some blood again, the final rat dangling off its jaws.

For some reason, the human reacted to the feeding with far less disgust than the previous times, and after eating the shredded remains of the rodent, the wolf settled by her side on its stomach, extending a paw to poke her in the side with a chuff.

The human sighed; a tired sound.

" . . . Discombobulate?"

It tilted its head, ears standing straight as it separated the sound into different, smaller parts in its mind.

Yeah, that sound was going to be really hard. Maybe a bit too hard. It chuffed and poked her in the side again, hoping for a different one.

"God-fucking-damn it . . ." she breathed out, and the wolf tilted its head.

That one was doable.

Yet when it started practicing, the human started making strange snorting sounds, which escalated into loud, rapid bark-yipping noises, her one functioning hand clenched around her convulsing stomach as she eventually started wheezing for breath.

Even then, she continued making that weird sound, completely uncaring of her own oxygen needs.

It growled in annoyance, poking her harder on the side of her waist to be quiet, but for some reason, that only made her wheeze harder and redouble her noises, so with a huff of annoyance, it got up and walked down the staircase to practice somewhere where it could actually hear the sounds its own mouth was making.

"W-Wait, no! I'm s-s-sorry. I won't l-laugh! C-Come *bhhhhhack!*" she wheezed out behind the wolf as it walked around the bend, out of sight.

What even *was* that cacophony supposed to convey? Some sort of happy bark-yip sound? Why was the human happy over the wolf practicing human sounds now, but when it'd first started, she had absolutely reeked of fear?

Humans just didn't make any sense.

CHAPTER 15

The long walk down from his manor was no less harrowing on his psyche just because it went through his own streets.

His boots echoed across the grimy cobbles with the steady beat of a metronome, his back straight and eyes cold. Peasants, mercenaries, and adventurers alike took one glance in his direction and parted before him as if an invisible wedge took point before him wherever he went.

As they should.

Even with Miaro's form tucked away in the shadow of his silver-embroidered trench coat, Kolak's stout frame by his side, and his personally chosen best soldiers behind him, not to mention every single protection he was able to come up with and place on his person—whether it be through enchantment, infusion, or artifact—the fact of the matter was that with every step, he got closer to entering the jaws of the Dungeon and the entities within which few to none knew about.

And he could only hope he would come back out whole.

Streets narrowed, houses and stores faded, and life petered out until all that remained were warehouses and groaning, creaking factories, faint lights of molten slag reflecting off into the smog above.

A fading soul dying by a drain, a gutter child shyly peeking through a broken window, a startled worker backing out of sight. On the other end of the third floor's substratum, the kingdom's teleporters would be admitting hopeful nobodies and experienced veterans alike to challenge the Factory, the active parts of this Dungeon they all lived in.

But his turf was far from such clamors.

And not all entrances to the Factory lay in plain sight.

His escorts were professionals, their steps light and quiet to draw attention to his own thundering ones, their visages faceless, every aspect of their stance and equipment formed and forged to accentuate his authority, his power. For all it mattered.

Across an alley, over a metal bridge that rattled under his heel, waste churning and bubbling under the arch. Down a staircase too tight for his soldiers to march through, instead forming a loose snake's spine behind his coattails, until finally, he turned the corner to see the entry point.

A single brown piece of fabric nailed to the iron wall, under which lay a familiar tunnel of jagged metal, no doubt the work of months. And across the center of the covering, sprawled atop a blood-red gear, a single eye gazing coldly down at him from its center.

He didn't know how they did it with naught but red paint and a messy brush, but that eye always looked *down* at whoever met its glare, no matter the position or angle. There was no magic, no real artistry, yet as he stared into the uncaring eye, he could swear the gear turned just a single degree to the right.

Even though it hadn't.

It was both annoying and unnerving.

Much like the cultists themselves.

Wordlessly, he extended an arm to Kolak, the man quickly placing a gas mask onto his glove.

He strapped it around his head like a helmet, hearing all of his soldiers mutely follow his lead with a shuffle of leather and fabric. After a moment to check that the purification runes and filter were functional, he clicked the button on the side of his mask to allow sound in and out.

"Kolak, take point," he ordered, his voice coming out in a tinny hiss.

His guard did as he was told, one hand on his sword as he marched ahead, pulling the tarp aside and ducking his head to pass under the jagged shards of metal unharmed, the entrance just barely wide enough for a large man like him to pass through.

He followed, knowing his itinerary was waiting for him.

If the relative silence of the lowest rungs of the third floor was one borne from absence of life, ahead lay a cacophony borne from death.

Light faded as the tunnel continued, the sounds vibrating the uneven metal underneath his feet, hissing, clanging, the rattling of empty conveyor belts echoing throughout the smog-filled cavern like the clicking teeth of a monstrosity eagerly awaiting its prey.

Kolak pushed aside another tarp on the other end of the tunnel and held it open for him, moving to the side.

Stepping out into the colossal cavern, he straightened once more, quickly checking his coat's enchantment again. After confirming his skin wouldn't burn and poison him from an unfortunate breeze, he fished in his pocket for the enchanted compass and reluctantly dug it out, extending his hand just a bit to hold it horizontally in front of his stomach, his head bending down to stare.

Burnished bronze met his eyes, the symbol of the Machinists carved into its gently curving dome. He flicked it open with his thumb, not wanting to see that eye for a moment more than necessary.

"Miaro, scout."

The viscous black smoke nestled inside his coat swelled and gathered at his abdomen, the buttons on the front unlatching with surprising speed and dexterity.

He suppressed a twitch of his brow as he watched the smoke burst out from the open gap of his coat like a thousand ravens' feathers, clumps of darkness exploding with impatience to shoot off in a hundred different directions.

In less than a second, all signs of the kid's presence were gone.

If Manos didn't have the ability to turn his muscles to steel in the fraction of a second, he would have never trusted Miaro to casually nestle inside his clothes, but he had proven his merit thus far.

Twelve men and women stood stock-still behind him as he simply waited, his hands in his coat pockets.

Five minutes later, a frenzied tide of shadows shot out from between every nook and cranny in sight, gathering like a whirlpool in front of him and coalescing into a thin, lean form in the span of a second. A blurry, wispy silhouette of black with two white slits for eyes glared at him with a cold, angry impatience.

Two months of guard duty were far more grating to Miaro than he'd expected they would be, but it was a necessary punishment. The brat had far, far too much lip and pride for his liking. The dubious nature of his abilities only made it more important for him to keep the little shadow thoroughly restrained under his lantern's bottom, unable to influence the light.

Manos never liked mysteries. They were always malicious.

"Nothing," Miaro dryly reported, his voice inflectionless, his featureless face unmoving.

"Keep a couple eyes out, just in case. Return," he simply said, and Miaro wasted no time, turning back into a cloud of wispy black and shooting down to the ground under his coat, some parts of him breaking off to slither into the gloom to act as their eyes. Then the assassin nestled back into whatever nook and cranny he could fit himself into.

Manos took the lead, hand loosely clutching the compass and checking it every few minutes.

Traversing the thin scars dug around the Bone Pits—where discards of the Factory's golems were thrown to rest in piles until they could be sorted and reforged into iron for the Dungeon's residents—was very difficult, even as one person, aside from some areas near the towers. As a group of fifteen, the downward crawl was unimaginably slow.

After three or four hours of mutely traversing the labyrinth, they had to stop for a short break to both recuperate their stamina and change their mask filters. It was a muted, subdued break, and they resumed shortly after.

The descent was sometimes steep, sometimes dangerous, but most of all, lengthy.

Another break—a longer one. Some light conversation was allowed as Miaro scouted, the tight confines of the Bone Pits not allowing his soldiers to spread themselves thin, basically huddled around an open center.

The lack of vigilance grated him.

They were a bit too trusting of Miaro. Something to fix later.

Soon, they began moving again, their sights and surroundings slowly but surely becoming a little more familiar as they got closer to their destination.

Eight hours of walking later, they came across what they were looking for. An iron gate, placed between two machines for seemingly no reason, blocked their path. Piles of wire were lying on the ground on either side, and painted crudely on the doors was the symbol of the Machinists.

The detailed painting of the gear and the eye in the middle further accentuated how unnerving the thing was.

Now that they were getting into Machinist territory, he put Kolak up front, regardless of their supposed *cordial* relationship. He just didn't trust them.

Bad form to trust madmen, no matter how needed they were for his goal. However, after a long descent down uneven and, at some points, barely *functional* terrain, they were all exhausted, so he ordered his men to rest up for an additional longer break before they got to their destination, making his healers pump everyone up with a little bit of healing magic to clear up any soreness and snags that might be lingering; just a bit of energy to ensure they were at the top of their game.

And eventually, the terrain flattened, the meaningless machines left behind by the Dungeon growing a bit more . . . organized was not the correct word. More utilitarian, perhaps.

Factories and machines the size of his manor were scrapped and hollowed out to act as communal homes within the vaguely rust-gray-colored environment, their symbol painted everywhere with bright red and yellow paint. Piles of unusable scrap were stacked high and fused or melted together as if to form a grotesque wall of metal around the cult's little village of sorts, nestled under pipes larger than warships and in the shadow of a broken aqueduct which had likely never seen an ounce of actual water.

Yet, nothing moved.

He walked his men down the catwalk flanked by a thousand eerie eyes, coming upon a circular area which was the closest approximation to an open square that one could find in such a place, scarred and bent metal showing just how many modifications they had to make to create a circular open space like this.

In a place built by the Dungeon, there was no cohesion, no plan, no logical shape. The factories were metal monstrosities more akin to someone grabbing six different shapes and mashing them together before drafting random bits of machinery and open, dangerous equipment all over them, running a thousand pipes around and *through* the structures, all interspersed with windows and walkways as if to pretend the constructs around the Bone Pits were ever meant to hold life within their walls.

Sometimes, the machines were out in the open, connected to others. Other times, they were just meaningless—things built just because the Dungeon *could* build them.

Like a child toying with its sandbox.

He, understandably, disliked the Bone Pits.

So, despite the unsettling appearance of the cult's residence and the countless drawings of gears with eyes sprawled across every flat surface, he couldn't deny that by comparison, this place was *almost* hospitable.

In the center of the square he and his men were waiting on was what he remembered to be the very lifeblood of this small community of madmen and fanatics. A cylindrical tower a hundred feet high, the side facing the entrance dedicated to water filtration, while the side facing their "chapel"—a metallic, crude imitation of gothic architecture—acted as a delivery system between them and their contacts on the third floor.

Which included him.

From the top of the tower rose a simple steel-wire lift which vanished off into the darkness of the Dungeon after just a couple hundred feet, no doubt changing directions dozens of times, until it reached another hole in the walls, where his men would load the carts with necessities and send them on their long journey down.

The first time he had found these folks, he'd felt like he was part of a fresh shipment of adventurers, gawking at the absurdity of everything and everyone down here. But by now, the roughshod aesthetic had grown on him. Like a rusting tumor.

Another couple minutes passed in silence, then from around the cylinder, the person he'd been waiting for walked out.

Archbishop Varmond.

A man who made most men shit themselves at the mere sight of his true form, hidden under that bulky black robe.

Frankly, he just found it fascinating, despite the initial surprise when he first saw him unfurl. He was like a brutalist work of art.

As he was right now, however, he barely came up to Manos's shoulder instead of towering over him at ten feet tall, walking toward them with his back hunched and his metallic legs curled up against his chest. Legs which tapered down to two round points of rubber like spider's legs.

A nonthreatening, courteous demeanor. At least for now.

As he drew near, the metallic hiss of his breath filled the respectful silence Manos and his men were maintaining. The archbishop's head rose, his black hood hiding his facial features, but a single, oversize golem's eye glowed with a sickly yellow light from under the murk of his hood, taking up almost a fourth of his head, the lens squarely focused on him.

"Welcome, Baron Manos Ironheart," Archbishop Varmond rumbled quietly, the sound gutturally deep and metallic, as if growled through a booming speaker on a low volume.

His metal hands split his robe down the middle just a bit, and his metal fists came to meet in front of his chest, only the knuckles of the ring and pinkie finger touching. Then, he unfurled his hands while rolling his wrists outward with the hiss of hydraulics, palm up, and bent his head down in a deep nod, his palms open as if offering something.

He simply bowed in return, as deep as someone of his status could within reason: a forty-five-degree angle.

"Thank you, Archbishop."

" . . . You seek audience with Him," the archbishop rumbled knowingly as they both came out of their greeting poses.

Manos nodded. For a man so fervently devout, he didn't beat around the bush, and he liked him for that exact reason.

"There have been untoward developments on my part that . . . *He* must know about. It pertains to our deal," he calmly said, and the archbishop nodded.

It grated to call the *thing* hiding inside the guts of the Factory a capitalized *He*, like it was a true god, but appeasements had to be made, on the prospect of its power alone.

"Follow. You know the rules," he warned. Manos set his jaw, giving him a grim nod, and the archbishop turned and began to walk deeper into the maze of distorted metal and broken stone.

They followed.

He could only hope the price of his failure wouldn't be too severe. They needed each other, so he was sure he wouldn't get killed. Yet none in sight were fooled as to who held the upper hand.

They could use Manos.

He couldn't use them. He *needed* them. Them, and the *thing* below their feet.

But its wrath would be hard to weather. Not only had he no excuses for his failure, but the presence below was not a diplomat nor something that could easily be reasoned with.

They moved down into unused air vents, rectangular tunnels of stagnant, humid air, then down even further through a dizzying labyrinth of steel pipes where their steps echoed into infinity, and eventually came upon a gargantuan staircase which led straight down into a pitch-black darkness, the steps slick with moss, the air a mixture of rotting death, engine grease, and smoke.

As he followed the archbishop down, he felt the familiar sensation of a noose tightening around his throat.

He'd done all he could. For six months, he'd been searching, but all he could find had been fleeting, messy, and impossible to track. False hopes and desperate reports that wasted his time. He couldn't find it; he couldn't catch it. It might be gone by now, for all he knew.

Sixteen people walked into the Dungeon.

Twelve hours later, three and a half came out.

CHAPTER 16

The wolf was starting to lose count of the days. Its internal clock had never been the most accurate, and without access to the light crystals and their cycles, it wasn't exactly sure how much time had passed.

It might have been the fifth day or the seventh; it just couldn't tell.

Additionally, while its routine had become rather boring and repetitive by now, it didn't really have anything else to do, its only entertainment coming in the form of some recreational rat killing.

It fed the human, moved its mana, tried to copy how the human moved hers to no avail, and slept as much as possible to accelerate its growth. Which was a very rapid one, because looking at itself now, it looked like any regular, decently fed canine, if a lot filthier.

The sudden break in the monotony came in the form of an unexpected level up.

That wasn't all that unexpected in and of itself, but the question of *what* had made it level up was one the wolf realized it had no answer to. It had assumed that killing things was what made it advance, and it had been doing *plenty* of that, but between its current nap and its previous one, it hadn't killed anything, only practiced on using the [Echoes of Oblivion] skill.

So practicing on its path-relevant skills also increased its level? Or was there some other hidden mechanics it didn't know about?

It hoped that humans knew more about the symbols than it did, because once again, all it could do was mentally dismiss those curiosities, throw the added attribute point onto Intelligence, and hope that its questions would eventually be answered.

Intelligence (+4)

It took the time to focus on its body, touching things up a little bit.

The scent receptors in its nose were an utterly mind-boggling number, one so high that it couldn't even count or imagine it, but the wolf decided to improve them anyway, experimentally *doubling* their number on one of the skill's phantom copies of itself. Then, after carefully confirming that there were no negative drawbacks to such a thing, it applied it onto its real body.

It healed any wear and tear of the miniature hairs in its cochlea—the organ behind the eardrum which allowed its brain to interpret the vibrations into sound—regenerated some of the torn-off micro hairs on its antennae, got rid of some of the scar tissue on its snout and legs, and then hastily decided to double the length of its antennae.

Having to glue its bottom jaw to the ground to sense vibrations properly was just too annoying, and added length wouldn't really have any negatives besides making the organ easier to snap and break, which would be an easy overnight fix.

Finished with its physical upgrades, it slipped back into the embrace of [Restful Awareness] and woke up with a yawn and a quick sniff.

And then immediately sneezed, not at all prepared for the absurd amount of information that flooded into and around its mind, immediately shutting off stimuli to adjust.

The human, who had gotten fairly comfortable around the wolf by this point—an observation of fragile interest—shifted.

"Good morning," it muttered, and the wolf chuffed in acknowledgement to whatever it was she'd said, taking another deep sniff of the air.

And sneezing again.

It grumbled, awkwardly turning its leg and lowering its head to rub its nose with the back of its foreleg. After the phantom itch had receded, it put its paw back down, took a *very* slow breath through its nostrils, and focused on the marvel of an overnight adjustment.

And realized that it had *probably* gone a bit overboard by doubling what was essentially how effective its sense of smell was. It would tone it down a little when it napped again; at least until it got more points in Intelligence. It wasn't quite an informational overload, but it was certainly difficult to focus on anything else but the insane, ludicrous amounts of subtle scents and aromas wafting into its olfactory receptors.

It closed its eyes and tried to identify as many as it could, snout to the sky.

A spilled patch of grease a couple steps to its left, just above the wolf. Weeks old. The almost spicy-sour scent of rust coating the edges of the railing mixing with the scent of uncorroded metal. The moss growing on the bottom of the staircase and piling onto some of the metal plates of the wall to either side of the pit. Rot, decay, death, and blood from below. Half-melted plastic, and the musky scent of some dusty building material from the trash pit mixed in with the scent of various bits of food discard and waste.

The scent of blood coating both itself and the human was very interesting, a familiar iron smell undercut by a sort of gamy, pungent organic odor that differentiated it from regular metals. From the pipes running up and down the pit, the faint, faded smell of vile poison. From outside the pit, human food, alcohol, body waste, stomach acid, a dozen different minor chemicals. Then the scent of ammonia from where the girl had urinated on herself, layered over the unique scent of the human itself.

That and a thousand more scents it couldn't name nor recognize wafted into its nose with every breath.

It felt like it didn't even need its eyes to navigate.

It flared its newly extended antennae out, their length now enough to go from the tip of its snout to just before its eyes. Even without reconstructing its environment from memory, it could navigate with relative ease. Scent allowed it to roughly feel direction and proximity, and vibrations helped with the finer details.

Not that it was planning on giving up its eyes. That would be beyond wasteful. It was just an observation of interest.

It quickly folded its antennae back into its fur and opened its eyes, quickly sitting down and shuffling to lie on the steps.

And it began to practice with mana again.

Even if a small doubt in its mind lingered that maybe it was just wasting its time, all it took was one reminder of the visions it had seen when choosing whether to accept its path or not and it faded, at least for a while.

The symbols hadn't lied so far, so the problem was on the wolf's end. It was doing something wrong, preventing it from succeeding. It felt like trying to grasp something with its jaws that was *just* close enough to have its teeth brush against it, but far enough to be unable to take it.

Routine continued—another dozen rodents killed, another couple bloody mouthfuls for the human, another nap which let it know that in just one more day or two, the tendons would be ready to stiffen and start functioning.

A sharp gasp startled it out of its rest, and its head snapped up, instantly awake and aware, ears standing straight as it hurriedly swiveled its head around for threats. After a few tense moments of silence without seeing anything amiss, its ears drooped as it grumbled in annoyance and settled back down to sleep.

"Sorry. I just—" the human started, and the wolf grumbled more forcefully, almost growling.

The human got the message and went silent, so it shifted with a tiny chuff of gratitude and settled back to rest.

It *really* wanted the new colors to appear already.

The condition of her body prevented her from meaningful rest despite her exhaustion, and the beast constantly waking her up for new words to mimic was another factor that had stopped her from hoping for anything more than short naps.

When awake, she would gently practice her remembered spells, followed by cancellation commands, making sure to never let her core become completely full with mana, something that everyone, mage or not, knew was a waste.

But after a particularly lengthy nap that had ended just moments ago, she'd come to realize why [Mana Tank] didn't appear to be doing anything.

The skill was waiting until her core had been filled back up entirely so it could start draining it, never allowing it to remain completely full, pooling the excess bits of her mana into her circuits, inert and ready to be used.

Her body *was* the mana tank, and her core was the battery.

That realization was already uplifting, and then she realized the implications of what this skill was doing, and could hardly believe what she was seeing. Mana constantly filling her circuits, automatically, meant many things.

For starters, the flow of mana through her circuits would improve, the capacity would improve, the capacity of her *core* would improve, and if she took a nice long nap with the skill at a high level, enough that her body would be stuffed full of mana by the time she woke up, she could technically have *multiple times* as much mana at her disposal than her core could store on its own.

From what she knew, most low-level mages didn't store mana in their bodies because it required constant mental effort and attention to keep it in place, which most couldn't do, not until they got their Intelligence high enough. And the rate of mana regeneration early on in one's career only made such a strategy viable if someone was expecting a fight hours ahead of time.

And she'd just circumvented every single one of those problems. The only worry was if the skill would stop on its own or just keep stuffing her circuits with mana until they burst.

At the moment, however, the process was very slow, so the chance of that being an actual risk would only pop up if she spent a couple days unconscious.

She suppressed her smile, reminding herself not to get too hopeful; reminding herself of all the various ways that tended to blow up in her face. Joy was quickly followed by despair, as she'd come to know, so besides that explosion of mirth when she'd heard the abomination say "god-fucking-damn it" in its creepy, ear-grating voice, she would do her best not to become too hopeful.

In the absence of positive emotions, the negative ones became all the more pronounced, so she simply suppressed them too, a resigned apathy slowly but surely taking hold of her as she shifted her mindset.

She was still stuck in a pit.

She was still blind and crippled.

And she still had nobody.

With an empty expression and an empty heart, she lifted her chewed-up fingers and continued practicing in silence.

After waking up once more and feeding the human her dose of blood, it decided to go for a different approach than usual to its mana practice. Instead of focusing on the mana itself, it focused on its source: its soul. Like an invisible, phantom limb that the wolf could feel but at the same time *not*, it sat in its usual position in the middle of its chest.

The wolf expelled mana, watching the process with the unseeing eyes of its mind.

The energy, the odd mist around its soul, gathered in the direction indicated, and its soul pushed it away with a mental order that was about as difficult as picking bits of gore out from between its teeth with a tongue it could barely control.

That was to say, *very*.

But the mana complied, and simply wafted out from within its flesh to harmlessly float away and dissipate into the foul air of the pit.

It repeated the process a couple times, then decided to try and visualize both the mana and its soul, just to see if it would help its mind with the process. Much to its surprise, it worked.

Its imagination probably had left much to be desired, as the wolf pictured the mana as some sort of oddly behaving yellow gas, and its soul as a blue light crystal like the humans used, but it was seeing progress for the first time and couldn't care less at the moment to refine or personalize the imagery any more.

As the minutes rolled by and it tested its newfound ease of pushing out mana, it eventually stopped and let its mind frantically run through various possibilities, trying to figure out what it had been doing wrong.

Even if it was easier to move mana around by visualizing the process in its mind, that still didn't help the wolf with figuring out how to properly use the [Echoes of Oblivion] skill, nor how to move mana the way the human did.

It turned back to its mental image of its soul, ready to give up, but just a bit too stubborn to do so. Minutes, hours passed, its mind empty of thought but the singular desire to feel and understand. And eventually, for just a fraction of a second, a sensation as subtle as the brush of a hair alerted its mind to *something* below its soul.

The sensation was a faint feeling of drainage. Like the feeling of its life-blood leaking from an open wound, but painless; not an injury but a natural occurrence.

Its curiosity and hope reignited, it tried to visualize that bleed, that sensation of its mana being sucked away into a place it couldn't perceive. It pictured its soul dripping a steady stream of mana into someplace down below, some void.

And it worked. The visualization in its mind came to life, the sensation quickly becoming easier and easier to feel the more it focused.

There was a tether connected to its soul leading down into *something*, slowly pumping mana into it.

Since visualization had worked so well thus far, it tried to picture a bowl catching the energy, and the barest awareness of something tickled at its mind. Then it imagined that its soul was feeding into some sort of vessel; a heart, perhaps. Remembering the organ in perfect detail and giving it the same blue coloration of its soul, it imagined that the tether led to such a heart.

And it felt it.

There was *something* tethered to its soul. A small thing, much smaller than the heart the wolf had imagined, but full of mana. And from it, just for a few finger widths, extended arteries and veins, before the feeling faded.

This unbeating heart of mana was small, but with much more capacity than its soul. The wolf experimentally drew from it and pushed the mana toward the phantom arteries, feeling with wonder how the energy moved along lines within its body that didn't physically exist, as if painting veins along the way while it traveled.

The wolf had had a vascular system but for *mana* this entire time. And it hadn't even realized. It didn't know whether to be angry or incredulous.

Grabbing hold of the energy in its phantom heart, it pushed it outward in all directions again. Yet unlike when it used its soul, the mana followed its newfound veins rather than just going straight through its flesh.

It was a very strange sensation to *feel* something in its body while knowing it wasn't *actually* there.

From its chest where its mana heart lay, one large vein went down its spine and out of its tail. On the other side, another equally large vein followed its spine upward until it was about to enter the skull, then diverged down to fade out of its mouth. Four other veins, slightly smaller, moved down through its limbs, fading off to nothing at its paws.

A direct command for the mana to leave through its flesh proved extremely difficult, its veins growing *smaller* veins to try and lead the mana out of the middle of its spine, an endeavor it quickly gave up on. It got up from its lying position and activated [Echoes of Oblivion], using the mana in its phantom heart rather than its soul, just to see if anything had changed.

The results were instant.

It yowled as its legs crumpled, barely managing to right its limbs, almost tumbling straight onto the human's injured legs, who let out an exclamation of surprise at the sudden sound.

With shaking limbs, it lowered itself onto its side with a shiver, gritting its jaws shut with a growl as it weathered through the sensation of its mana forcibly making a billion tiny little mana veins across every hair's width of space in its body.

It was the worst sensation it had ever felt. A sensation of such supreme discomfort it was borderline painful, but somehow *worse* than any pain, making its legs shaky, its stomach clench, its arteries wriggle under its skin. It felt like an uncountable amount of burrowing worms moving through its flesh after it had deprived itself of its sense of pain, feeling the uneven lines move through its flesh.

It panted and growled in agitation, tilting its head and biting into the iron plank it was resting on, the pain of its tearing gums helping it ground itself, the shriek of tearing iron a comfort in the storm of unease. It jerked its head around, the metal being shredded and spit out of its bleeding mouth, the wolf having just enough presence of mind to not bite *too* deep and sever the plank.

It turned its discomfort to anger, and its anger into pain and catharsis, drowning out the sensation.

Then murky blackness covered its eyes, its mana finally breaking through its fur after saturating every tiny bit of its body, and the sensation disappeared like it was never even there.

It froze, unlatching its teeth from the metal, and got up, tilting its head down to look at its paws.

A black void in the rough, wispy shape of a canine foot.

Its tail started wagging, hesitantly at first but quickly growing to a furious whirl of motion, the canine in complete and utter disbelief and elation.

It reared back on its hind legs, lifting its upper body clean off, and purposefully stomped with its full power and body weight down onto the iron.

Nothing.

It chuffed, growled, barked, howled, ran up and down the steps—all in complete and utter silence.

Unable to contain itself in its pure glee, it turned off the skill, turned its head up, and did something instinctual it had never done before.

Gathering as much air into its lungs as it could, it howled in celebration with all its might. Then, just because it felt like that wasn't enough to express its feelings, it moved mana down the phantom veins that went through its lungs and out of its throat, pouring its intent to share triumph into the howl, the joy of victory.

The howl quickly grew to be almost twice as loud, the mana intertwining with the sound waves, carrying its joy to all who would hear.

After a few seconds, it ran out of both mana and air, and panted in joy with its tongue hanging out of its mouth, not letting the human's surprise and fear sour its mood as it quickly trotted down to kill some rodents in celebration. Then it remembered that its mouth was bleeding and quickly sat down for a nap to fix that.

Thirty minutes later, it got up again and went to enjoy itself with the squeaking vermin.

It feasted, brought up one for the human—who was, strangely enough, almost *eager* to drink now—then let the skinned corpse sit next to her, just in case she wanted it, and went to sleep.

-Acquired Skills:
You have gained the Skill [Logotexnia - Level 1]
[Mana Manipulation] has Leveled Up. Level 3 → Level 4
[Echoes of Oblivion] has Leveled Up. Level 2 → Level 3

Although *immensely* pleased, borderline ecstatic over its progress, the new skill was what drew most of its attention. [Logotexnia] was a rather odd skill, according to the symbols.

It was basically about controlling the sounds it made using its mana. It could muffle things, make them louder, or even alter them to be entirely different. It could let it pour *feelings* into the sound; intent. Its range of application was just absurd. As long as the sound originated from the wolf, it could twist it into whatever it wanted, and the ability to use feelings and intent was one which transcended all language barriers. Immediately, its thoughts moved to its ongoing attempt of human speech, and it decided to try using the skill on that as soon as possible.

There was little in the way of information explaining *how* the skill worked beyond some vague notion of *willpower* and *understanding*, but it would make it work, just like [Echoes of Oblivion].

Eventually.

The scent of cooked rat and the sensation of the girl's mana being expelled, coupled with the sound of her spark spell, confirmed she was most likely eating the rodent it had left her, so it continued its sleep unperturbed, mentally signing off the racket as nothing to be concerned over.

But maybe it was getting a bit too comfortable with having the human around . . .

And that thought gained a lot of merit when it woke up to the feeling of something faintly brushing against its leg.

Its eyes snapped open to see a dainty human paw faintly brushing against its foreleg, the fingertips hesitantly brushing over its fur, and it tensed. It had lain down on her left side this time without giving it much thought, as the step above her had been mutilated by its jaws a few hours ago.

The human felt the sudden tenseness of its muscles and momentarily paused, but then continued on regardless, her fingertips faintly brushing over its nails—which it barely remembered to mentally blunt in time—and forelegs as it watched her, unblinking. Eventually, it relaxed, and the human grew a bit more confident in her movements.

Honestly, it felt nice. It was tempted to offer its head for some good pets, but it did not want her fire-spewing hand *anywhere* close to its vitals. Some instinctual part of itself just *didn't* like fire. Sure, it had grown used to her, and had even grown to like her quite a bit, as it had never spent such a prolonged period of time around a single particular creature, but it wasn't forgetting that sneak-attack attempt. Not any time soon.

And it wasn't out of some grudge. Just as a reminder that the human *could*, and maybe *would* grab an opportunity to hurt it, even if the wolf was helping her.

No mana entered her hand, however, so it shuffled a bit to the side, thankful for how wide the planks of iron were, before extending its legs toward her left flank for better access. Her fingers gently curled around its paw and rubbed at the soft bits underneath, which felt *divine*. Its tail started thumping against the iron, just a bit.

"You're so . . . *small*," the girl breathed out with an odd sense of . . . awe? Confusion? It couldn't tell.

An hour went by in what felt like a minute, and it eventually decided to try using its new skill as the human kneaded its paw.

And much to its surprise, using it was incredibly easy. It had been expecting a complete and utter *slog* of hard work and practice, but all it had to do to make the skill change the sounds coming out of its throat was roughly know how they were made and mentally order it to change the sound wave to what it wanted it to be—the rattle of metal; that blasted *P* sound it couldn't ever properly do because of its lack of cheeks. As long as it understood how a sound was made, it could replicate it with relative ease.

The knowledge of how sound waves worked proved utterly invaluable.

Sure, it required mana, and a *lot* more focus than making human noises the normal way, but as soon as its mental acuity was higher, either through modification or simply by dumping points into Intelligence, it was sure that it could just . . . *growl*, or some equally simple sound, and twist it a hundred different ways to form whatever sound it wanted *while* doing other activities.

And it wouldn't even have to modify itself.

It wouldn't say it was through luck that it got the skill—more of an *accident*, really—but the circumstances lining up the way they did, from its knowledge of what sound waves were, allowing it to understand and better use the skill, to getting said skill *right* when it was starting to give up on making some human noises like *P* or a sharp *B* . . .

It felt *great*. It was used to circumstances lining up in the worst way possible, so this break in the pattern was more than welcome.

It still needed some practice, but after an hour or so of making human sounds with surprising accuracy, it felt like it could make most simple sounds. So with intense, *intense* focus, it poked the human on the side and let out the sound it had practiced the most.

"Thankyou," it howled lowly, the skill twisting the sound waves into something more intelligible to the human, pouring a bit of extra mana to convey a sense of curiosity through the sound.

The human stilled, the scent of fear entering the wolf's oversensitive nostrils. She gulped and resumed her previous activities after another moment of tension.

"Y-Yeah . . . um. No problem. Even if you probably don't know what *thank you* or *no problem* mean," the human whispered back, a long, complicated series of sounds that it was neither going to attempt to interpret nor mimic.

It chuffed and poked her again, and the human sighed.

"Um . . . discombobulate?"

Thankfully, she understood what it was asking for. The wolf considered it for a moment, then decided to try it this time, fairly confident it could make whatever sound the human threw at it, as long as it didn't run out of mana.

As they relaxed side by side, the human petting its legs while it pestered her for words to try out with its new skill, it felt . . .

Relaxed, comfortable.

Even the constant, barely perceptible hunger from the [Devourer] skill faded as they continued, until they both fell asleep.

Their rest didn't last long, however, as the gears below began to spin, and the most horrific, vile poison it had ever smelled suddenly entered its nostrils, making its eyes fly wide open.

CHAPTER 17

The beast's rate of progression with speech was ridiculous.

Maybe it was five, maybe it was fifteen days, but even if she took the higher end of that estimate, learning to speak so *quickly* and legibly in such a time frame was an absurd feat for something that was decidedly *not* human, and most likely less intelligent than one as well.

She hesitated to call it a dog, because while its legs and paws *felt* like a dog's, it was much, much too smart, and that was without considering its strength comparative to its size, as well as the fact it had some skill for tearing apart *iron*.

Whether it was a dog or not, however, she could think of at least four scientific institutions and noble families each that would be losing their minds just to get their hands on the beast.

As for her, she was just hoping it would stop talking already.

Understandable or not, the sound was *horrendous*. It made her skin crawl and her eardrums squirm inside her ears. It had, very suddenly, improved in its ongoing attempt at human speech, but that didn't make its "voice" any better. It was a concoction of growls, quiet howls, grunts, and whines mashed together and twisted to form words, and she would rather glue her ear to a loudspeaker as it broadcasted someone scraping their nails against a chalkboard than listen to it speak for any prolonged period of time.

At least at first. Much like she'd grown used to the pain, she eventually got used to the horrific mimicry of human speech, and it was a lot less terrifying to listen to when she held its paw in her hand, the beast no longer some unknown entity but a small, albeit *extremely* disturbing creature of a vaguely canine build.

She even managed to make it fall asleep eventually, and soon followed suit.

Once she woke up and started practicing, she had to stop in puzzlement as she felt a surge of mana nearing her location, hurriedly using cancellation commands as her heart started slamming into her ribs.

For her to feel that mana from the other side of the pit, whatever was coming was *big*. Some field effect? Or . . .

Or poison cleanup, for when the rats were too many to clear with mercenaries and adventurers for a reasonable price. The realization was almost disbelieving, a faint feeling of betrayal nestling in her heart. Had they even sent someone to check for survivors? Had they done so and then decided to kill her anyway?

She was going to die, trapped in a metaphorical box, gassed like a rat.

Everything she'd been through, all that training, twenty years of living, just for that.

"*Ffffuck*," she half laughed, half sobbed out, her breaths stuttered and her chest quivering from nerves, her mind and body unable to pick between sobbing or laughing hysterically, her body trying to switch between them with each stuttered, tiny breath.

With a hurried, panicked train of thought, she tried to come up with alternatives which didn't make her fear a slow, agonizing death, but her mind remained stubbornly attached to reality, telling her insistently that there was hardly anything *else* that would feel like that.

She didn't get the chance to further attempt to delude herself before a pair of canines chomped through her torn garment, *somehow* not chewing into her flesh, and dragged her down the stairs with haste she hadn't been expecting, letting out a short cry of anguish as her broken legs slammed into each step with loud clangs of metal.

Gritting her teeth with an agonized gurgle, she jerkily lifted her hand up to the beast's neck, and before it could pull away this time, she used a mildly overcharged [Haste] spell on the beast. After a single second where it froze in surprise, it continued, practically flying down the stairs.

Through her panic, she only barely managed to open her System screen and put her spare attribute point into Endurance in the hopes that she wouldn't come out of this without legs, feeling her broken bones grind against each other inside her flesh, nothing but the snug fit of her iron greaves and thick pants preventing her bones from splintering out of place.

* * *

The most horrific, vile poison it had ever smelled suddenly entered its nostrils, making its eyes fly wide open.

Its nails scraped loudly against the iron as it hurriedly jumped to its feet, struck with a sudden bout of panic and indecision.

The scent was overpowering. And it was getting closer, fast.

It dashed to the railing, ignoring the strange sounds of the human, and tilted its head to look up.

It flared its antennae, aimed its ears to funnel the sound into its eardrums, and took a deep sniff, just to confirm what it dreaded.

It quickly located where the scent and the extremely faint sense of mana was coming from—four relatively thin pipes bolted to the corners of the pit. Its eyes trailed up along them until its head was tilted upward, where the pipes curled inwards, snugly fitting under the metal walkways above where the humans would hook their trash carriers. Along the cube-shaped frame of the pipes were spots where rectangular metal blocks extended, pointing down, covered in small circular holes.

A design it had seen many times before. One definitely intended to spray out some form of gas or smoke.

And not all gases floated up; many floated *down*.

Its understanding of what was happening was swift and decisive. The humans were going to wipe the pit clean using poison, and it was poison that neither itself nor the human could survive.

Maybe the scent was much worse than how strong it actually was, but if it wasn't, it was much worse than almost anything the wolf had run into so far. This was poison *made* to kill, not a byproduct of the human machinery.

So it had to leave, *now*.

Tilting its head down, however, presented it with another problem. The spinning gears were crunching away at the several-feet-tall pile of trash, and that made any and all rats occupying the pile rush up to the surface, likely done so on purpose by whoever was controlling everything.

Just from a cursory, rushed head count, it could see at least as many rats as it had killed with the staircase, with more rushing out of the slowly lowering mound of trash, climbing along the ridges, and squeezing out of the grates one after the other.

There were *hundreds* of them.

And it was, once again, completely stuck.

If it took one step down there right now, all it would take would be a single rat to alert a small horde of its kin to tear the wolf apart.

But the only way to escape the poison was to go *down*, ride the trash, hope it didn't lose its footing and get crushed, and manage to scramble to a pipe large enough to squeeze into.

The topmost row of gears inside the trash pit had a gap of about a human's height in the middle, and the rows tightened in increments of about a foot from what it remembered. So while difficult, it could probably survive all the way down as long as it kept its footing and its body in the middle of the gap. However, all it had sensed underneath the gears when it had been sniffing around with its antennae was a gigantic nothing. The drop below could be twenty feet or two hundred; it had no way of knowing right now.

Additionally, the human.

It wasn't sure of how it would save her.

It certainly had the *strength* to do so, as its new tendons had finally finished during its most recent nap—not a moment too soon—but saving her would be difficult regardless.

It needed more time to think.

Tilting its head toward the pipes, it saw the first wisps of the poison puff out in a steady stream which lazily floated downward, blotting out the human nest's innards one inch at a time.

It turned, bit into the human's garment while making sure its teeth were blunt to her skin, then hurriedly dragged her down the steps, ignoring her exclamations of pain, hoping to take her down to the second floor to buy just a bit more time to think of a viable plan of escape. If not for both of them, at least for itself.

Halfway to the second floor, her hand raised to its neck in a familiar manner, but it was too distracted to react in time, only managing to freeze as her fingers tapped its fur.

Her mana did *something*, and suddenly, the world was far more vivid, far more *slow*. Whatever she had done was only beneficial, so it didn't bother wondering, simply resuming its hurried pace.

After positioning her body sideways on one of the steps on the second floor, it unlatched its teeth and peeked through the bottom gap of the railing at the rats.

From what it remembered, their scent receptors were much lesser than its own, but far more than a human's. So they would *eventually* smell the poison, likely soon, and hurriedly throw themselves into the pit, assuming nothing alive caught their attention.

It didn't have much time to test its newfound strength, nor did it know its limits at the moment, but it did *not* want to let the human die. Getting another one would be an utter pain, especially a blind one whom it could easily isolate and spend time with. If it could save the human without sacrificing its own survival, it was going to do so.

Even while its eyes flickered back and forth from the rodents to the steady stream of poison, it could faintly feel where the human was, a curious feeling it didn't care to question at the moment.

A plan quickly began to form.

A mildly risky one, but the only one it could come up with which would make both itself and the human survive the coming ordeal.

Speaking of the human, she was starting to hyperventilate behind it, so the wolf chuffed as low as possible, its snout turned toward her.

"Oh . . . I thought you'd left," it whispered, barely audible even to its own ears. She sounded relieved, and her breathing slowed a little, so it chuffed low again before prowling down the stairs, gleaming gold orbs focused on the vermin littering the pit floor.

It just needed to get its antennae to touch the stone. The vibrations didn't travel well between different materials. All it could sense when feeling the metal staircase were a dozen or so feet of stone, and the entire staircase itself.

Slowly, it activated [Echoes of Oblivion], trying to restrict the skill to only cover its eyes to conserve mana, to middling success.

With its head as a wispy effigy of darkness, it flared its antennae and extended its neck down to the stone at the last step of the staircase.

And quickly realized this might become the most bitter fight for survival it'd had to date.

The rats in the pipes were *everywhere*. No matter what pipe it picked to scramble onto, there would be rodents waiting to pick its bones clean. They were even more numerous than before the humans had come to cull them.

The constant vibrations of the gears provided the wolf with a mental image that was extremely detailed, even if the Perception bonus it had gotten from the human's skill had faded, so it quickly located the single best pipe in the interweaving network underneath. One just big enough for the human and itself to fit into and maneuver, with only a few rats scurrying about inside, likely because of the thick iron grate which prevented the rodents from fleeing, but that wouldn't be a problem for the wolf.

It tilted its head up.

The poison was almost halfway down the pit.

It needed to wait just a little bit more.

It covered its legs in silent darkness as it dissipated the mist around its head and quickly scrambled up to the human, chuffing again to notify her of its presence. She murmured something the wolf didn't pay attention to, her breaths still rough and stuttered from the pain.

Nothing the wolf could do about that; she'd just have to endure.

The relative silence felt suffocating as the seconds rolled by, its eyes nailed to the horde.

As the poisonous cloud descended to just after the middle point, a few rats started sniffing the air and looking up, squeaking in alarm and becoming more animated, as if unsure of what to do.

The alarmed squeaks which signified danger multiplied quickly, and soon enough, most of the rats on the surface were scrambling into the tiny grates at the edges of the pit; at least those that could fit.

The rats scrambling up from the shifting, rumbling mounds of trash caught up quickly and started trying to burrow downward to the pipes, snaking between bits of discarded metal, with many of them quickly getting crushed by the gears.

The gas was now two thirds of the way down, and every sniff of the poison made its nose protest as if doused in acid, despite the amount of particles it was inhaling being only the absolute minimum for any scent to even register for most creatures it knew of.

That stuff was probably strong enough to *melt* the human, never mind just killing her.

Some rodents squeezed into the metal guides on the sides of the pit walls to make their way down to the pipes below for more safety; most of the bigger ones, however, simply jumped off to burrow into the trash and get crushed.

Truly stupid creatures. Waiting on top was the only way to survive.

The garbage heaps were steadily lowering, and the wolf quickly regarded the falling poison and the speed at which the mounds of trash were moving, and . . .

They had a chance. A fairly slim one, but it was there.

It bent down to bite onto the human's garment again, tilting its head to check up on the cloud of gas and the rodents.

Twice as strong as yesterday with its new tendons in full function, it didn't need [Bloodrush] to move the human, so it saved the skill for later and dragged her down, slowly, making sure not to be sudden and have the human make some loud sound of pain which would attract the rodents before the wolf was ready.

Its heart hammered in its chest while [Devourer] whispered in its ears, begging for a feast, for action, and adrenaline ran thick in its blood like glue.

Its body was almost shivering from the wild mix of dread and anticipation, but it refrained from any hasty actions for the moment.

Dragging the human off the last step with a light rattle until her shoulder was parallel to its own, it spent a moment to fix its grip, then with its head sideways, prepared itself for yet another close brush with death.

The smell of the poison was overpowering. The rodents covered the sides of the pit like an undulating blanket of filth as they scrambled to find some random pipe to escape into, dozens of them slipping off or being pushed off onto the retreating mounds of trash below. The ones that were impatient simply jumped off on their own to try their luck with the gears.

The wolf raised a hind leg to tap the human's left wrist, a short grumble rumbling out of its chest. A wordless request.

Her hand rose to hesitantly tap its hip, yet no skill infused its limbs, the motion almost like a question of its own. It tapped her again with a growl, and the human made some short sound of realization before tapping its leg once more. The wolf felt the world become brighter, more colorful, *slower*, louder, and more tactile, every minute shift of its body increasing in speed it wasn't expecting.

While the previous boost felt like its body had become lighter, this one felt like its body was utterly weightless, the feeling twice as potent.

The human started coughing, *finally* able to smell the poison, presumably.

The metaphorical clock was ticking, and the wolf realized it couldn't wait any longer. There were only about twelve feet of air between them and the poison cloud.

The blanket of death blotted out all light as it descended, and in the darkness, two gleaming golden eyes narrowed as the wolf bent its legs in a crouch, its body pointed straight at the trash pit with its head wrenched to the side, canines tightly holding onto its human charge.

It started slow, so as to not dislocate the human's shoulder, then quickly sped up within three bounds, thankful that the absolutely deafening clamor of the trash pit was covering the sound of the human's pain and discomfort, as well as the scrape of her foot coverings against the stone.

Despite the awkwardness of running while hauling a heavy human at its side, destroying its balance, the girl's skill made it so blindingly fast that it didn't matter.

The panic and the deafening racket of breaking and bending materials covered for their charge perfectly, the rodents only noticing them once they were ten or so feet behind them. Far too late to stop their charge.

One shrill squeak prompted another in a chain reaction that took less than a second as they quickly abandoned any notion of self-preservation and charged at them mindlessly.

[Bloodrush] activated, and the wolf's eyes bulged, the bonuses in Perception, Speed, Strength, and Endurance all combining into an incredible feeling of absolute *power*. The world slowed to a crawl, and the wolf sped to a blur.

It could feel every vein pulsing under its skin, every individual hair tugging back from the wind. Could individually count how many rats there were in and around the pit from a mixture of hypersensitive vibrations, the sounds of their breaths, and the scents wafting into its nostrils. Its vision sharpened, and it could probably individually count each hair on the rodents' hides.

Not that it needed sight.

Every sound wave brushed the microscopic hairs of its antennae, every vibration of its paws smacking into the stone moving through its muscles and bones to rattle the base of the organ, feeding the antennae information without any actual touch. It could run through the human's nest with its eyes and ears shut if it wanted.

It felt, in one word, amazing.

Lowering its center of gravity, it pushed its limbs to the limit. Just before it collided with the semicircle of rats rushing at them, it used its lower body like a whip, kicking forward with its back legs before curling them up to the side of its stomach while its forelegs turned to the left and dug into the stone to add to its momentum, its nails acting like razor hooks to stab into the stone.

Its right side—hip and legs—smashed into the rats, its speed and power allowing it to weather the hit with nothing more than the dull ache of a bruise as half the rats went flying into the pit. Before its momentum could bleed off completely, it slammed its back legs onto the stone and pushed itself backward, digging its nails into the ground, and yanked the human away just as the remaining rodents to their right were about to leap onto her, adding almost three feet of distance.

Just half a foot away from the lip of the trash pit now, it was relieved to see the human using that fire skill to blow the rats back for a moment, buying the wolf the moment it needed.

It forcibly tugged the human away again, just enough to get itself into the right position. Its lower legs moved back and met air before curling in to press against the wall, the wolf's lower body hanging over the trash pit.

The human suddenly jerked with a guttural battle cry and blasted the rodents again, the scent of burnt fur and fabric momentarily cutting through the poisonous miasma in its nostrils.

That sudden movement, however, caused the abused fabric its teeth were clamped around to tear apart, the wolf barely managing to hook its foreleg's nails into the stone to delay its fall by a second as it jerked back, its elbows digging into the sharp corner of the pit. The tiny scraps of fabric its jaws were holding on to were the only thing keeping it suspended, and those were *quickly* tearing.

A flash of panic chilled its gut, and it swung its head onto the human's right shoulder, only to remember a moment too late that the right side was ripped too.

With its nails sliding out of their stony sheath, there was no time to think of an alternative.

It bit down on the collar of her coverings, barely managing not to sever an artery in its panicked chomp, and dragged its forelegs down to brace against the wall, curling all four of its legs under its chest.

It had been expecting a blast of fire to the face, but besides some short yip of surprise, she didn't react, still blindly shooting sparks out at the rodents.

With a growl of exertion, it pushed with its legs as hard as it could while wrenching its head back, throwing the biped backward into the trash pit.

She screamed as she was launched over the wolf, a sound that was somehow still only barely audible past the cacophony filling the pit. It opened its jaws and let go of her collar to let her tumble off into the trash pit, a movement that it followed, with much less momentum.

For all the power the boost gave the wolf, it only managed to flail midair enough for it to land in a diagonal with its legs extended, the impact of a twenty foot drop not nearly as painful as the dozen sharp metal edges and bits of glass that slammed into its hip and then its side, bruising its bones and tearing its skin as it sank into the fragile waste with the sound of a thousand and one things breaking underfoot.

Midair, it'd managed to catch a glimpse of the human landing legs first on some of the softer bags of trash; a small mercy.

It scrambled to its feet and extended its neck to peek over a thin sheet of sharp metal, and its eyes rested upon her squirming, sobbing, and groaning figure.

Groaning and sobbing was good; it meant she was alive and conscious.

Letting out a loud bark to be heard over the cacophony, the wolf rushed forth to climb out of the crater it had formed. It kicked once, twice, allowing its nails to partially cut into the trash for a better grip, and quickly scrambled out, battering and kicking rodents out of its path as it moved to her side. After a few stumbling steps, it half hovered above her, quickly checking her for any urgent wounds, of which it found none. Then it lifted its head to swivel around and keep an eye on the rodents for what little time it had to spare.

It hadn't been expecting the fabric to tear, for some reason. It should have seen that coming.

Despite that hurdle, however, they were right where they should be—on the top, and right between two rows of spinning gears—even if it had to shift its footing every other second to not lose its balance.

They just had to hold their ground until the pipe revealed itself.

It growled, an almost instinctual sound which served no real purpose, as it watched a couple dozen rats jumping off their perches on the surrounding walls to charge at them. Thankfully, most of them were not paying attention or just didn't hear them over the deafening racket of the gears.

Some landed badly and got injured. Some fell through the cracks and down into a cage of metal trash, getting lost and buying them precious time. But most of the rodents landed perfectly fine, blazing a maddened line straight toward them.

A chorus of shrill squeaks from behind made the wolf turn its gaze back to the wall they'd just jumped off of, and its eyes narrowed while its lips curled into a snarl at the sight of more than half a hundred rodents, the vast majority of them now jumping out of their pipes and metal indents into a messy pile of filth just a few feet away.

Maybe it should have done something differently. Maybe there was some option it hadn't considered whatsoever. But there was no time to ruminate on such thoughts nor gain its bearings; this was the best it could come up with. It chuffed to the whimpering human, moving a hind leg to poke her in the back while lowering its body in preparation.

"Fuuuuuuuuuck," she sobbed between gritted teeth. "You p-piece of . . . *ffnughngn psycho!*" she grunted, lifting her upper body off the unstable ground with one arm to flip over onto her back, panting. "Damn it . . ." she groaned, her left hand reaching out to clutch its leg in a tight, desperate grip.

They were surrounded by vermin, but the vast majority of them were coming from the wall fifteen feet away, something the wolf was going to deal with. It just hoped the human wouldn't panic and throw sparks at its back.

She would just have to deal with whatever rodents were behind them. Its eyes swept over the shifting terrain one more time, forcefully shaking off her hand with a jerk of its leg, knowing it had mere seconds before the onslaught started.

The image, one of a giant mass of five dozen rats squeezing between, under, and through garbage in a stuttered, split charge, was one that seared into its mind, a momentary panic freezing its limbs.

A panic which shattered like glass when a small rodent it hadn't noticed bit into its right paw. With a yowl, it snapped its leg up to its mouth, bit the rodent hanging off its bleeding toe, and threw it into the horde with a whip of its head to buy time.

And so, the fight began in earnest.

The rodents' footing and movements were horrendous, even worse than its own, the tunnel vision making them utterly blind to everything besides tearing the wolf apart, which only made them stumble and fall over each other. A fact the wolf decided to exploit, hoping to catch rodents and use them as projectiles to break their semicoordinated rush.

An isolated, speedy little rat rushed at it at the forefront of the charge. The wolf used its speed to dash forward, snapping its jaws shut over its neck and spine, ready to twist its neck and toss the vermin back to its kin. However, the moment it bit, it stumbled forward as something under its front paw broke from the gears, sucking the first section of its leg between fragile glasslike material before it could hop backward.

It clumsily put its weight onto the squeaking, writhing rat with its neck to quickly dig out its leg, then flicked the soon-to-be corpse into the horde, managing to scatter and break a small cluster of rats as it hurriedly jumped back.

And now it was basically stuck because the human was right behind it. It'd moved too far back.

It *could* retreat. It could run away and let the human get eaten, just to buy itself some time. But the thought, for better or worse, didn't even cross its mind in the heat of the moment.

To its right, a rat scurried with surprising speed to snap at its right foreleg, which the wolf curled up to its collarbone before leaning its body forward and slamming its paw into the middle of the rat's back, its entire strength and body weight behind the blow. The smaller rodent's spine snapped with a small, albeit satisfying crack.

It turned to see four rodents scurry toward it side by side. It quickly battered the leftmost one with its right paw, which tumbled away into shifting garbage, and extended its paw toward the second to bait it into snapping its teeth, pulling its paw back at the last moment then jumping forward to snap its jaws shut and stab it through the upper spine with its canines, using its right leg to sweep the other two rodents away in the same motion.

Although that worked remarkably well, that's when it made the same mistake twice in a row.

The wolf moved its hind legs forward to kick its body back, but one of its paws slipped off some wet, metallic surface as soon as it extended, continuing with its momentum to almost smack into its own ribs, making it overcompensate to keep itself stable by using its left paw to catch its body weight.

Whatever its foot landed on, it folded inward before tearing apart, further destroying its sense of balance and making it slam shoulder first into a sharp-edged piece of stone.

It barely managed to unlatch its jaws from its latest victim to let out a barking snarl, when a rodent jumped onto its right shoulder while another bounded up toward its head. The wolf thrashed its body wildly to buck off the vermin, and with the savagery of instinct, chomped down on the rat in front of it, its canines phasing through its sides and stabbing into its organs and legs.

But its head was left untouched, and right beside the wolf's mouth. The rodent twisted in its grip and bit into its jowls, and as the wolf wrenched its head to the side to throw the vermin into the horde, it felt the rat's teeth take their cut of flesh. The wolf finally managed to right itself with a snarl, its back fur bristling so harshly it resembled a mound of spikes atop its spine.

It was, for some reason, genuinely furious.

The rodent it had bucked off recouped and bit into its hind leg, its teeth only barely managing to pierce through its fur and skin before the wolf twisted its hip and kicked it away like a pebble, hearing its squeak cut abruptly with a wet thud.

Fury, its new tendons, the [Devourer]'s hunger, and [Bloodrush] all combined to boost its Strength to lengths it was unprepared for. But as the rodent horde neared, it wasn't sure if that was going to be enough to overcome sheer numbers.

In the darkness, only brief flashes of orange light illuminated the pit, the human panicking and squirming closer to the wolf with every step as she blasted away stray rodents from her side.

They just had to stand their ground until the pipe was revealed.

A large cluster of vermin neared, and the wolf engaged them instantly, each swipe of its paws sending multiple rodents flying, despite the awkward motion.

The hunger in its innards flared, and with every passing moment, it felt like its stomach was turning into a furnace, a roiling, restrained heat in its gut.

It snapped its neck forward like a snake to bite the head off a rat, then smashed another with its paw, the rat's abdomen bursting open with a wet squelch on a sharp piece of metal, its pathetic squirming as it succumbed to its injury only furthering the thrumming bloodlust in the wolf's heart.

A rodent larger than the human's head let out a squeak so shrill that it cut through the chaos to scrape against the wolf's eardrums, its beady eyes glowing a faint dark red as it barreled through its own kin with speed that was unnatural, breaking their charge to continue its own. But it was still far, so the wolf continued with what was in front of its snout.

Another swipe that threw away a couple rodents. Another rat bite on its legs. Another three swift disembowelments as the wolf braced itself and used its relatively stable footing to snap its head in and out of the quickly thickening wall of vermin, breaking their charges, throwing their bodies away.

As long as it kept moving, using its body like a battering ram to knock the rodents away before putting its head into the mess, it would only suffer some minor cuts and bites. At least, so far, that strategy was working.

The bumpy expanse of trash swelled, the "ground" turning more unstable as the gears started bulging out the mounds of trash.

The human behind the wolf screamed, the scent of charred rodent and blood cloying the air, another burst of light illuminating the massive rodent as it clambered onto a metal pipe that jutted upward in a diagonal, towering over the wolf.

Then it jumped forward, a rather clumsy move from a body not made for leaping, powered by frenzied bloodlust and little else.

The wolf didn't hesitate.

With the rodent in the air, belly down, it was nothing but a bag of meat.

It extended its hind legs, curling its forelegs to its chest as it opened its jaws and tilted its head to align its canines. Then it snapped them shut around the rodent's neck and head. Using both its own and the rodent's momentum, it curled its waist to the left, lowering its torso and using the large rat like a sweeping broom to send half a dozen rodents flying.

Its eyes flicked to the human in between swings of the rodent, each strike sending mangy fur flying away, even as its battering tool tore and crunched. It saw her hyperventilating form desperately pouring her mana into bursts of searing sparks, which had far more stopping power than any fire should have, blowing any stray vermin away and buying the wolf precious time to maneuver around.

Something the wolf doubted she could keep up for long. They weren't gaining ground nor respite, only buying time.

With a continuous, thunderous rumble, the trash slowly rose higher and higher, slowly pushing toward them, the rotation of the gears trapping them in an improvised trench as the terrain beneath their feet swelled, snapped, and tilted at random.

The sound was deafening, the air choked with the miasma of poison and burnt fur.

They had even less room to move, the human's blasts only growing less accurate and less powerful as she struggled not to be sucked under with three useless limbs.

The tide of rodents was stemmed for a moment by the deteriorating ground beneath their feet, many of them losing their footing or falling over in clumps of wriggling filth. The wolf continued moving its head from side to side in wide swings, even as its neck muscles grew sore, its breaths heavy around the corpse in its jaws.

But the horde of pushed-back rodents also had the high ground now, burrowing out of moving and crunching garbage.

And at that precise moment, the human's spell ran out.

The vermin were so much faster, its body so much more sluggish. Its balance was off, the constant shifts and snaps making its paws slip and over-extend. Then its legs buckled when the terrain underneath it surged upward with a force it wasn't expecting, its extended limbs unable to muster the strength to prevent its chest from smacking into the metal refuse underneath.

From above on both flanks, and in the groove before it, the horde stepped on each other just as much as they stepped on trash, the first coherent rush in the fight so far.

A tide of black-gray fur washed over the wolf as it flailed under a mass of writhing vermin. It let out a sharp, guttural bark as it used its strength to buck wildly, then hastily planted its feet and slammed its shoulders into the rising garbage on the left then the right, feeling the sharp crunch and squelch of viscera wash over its sides. It continued its wild motions, using its limbs and body like a battering ram to physically squash or throw the rodents away, eyes clenched shut as black squirming clumps scattered and flew away into the darkness.

The ferocity might have worked to keep them from latching on, but not all of them.

A rodent bit into its hip. Another latched on to the tip of its tail, its teeth hooking into the space between the bony segments, almost severing it. One managed to bite onto its testes, while another held onto its neck and bit onto the base of its ear. Five others had held onto its fur, biting its sides, trying to dig deeper. Another quickly bit its leg as the wolf prepared to slam its chest into the trash below to squash a rodent dangling off its rib, its teeth uselessly scraping against the bone, too tough to snap.

Before it could do so, before the pain could even properly register, a bloodcurdling shriek sounded out from the human, and the world was suddenly washed away in a wild spew of sparks, a million tiny explosions burning into its retinas. The wild spew sporadically swung side to side, bouncing off the walls of trash on either side before impacting the wolf itself, throwing away some of the rats and momentarily making the wolf stumble away.

It snapped its feet out just in time to prevent another fall as chunks of its flesh were torn off by the removed rodents.

Barely staying on its feet, it roared out a bark that hurt its throat, thrashing and bucking its body. Another couple of rodents detached, and it raised its head before swinging it downward, the rodent chewing off its ear detaching with the momentum with a spray of blood, leaving only a thin film of cartilage to keep the wolf's ear connected, blood quickly pooling into the eardrum.

It swung its hips for added momentum to slam the rodent attached to its tail into its dazed brethren, uncaring of the tip going with it. Its legs were used to batter, make space, gut the rodent hanging off its privates with a lucky scrape of its nail.

It used the last few seconds of [Bloodrush] to get onto the hysterical human, its stomach over her head, battering away rats with all four legs in rotation, bucking to throw them off, just buying time, eyes wide and teeth bared in a furious snarl.

Something in its soul thrashed against its chains, and the wolf felt [Mental Resistance] strain for a moment.

By some miracle, the human had enough mana to slap her palm onto its stomach as it rotated in place above her, giving it a weaker boost than before but a very well-timed one, as [Bloodrush]'s Strength, Speed, and Endurance bled out, leaving its limbs feeling lethargic and slow, uncooperative, the communication between brain and limb feeling slow and sluggish.

The human's skill helped, but not enough to continue as it had been, the loss in Endurance being felt especially hard as its muscles burned with exertion.

Its blood had more adrenaline than water in it, and despite the danger, the wolf couldn't help but break from its protective movements, snapping forward with its jaws, whipping its head to the side in a small, jerky motion to throw a rodent away, and in the same movement, clamp onto another one.

It continued, snapping its teeth shut, flicking rodents away, and instantly grabbing onto another in a frenzied mess of blood and viscera, only pausing to use vermin as a sack of meat to batter their brethren away.

Despite only two of its limbs ever being used to support its body—the other two kicking and rending shallow cuts in the squirming mounds of fur scrambling for them—the wolf managed to keep itself relatively grounded, its center of balance only wobbling slightly during the fight. Some instinctual part of itself remembered how to keep its balance, only ever keeping the upper parts of its limbs stiff and letting the lower parts move with the bob of the terrain. Its movements grew less restrained, more confident.

It swiped two rats away, one of its toe pads paying the price in blood when one of them quickly turned and bit down before the wolf's paw smashed its teeth out of its mouth. Behind them was another monstrously large rodent, almost half the size of the wolf itself, and twice as large as the previous biggest it had seen.

The heat in its stomach felt like liquid magma eating away at its insides, a blast furnace contained in far too small a vessel. It was the only thing its body felt besides a strange, scared sort of excitement. A savage satisfaction in a fight to the death.

And it *hurt*.

The rodent lunged for the head, its stubby legs only barely managing to lift its upper body off the ground, its teeth just barely high enough to reach the wolf's neck.

In a moment of pure instinct, the wolf turned its upper body to the right, lowered it as much as it could, and the moment the rodent's teeth latched onto its neck fur, exploded to the left, pushing with its shoulder, neck, and legs, uncaring of the two thin cuts on its neck as teeth dragged through its fur.

The rodent was thrown off-balance, head to the sky, and the wolf plunged its canines through its neck and eyes, using its momentum to continue the motion while using the rodent as a sweep once more, battering away dozens of rodents before they could get to the human from both the left, right, and sometimes above.

Even the new tendons woven around its neck and curled around its spine were feeling the strain by now, but it held its ground, protecting the human and itself with all it had, even as the rapid swinging started making it feel a tad dizzy.

The blood loss was probably as responsible for that as its motions were.

The trench deepened, tightened, the trash momentarily burying the human's legs. The wolf barely caught it out of the corner of its eyes, instantly letting its canines phase through the rodent as it kicked with its hind legs to pivot and dash forward.

Curiously, even as the human spent every ounce of energy and mana she had blowing or throwing rodents off, she didn't attack the wolf when its jaws tore through her charred pant leg and scraped against her skin, nor as the wolf hauled her broken limbs out the trash.

Instead, she let out a guttural groan of pain and blew a wide burst of sparks around her in an awkward semicircle, her injured arm curled around her head protectively.

The wolf kicked away a couple rodents—with much more difficulty than before—as it did the same with her other leg, the fabric tearing from the strain. The human's voice quickly grew hoarse, but it pulled her leg free after two seconds of struggling, and it quickly dashed over her torso to bite into a rodent about to bite into her scalp, tossing it away.

Then, with a thunderous rumble, the trash went too high, got too unstable, and a tide of uncountable bits, big and small, toppled on top of them like the lid of a coffin, mashing them together, the rodents completely buried all around them.

The human had lost her voice by this point, and clumsily threw her hands around the wolf, whose brow was split open by the sharp corner of a metal box, its left eye blinded by its own blood, dizzy and confused.

The sudden lack of rodents, the pressure on its upper back, smashing its chest into the human's face, as well as the rather sudden perception of its injuries made it quickly snap out of its confusion with a growl, flaring its antennae for more information.

It was only the Speed and Perception boost which made the wolf realize what was to come just a split second before it did, and it hurriedly dug its hind leg's nails into the human's garment, despite feeling a piece of rebar trying to pry its rib cage open.

Even if they were in the middle, it quickly became hard to breathe as their sides were squeezed, harder and harder, the wolf's bones creaking under its flesh, slowly getting bruised by a wall of sharp corners and rusted waste as dust hung thick in the air, like trying to breathe in slime.

It might have been just ten or so seconds, but in its entrapped state, it felt like a hundred times longer.

Then the world dropped out from under them.

With the coffin of discard no longer suspended between the gears' crushing pressure, they simply dropped, falling like a conjoined pair of stones in a shower of dust, metal, glass, plastic, and a million other less savory things.

The impact might have been lesser had the human not accidentally used the wolf as a cushion for their spinning fall.

It was only six or seven feet, but the added weight of the human was enough to make the wolf let out a shrill, sharp yowl as it felt one of its ribs land onto an iron pipe, the snap reverberating through its bones.

The human's injuries forgotten, it curled its feet inward and kicked her off, scrambling to its unsteady feet as it panted, blood both foreign and familiar dripping from its mouth.

And in the scattered, seemingly nonsensical pattern of holes in the walls, it found the pipe it had been looking for this entire time, half hidden under a piece of debris, slowly inching upward.

It only wasted a moment to grab onto the human by her collar, its teeth lodged into the tough fabric, and on unsteady, trembling legs, it pulled her along, step by step, getting closer to salvation, feeling a slow, insidious chill slowly move into its body, adrenaline slowly starting to fade and pain slowly creeping back in.

If the wolf was tired, the human was exhausted, barely conscious, her head limply hanging down as she muttered gibberish. The wolf's blood dripped down its teeth to slowly coat her neck.

Its tendons strained like frayed ropes as the wolf dragged her closer to the pipe foot by foot, the scent of the poison slowly filling the air as bits and pieces of trash continued to rain down from above, caught or squished into the gears, occasionally impacting its numb backside.

The rodents trapped in the pipe, eight of them, spotted them just ten feet away and quickly jumped off. The wolf felt their squeaks tickle its antennae, the ringing in its ears drowning out most sounds.

The trash continued to scrape down the walls inch by inch, and the wolf let go of the human just as her skill faded away, its limbs feeling like they were made of lead. A mass of rodents as large as itself rushed at it, and it could only glare at them with a defiant anger.

It didn't have the time nor the energy to fight the rodents and drag itself and the human to the pipe before it would be too high for them to jump into. It also knew the other pipes were stuffed full of rodents, even if they weren't near the entrance.

In its hazy-eyed state, with one ear and one eye made useless by blood, and feeling like a clawing, tearing void was ripping its stomach apart, it gathered all it had—all its fury, all its mana, its breaths ramping up into snarls, one eye glowing red under the veil of its lifeblood, and the other gleaming gold as mana flooded its lungs.

It needed more.

And so, it reached deep into the recesses of its mind.

Hazy recollections of its old weakness, of running from rodents until it could barely breathe. Of a gnawing, empty pit in its stomach; of shivering as its insides chilled to ice despite the sweltering heat of whatever machine it was nestled against. Of vomiting until it could barely breathe, poison and blood mixing with whatever scraps it had found to eat pooling around its snout.

Of hatred, buried deep from necessity. Hatred of its kin, biting and chasing it away. Hatred of the machines that burned its eyes, its nose, its lungs. Hatred of the structures that speared into the sky, as if their existence was there simply to remind it of how small and insignificant it was. Hatred of the human's nest.

Hatred of itself, when it was too weak to survive.

Too weak to find food, too weak to take it from others.

So the wolf grasped tight around the lid of the coffin it had trapped its hatred within and dragged it out, fanned its flames and plastered it to the forefront of its mind.

They used to be memories, unimportant and fading, emotions fleeting and unnecessary, but for this moment, the wolf gripped onto them with bloody teeth as its lungs burned and swelled with more than simple air.

And it waited one, two, three seconds, until the rodents were just a foot away. [Bloodrush] activated.

The mana coiled around the air in its lungs, latched on to it like a rabid passenger. Mana turned to sound, and the passenger roared with a hundred different shades of fear, fury, hatred, and desperation as it rode upon the air that screamed out of its lungs. The pressure felt like a fist being driven through its throat.

Its vocal cords snapped like strings almost instantly, trampled underfoot as the mana vein of its throat reinforced the sound waves, propelling the air forward. The tight ball of emotion, sound, and mana finally left the entrance to its mouth.

And without the confines of the wolf's circuits, the proximity of its control, it promptly exploded.

Blood spewed out of its throat and mouth in a fine mist as a sharp crack of sound drowned out all else, the sphere in its mouth expanding in less than the blink of an eye.

Its jaw broke and detached from its joints to dangle lifelessly, the muscles tearing open as one of its canines ripped out of its mouth. In the last millisecond, whether by luck or instinct, it wrenched its head to the side just enough so the air wouldn't go back down its gullet and rupture its lungs.

That didn't stop its neck from being violently wrenched to the side before it could even see the effects of the explosion as it was blasted back by its own skill. Its body spun and flipped in the air chaotically for a few feet before its hind legs smashed into the trash again, promptly crumpling and leaving it to tumble awkwardly onto its side.

If nothing else, the agony helped it stay awake.

With shrill wheezes, it forced itself upright, tilting its blood-filled ear to the side for the crimson liquid to drip out, simply to regain some sense of hearing, as the other one could only hear a high-pitched whine.

The pain was . . . not something it had *never* felt before, but definitely equal to its worst experiences. Yet, the way forward was open, few if any still-moving rodents in sight.

Step by stumbling step as its sense of balance returned, it managed to drag itself back to the gibbering human, and with some fiddling, hooked its top canines into her garment. Through blurred eyes, it succeeded in seeing what its skill had managed to do—from the splattered corpses of the rats that had popped open against the stone wall, to the eight-foot-long cone of destruction that had formed a convenient ramp of trash, straight into the drifting pipe.

The rest was a blur of awkwardly adjusting its top canines to properly drag the human. Of being thankful for its hanging jaw allowing it to easily spin its canines and cut through the grate. Of one long, final stretch of agony as it dragged itself and the grunting human into the city's underbelly.

And finally, rest.

CHAPTER 18

She'd long since stopped caring about what was happening around her, or even trying to understand it. There were no shrill screams, no chittering, no wriggling horrors trying to eat her piece by piece, and so, she just . . . sat there, and waited. Wherever "there" was.

She couldn't really say she was *resting*, however.

It wasn't just the pain, nor the slowly encroaching feeling of wrongness in her body. It was the start-stop nature of her rest, which left her feeling like she was slowly detaching from reality.

Every time she woke up and fell asleep, she felt like there was no transition period, moving seamlessly from one to the other in increments so small she barely had time to process whether she was dreaming or back into the land of the wakeful. Three minutes of dreams that were a mixture of bizarre concoctions of her subconscious and simple replays of her memories; two minutes of hazy but *real* sensations, then back again.

And as this continued, she started losing that distinction. She no longer *slept* or *woke up*; it was a chaotic jumble of awareness which took her from talking to a faceless acquaintance and back to a damp, foul-smelling tube of iron where she'd absentmindedly pet blood-soaked fur until her mind took her away again.

So she indulged herself in sight, in sound. Whether it was real or a melting fragment of her memories, it didn't matter.

That withheld thought of the System tickled at her mind constantly, but she ignored it. Some weak, withered part of her screamed at her to keep going, to keep moving.

And she heard that, too; she just didn't listen.

The metaphorical limbo she found herself in had many layers, and she was slowly being torn between them.

To struggle or give up; reality or a dream.

The more the cycle continued, the more discontent she felt, her dreams going from comprehensible, to memories, to a mess of impossibilities, and back. And as she used that thin sliver of awareness which came with being "awake" to think back on her life, she couldn't help but think it was . . .

Meaningless.

Empty faces, inflectionless voices that spoke but said nothing. Dozens of connections, thin as strings, snapping under the weight of a gaze full of scrutiny—all but one. Buildings of brass, brick, burnished bronze, and glass. Foods that were more of a social statement than nutrition. Clothes that hurt to breathe in, that choked her in the stifling heat of summer.

A life of slavery.

Should any real slave hear that thought which whispered in her ears, she knew they'd snap her neck out of rage, and they'd be justified. Maybe it was her highborn status which prevented her from seeing just how vast the difference between the two scenarios was. But exchanging a golden birdcage for a dress of rusted chains didn't hold any real significance to *her*, even if it did to other people. Whether it was nobility rocking her cage and poking their fingers between the bars, or a sleazy bastard like Ghar yanking at her leash, what was the difference beyond the conditions?

Powerless in one and powerless in the other, unable to do what she really wanted.

Not that it mattered. She was probably going to die like this.

Forgotten in a rusty pipe.

The hazy call to let her mind fade away grew more insistent, and she indulged it, letting her twisting mind take her hand and drag her through the labyrinth it had crafted.

She glanced at her teammates as they strolled back to the guild, her steps slowing. She quickly dug out a bronze crown, bending down to offer it to the skeletal child with a wooden cup sitting by his legs. He didn't have a reaction whatsoever, and after another quick glance at her team, she simply put the coin into the kid's empty cup.

Still no reaction, his head hanging down. Her heart ached at how exhausted the poor kid must be. But she had also learned of how cruel life was on the third floor, so she shook his shoulder to wake him up, just so the kid wouldn't have his money taken by some random passerby.

"Hey, kid?" she whispered with a small, friendly smile, expecting him to startle awake. He didn't react, completely limp, his head swinging in time with her movements.

He was . . . too limp.

She lowered her hand to touch his arm—

And it was ice cold.

She jerked her hand back, eyes wide.

As if in slow motion, he fell sideways, his rough, dirty rags scraping against the wall as if they were made of wood.

Two empty, lifeless eyes stared at her boots.

She jumped to her feet, staggering back, hyperventilating. The world swam like paint dissolving into water. A slap that almost threw her to the floor snapped her out of it, Ghar's scowling face blurring into sight, his fist bunching into her robes and dragging her away.

Some part of her understood; acknowledged it. Yet, another refused to accept it.

She hastily wiped the tears out of her eyes and started to turn her head around. She knew that she would find a shivering kid staring in wonder at the bronze crown, and he would flash her a thankful grin, full of childlike innocence in the hellish pit that was this place, and everything would be normal.

But all she saw was someone bending down to take the coin before continuing on their way, not even sparing the corpse a second glance.

She stared at the coins in her hand. Furious green eyes flashed up to glare at a faceless man, only vague outlines of his features showing.

"What the hell is this?"

"Payment." He shrugged, a smug, shit-eating grin on his face. It somehow felt much more sincere than his friendly, charming smile, and she cursed herself for not seeing it before.

She gritted her teeth, nostrils flaring.

"This is one bronze coin. The payment for the job was one silver. You said we'd all take an equal cut."

"Yeah. I did. Never signed anythin' though, did I? You did." He shrugged again, gesturing with his chin at the book hanging off her hip.

Her shaking hand clutched the coin in her palm as she closed her eyes, a hissing breath of fury leaving her. She wouldn't be able to pay off the debt. She'd become a slave, to **them,** of all people. How could she have been so stupid? Of course this had happened. Why did she always assume the best of people?

She opened her eyes to a room of opulence. Her all-too-familiar cage, drowned in the pale orange of dusk as a silken pillow cradled her head. A knock on the door shook her out of her restless thoughts.

"My lady?" a shaky whisper came from the door, and her eyes widened. She knew what that tone meant. She'd dreaded when the time would come for her to hear it again.

She launched herself out of the bed, uncaring of her covers hitting the floor, and she almost joined them in her haste to throw herself at the door.

She swung it open, and her eyes widened in horror.

Her sight blurred with tears.

"Oh god, Katherine . . . " she croaked out, her eyes tracing the black mess of bruises that covered half her friend's face.

"It's not your fault," her friend, maid, and shield said in a whisper full of conviction, her features showing more pain for Emhreeil than herself.

She choked down a sob as she ushered her in and forced her still-bleeding form to sit on her bed, dragging out a chest of medical supplies out of her closet, her tears almost choking her as she applied the healing paste on the whip marks covering her friend's back side.

"It's not your fault, Emhreeil," Katherine would whisper, each repetition as painful as a shard of glass being driven into her chest.

Because repeating something didn't make it true. It simply made the words lose all meaning.

Despite her protests, she didn't let Katherine lift a finger that night, and long after she'd fallen asleep on her bed, face down and having difficulty breathing right, she could only stare at her friend's injuries in horror and dig her nails into her scalp until she felt the warm trickle of blood mar her fingers and stain her auburn hair.

Her parents had seen how close she'd gotten to her maid. So why waste money on healing Emhreeil from her beatings for public appearances when they could instead use her maid as a punching bag?

Every mistake was a slap. Every month's end that she didn't unlock the skills and paths her parents wanted her to get was another night that Katherine spent tied to a wooden post, whipped until she could barely walk.

She hated her family. She hated them so much. She wanted to put them in a cage, cover them in midnight oil, and burn them to a crisp; inhale their exhumed flesh as they begged and screamed and burned.

She needed an outlet for her anger, so she simply stood in silence, hands clutching her hair as she imagined her family dying in all the most horrific ways she could imagine, even if she knew she'd never have the guts or conviction to ever do such things to anyone.

She blinked.

She stood opposite to her maid, a bittersweet tang in her heart as she cast a low-power [Sparkburst] to light her papers of ownership on fire.

"You're free," she whispered to her friend with a smile full of happy tears.

Katherine just stared wide-eyed, stunned, at the fading embers of her shackles as they flew off into the afternoon breeze, the orange motes of light reflecting in her brown eyes. The bag she'd given her fell from her limp fingers, the clinking of coins impossibly loud in the quiet, disbelieving silence.

"And . . . so am I. I'm sorry for everything. You deserve b-better. You always did. A-A better friend. Someone who had more spine, who could . . . prevent the scars on your back. Someone who would have done this sooner. I-I'm sorry. Goodbye," she eked out, her voice warbly and her heart torn between feeling joy and agony.

She turned away, walking toward the Dungeon, praying to gods she didn't believe in for Katherine to find and lead a happy life away from her. A life free, away from someone as worthless as she, as powerless, as cowardly, as passive, as defeatist, and a million other insults that all rang true.

Some deep, selfish part of her wished that Katherine would stop her, demand that she come with her. Tell her she still wished to come with her, to brave the wonders and horrors of the Dungeon together.

But that never came, and she held the fragments of her heart in place until she booked a room and cried into a pillow for a day straight.

A shove against her uninjured shoulder startled her awake from her half sleep, and she tensed for a moment until the breathing of the beast reminded her of reality.

It chuffed and poked her again, albeit with less force.

She resumed petting its bloody hide, and it grumbled before going still, whatever she'd been doing to disturb it assumedly having been dealt with.

Her mind wandered back to the strangely clear memories her mind had confronted her with.

And in them, she found a spark.

Albeit she kept the emotion buried for the most part, she knew she had an abundance of self-loathing. She hated how easily she gave up in the face of adversity, how easily she folded under social pressure. How easily she shied away from confrontation, and how easily she let others trample over her and all she cared about, both because of mental and personal weakness.

She wanted to live, to change. To see her best and only friend just one more time. To enjoy a free life. To help whoever deserved it.

It was a vague outline of what she wanted, but it was enough.

It was somehow telling of how pathetic she was that the motivation, drive, and determination to change her life came when she was at the very brink of losing it, but she could work with it.

Despite those bold words, however, her mind and body were still battered, and her awareness quickly grew hazy and forgetful, fading away as her fingers grew still in the beast's fur.

Her last conscious thought as she was whisked away into another dream, buried under a hundred unpleasant emotions and sensations, was that she was probably dying from infection and starvation, and that's why she couldn't stay awake despite the pain.

That was actually funny, for some godforsaken reason. She snickered as she was swept into another dream.

Her eyes raked down a page covered in passages that her brain refused to interpret or ascribe meaning to, and she hissed in frustration, pressing her palms into her eyes.

She tried again.

Words turned to syllables before her tired eyes, syllables turned to letters, letters turned to meaningless symbols. She couldn't read a single word.

She tried again.

With great effort and grit, she got herself to read the paragraph at the speed of a snail, but correctly. And the moment her eyes landed on the final dot, she realized she had no idea or recollection of what she had just read. A pure, empty blankness.

"Recite the page for me. Or at least that paragraph you've been looking at for the past hour," her mother instructed, a thin veneer of calmness in her voice which couldn't hide the overwhelming weight of disappointment in her gaze. She gritted her teeth, struggling to withhold a childish tantrum.

"I can't," she forced out, resisting the urge to sob.

How many hours had it been? Seventeen? A full day?

All she knew was that her brain refused to function anymore. Her studying for the past four hours had been utterly meaningless, and still, she was forced to continue.

"I see. And you have not gained any skill so far, correct?" her mother coldly asked, less of a question and more of an accusation.

"No," she answered for the fiftieth time.

"Again."

"No," she growled, her eyes and fists clenched shut.

" . . . Look at me," her mother said, her voice calm yet sharp and dangerous, like the edge of a drawn blade. Emhreeil tensed and gulped before gritting her teeth, her anger far outweighing her caution for a moment. She turned to her mother with eyes that refused to focus, narrowed in a glare.

A pulsing agony which covered half her face and her sudden change in view were the things that made her shocked mind understand what had happened, the sound of the slap still echoing down the hallway. Tears ran down her face as her teeth gnashed.

"I was not asking. **Again.**"

She snapped back into the land of the living with a gasp in her throat and a strange-sounding snarl in her ear, the beast's fur bristling under her fingers. She felt that its attention was on her, somehow, so she didn't move nor breathe, shocked out of any kind of rest.

The strange snarl quickly died down, and the beast chuffed, its fur settling down.

A light, barely perceptible sting accompanied the pounding headache in her mind, and she idly realized she was crying. Stupid nightmares.

Her groggy mind slowly realized that she'd probably been making noise in her sleep, as she couldn't find any other reason for the beast to be growling at her. The sudden kick of adrenaline helped startle her body and mind into activity, at least, and despite feeling like she could barely even think, much less make any sort of decent decision, she focused on that background process of her mind dedicated to the System, and her progress revealed itself.

She had wallowed in self-pity and self-loathing enough. She had to focus on getting out of this shithole first, however unlikely.

You have progressed on your Path.
[Infuser] Level 8 → Level 12

-Available Attribute Points: 4
-Attributes:
Strength (+0)
Speed (+0)
Dexterity (+0)
Endurance (+1)
Perception (+0)

Resolve (+1)
Intelligence (+4)
Soul (+2)

Impressive as it was to gain four entire levels in a single fight, she couldn't find it in herself to be impressed or even happy about it. She quickly threw her points according to her current situation and moved on.

Endurance (+3)
Perception (+2)

Or would have, had she not been momentarily stunned by how much better she felt by adding two points into Endurance. Aches lessened, the squirming of her insides became less prominent in her mind, the shivering cold of hunger in her gut decreased, and the uncomfortable heat became a little more bearable as a surge of energy rushed through her. It felt like her limbs were made of timber rather than weak flesh as her heart swelled with blood and vitality.

Even her mind cleared up, if only a little.

The sensations from Perception's upgrade were empowered. Sounds became louder and easier to tell the direction of; scents became annoyingly easy to notice. Yet, much like she'd overheard from people's conversations, it didn't feel attention-grabbing nor overwhelming.

She focused back on the letters in front of her as soon as she was done noting the various, if small, improvements.

-Acquired Skills:
You have gained the Skill [Tough Skin - Level 1]
You have gained the Skill [Infection Resistance - Level 1]
You have gained the Skill [Disease Resistance - Level 1]
[Infection Resistance] has Leveled Up. Level 1 → Level 2
[Disease Resistance] has Leveled Up. Level 1 → Level 2
[Sparkburst] has Leveled Up. Level 13 → Level 16
[Haste] has Leveled Up. Level 10 → Level 14
[Pain Resistance] has Leveled Up. Level 14 → Level 18
[Poison Resistance] has Leveled Up. Level 8 → Level 9
[Mana Tank] has Leveled Up. Level 1 → Level 2
[Mana Conduit] has Leveled Up. Level 1 → Level 3

-Acquired Traits:
Enduring (1/5): You have felt the chill of death multiple times and survived. You are slightly tougher.

The System unfortunately told her what she'd known and had been fearful of admitting in the form of two resistance skills. She had an infection.

Honestly, she'd be more surprised if she didn't have one, or multiple. During that chaotic mess of a fight, her broken hand had been used as a chewing toy for the **worthless fucking vermin—**

Her train of thought stopped for a moment as she took a moment to parse her surprise. That thought was a little . . . sudden. She couldn't say it wasn't genuine, but even in her own mind, she rarely thought of anything or anyone with such intense hatred, except her parents.

She remembered her earlier dream and the fleeting thought of burning them, and as a thought experiment, imagined a cage full of rodents being tossed into an open fire.

The amount of savage glee she felt at the thought was, quite frankly, a little terrifying.

She couldn't care about her deteriorating mental state, however. Not right now. She instead focused back on the steady, pulsing pain in her right arm. With much difficulty and strained grunting, she managed to bring it up next to her head, using her working arm to poke and prod it.

There were multiple spots where new wounds and bites had been made, and despite their small overall damage, the problem was in the very, very obvious infection. If the throbbing waves of pain in her arm were enough to punch through a level *eighteen* [Pain Resistance], she knew she'd probably be screaming in pain if she lowered the skill's power.

Gingerly, she poked and felt around the skin, the mental image growing more vivid and more dire by the second. The skin felt like it was overlaid atop a furnace rather than her flesh, hot to the point of concern. And around each bite mark, big and small, was a far more concerning numbness, a certain wetness and toughness to the injury that couldn't be justified by congealed blood.

Infection was often the first step, occurring when filth or disease entered one's body and began to spread. Disease occurred when the body was damaged—as a result of the infection—and signs and symptoms of an illness appeared.

Which meant that [Infection Resistance] was a lost cause by now; she was already infected. The skill would hardly help her. All she had to deal with this problem was [Disease Resistance] and her own body's natural defenses, whatever they were. Even if she knew what had to be done, it was difficult to visualize, much less seriously consider. And there were so many things that could go wrong.

While the beast could somehow cut iron, she didn't know if she could get it to cut her arm off; not without sight and unable to make it understand her. At worst, she might even make it think she was inviting it to eat her, absurd as that sounded.

She also didn't know if she'd be able to bear the pain of cauterizing it either, despite her skill almost tripling her pain tolerance.

What she did know was that at this point, her right arm was disposable. So she could experiment as she wanted, really. It was inflamed from the constant agitation of her broken bones, full of filth, and infected. Sooner or later, it would kill her.

The least she could do was put the damn thing to use before she got rid of it, one way or another.

The problem was that she had no idea what to experiment with. She'd long since forgotten all her harebrained ideas, speculations, and random bouts of inspiration when it came to magic, beaten out of her by quill and fist.

Her thoughts wandered to the single common point all mages had, which was a minor form of telemancy—moving things with their mana.

And an idea began to form.

She gingerly moved some mana out of the exit point in her palm, feeling it appear like a thin coating around her arm.

"Like a potentially teleporting, intangible, immaterial gas that isn't affected by air, gravity, or most natural laws. Quite simple, really."

She remembered those words clearly and struggled not to snort. Her teachers had rarely indulged her undying curiosity of magic, as they had been instructed not to by her parents, but when they did . . . it was both enlightening and baffling.

She gripped the sleeve of mana with her mind and began pressing. She knew the break was roughly in her forearm, but she wanted to see if she could get a more accurate spotting of the issue. A poke at her elbow sent a spike of pain a little above the joint, so she gingerly poked there, too. She felt neither a shift nor a grind of bone, so she mentally noted that to be a fracture at worst.

She pressed a little higher and felt a much more violent spike of pain, followed by insistent pulses of the feeling all along her limb. A poke a little bit above the previous one made her shoulders tighten and jaw clench, the pain accompanied by the extremely uncomfortable sensation of broken bones grinding against one another.

And then she got another idea.

The thin coat of mana around her arm tightened, thickened, and with careful, careful precision, she pressed down gently along her forearm in a firm cylindrical shape. Then she shifted, moving her hand just a bit, a cautious press of mana keeping the bone set.

Of course, the mana splint was far from perfect. It was very mentally taxing to keep it going, to keep the pressure rigid and consistent. And despite her best efforts to control the mana properly to minimize energy bleed, even a small splint like this was draining her mana a little faster than she could generate it, even while using [Mana Conduit] as soon as it was available.

It wasn't quite as delicate as some of the common exercises for mana control, like spinning a pen in place, rolling it, or spinning it in all of its axes without dropping it or launching it at herself, but the wider scope made it harder for her mind to focus on all of it at once.

Still, it was something.

In a moment of free fall, or perhaps while getting dragged, it could help save her legs, at least, even if the arm wasn't salvageable.

Telemancy was a strange but common form of magic. Inefficient in how much mana it burned to move things, with a very high degree of control needed to be used offensively, and easily disrupted by other mages. It was considered more of a show of mastery and a good way to train rather than something genuinely useful in any offensive capacity, regardless of skills.

Considering that "mancy" meant that it was *learned* magic, there was a lot of debate on whether it should even be classified as a "mancy," when even the most untrained of mages could make a pen slide across a table with mana, for example.

A "kinetic," for its part, implied someone who was locked into their inherent magic type. A telemancer to a telekinetic was the difference between a kitchen knife and a greatsword in terms of danger. The control and power that one gained by being born with inherent magic was nigh impossible to match, even if it restricted them from using any other type of magic.

If only she'd been born a telekinetic, she wouldn't be mentally ranting just to pass the time. She'd be delving into the Dungeon and tearing apart iron golems like they were made of paper.

With a shift of her hips, which had been hurting less and less, surprisingly—and were probably *not* broken because of that—her attention was drawn to the stifling tightness of her pants and iron greaves.

The latter was actually good, as the knee-length iron had kept her lower legs relatively safe from jostling. It wasn't exactly a splint, but it was tight enough to let the bones heal, albeit slowly, as long as she didn't contract the muscles that made her feet move.

The former, however, was simply because her pants were burnt; pretty badly, too. They were made of thick, threaded wool, so while they offered great protection from cuts and stabs, they burned pretty easily. In some spots, she could even feel the humid air meet her skin, which was definitely not good.

In the heat of the moment, it wasn't like she'd had any other option to get the damn rats off her. She just hadn't realized how strong [Sparkburst] had been getting lately. At the first couple levels, she distinctly remembered how it would only light a paper on fire two out of three times, usually just tearing it up into lightly smoking bits of paper with the microexplosions of the sparks.

The progress was a balm on her soul, even if it cost her the protection of her leggings.

She sighed, a low, croaky sound, and continued applying the mana splint on her arm, adding a repulsion field around it just strong enough to have it float off the ground a little. Mostly because she felt like a repulsion field would be extremely effective in breaking any strong shocks before they snapped her bones back out of place.

With any luck, she might even get a skill to make this stuff easier, but the System was a cruel, unpredictable, and impossible to figure out little bastard, as evidenced by the fact she'd spent literal years without getting a single one of the skills that would have made life easier for her, while some people got them by doing something once or twice.

Some people got skills about telemancy after spinning a pen for a couple minutes, while others just *never* gained them. There was a loose understanding of *desire* and *struggle* being the two foremost things which decided on what the System gave someone and how quickly they leveled it, but it was all conjecture and speculation.

Whatever justifications the Scions gave for why the Eye and the stupid System it had made were the way they were, she was never *not* going to be resentful that she'd never gotten a single medical or studying-related skill, even though she knew damn well that she genuinely wanted them, at least at the time.

She could almost hear some snooty priest recite the whole "The Eye knows us better than we know ourselves" spiel. It kind of pissed her off.

Deciding not to waste her mana, she lessened the repulsion field and softened the grip of energy around her arm, using just enough to keep the exercise going for as long as possible while keeping herself topped up. She didn't know if her body had a limit on how much mana it could store in its circuits, but she felt like she had about half again her normal mana capacity at the moment.

And now to just . . . keep practicing, with the vague hope that the beast would continue to cart her around.

Yep.

Just keep going . . .

. . . Gods, she was so *bored.*

It felt absurd to say that she was bored in her situation, but now that she was somewhat awake, the only thing she had to focus on was the telemancy splint she'd fashioned for herself. It was rather tempting to make the beast say some stupid stuff just to pass the time, maybe relieve some stress through the humorous absurdity of such things, but it seemed to be very grouchy at the moment, so she opted not to bother it any more.

CHAPTER 19

Sleep was near instant. The moment it deemed its environment safe, it simply collapsed like a puppet with its strings cut, uncaring of the human's pained grunt as it accidentally flipped her onto her stomach from its sudden yank at her collar.

You have progressed on your Path.
[Hound of the Keeper] Level 9 → Level 16

-Available Attribute Points: 7
-Attributes:
Strength (+0)
Speed (+0)
Dexterity (+0)
Endurance (+2)
Perception (+1)
Resolve (+1)
Intelligence (+4)
Soul (+1)

The wolf didn't spend even a moment to "read" or consider the symbols, brushing them aside, forcefully telling them to leave it alone.

Surprisingly, it worked, and its body came into view. Or feeling, rather. It was still a strange sensation.

The damage was much less dire than it had assumed it would be, the points it had in Endurance showing their worth. The problem was that its wounds were still very much open, and bleeding *very heavily*. It was a wonder how it even had the presence of mind to fix itself . . .

Thankfully, pinching veins shut was a matter of seconds, however numerous they were, and in short order, it felt like it had at the very least stabilized itself for the blood loss to no longer be a threat.

It started on a quick overall assessment of its injuries. Its bottom right canine had been ripped out of its mouth completely, and its jawbone had broken at the middle point on both sides. Creating a thin sleeve of cartilage around the bone and its fragments to keep them pressed together, before urging its body to connect the bone again was a matter of a couple minutes. It assigned the cartilage to be cannibalized by its skill, slowly, just to make sure the bone fixed properly.

Turns out, the amount of tissue lost when bones snapped was actually minimal. It would be very different if the bone was pulverized or outright removed, but a simple break would heal faster than even a flesh wound. It was too microscopic an injury once it forced its bone pieces to press together.

At the thought of a flesh wound, it focused on where its jawbone limply hung, connected to its head by skin and little else, and proverbially growled in annoyance.

The muscles, tendons, and joints were *all* damaged. The muscles were torn apart, one of the tendons on the right side was snapped clean, and bits of cartilage around the joint were broken and stripped from the bone, not to mention the obvious problem of it being detached.

Pushing the bone back into place was fairly simple, and fixing the torn-up bits of cartilage around the bone was a fairly quick process. The muscles would take a bit longer to repair, as the damage was more extensive than simple muscle fibers being snapped, but the tendon was a relatively quick fix. It just had to grab the two ends and stick them together before focusing as much essence as it could into reconnecting the two pieces. It knew that slower healing took less essence to complete, as speed seemed to cost just as much essence as fixing the wounds itself, but it had plenty of material in storage, so it could afford to be a bit wasteful.

Its tail would take a couple days to return to its previous state, but it wasn't a particularly necessary limb, so the wolf didn't bother speeding the regenerative process along, just giving it an average amount of essence.

Thankfully, it only lost a single canine from that ill-thought-out blast of sound, and it sped up its body with the process of making a new one, hoping that the cutting power of its old tooth would somehow transfer.

Because no matter how much it looked into its teeth, it couldn't find out anything about them. Not really. When nearing a bone, it could see the microscopic fibers it was made up of, but there was no such thing for its teeth. They were just . . . perfect. Perfectly smooth, perfectly dense; it couldn't even tell if they were made of bone at all. Just some white, inscrutable substance, harder than anything it could even imagine. It didn't know how to replicate them.

Fixing its right ear was also a rather quick fix, only taking a couple minutes. It just had to grab on to the flopping part with its mind, yank it back into place, and then use tiny bits of stretchy muscle to connect the pieces and rebuild the veins, cartilage, and skin.

Then it suddenly realized that it had been moving its body in its sleep this entire time, in a way. It had made muscles and used them like tentacles to connect to the other piece of its ear to fix the cartilage and skin. It had grabbed pieces of its bones with its mind and pushed them into place; used muscles to adjust and tighten them together.

So . . .

Its leg, from where it was mushed beneath its chest, restricting the blood flow and making pins and needles punch through the skin, slowly moved.

A sense of jubilation and absurd giddiness went through the wolf.

It could *move in its sleep.*

It activated [Bloodrush], disbelieving of the fact that the skills *worked in its sleep.* Then it grabbed on to its body and slowly pushed its leg out from underneath into a better position.

It was a strange sensation. Unlike moving normally, where the mind put forth a command and the body followed, this was a far more direct method—no middleman in the form of nerves; no muscle memory to guide its movements with the force of habit. It was awkward and stilted, and it took a *lot* of focus, but as long as it was in the [Devourer] skill, it could quite literally walk while asleep, judging by how it made its legs trot in the air as it lay on its side.

Of course, it couldn't shake away that mental dismissal of its senses, its hearing and smell incredibly muted, and its sight . . .

It forced its eyelids open. A blurry mess met its vision, and the shackles of sleep threatened to slide away the more visual stimuli its eyes encountered. But in the dark iron pipe they were in, that was hardly a problem. The problem was that the attempt to focus on both the sensation of its body and the visual stimuli was quickly giving it a headache.

Maybe it could do something with this in the future. Walking with its mind, albeit mildly dangerous due to the loss of senses, could be useful for exercising in its sleep, or such things. But for the moment, it was a distraction, so it simply stopped, trying to remember what it'd been doing before.

Ah, fixing itself.

Some repairs other than the ones it had already done would take a day or two, like the chunks of meat missing, the tip of its tail, and its vocal cords, but the most annoying part to get rid of would be its own reproductive organs.

Because as it had learned, those were nothing but a weak point that it had simply not thought of removing until now. Cannibalizing the organ was a matter of a few days, and rebuilding it for . . . whatever reason, wouldn't take much longer. Actually, if it wanted to make pups, it could just give itself a womb and inseminate itself without having to worry about finding a female canine and protecting her, so its reproductive organs weren't even useful for *reproduction*.

It paused for a moment, genuinely considering the idea.

It was . . . weird. Its mind rejected the notion out of some odd sense of revulsion, as it was a male, but it couldn't deny that having an actual pack of kin at its side was an appealing idea, and that impregnating itself was the safest and best way to achieve that, regardless of how uncomfortable the notion made it.

It was also impractical, as food was already relatively scarce around the human nest, and the wolf had no real idea of how to raise, control, or care for pups, since it had no memory of even *being* one, but it was an interesting idea for the distant future, perhaps.

Putting that thought aside for now, it focused on another weak point it had felt acutely during the fight. Endurance. Not the attribute, but its body's capability to keep going. In a fight that had lasted a mere two or three minutes, it had gone from fresh and hale to completely exhausted.

It had grown, its muscle mass almost doubling since its acquisition of the symbols, but it hadn't properly gained the energy to sustain that meager mass and power.

So it focused on its cardiovascular system.

Veins widened and thickened, stabbing deep into muscles not supported by a proper blood flow until now—a terrible oversight. Its lungs expanded, as much as it could spare without squishing other organs. It moved its diaphragm down, let its organs shift lower to make some space, and the muscles of the diaphragm itself were strengthened, the muscle fibers hardening, toughening, but not multiplying, just to make rapid breathing easier.

It knew that exercise would vastly improve its cardiovascular system, but it didn't know how exactly, so all its changes were mere approximations and imitations. For all it knew, it could barely be improving itself compared to normal exercise.

When it had some free reign to run around and test its endurance and what effects exercise would have on itself, it would do so, but at the moment, this was the best it could come up with.

There was so much more it could fix, the wolf felt a little overwhelmed with the possibilities, and that was without considering things it could outright change.

It spent much time considering the natural chemicals its body produced, one of which had greatly helped it during the fight. *Adrenaline*, which had made its veins sing in ecstasy. Which helped its muscles push beyond their limit. Which made it want to throw away caution and charge into the bloodbath. It was the equivalent to a minor [Bloodrush], without the added Endurance.

Additionally, its abdomen was still mostly empty, so it quickly made some glands within the flimsy cage of bone that would slowly but surely produce this chemical and store it in sacs just beside the glands. The sacs connected to the bloodstream with a simple one-way valve system used in various other parts of its body, and it surrounded them in a thin sleeve of muscle which could squeeze and force adrenaline into the bloodstream. Getting muscle memory to connect to its brain took a bit longer, but it would be complete sooner rather than later, and then it would have adrenaline whenever it needed it.

The sacs were rather large, and the glands were rather small, but that was alright. It expended some essence from [Devourer], a tiny amount, that would be dedicated to creating the chemical alongside the glands just to boost production.

If and when its body started building a tolerance for this natural chemical, it would simply wipe that tolerance away to maintain its potency, allowing the wolf to always have an additional, natural boost in any fight it got into.

After applying these changes, it was displeased to note that they would, for one reason or another, take a couple days to be made. It still wasn't sure of what factors made a change take less or more time, but the skill wasn't very forthcoming with how it worked.

Another quick check of its injuries revealed some sort of . . . blight. An unknown *something* that the wolf knew was detrimental to itself; some sort of infection, or poison. Destroying it was laughably easy, however, as the wolf simply turned to its own immune system and buffered it with as much essence as it dared to, with the vague direction of attacking the foreign filth.

The infection would soon be gone entirely, so—

The hand that rested on its fur suddenly tightened to the point of mild pain, and the wolf was thrown out of its rest. Its eyes flew open, and its head rose and swerved to observe its surroundings. The downward-tilting pipe was secure from the poison, as it couldn't rise upward, and it could neither hear nor feel any rodent approaching, just a few of them in neighboring pipes.

Seeing no danger, it flattened its antennae and turned to the whimpering, squirming human as her hand tightened and jerked, her paw clenching its fur. Likely having a nightmare. It carefully aimed with its hind paw and roughly shoved her uninjured shoulder, simultaneously annoyed and sympathetic.

It had things to do, and while it knew nightmares sucked, its rest was far more important at the moment.

The human thankfully startled awake, so it went back to sleep with a grumble, ignoring her words again.

It took a minute, but it returned to its body—just observing, not doing anything for a few minutes. Absentmindedly, it fixed all scrapes, bruises, and minor injuries, then returned to a mindless fugue of hesitation.

Its changes would kick in, some soon, some later. But now it was out of ideas, and the wolf was more concerned with a different problem.

Frankly, it had forgotten about the human until now.

And it wasn't sure what it wanted to do with her.

It didn't particularly need her. She'd helped it finally understand how to use the [Echoes of Oblivion] skill, and it was extremely grateful for that, but her usefulness had pretty much expired now. The wolf could learn words and how to speak them, as well as what they meant, simply by observing other humans, and watching her move her mana around had stopped being useful to the wolf.

Until now, she hadn't been a liability. In that fight to escape the poison, she'd more than proven her worth, even with three semiuseless limbs, by keeping the rodents off its back and giving the wolf some boosts in Speed and Perception that had greatly helped.

But now, it was in unknown, unfamiliar territory. Dangerous territory. Dragging her around would slow the wolf down, hurting its stealth capabilities. And the tightness of the pipes would make it difficult to properly drag the human along.

This was territory in which the human would be nothing but a liability.

And yet, despite all that, it didn't really want to leave her here.

It could acknowledge that at this point, it was simply acting on emotion, but it had never spent so long with another living being, never slept alongside them for days on end, never shared its food with another.

This was the first connection it had ever made, and some primal, social part of its mind that had grown atrophied was now preening in contentment just from being around the human. If anything, she was like a . . . giant, weakling pup whom the wolf had been taking care of for a week or more.

In the future, this connection could yield great things for the wolf. Maybe the human would give it food on a steady basis, allowing it to taste and experience more things without putting itself in danger. Maybe the human would give it ideas and talk to it, when it could finally talk back to her. Maybe the wolf would be the one to need her assistance, and she would come.

But truthfully, all those thoughts were merely the wolf trying to justify why it was prepared to put in so much effort into keeping her alive. It was well aware of that fact, but it couldn't help itself.

It liked having her around, even if she'd tried to attack it once.

In what felt like a lifetime ago, it remembered understanding just how truly alone it was, the last of its own kin, the only wolf it had ever seen, feeling its heart crushed by loneliness. That emotion felt so far away now, so muted when it stuck around the human, her petting hand like a brush that painted over that feeling with every stroke.

Maybe once she was better, she would turn away and never come back, but that was fine. It still wanted to try.

Sure, it knew damn well that if push came to shove, it would turn tail and run to preserve its own life, whether the human survived or not. But until that moment came, it couldn't find it in itself to abandon her just because she was mildly inconvenient.

It could eat any human, any one of its canine kin, but this *particular* human was . . . it was the *wolf's* human. As long as she acknowledged that the wolf was in charge of this bizarre, makeshift pack, it would protect her.

That was a good point for its thoughts to reach absolution, it believed.

Then the human started making her sad yipping noises again, and the wolf woke up once more. It tried to snarl, only for a wheeze to come out.

Right, it forgot about that.

It activated [Logotexnia], and with a bit of focus, managed to push some air out of its throat and use the mana to weave sound waves into a rough approximation of its snarl, letting its fur bristle in warning. Getting woken up constantly was getting *really* annoying.

The human woke up once more and stiffened, the light scent of fear entering its nostrils as her sounds stilled.

And now it felt bad.

Great.

It let up and relaxed, cutting off the sound of its snarl. It quickly fell asleep again, the human petting its fur, a luxury it was unused to.

With one last check to make sure it hadn't missed anything to improve or fix within its body, it called the symbols back with a thought, which surprisingly worked.

-Available Attribute Points: 7
-Attributes:
Strength (+0)
Speed (+0)
Dexterity (+0)
Endurance (+2)
Perception (+1)
Resolve (+1)
Intelligence (+4)
Soul (+1)

Seven whole points. And it knew *exactly* what it was going to put them in.

Speed (+1)
Endurance (+7)
Intelligence (+5)

For a moment, it felt its bones turn to steel; its flesh harden into marble. The beat of its heart became a thunderous boom, its very body suffused with a feeling of invincibility. Unfortunately, the feeling faded quickly, yet not entirely. Its body felt harder, tougher, lighter. Every breath felt unnecessary, as if it could just stop breathing and its body would keep working for hours on end, vitality and power seeping into every fiber of its body.

It was intoxicating. Addicting.

It wanted more.

Knowing that it had no more points, however, it ushered forth the rest of the symbols.

-Acquired Skills:
You have gained the Skill [Sonic Blast - Level 1]
You have gained the Skill [Tremor Sense - Level 1]
[Pain Resistance] has Leveled Up. Level 17 → Level 19
[Restful Awareness] has Leveled Up. Level 6 → Level 15

[Tough Skin] has Leveled Up. Level 2 → Level 4
[Mana Manipulation] has Leveled Up. Level 4 → Level 6
[Bloodrush] has Leveled Up. Level 3 → Level 5
[Logotexnia] has Leveled Up. Level 1 → Level 4

It stared at [Restful Awareness] in mild confusion tinted with disbelief. Nine whole levels. Just for moving around a bit in its sleep? That was absurd, if it actually had any effect. And the [Tremor Sense] skill meant that . . .

It could get more abilities out of its [Devourer] skill by changing its body? If it added a venomous tooth, would it get some skill about venom then? That seemed like it was *heavily* incentivizing the wolf to stray from its original biology, even if the only thing [Tremor Sense] did was make interpreting the signals its antennae picked up a little bit easier and a little bit more accurate.

With the symbols having nothing else to show it, the wolf returned to its body and got to work on making a skin sac full of hypernutritional blood for the human to drink. Just to make sure it wouldn't be a hindrance, the wolf made the sac thin, without blood vessels, and without any pain receptors. The blood it put in there was . . . not exactly blood. It removed much of the blood plasma and filled the liquid with tons of nutritional things it usually found in meat—even if it wasn't exactly sure what they were—a lot of water, and filled it chock-full of vitamins, as many as it could.

The change would take an hour or two, so it simply allowed its body to fade away, its mind finally resting along with its body.

When it was done sleeping, it got up, letting the human's petting hand slide off, and with a low groan, put its butt high in the air and stretched its forelegs as far away as they would go, its chest brushing against rusty iron with a low yawn.

Nothing felt quite as good as a long nap.

Its jaw wasn't hanging anymore, the jawbone back in place and the muscles mostly repaired, but it was still quite tender and painful. It poked the small nub of bone coming out of its bottom right canine with its tongue, noting that it felt exactly like its other teeth, much to its relief.

It turned around to the human, who was still doing something weird to her arm with mana, and lowered its head to hook its top canines through her right shoulder garment. With a minor bit of readjustment, it wrenched its head to the side to flip the human onto her back.

With a bit of groaning and a lot of effort on the human's part, they managed to turn her around, despite the pipe's relatively narrow confines.

The wolf lifted its right paw, staring at the jiggling sac of skin attached to the inside of its foreleg. It was *weird.* And mildly repulsive, which was a rare thing for the wolf to think of anything when it'd had to swim through literal rivers of shit more than once in its life.

Regardless, it wasn't like it was going to wound itself to feed the human some blood, so this would do.

It lowered its right paw and lifted its left to poke the human's mouth covering. After a moment of incomprehension, she understood, voluntarily lifting the fabric and opening her mouth. Putting its left paw back down and lifting the right one again as far up as it could, it awkwardly twisted its head, trying to find a decent spot to pierce. After a moment of visualizing, the wolf quickly teared a hole into the sac and hurriedly lined up the thin stream of pinkish blood to land in her mouth, some of the liquid being wasted on her collarbone and hair.

Its consistency was more like water, and the human's confusion was almost a tangible thing that hung in the air as she hurriedly gulped down the liquid.

The steady stream slowed to a trickle, and the wolf, deciding the human had had enough and growing annoyed with holding the awkward pose, curled its leg inward and quickly bit off the skin sac, chomping it down and hurriedly swallowing it.

It had a very strange taste.

"What the fuck . . ." the human whispered, sounding awed and seeming far more . . . energetic, than before.

That was odd, especially considering that her arm was infected, but the wolf didn't pay it much mind, flaring its antennae and using the help of [Tremor Sense] to figure out a decent path to the surface, almost dragging its snout across the pipe's confines. It didn't find much.

The pipe they were in continued to climb upward for two hundred or so feet at a thankfully low angle before curving to the left and going downward. Dragging the human up a steep slope would have been a pain, even with its nigh-inexhaustible body.

It couldn't really feel anything beyond that, so it focused on what was around them, just in case. Which ended up being a bunch of haphazardly, chaotically placed pipes that were either just holes in the stone or pipes of iron that snaked *through* the stone, none of them leading to any kind of open air, and more often than not, having more than a couple of things walking around within them.

As fun as a fight was, the wolf wasn't exactly *looking* for one, so it was going to avoid anything alive for as long as possible.

The pipe they were in was relatively safe, at least, so it was going to drag the human and itself a bit further along and then stop to rest again just before the bend. It didn't really want to explore the unknown with half-healed injuries and with half its minor improvements not having kicked in yet.

As it hooked its canines onto the front of the human's collar and started dragging her up, it was mildly surprised at how helpful and aware the human seemed, using her left arm to assist the wolf, and barely making any sounds. She even gave the wolf one of her buffs to speed them along, which made the awkward backward shuffle a little less tedious.

Maybe she wouldn't be as much of a liability as it thought.

CHAPTER 20

Constantly creating skin sacs full of modified blood to feed the human, eating them, and then repeating the process a couple hours later for what must have been a day or two was fairly boring.

But at least that rest had let it realize some of the mistakes it had made early on before they became a problem.

To start with, the wolf finally realized why its rib had snapped from a mere six-foot drop back in the pit, something that shouldn't have happened from its meager weight and Endurance points, even if the human had added some of her weight onto it.

It had made its bones *too* hard. Bones didn't snap and crack at every impact because they could *bend*, and the wolf had somehow just . . . not considered that. In its attempt to make its bones as hard as possible, it had also made them brittle. Thankfully, taking the connective tissue that made up its bones and making it a little bendier would be easier than it had expected. The idea, surprisingly, came from its eyes.

The insides of its eyes had smooth muscles, which were muscles that were small enough to be on the cellular level, and were numbered in the "billions," a number it couldn't quite conceive of but vaguely understood. These muscles were called ciliary muscles and helped with altering the shape of the lens.

And technically . . . it could also make tendons small enough to be on the cellular level, with them being some of the stretchiest while also relatively tough tissue that bodies had.

It just had to grab a bone and weave microscopic strings of tendon tissue throughout the white strands, partially fusing them together.

And that thought brought it into a rather sudden contemplation.

The new way of using its skill that it had discovered after the fight.

It could directly grasp onto its current body and start making changes, which were affected by time in a normal fashion, like when it stuck its bones together and healed them in a matter of minutes while asleep by using its mind like a physical force, a direct and immediate approach that was severely limited due to the gradual nature of most changes, while this method of use was almost entirely manual.

If it wished to give itself an eye using this method, for example, it would have to sleep for the entire time the alteration took place, or the change would simply stop the moment the wolf stopped paying attention to it. It was only really good for moving in its sleep and for emergency fixes, which it'd never had to do until just now, and probably why it hadn't even unlocked this way of using the skill until then.

The usual way the skill worked was by grasping onto a more conceptual body, with far more time to consider and tweak changes that would only start applying themselves as soon as it decided it was done altering itself.

So, manual, real-time change, or conceptual dreamscape change that would only truly begin once it decided that it was fine with said changes and had let the [Devourer] skill fade away.

Unfortunately, neither option would allow it to just . . . make a copy of its body and test how its new experimental bone would work in practice. So it would have to make a sacrifice.

It picked its right foreleg's humerus, one of the few isolated and relatively easy to break bones, and changed the bone's connective tissue to match its test bone's structure. With that done, and after realizing it'd gotten side-tracked, the wolf went back to what it was doing before the sudden bout of inspiration.

Fixing its mistakes.

The second mistake it had to fix was that it had forgotten to allocate some of the [Devourer] skill's essence to replace the hormone production that its reproductive organs were responsible for, so it quickly did that as well. It could just put the organs in its abdomen, but it preferred to have that space available for something else, whenever it got a good idea.

And after that, it was back to its routine. Create a skin sac full of modified blood, feed the human, bite it off, sleep for the changes to come faster, repeat.

It was boring.

Resting had become boring, a thought it never could have possibly imagined its mind would have.

But its test bone was done, so it had to . . . well, test it. And the only way to test how much damage a bone could take was by trying to break it. The problem was that it *couldn't*. Its body was far, *far* too tough, and the wolf didn't have the strength to snap its right humerus or even *bend it* enough to see how far it could go before snapping, no matter which way it bit itself or tried to find something to slam its leg against.

It was frustrating.

So it went to sleep and decided to use its mind, entering the manual, real-time mode. As it had done before, it manipulated its body now, gripping onto the humerus and using the full force of its mind to grab the two ends before pressing down in the middle of the bone.

It felt the start of a headache at the mental effort, but it *worked*.

Then it used more force, bending the bone as much as it could go. The damage was done on both sides as the strands of hardened connective tissue fused with microscopic tendons strained and frayed, but much to its utter astonishment, the wolf almost managed to take the curved bone and turn it into a gentle crescent shape in the complete opposite direction before it broke.

Even the *way* it broke had changed. Instead of snapping in two on the point of pressure, like a normal bone, it instead pinched and flattened on the sides of the point the wolf was focused on, allowing the bone to bend even further, just a bit, before the strands all started snapping apart.

When the wolf let go, the bone simply moved back into place, albeit slowly. It was damaged, with a lot of the connective tissue snapped and bent out of shape, losing structural integrity, but still able to support weight; still structurally well enough to be useful, not sliding and scraping around in pieces like a normal bone would.

And the bendy nature of the bone would naturally diffuse impact, so while it was softer than its current bone structure, it was far more difficult to break, far more useful *after* breaking, and it was also a natural defense against any attack. It would have to expend some essence from the skill to supply these microscopic strands of tendon tissue with blood and energy to prevent them from drying out, but that was hardly an issue for the foreseeable future.

This . . . was amazing. And it hadn't been anything more than a whim; a random idea it'd decided to test. Despite the pain and the extremely uncomfortable grind of frayed bone writhing in its flesh, it was absolutely ecstatic.

It quickly set the bone to fix itself, which took a few minutes more to heal than its current ones, and after having confirmed the usefulness of its experiment, it changed every single bone in the same way and applied the change, which would only take a day to fully complete, before setting the skill to take whatever essence it needed to keep the fused microtendons from atrophying and drying out.

It wasn't a lot, thankfully. A rodent a day, maybe?

Then it woke up again with a massive, satisfying stretch, feeling like it was finally ready to face whatever mess its antennae were informing it of up ahead.

It wasn't difficult to interpret; it was just strange. After a hundred or so feet down from the bend of the pipe, the sensation of rock tightly surrounding the pipes suddenly cut off, which meant open air. It was some kind of cube-shaped vertical tunnel through which went a ton of pipes, many connected to something distant and many just rusting away. Dangerous terrain at best.

Still, it wished to make sure it wasn't passing by an easy opportunity to get to the surface, and they would have to go through there to continue anyway.

It bent down and hooked its canines into the human's clothes, but before it could drag her, she started struggling, putting her hand on the iron pipe and pushing away.

"Wait, wait. Stop," she said, and the wolf stopped with a confused grumble, unhooking its teeth from her garment.

She brought her injured arm to splay out by her side using some weird mana technique, then started making a strange . . . sawing motion?

"Cut. Uh . . . bite. Bite this off," she whispered, gesturing and poking toward her injured arm's shoulder.

It tilted its head. Did she want it to lick her wounds?

It moved forward and nosed her left hand away, hooking its canines on the shredded remnants of cloth around her arm.

Mentally ordering its teeth to not cut through skin, a command of dubious effect, it quickly but carefully moved back, cutting through the cloth. It stopped at her shoulder then straightened, letting the crusty fabric peel away.

It didn't really need its eyes to know the limb was infected beyond saving. The stench was quite vile. Licking it wouldn't really accomplish anything but leave the wolf with a bad taste in its mouth.

The human was starting to breathe harder, but after a moment of inaction, she resumed with her strange motions, making her hand and fingers flat before making a chopping motion at her shoulder, repeating that *Cut* word constantly.

It had no idea what she was trying to convey, and just continued staring at her, tilting its head this way and that.

Then she curled her fingers into rough approximations of claws and closed them around her upper arm before making some sort of sudden jerky motion by twisting her wrist outward.

"Come *on*, please. I'm sure you can understand. Cut!" she whisper-hissed at it, and the wolf grumble-growled at her, perplexed.

She growled, much like itself, then blindly extended a hand toward its snout. Confused but not particularly alarmed, it allowed her to paw at its neck before finding its muzzle, which she gently but insistently guided toward her arm.

With a sort of baffled curiosity, it lowered itself into a crouch and allowed the human to press its snout into her upper arm, despite the ugly scent clogging the air. Then she jammed her fingers under its jowls, and it grumble-whined in confusion as she tried to wiggle her fingers between its teeth, curling its lips open and tonguing at her filthy fingers out of instinct.

It was beyond confused at this point, so with a mixture of confusion and curiosity, it relaxed its jaws, ordering its teeth to be blunt. The human hooked her finger at its bottom canine and twisted her wrist to use the back of her palm, forcing the wolf's jaws open. With its mouth stupidly hanging agape, it waited to see what she was trying to do.

She raised her hand, clumsily pawing at its newly healed ear, before grabbing onto its fur and tugging down until its jaws were surrounding her arm, then she used some sort of mana pressure to close its lower jaw, a fairly gentle touch, and pressed down on its snout with her functioning hand.

Then she tightened both of her holds, grinding its teeth against her arm, and pushed away.

"Cut. Cut."

The realization was sudden.

It was mildly embarrassing that it hadn't understood sooner. The human was asking it *to bite her arm off*. Of course she was; the thing was completely useless at this point, just weighing them both down, and infected on top of that.

Its mental evaluation of the human went up a little bit.

Just to show her it understood, the wolf tightened its jaws on its own and allowed its teeth to cut *slightly*, just breaking the skin. The human's breath hitched before resuming, fast-paced, as she settled back on the pipe, lifting her hand to the top of its head and aggressively petting it between the ears. Some . . . form of approval?

"Yes, yes. Just . . . bite it off. C-Cut."

It chuffed as best as it could around her rather thin arm, testing with its tongue to make sure it could cut through her arm in a single clean yank. It was rather surprised to note that it *felt* like it could, just a thin strip of flesh maybe remaining after it pulled its head back, its canines just a *little* too short to meet.

. . . When had its canines grown so large?

Actually, had the human become smaller?

Leaving aside those thoughts, it lowered itself and lightly growled in warning. The human's hand left as she placed her wrist in her own mouth.

"Cfuuht," she urged, muffled by her wrist, and the wolf did exactly that.

It let its teeth cut at full capacity and yanked its head away, backing up a step. Thin strings of flesh and two thin strips of bone kept the arm connected, so it quickly jumped forward and bit down on the arm, twisting its head to break the bone and yank it away, snapping the thin strings of muscles and leaving behind a flat, bleeding surface. It quickly dropped the arm by its side, mildly concerned about how the human would stop the bleeding.

Surely she had *something* to fix the problem.

Before it could be concerned about blood loss, the human placed her functioning arm to the stump through panicked, gurgling breaths that barely held back screams of pain. Sparks filled the tunnel, making its unadjusted eyes snap shut, light bouncing around its retinas as it shook its head.

This time she couldn't hold back, letting out a long, guttural groan, her back arching, her neck tendons standing out under her skin like strained cables as her body jerked and heaved. Wheezing, harsh breaths were let out in rapid succession as blood dripped down from the stump, and with a determined snarl worthy of a wolf, the human activated the spark skill again.

Before she could make any more sounds, the wolf darted forward and turned its leg to the side before it shoved its foreleg in her mouth just above its elbow, activating [Echoes of Oblivion] to devour the sound waves coming out of her throat. It wasn't just grating to its sensitive ears; the wolf was mildly paranoid about someone or something hearing them.

It did *not* want to fight anything in a pipe.

It hadn't considered the human's bite, but besides hurting a bit, it didn't do much, so it wasn't concerned, instead trying to figure how to best get rid of the light swimming across its vision. Light that had a couple of shades of yellow more than it remembered ever seeing, which meant the changes to its eyes' color spectrum were close to finishing.

Blinking rapidly did nothing to get rid of it, though, and it couldn't use its other leg to rub its eyes unless it wished to put its entire weight on the human's mouth and teeth, which it didn't.

The majority of the human's sounds were eaten by the wolf's skill, but her hasty, wheezing breaths, intermingled with whimpers and groans, were still impossible to silence completely, escaping from her nostrils and through her chest, muffled.

It was also more than a little confused on why the human was using sparks on herself, so it bent forward to investigate, peering between her quivering hand and the stump with an awkward half hop.

The stump was cooked black, and much to its surprise, it wasn't bleeding at all, even if its shape had changed, a far more uneven surface from before.

Actually, it shouldn't be surprised. Burning the blood vessels would obviously seal them and stop the bleeding, but there was a certain detachment between the knowledge provided by its skill and its own inherent naivete of the world.

The wolf still wanted to get going. It was getting rather tired of being stuck in one place or another. The human was still recuperating from the loss of one of her limbs, however, so it grumbled and opted to wait a little, even if she wouldn't be doing any of the work. It yawned, only having gotten up from its sleep a couple minutes ago, and clacked its teeth shut before turning to the infected limb it had discarded. The scent of fresh blood and burnt meat was making it hungry, even as it mixed with the cloying stench of infection and rot.

The human definitely had no use for the limb anymore . . .

It lifted its foreleg out from between the human's clenched teeth, pleased that she was only panting and groaning now, and lifted the murky darkness from its leg to conserve mana, quickly trotting over to where it had dropped the sickly limb and snatching it up in its jaws.

Then it circled once, sat down, and placed the arm between its front paws to gnaw at it.

The taste was mostly the same, simply undercut by a slimy, tough texture and an oddly chemical smell, all on the outer flesh. Pus just tasted like mucus, thankfully, so that was easily ignorable.

The human started making some strange sounds like hissing grunts again, and it clicked its teeth shut before chuffing in acknowledgement. The wolf wasn't sure if she was trying to draw its attention, but it might as well let her know it was listening.

Then it continued eating.

"Y-You . . . you are eating . . . *pffttt* . . . ahahaha . . ." She trailed off, her barking yips gradually combining with a long, drawn-out groan, then transitioning into coughs. "Sha-meless m-*utt*," she muttered through her coughs before continuing her slow, wheezing breaths.

Minutes passed by in relative silence, the quiet only interrupted by snapping bone and tearing flesh, until the wolf eventually finished the limb and licked up a stray finger it had missed.

It quickly chewed the appendage and swallowed, observing the human.

With its snack finished and the human relatively quiet, it licked its chops and moved toward her, quickly finding a decent spot to bite on before awkwardly shuffling until the human was side by side with the wolf.

This . . . wasn't going to work. The pipes were too narrow to let the wolf face whatever was ahead *while* dragging the human. It shuffled around a bit more, struggling to find a decent position where it could use its eyes, before it promptly gave up and returned to its previous position, back end facing toward the unknown.

The scrape of the human's coverings against the rusty iron, including her metal-clad feet, were worryingly loud in the silence that surrounded them, but the wolf ignored it, as the scrape rattled the pipe a bit and allowed it to get a half-decent feel of the layout with [Tremor Sense].

The human gave it one of her boosts, and their trip toward the open-aired section of the pipes hastened, its confidence from the Perception boost helping just as much as the boost in Speed.

Even with that and the rather steep downward curve, it took a couple minutes to get to where they should be.

With one last, long drag, it let go of the human, lowering its head to brush against the bottom of the pipe, antennae flaring.

A foot or so behind them, all sensation in that direction just *stopped* before the vibrations snaked around the cubic hole and continued. Twenty or so feet wide, with multiple pipes snaking through, and very, *very* deep.

It turned around and, with a mild sense of nervousness, stepped away from the comfortable grip of the stone holding the pipe in place over an endless drop. Not being able to see said endless drop, surprisingly, didn't help all that much in quelling its nerves. It gingerly tapped with its foot, feeling the vibrations travel through the metal, telling it what he was dealing with. Nails, metallic tubes framed around the pipe, thin sheets of metal bracing—all relatively firm, but rusted and far too jittery for its liking.

It took a couple feet before it found a spot it knew was safe enough to cut a hole into without accidentally damaging the bracings; one that it was picturing as just large enough to stick its head out of and see if there was something outside that could help them reach the surface.

Actually cutting the hole was a lot more annoying than it had expected it would be, mostly due to the thickness of the pipe, but after a couple minutes of awkwardly tilting its head side to side and scraping its nails against the iron, it had a round, jagged hole to stick its head through. And a lot of small cuts on its gums, but it had grown used to it at this point.

The fact that the iron piece it had cut out only hit something after a solid ten seconds of falling was almost as concerning as the sight of a hole that had no start or end, its head tilting up and down in disbelief.

They couldn't have gone *that* far down . . . right? The pit was deep . . . and then they'd dropped a bit more, then gone up, and then they'd gone a little bit further down . . .

No, they didn't really go down *this* much. There was no way. Was there?

Unless the surface above tilted upward in the direction they'd moved in, this didn't make much sense. Either that, or the wolf hadn't been paying enough attention.

The view was almost reminiscent of the terrain around the burning rivers. Just an endless expanse that faded out of sight. And its eyesight was *better* than then, too, even if only a little bit, yet it still couldn't see the top or bottom.

It swiveled its head. Pipes—some metal, some steel, some smelling faintly of lead, all rusting away. The metal rods supporting them were so warped by rust they were almost deformed, lumpy, as if infected by tumors. Foul-smelling water tainted by something that smelled faintly like the rivers of fire dripped down from the inscrutable expanse above and slithered from one pipe to the next in a slow descent, the tapping of drops hitting metal the only sound in the foreboding silence, aside from the faint echo of the metal circle the wolf had cut out impacting things from below.

The only illumination in the entire hole came from the odd, tiny mushroom clinging to a pipe, glowing a faint yellow green. Though for all it knew, it could be glowing in any one of the colors its eyes couldn't quite perceive yet.

Seeing nothing that would help them, and with some instinctive part of itself squirming in discomfort over being suspended over such immense height, it carefully moved its head back through the hole and turned to move deeper down the pipe, see if there was anything of note or alarm before it stumbled into it back end first.

"W-Wait. Hello? Don't . . . don't leave me here . . . please? Hello?" the human called out from the other side of the pipe, sounding oddly scared and pleading. Likely scared of the wolf just leaving her there to starve.

Some small part of it was pleased that it was starting to properly interpret emotion from the human's sounds.

The wolf gave her a short, howlish bark in reply, which it suffused with a feeling of reassurance from [Logotexnia], before turning around and continuing to move down the pipe.

The human said nothing more, thankfully, and it stomped its feet a couple times with its nose brushing against the iron.

The pipe was surprisingly sturdy, so it wasn't particularly worried about bringing the human over. Up ahead, however, the pipe continued downward, flanked by mostly stone, with the odd sensation of another pipe brushing past its senses. It didn't want to go *down*, but it didn't really see any other option. Even if it had *no idea* how deep this stupid pipe went.

With a faint grumble of annoyance, a vocal habit it had picked up by constantly being around a creature who needed sonic reassurance of its presence, it trotted back to the human, preparing itself for another long bout of boring dragging.

It was almost *wishing* that some annoying rodent would pop up already just to have something to toy with for a couple minutes.

She didn't quite know what the hell the dog-shaped beast had been giving her to drink, but it was either some expensive potion or some *extremely* high-quality blood. Where it had gotten it from, she also didn't know.

What she did know was that that absurd boost she'd gained from the Blood Drinker trait was the nail in the coffin that had sealed her decision. It had been as good a time as any to get rid of the arm, and she had, with a grit and tenacity that would have at least gotten an approving nod from her father, were he around. Even if she'd fallen asleep a couple minutes after.

The cauterized wound still hurt *so goddamn much* that she could only try and find other things to focus on, lest she make more noise than she already was making. She focused on the strange, tasteless caress of thick, misty smoke that had filled her mouth when the beast had put its leg in her mouth to bite on. She focused on the fact that they must have been travelling for at least a full day, and they just kept going *down and down*, farther and farther from the surface, as if they were descending to the depths of hell itself.

Moving her focus from pain to anxiety wasn't the best trade-off, but it worked to some extent.

She used a bit more mana than could be justified to add a slight repulsion field to her iron greaves, just enough for them to float off the pipe, taking the short stops the beast frequently made to recuperate.

Part of her really wanted the beast to give her more of its superblood, because the boost was slowly fading—like blood slowly leaving her body from an open wound—and she hated the feeling. The sensation of every attribute getting a boost whenever it gave her the blood was like a punch to the senses, the crack of a whip, the rush of a drug, and a pleasant sensation she felt like she could *really* use right now.

The beast unhooked its teeth from her shredded clothes and walked away again, likely just scouting ahead, exactly as it had done all the other times.

But it went a lot farther, until she could barely even hear its claws tapping away at the pipe.

And farther, until only the faint echo of its steps caressed her ears.

And even that faded.

It didn't make sense for it to leave her here after all the trouble it had gone through to help her, after the . . . the connection, the *something* that had built between them. She knew that; she knew that it didn't make sense for it to just abandon her here.

But the beast never made sense. It rarely played to her expectations, and the thought made her chest tight and her guts coil into a ball of anxiety and stress.

A minute passed, each second stretching to infinity to become an hour.

Two minutes passed, only the whispers of her mind to keep her company.

And it whispered, mocking, yet concerned and truthful. *What if it never stops walking away and leaves you here to die and rot in a pipe where nobody can hear you scream, and the chitters of rats creep ever closer as the pipe tightens around you, and you can't even crawl away—*

Oh, she knew this feeling.

She was panicking.

She breathed in stuttered gasps—feeling like a smithy press was crushing her rib cage, like her heart was being pulped in an icy fist—and she raised a hand to ground herself, her trembling grasp pressing into uneven, wet rust.

The air was humid—too humid. Like water, like slime, like blood, and she couldn't breathe.

Her next exhale came out in a sob.

"H-Hello? Pl-please! Please, please, come back, please come back, please come back, pleasecomebackpleasecomebackpleasecomeback . . . ease . . . ack . . . " she babbled, her voice lowering with every word, replaced by panting, wheezing exhales as the tunnel closed in around her.

Her hand remained at a constant distance, but her mind didn't care; it *knew* that a vise of iron coiled around her, crushing her, and she couldn't breathe. She opened her mouth to cry for it to come back, cry for help, and she couldn't. She could only wheeze uselessly, as if her vocal cords simply didn't exist, and she couldn't scream, she couldn't see, she couldn't smell anything but the stabbing scent of iron, of copper, of blood and rot. She couldn't move, she couldn't breathe, she couldn't see, shecouldn'tmoveshecouldn'tmov eshecouldn'tbreatheshecouldn'tseeshecouldn'tmoveshecouldn'tbreatheshecou ldn'tseeshecouldn'tmoveshecouldn'tbreatheshecouldn'tseeshecouldn'tmovesh ecouldn'tbreatheshecouldn'ts—

The steady pound of steps approached rapidly, a loud, reassuring bark echoing through the tunnel, snaking through the iron, vibrating in her bones.

She gasped in air, sharply, as deep as her lungs would allow, until something in her rib cage popped, and a sliver of sense returned to her frantic mind.

The freezing, lumpy press of iron receded against her skin, let go of her shoulders, lifted its steel boot from her ribs, just a little bit. Just enough to recognize the rapid clinking of nails impacting iron.

Her mind swam and twisted, and her hand, already rubbed raw from trying to help the beast move her, finally bled, warm drops of liquid pooling in her scrambling, shaky palm as it pushed desperately against the constricting steel pressing into her. It tickled, running down her malnourished forearm as she wheezed in rapid, desperate breaths.

It was fine. It was coming back. It was fine, it was coming, it was fine, it wasn't leaving her behind—

A snout nosed at her face covering with a concerned whine, and the iron bent away, just a bit, just a bit, just enough for her to let go of her grip and latch on to whatever furry part of the beast she could reach and yank it onto herself, feeling its chest and scrambling legs impact her collarbone and squirm against her chest as she curled her arm around its neck to grasp onto its opposite shoulder as she just . . .

Held it there; held it against her chest, burying her face into its fur, the scent of filth and wet dog being the single best thing that had ever graced her nostrils as she sobbed in relief.

It was back; it was fine. Everything was fine. She wasn't alone; she wasn't going to die without anyone to even know or care. She was fine. It was all okay. It was good; she was fine. And the dog, the beast, the monster—she didn't care anymore. It could be a horrific abomination from the deepest depths of the void for all she gave a shit. She was just happy that it didn't abandon her.

She let it grumble in confusion as she just held it with one arm, uncaring of its shuffling legs bruising her sternum, babbling thankful gibberish into its ribs, into its fur, frantically petting its back down to its head and tightening her hold whenever it tried to squirm out until it stopped trying, until her burning lungs stopped spewing her panic into the rust-scented air.

Maybe later she would be embarrassed about her behavior or would chastise herself for treating a dangerous beast like a hug pillow. But at the moment, she couldn't care less.

CHAPTER 21

While it had been rather uncomfortable at the start to be restrained against another living being, despite the obvious lack of any hostile intent, the wolf quickly grew to appreciate it. It reminded it of hazy, barely comprehensible memories of doing the same thing with kin, so distorted and distant from what it knew that it was half certain they were just some vague concoctions of its dreams which the wolf had fooled itself into thinking were memories.

Which was quite likely.

Regardless, the urgent need to move remained at the forefront of its mind, because it had *finally* found what it had been looking for this entire time: an ending to this absurdly long pipe in the form of some strangely large metal fan cowering behind a rusted grate. That was the whole reason it had gone so far to check, which it suspected was the cause of the human's delirious panic.

Eventually, her breaths evened out and her hold grew loose, so the wolf squirmed and wiggled off from its awkward position atop her sternum to start dragging her again.

They had about five hundred feet to go still, which would take . . . a lot of time. Maybe a day, actually.

Where were the damn rodents when entertainment was needed . . .

With a heavy exhale akin to the human's sighs, it bit into her garments and began pulling.

It unhooked its canines from the human's coverings and turned around, stomping one foot with its antennae brushing against the dusty, wet confines of the pipe. The complete and utter lack of any light down here really made it all the more appreciative of [Tremor Sense] and its antennae.

Unfortunately, it inhaled through its nose without thinking, leading to a minute-long bout of uncontrollable sneezing, the human's happy, barking yips oddly successful at lifting its mood, even if it was pretty sure she was having fun at its expense.

With a dry exhale from its nose, it moved forward a few feet, focusing on the idle machine a couple dozen feet from where it'd left the human.

It could just cut through the outer grate with its teeth, but frankly, that would both be extremely annoying—simply due to how much wet dust was clinging to the iron—and time-consuming.

Maybe it was being too thoughtless, but it had been stuck dragging the human for . . . it had no idea how long by now. It was extremely, unimaginably bored, extremely irritated, and extremely impatient, feeling the beginnings of delirium starting to slowly settle. The tension and unease of constantly skulking through an endless pipe had long since worn out, especially after it had straightened. The wolf just wanted out, ***now***.

So it lowered into a crouch, activated [Bloodrush], and charged at the grate.

It had enough room to turn so that its shoulder took the impact, so it did just that. The thick, crisscrossing metal wires bent and even broke apart at some points, but still held. It hastily stepped back and repeated the process, a deafening, short screech rushing through the tunnel and the giant room beyond the machine as the grate tilted back, only a couple fragile nails holding it in place as dust and rust powder flew everywhere, choking the air.

Even if it got through the grate, there was still a fan behind it, and then another grate.

Remembering the human's skill, it backtracked to her and put its hind leg on her shoulder, lightly pushing her with a chuff, insistently poking her arm. After a couple seconds, she understood, giving it the Speed boost by tapping its thigh.

Its perception of the giant room beyond became clearer, sharper, and with a hundred more details than it needed to know. It was a gigantic rectangle filled with all manner of trash and containers, its height cut into two equal parts by a thin floor of metal with staircases on either end, a few rods of thick, sturdy iron running across the room to support the sheet floor.

And the outer grate hiding behind the rusty fan was a lot less shaky than the first, it idly noted.

It prepared itself for a nasty bruise, then charged again, dozens of feet of distance vanishing in an instant as it engaged every muscle and tendon it had at full force, the rusty iron below its feet breaking as its nails dug in for added traction.

The grate gave in instantly, caving in before detaching and slamming into the fan with the deafening, rattling boom of metal protesting its fate. The thin metal rods holding the fan in place broke as well, sending the combined weight of the wolf and the shattered scrap slamming into the outer grate.

It was at this moment that the wolf realized it had *vastly* overrated how strong the outer grate was, and that it had put far too much power into its charge.

It hastily tried to throw a paw out to dig its nails into the pipe, but it was going too fast, and its capability of bending its leg sideways was as useless as ever, only barely managing to graze its nails against the edge of the pipe before it disappeared.

With a surprised yelp, it tumbled through the air for a second, full of mild panic and uncertainty, only to smash into the rusty metal flooring shoulders first, its tailbone slamming into the sheet right after. The concentrated force punched through the thin rusty metal and made a jagged hole that cut off at the middle of its back.

Its bottom half immediately plunged through, and its momentum combined with the weight of its lower body to yank its upper body through the hole, getting a thin cut on its chest from slamming into the sheet as its forelegs scrambled to find something to hook its nails into to no avail, tumbling backward.

The second drop wasn't nearly as forgiving as the first, the hard stone not bending in the slightest under its weight as it struck the ground with a meaty thud.

Its lungs expelled all the air out in a sharp, short wheeze. The wolf could only lay on its side in shock for a moment at the sensation of impact traveling through its body to punch into its heart, prompting it to skip a beat before it redoubled its pace.

That was a *horrible* sensation, even if its Endurance made sure the wolf's body tanked the drop with only a bunch of bruises and a minor cut across its chest.

Flakes of rust and miscellaneous debris rained down on the wolf as it rolled onto its feet and started lightly coughing, trying to get its lungs to recuperate from the impact and start functioning normally again, even through the dust and rust powder utterly saturating the air.

It was under the impression that it had a few moments to take stock of its situation and recover, figure out how it was going to get the human down, and maybe get a better understanding of the layout of whatever strange place they'd stumbled into.

That notion was quickly invalidated by the rapidly approaching taps of something hard impacting stone, making the wolf go rigid as it quickly bent its head down with its antennae out, tail stiff and pain forgotten as it strained to calm its breaths.

Like ripples of water in an ocean made of stonework, the vibrations traveled through the distant floor, crawled up the wall separating them from the entity, slithered between pipes and wires, then eventually reached the wolf.

Six tapering points would slam into stone before repositioning, leading up to a roughly oval-shaped segmented body, the added boost to its senses allowing it to feel how the vibrations moved through the entity's body before losing cohesion when they entered its almost . . . liquid insides.

Useless information. As it rapidly approached, the wolf ignored the minute details and the human's calls, focusing on what it could discern that would be to its advantage. The insectoid-seeming creature was fairly fast for being a little larger than the wolf, about twice as heavy, and covered in some sort of external skeleton, but nothing that could outrun the wolf.

Some primal part of itself, a feral animal that was always at the edge of its consciousness, grew fearful. In the dark, with its nose choked by dust and rust, with *something* it had never seen before steadily approaching, it grew stiff, unsure of what to do, and overcome with the urge to hide or run.

Seeing as it didn't have anywhere *to* run, it activated [Echoes of Oblivion] and gently lowered itself into a crouch, antennae still caressing the floor. As it got closer, the wolf grew even stiffer, the sound of the creature's steps unfortunately drowned out by the human's calls.

It was *very* tempted to bark at her or something similar just to tell her to stop giving the enemy a clear direction to follow, but it didn't wish to reveal its presence yet, focusing instead on what it could tell about the approaching threat.

The creature sped up, likely lured by the human's increasingly panicked calls, and the wolf remained stock-still. It recalled all it knew about insects, which was . . . more than most, it assumed, but not that much. This thing wasn't a cockroach.

It had, frankly, nothing to work with.

The insectoid approached, and the wolf focused on the wall separating them, scanning for entry points. There were a few rectangular holes filled with broken shards of something on the top of the room, but they were far too high. The most likely point of entry was the thin metal door sitting on the right end of the room, something the wolf was certain the insect could easily crash through.

As the enemy came closer, just a dozen feet from the wall, it seemed to suddenly stop, its acceleration suddenly vanishing as if in defiance of physics, a startling, unnatural thing to feel. Its legs had definitely taken the force of a sudden stop, as the wolf felt that through the floor, but it was still just . . . a tiny bit too unsettling to feel like a natural movement.

Or the wolf was simply uneasy with its lack of sight and projected that emotion onto random details. That felt equally possible.

For a long couple seconds, the creature's legs changed position, showing the wolf how it seemed to be swinging its body from side to side a little, as if observing the wall with eyes it shouldn't have, considering the absolute absence of light so far down into the earth's guts.

Then it resumed, but its movements had changed, the frenzied pace replaced by a steady, predatory prowl which made the hairs on the wolf's back stand up in a bristle. The creature approached the wall, then seemed to get up on its two hind legs, its four frontal limbs settling against the surface.

And after a second of inaction, it started *crawling up the wall.*

The wolf's antennae froze in place, its mind sputtering in confusion.

. . . That thing was at *least* twice as heavy as the wolf, or so it felt like. Probably almost as heavy as the human. There was *no way* it could just . . . walk up a vertical surface. That didn't make sense. How? Mana skills?

Its antennae resumed their frantic writhing, noting the insect was losing that cautious hesitance in its steps, moving faster and faster and quickly crawling up the twenty-foot wall. Yet, there was a strange pause each time it put one of its legs down.

The wolf focused on that pause and noted how the pull of its weight would somehow be dispersed along a flat, circular area at the tip of each foot. That area would then slowly retreat back to the tip of its leg, and the insect would reposition it higher before spreading that circle of influence again.

And once it got through the holes on the top, it would be on the iron floor above the wolf, with a clear and simple path toward the human.

There were stairs on both ends of the room that lead up to the metal floor above, so the wolf quickly bounded over to them before gingerly, and with the utmost attention paid to the vibrations at its feet, moving up to the second floor.

The wolf's skill might make it soundless and sightless to others, but its weight still had impact, it still caused vibrations, so it needed to get into position as fast as possible, lest the insect notice lingering aftershocks—assuming it had some kind of vibrational senses like the cockroaches it had consumed.

The pipe the human was yelling from was at about the middle of the room, along with two others on either side, equally spaced out near the ceiling and parallel to the rectangular holes on the other side of the room where the insect was about to go through.

The wolf gingerly tapped at the rusty iron below its feet to locate where the supports were hidden, and hopped from one to the other, the thin sheets they were supporting obviously unable to take any weight at their center. It had to get to . . .

It paused, its legs still tense for a jump.

It didn't know where it wanted to be. Why was it even up here? What was the plan. How was it going to ambush a creature when it didn't have a single clue where its vitals or weak points were, much less what senses it had?

The wolf was going to be fighting something it couldn't see, and after the fight had started, vibrations, hearing, and smell wouldn't help it all that much. It would be fighting something while effectively blind. Something heavy, foreign, and dangerous, in territory it was unfamiliar with.

But what was the alternative? To just . . . let the insect eat the human while the wolf smashed through the door on the bottom right of the room and ran for its life?

For a moment, it considered it.

The sound of crunching glass only made its breaths deeper, anticipation, dread, and a hesitant sense of eagerness bubbling in its chest.

It could just run. The human was making a racket; it could easily slip away and trundle through endless corridors and tunnels until it found its way back to the surface.

The room was filled with sudden banging, the tapping of the insect growing frantic for a moment as its leg punched through a sheet of metal and it hurriedly righted itself before cautiously testing the terrain with every step, slowing down even further.

The wolf could run away. The creature was still on the other side of the room, almost fifty feet away, and stuck in a grid of rusty pitfalls.

But why would it?

Why *should it* just let whatever fancied itself as a predator threaten its pack, bizarre as it might be? Why should it continue to be timid in the face of genuine danger, only hunting within its comfort zone and running with its tail between its legs whenever it faced something new?

Besides, it had spent hours on end fantasizing about getting something to fight—getting to feel that adrenaline rush again, that tension and exhilaration it had felt when wreathed in screeching rodents; that sick rush that danced the finest of lines between ecstasy and despair, where one wrong move would lead to death—simply to alleviate its boredom in that endless pipe.

Not to mention all the things it could gain from eating this thing. What if the wolf could learn how to just *walk up walls?*

A bone-deep greed urged it to tear this insect apart for its own benefit.

The creature was twenty feet away, minutes passing in what felt like seconds as the wolf stood still, frantically contemplating.

The human's clothes scraped against the pipe as she slowly—and with a lot of struggling—dragged herself toward the mouth of the pipe, the observation only a mild background process as its thoughts continued to race while the foreboding taps crept closer.

It couldn't detect many more details, despite the close range. Segmented chitin plates, tear-shaped body, six legs, and two chitinous fangs on the front. No antennae it could feel. Very little to go with.

Until it realized something obvious. For it to be following the human's voice, it obviously had to have ears of some sort. It could have come here from the vibrations caused by the wolf's fall, but if that was the case . . .

The wolf, muscles tense and lips curling into a soundless snarl in preparation, tapped the metal with its paw.

The creature didn't react, continuing its prowl in a straight line toward the human.

No vibration senses. The wolf's lips fell to cover its teeth again.

A plan began to form. A crude, haphazard one, but it didn't have all that much time for thinking at the moment as the insect moved past the wolf, only ten feet in front of it and a couple feet from the wall. The human was still only halfway to the pipe's exit, thankfully.

It tapped a paw, visualizing the grid of metal supports and where the plates were at their weakest, idly noting a small rusty canister a foot to its left, among other bits of useless debris littering both floors.

Its thoughts lingered for a fraction of a second on the can.

The wolf stretched its neck and weight as carefully as it could manage, bit through the can's circular corner, and with a flick of its neck, sent it crashing and rolling across the floor behind the insect, to its left.

The creature stopped in its tracks, one of its legs no longer touching the metal, sitting frozen in the air.

A stalemate.

The insect had definitely heard that, but it had no real information besides thinking that *something* was at its left side, while the wolf was actually positioned to its right. So it just froze, despite the obvious prey just a few feet in front and above it making a racket with her grunts and huffs.

A far smarter foe than the stupid rats.

But it didn't matter, because it had coincidentally stopped exactly where the wolf wanted it to—right beside a six-foot-wide square of wobbly iron. A heavy enemy with a hard exoskeleton on fragile terrain? It was just *asking* to be exploited, and if the wolf made it crash on that plate with enough force, it would probably fall through.

A ten-foot gap stretched between them, with an awkward running start but then a clear path.

Its boosts had already faded during the tense, long minutes it had taken for the insect to climb up the wall, down, and crawl across the metal floor. [Bloodrush] was ready and begging to be used again, so the wolf obliged, its nails partially cutting through the supports for added traction as it charged forward, putting its feet only where the support rods would bear the sheets and its weight.

Two, three bounds, and it turned its head, ready to shoulder slam the insect into a ten-foot drop, hopefully injuring it enough so it bled out, or whatever it had in place of blood. Or at the very least disabled it somewhat.

Instead of smashing into its legs from the side, however, the wolf found its shoulder smashing into the insect's abdomen, its pointed legs curling inward from the impact and stabbing through the wolf's fur and skin, one at its left shoulder and the other at its right side, while the others flailed for purchase.

But it didn't have the leverage to bite the wolf with its weird chitin fangs, and the creature's legs were barely half an inch into its flesh, so in that fragment of a second before the insect was launched away, the wolf was certain its plan had worked. Only, it was disproven yet again when something goopy and unimaginably sticky came out of the insect's legs, pulling it alongside as they tumbled over each other back onto a fragile sheet of metal, which bent and cracked under their weight.

On top of a writhing mass of chitin, the wolf bucked and twisted, struggling to get a grip on something or at least try to bite a leg off, but the insect quickly yanked it around by the shoulder and side, not allowing it to orientate itself nor properly twist around to bite it, the wolf's legs simply flailing in the air.

Its struggles became even more desperate as four more legs stabbed at its fur—one on its chest and the rest on its sides—secreting that sticky goop and pinning the wolf even more. Maybe if its fur was more fragile, it could have simply twisted until the goop tore it off to allow the wolf to maneuver, but its body was so tough because of Endurance that it simply did not have the strength to, only able to twist its upper body away from the searching fangs of the insect.

The metal underneath them made another cracking sound as it bent outward even more from their struggle, and the wolf deactivated [Echoes of Oblivion] to snarl as loudly as it could and buck its hips up, then down, with enough strength to feel its muscles burn and protest.

The sheet finally broke, and the wolf fell for the third time, pinned in place on the insect's hard underbelly.

An underbelly which cracked alongside its back plating when they quickly slammed into the floor, the impact once more stealing the wolf's breath.

The human was yelling something, questioning. Meanwhile, the insectoid didn't let out a single sound as it pushed the wolf off its belly into the air before swinging it to the left, then the right, its goopy liquids spreading over the wolf's writhing limbs and body. It slowly built momentum while the wolf snarled and struggled, and with a particularly wide swing, it used the wolf's weight to turn itself over onto its side, the wolf's ribs smashing into hard stone.

Despite having contact with the floor, the wolf could barely even move, the goop moving as if sentient to restrain it, even working against its every movement. If it curled its spine inward, it pulled outward; if it curled outward, the goop pulled it inward, and combined with the insect's legs, it couldn't even try to brace its legs against the ground.

Its lungs burned, its eyes bulged, and its breaths came out in snarling pants as the goop on its chest crawled up its throat, fear and panic starting to claw at its mind as every movement became harder by the second.

The human's yells gave it a single second of clarity, and it quickly gathered air in its lungs and infused them with mana, a sense of desperation and fear, before letting its vocal cords shape it into a loud yowl toward the human, hoping she'd have . . . *something*, some way of helping it.

The slime reached the middle of its forelegs, pulling them together before connecting, tightening them against its chest while it let out sounds of panic, snarls, and whimpers as it uselessly tried to twist its neck to bite something, anything, each sharp crack of its teeth vainly slamming into each other feeling like another nail in its coffin. It couldn't even reach the leg that was digging into its chest.

Something like a complex network of ropes was running through the sticky goop and tugging the wolf into whatever position it wished, giving the slime far, far more durability than something of that consistency should have.

The rush it had felt when the fight started had turned into nothing but naked dread, the encroaching possibility of death scraping at its mind like jagged shards of glass, higher thought flaking off with every scrape as it wriggled in its bonds, barely able to move.

The insect curled its legs in, dragging the wolf closer to its fangs.

In a moment of panic, it poured every single drop of mana it had into a [Sonic Blast], the air coiling in its lungs like a serpent ready to strike, then slammed the ball of air and sound through its throat, once again tearing out its vocal cords in a spray of blood.

With its mind and proximity keeping the air and sound compressed into a tight ball, the wolf tilted its open maw toward the insect's face—up and to the side, its snout almost brushing against the creature's fangs—and barely managed to maintain a connection with the blast for long enough to tilt its head away before it detonated, wrenching its head down to almost smack into its own chest as something went *crack pop* in its spine, causing its limbs to spasm in their restraints before going limp.

A sharp crack of thunder rumbled throughout the underbelly of the third floor as the rusty metal above them exploded outward with a deafening cacophony of sound that the wolf couldn't hear, entire sections of the metal flooring above losing or bending their rusty supports from the overpowering blast.

A moment before unconsciousness consumed its damaged brain, it felt the straining press of a single fang struggling to pierce through its skin and fur.

CHAPTER 22

She'd already spent almost half the mana in her body to get to the lip of the damn pipe, and now, she didn't know what to do, panting from exertion as she deactivated [Telemantic Construct], the only thing which had allowed her atrophied arm to drag her body the distance.

An almost frantic sense of urgency pushed her forth, and she spent a quarter of the mana in her body on a self-applied [Haste] spell, casting [Mana Conduit] the moment it came off cooldown again.

Her hearing was already little else but a steady whine which dug into her brain like a drill, so the Perception boost quickly made her realize just how loud things could become beyond her usual audial range. Yet, due to how Perception worked, she didn't have to worry about a headache so much as the creeping suspicion that she'd be hearing that whine in her mind for months even without it existing.

Letting out a groan as she cracked her neck, she then dragged her collarbone over the end of the pipe with her rubbed-raw hand and extended her arm down, excreting a light wave of mana and struggling to feel how it conformed to the stone below her.

"Hey! Mutt! Beast! Dog! Fleabag! Void abomination!" she yelled once more, barely able to hear her own voice over the whining shriek drilling into her ears, but still hoping to hear something, *anything*, to confirm that her companion was still alive, the memory of that panicked yowl bouncing around her skull like a pinball.

Nothing.

She could *feel* exactly where it was, from the strange, curled up position its limbs were in to the distance that separated them, and she could feel how something foreign was tugging its limbs around without any input from her beastly companion. But she couldn't feel if it was alive. Whatever skill the beast had that allowed them to share awareness of each other simply didn't extend that far.

She pushed the mana out of her palm with more force, expecting results and feeling the blunted claws of panic start to brush against her throat with every passing moment.

A couple feet from her hand, everything worked perfectly, feeling like she had a dozen hands brushing against the rock beneath her. But then the feeling faded to nothing before it could meet anything substantial.

It was more akin to trying to extend her senses throughout a strand of smoke. Like trying to grasp the hazy, crumbling memory of a dream. Like a word that was on the very tip of her tongue but refused to come. She could feel it brush against her fingers, against her mind, but it could never press down hard enough to give her information.

With a growl of determination that hurt her throat, she poured the remaining quarter of her body's mana and violently expelled it out of her hand, *finally* meeting some sort of cracked flooring, small hints of her mana managing to slip through the cracks to lick at the air before she lost sensation. So the beast *had* crashed through something twice; her ears hadn't been deceiving her.

As the whine in her ears faded, she could hear the sound of faint scraping—the clicking of something hard impacting stone in a frantic tempo—and she gritted her teeth as her imagination ran wild, gigantic spiders with eight spiked limbs and glowing eyes invading her thoughts. Or centipedes. Centipedes were even worse.

But the way the wolf was being restrained felt exactly like a cocoon.

And as she imagined her beastly companion being wrapped up in a cocoon and tugged around by such disgusting monsters, all hesitation and fear faded, even if only for a moment.

She gripped onto the rusty pipe with her shaking fingers, used telemancy to push her stomach off the metal, just a little bit, and heaved, pushing herself away from safety. Her shoulders cleared the lip, then her shoulder blades as her elbow started pushing outward, her body tilting toward the right.

She paused for a moment to prepare herself, then remembered something of no real consequence; a distant memory of Katherine telling her that the only way to bathe in cold water, as slaves usually did, was to dive right in without hesitation and deal with the aftermath until the body adjusted.

A bad analogy, but she'd held that conversation and belief dear to her heart for a long time. And it strangely fit in this scenario. Just dive right in.

She could only hope that the fading boost she'd gotten from the beast's blood would spare her more broken bones.

She curled her waist to turn her body to the left before lurching to the right, pushing with her arm and throwing her weight downward, feeling her torn garments strain as they ground against rust, slowly dragging herself out of the pipe, her stomach digging into its edge.

Another push, and her balance shifted as her weight dragged her out of the pipe by itself. She swung her body to the left, splaying her fingers at a flat ninety-degree angle at the edge of the pipe, and allowed her body to slide out, her legs painfully grinding against the top of the pipe as they did.

Then she did her best to lighten her weight with [Telemantic Construct], barely managing to hold on to the pipe with a strained, throaty grunt. She was oddly thankful of her malnourishment and lightweight armor as her hand shook and painfully strained to keep her meager weight from collapsing.

She took a deep breath, mentally choreographing her fall to hurt as little as possible for a quick moment. Right side first, cover her head with her arm, and try to land on her hip and roll to the left.

She was *so* going to break something important; she could fucking feel it.

After mentally preparing a two-way repulsion field around her body for a few moments, she weakly swung her legs to fix her momentum. Once her right side was just a bit extended, she let go with a small yelp that didn't escape her pursed lips, hurriedly curling her arm around her head.

She crashed through the first floor—much like she assumed the beast had—the impact surprisingly weak, only feeling like a really strong slap on the back. Which was terrible, as she'd been banking on the first impact softening the assumed second one.

She barely managed to send a pulse of mana out of her palm to feel the floor and process the information before she slammed almost half of her core's mana into the construct at the last three feet.

Although the force of her own energy crashed into her back like a particularly unwieldy mattress, completely knocking her breath out of her lungs, she continued her fall with bleeding momentum, and with a reaction time that was equal parts luck and anticipation, she managed to roll once her right shoulder hit the stone, the construct dissipating immediately after.

Her legs had been mercifully saved from even hitting the ground.

For several seconds, she simply lay on the floor, gasping and wheezing and choking and coughing like the useless pile of bones she was, gathering mana into her fist just in case the spider came closer.

She felt her companion's limbs slowly loosen from their rigid positions against its own body, as if the cocoon was being undone, and grew even more paranoid, straining her ears past the lingering whine to listen for the insect's steps.

Gathering the dread in her stomach and chucking it to a distant corner of her mind, she tried to figure out where the spider was.

Was it gone, or was it repositioning to shove her in a cocoon as well? She was close to the beast, only eight or so feet away; she should be hearing *something* other than faint echoes of the explosion and the beast's labored breathing.

She'd been hearing the odd tapping the entire time she'd been dragging herself to the pipe's exit. She *knew* this damn thing made noise. If it wasn't making any, it wasn't moving.

So she would move instead.

Trying to force her legs to curl felt foreign, as if they'd forgotten they weren't just useless sacs of flesh hanging off her torso, and her body wasn't sure of how to force them into action.

She quickly formed two sturdy sleeves of mana with [Telemantic Construct], powerful enough to make sure nothing broke further than it already had, and stuck them to her broken limbs. Then, with a heaving groan of both exertion and pain, she staggered upright for what might have been the first time in gods knew how long, swaying side to side as she readied herself, ignoring the burning, pulsing pangs of agony that raced up and down her legs.

A halting, shuffling step forward, palm open and aiming just above the wolf, where she assumed the spider to still be. Her heart was slamming into her rib cage with near-audible thuds, feeling her blood pulse from the tips of her fingers to the sides of her skull as she pushed through a feral, instinctual fear.

But she held, patient. She only had one singular, powerful shot, and if that didn't work, they were both dead. She had to confirm where the spider was, even if she had to do so by getting tackled by some vile, eight-legged nightmare. Worst-case scenario, the beast had already been killed by the damned thing, and she would soon die alone anyway.

Her right leg was broken in two parts, and she felt the grinding of bone as her muscles pulled ever so slightly, her left slowly joining in her meandering shuffle.

Another step forward, her heavy, dust-choked breaths coming out with a rolling *R* sound, as if she were snarling, every drop of mana she could store in her core gathering in her hand and straining her circuits as her body quivered with adrenaline and fear.

The beast's upper body was suddenly yanked forward as the loud sound of something hard scraping against stone filled the room from just in front of her. With her nerves on a hair trigger, she didn't hesitate at all to straighten her hand out, aiming a lot lower than she probably should have, and using [Sparkburst] on reflex with a barely restrained yell.

The heat felt as if her hand had been dunked into boiling water, despite almost none of it being directed toward her, and her ears were consumed utterly by the sounds of a million tiny explosions going off at the same time, combining into a single deafening crackle which didn't at all sound like a pyromancy spell should.

And then she stood in place, panting, on quivering legs that only just managed to not crumble as her lungs burned.

Her body sagged with exhaustion, and she took a few stumbling steps toward her companion, letting her hand drop. If her blast hadn't killed the thing, then they were both dead. Nothing more she could do. No weapons, no strength, no mana.

On her third step, her right knee crumbled, and she bit down on a cry between her teeth, refusing to let it escape as she stumbled, scarcely achieving to regain her balance by putting even more weight on her left leg. One more stumbling step, feeling like hundred-pound weights were attached to her ankles, and she slowly lowered herself to her knees with all the strength left in her atrophied thighs before surging forward, her chest hitting stone as she stopped her head from smacking into the beast's with her oversensitive, stinging hand.

She lowered her forehead to the beast's slimy neck, regaining her breath. As the seconds continued to tick and no unseen horror came to bite her head off, she felt a cautious sense of hope flicker in her chest, an odd, unfamiliar sense of accomplishment welling in her heart.

She'd done it.

And the steady rise and fall of its chest against her shoulder assuaged her most prominent worry. It might be poisoned or unconscious or temporarily comatose, but it was alive.

A trembling hand moved up to pet along its back, moving through quickly thinning slime and odd, veiny protrusions that covered its shoulder blades, to eventually brush against hard, smooth material utterly out of place on its fur.

With a faint, exhausted sense of confusion, she gripped the sticky limb. Following up along its tapering length, her fingers ran over veins which seemed to come *out* of the protrusion, until her fingers felt the first joint, and she realized what she was touching. A surge of overwhelming revulsion filled her gut as her hand jerked away.

She fucking *hated* spiders.

And for that precise reason, she waited only a second to psych herself up before grabbing on to the disgusting, slippery appendage and yanking it off the beast, who didn't react as she grunted with effort to shove the damn thing as far away from them as possible.

The fact that there was a limp spider corpse *right next to her* prevented her from truly being at ease, but as she laid her head on the beast's shoulder and neck, her hand idly sitting on its slimy coat and playing with its fur, she gradually felt her heartbeat slow down, enough for her not to feel like her body was one scare away from a heart attack.

Yet, through the dust, rust, and acrid stench of slime and dead spider filling the air, her nostrils caught a faint whiff of tangy copper, and she felt her breath hitch. With a dry gulp, she extended her neck toward the source just a bit, just enough to feel the beast's wet fur under her cheek, her nose nestling into glorious, blood-soaked fur with a deep inhale.

An intense craving slammed into her like a sledgehammer as her nostrils flared; as her heartbeat started picking up once more. The insides of her throat turned into sandpaper, like the driest, most barren earth. Like a tube rubbed raw with sand.

Without even thinking, her hand ripped the cloth off her face, and she extended her tongue out to lap at the cooling blood, only to freeze in place from shock, tongue pressing against dirty fur as her mind raced.

What did I . . .

Her body had just acted without any thought or input on her part. It was startling, and the intense desire she felt for the blood was equally so.

Despite that, however, as she felt her taste buds sing in pleasure, felt her nostrils flare to inhale the delectable scent of blood, and felt the tantalizing prospect of another attribute boost dangling before her mind's eye, taunting her with how *weak* and *useless* her body was right now, she couldn't deny herself.

It was . . .

Dehumanizing. Addictive.

A balm to her scorched, dry throat.

She licked at the beast's fur like an animal, uncaring of the faint undercurrent of chemicals in the blood mixed in from its dirty coat, her slime-coated hand clutching at its fur.

Each lap of cooling blood filled her limbs with a little more strength, made her soul swell just a little bit more, made her body feel just a shred tougher. So she continued, her hand gradually tilting the beast's neck as she slowly trailed up the path of dripping blood, cursing her tongue's short nature for being unable to lick off the crimson that coated her nose.

Time ebbed and hazed in her mind. In what felt like only a few moments, she'd basically licked its neck clean, blood and slime coating the inside of her mouth in equal measures, any liquid long since swallowed. Her jaw and tongue were sore.

She should be disgusted by both herself and her behavior, but she just . . . couldn't. She couldn't feel that revulsion. She simply sniffed the air as she placed her head back on its shoulder, her nostrils luxuriating in the scent of gamey copper, feeling a sense of satisfaction and accomplishment.

Her first real kill. Her first meal, *taken* rather than given, even if it was from her only ally, with no fight nor conflict to be had.

The only judge in this empty court was herself, and she had no cares left to give toward propriety, dignity, or social expectations hammered into her for two decades. In this humid, dusty grave, there was no outside world, no culture or civilization, no humanity to judge or temper her, nothing but survival and the comforting song of her companion's breaths.

Whether her actions were driven by some sick addiction—some inherent, desperate desire to feel a little stronger even if just for an hour or two—or the increasingly sharp knife of delirium gently scraping at her mind, she felt not a shred of shame or disgust.

And as she fell asleep, she felt the distant pull on her attention of the System telling her she'd progressed, something that she temporarily ignored.

CHAPTER 23

For the surface dwellers, cremation was a ceremony, a religious duty of those who followed the Six-Winged Dove. To assist the soul in escaping its fleshy vessel and hurry it along to the afterlife, whatever that may be.

The unspoken implication that they didn't wish for anyone from the Six-Eyed Crow's church to get their hands on a corpse was a strong, if paranoid, concern of the upper capital Carmerans. Stigma did wonders for stoking fears of something that wasn't all that bad once someone got over the shock factor.

He'd worked in the borderland between the upper capital and the Dungeon a long time ago, when the entrance hadn't been utterly dominated by trading companies, merchant families, and noblemen-backed businesses that would resell Dungeon goods to the upper-city folk for ridiculous prices.

A century, he believes, but he'd long since lost count of the years and his age. Being a half troll, he aged . . . not like an elf, but close enough. It wasn't all that uncommon for trolls to survive to a four-digit year, and he had the privilege of having around half that lifespan, or so he anticipated.

Shaking his head to rid himself of those useless thoughts, he focused back on the comparison he was pondering as he absentmindedly took a cleaver to an old man's corpse, cutting him up into efficient, clean-cut chunks that could fit more comfortably in a bag.

Right, the Dungeon and the surface city.

For them, a part of the capital that was, for the most part, dominated by the Dove's church, cremation was a duty; a revered ceremonious process.

For the people of the Dungeon, cremation was either a necessity to prevent diseases . . .

Or a *waste*.

Cutting off the man's ankle with one last clean chop, he quickly slotted his cleaver into the sharpening tool, pressing the button on the table to start its whirring, before he swept his arm through the chunks of meat on his table to funnel them into a thigh-high bin of parts at his side.

Well, *his* thigh. It would probably be waist-high for anyone else.

Regardless, he still had about two more people to go for the order. Thinking of said order, however . . . it was one of the few times he couldn't help but question if this way of treating the dead was perhaps just a *tad* . . . wrong.

Maybe at one point in his life, he would have considered this job a lot more appalling and immoral, but time and reading the religious texts of the Crow's church had served well to acclimate him to how the dead were treated down here. Not just acclimate; understand, even.

And it made sense, even to a rather sentimental guy like himself.

Why would you burn organs when they had so many uses, despite their owner's expiration? An unfortunate young man's lung could, for an appropriate price and by someone with appropriate expertise, be transplanted into someone else and give them decades more to live. His heart could be sold to witches and those who conducted rituals for one thing or another.

His brain could be sold to men of . . . ill repute, like the doctors of the Santhin Clinic, for studying. His eyes could be given the same treatment as his lungs, giving some random unfortunate his sight back for a price and time investment that was costly, but barely a drop in the bucket compared to what the Dove's church would have someone pay to get their vision back.

And why stop at his organs? His body would be of much use to a young, budding necromancer who wished to practice such craft without falling into the stereotype of being a grave-robbing, murderous psychopath. Perhaps with enough time and societal change, Carmera would stop using slaves in the mines and sewers, instead having unthinking corpses do such dirty, unsafe work.

It was an efficient system. The local authorities would pay a decent fee to take fresh corpses, depending on their quality, then give the bodies to semi-independent companies like his own. Then the corpses' contents would be processed and sold, the authorities would take a cut of their earnings for providing them with material to work with, and *mostly everyone* was happy. Those who weren't took their loved ones to the crematoriums, something not everyone could afford to do.

So yes, he could understand, and even list off the reasons he had no problem doing this grisly work, treating the dead as another resource.

But even so, as he carefully cracked open a thin young woman's chest cavity with his cleaver, her body wrapped in the usual enchanted preservation bag, and delicately started removing her organs with a thin knife to place in containers on the rack to his left, he felt a slight prickle of discomfort at cutting people up for some freak to *eat*.

It was just . . . not necessary whatsoever. It did nobody any real good.

He could justify his work by telling himself that with every organ sold, more was understood about the various biological quirks and differences of the humanoid races; that another man, woman, or child regained something; or at least, that some witch used them to empower either herself or another. The latter wasn't exactly necessary, but it still did some good to the world while providing him and his wife with a decent living.

Selling people's bodies for that freak to *eat* . . . it just somehow felt like a step too far. It was far from wasteful, but it just wasn't necessary.

Most people could feed themselves just fine for a fraction of the cost it took to eat human flesh.

There were colossal factories dedicated to nothing but cultivating and supplying the people with super mushrooms, some magical, rapid-growth fungi species found in the Dungeon centuries ago. Then there were enclosed, industrial slaughterhouses all over the second floor, a certain factory using a Dungeon artifact to endlessly grow tough, stringy flesh to sell for cheap to whoever needed some meat in their diet. There were even some newfangled "greenhouses" made by some particularly creative half-dryad mage on the first floor a . . . few years ago? He didn't keep up with outside life much.

He thought the lad was a wealthy merchant now, actually. Selling "home-trees," another interesting concept that was sweeping through the Dungeon, according to his ever-gossiping wife. Or rather, it was sweeping through the Dungeon for those who could afford such things. Which . . . he was a part of, actually. It would be a good anniversary gift. Hm . . . He did miss the green of the forest, honestly.

He was getting distracted again.

Point was, things rarely, if ever, got so bad that anyone above the third floor would have to resort to cannibalism to keep oneself fed. It felt wrong to sell human meat like livestock to be eaten without some underlying reason or result.

He sighed as he expertly cracked open the woman's skull, cut through the meninges, and cut off the brain stem before delicately placing the brain into an enchanted metal container, swiftly closing the lid. He'd wipe the blood off later, and then sell the remains of the scalp with the other waste of the corpses to the mushroom factories. They could always use more organic material, and he could always use more crowns in his pocket, even if it was *barely* worth the hassle.

Before he knew it, he was just one chop away from finishing the order, paying attention to the elbow joint to not mutilate the flesh too much. It was just a point of pride for him to have his work seem clean despite its brutal nature.

He jumped slightly when a tinny ringing sound filled his workroom without warning. Were his skin not made of stone, he'd have cut his wrist open. He quickly dumped the cleaver next to the last limb on his worktable, took off his bloodied apron, and rushed over to the sink, turning on the tap to clean his arms.

The door opened, and he twisted around to see his wife poke her brown-haired head in, lightly grimacing at the grisly sight of his workspace.

"Honey? The uh . . . client is here."

He smiled and nodded at her before quickly turning to scrub off the scent and feel of blood from his hands.

"I'll be right there."

He could never quite get it to leave, no matter how hard he scrubbed and lathered his fists and forearms in soap, but he didn't want to greet his clients stinking of gore.

Though, knowing this guy, he'd probably find it appetizing.

The door gently shut behind him, and he hurriedly grabbed one of his largest cloth bags, a black one to mask the blood, and settled it over the cart. Then with a cautious heave, he pushed the cart onto its side, his fingers keeping the bag in place, and turned the cart over upside down to pour its contents into the bag, bracing the cart's bottom against his gut.

It might drip a little, but the guy liked his food "fresh and wet," so he'd just have to suck it up.

Damn creep.

He quickly set the cart back onto its original spot and tied the giant bag closed, making sure to keep his hands as clean as possible.

With a confidence he didn't feel, he took the bag and opened the door, briskly walking across the small corridor separating the workspace from the front. It wasn't exactly a store per se, as they handled most of their business through couriers and cable mail, but it was roughly styled like an office, a haphazard one with a single unused desk in the corner and too many metal chairs to ever realistically be used.

Very hole-in-the-wall kind of place, but again, businesses like his own didn't require visibility; they just needed accessibility.

As the walls retreated to his sides, he stepped out of the corridor and cast his gaze to the left, where his client was sitting still as a statue, his head hanging limply to stare at the floor through his creepy metal faceplate.

He might be eight feet tall, but the bastard just made his *everything* crawl in discomfort. Still, he paid *really well,* so he sucked it up and walked forward with a forced businessman's smile until they were just a half dozen feet apart.

The . . . man finally looked up, then stared at the bag, his head tilting just a bit.

Damn creep.

About six feet tall and covered in a twisted, tattered mess of cloths and cloaks on his upper body, with a torn pair of pants, and no shoes, anyone with half a mind would dismiss him as some random vagrant or another homeless drunk with a weird helmet.

Until they looked closer and saw the grayish skin, the rippling muscle barely concealed by his scrappy clothes. Noted how the metal was bolted to his skull and face, a smooth surface that covered his head from just above his lips to the back of his head, with three metallic protrusions equally spaced along the top of his metallic scalp and seemingly melted at the tops.

His jaw was inordinately squared, and his mouth looked like someone had cut up his cheeks until they met the jawbone and gave up, a normal mouth that continued into a creepy, endless line that almost touched his goddamn neck.

And just to complete the creepy look, his faceplate proudly showed the numbers "762" in white industrial lettering on the front, where his eyes and nose and face should be.

He *really* disliked his guy. So much so that he still couldn't muster the curiosity to want to ask how the fuck he could see and hear him without eyes or ears in sight.

After a few more seconds of awkwardly standing across each other, his client jutted his scarred chin at the bag.

"Are you going to give it to me or not?" he asked quietly, his voice uncomfortably average. Not gruff or gravely, nor light and girly. Just . . . normal. Like any other random guy on the street.

Somehow, that was a little more unsettling than if he'd spoken like a raspy wraith.

Despite his discomfort, and with a fake smile still on his face—whether the man could see it or not—he extended his hand. The man took the bag, his black, slightly-too-long fingernails grazing Gaphit's skin, then quickly untied it with surprisingly dexterous fingers before opening it and fishing out a hand.

After observing it and turning it over this way and that, like a merchant inspecting the goods, he opened his mouth, and Gaphit learned what a human shark would look like, were they a cannibalistic creep with only one row of metal teeth that reached back to their jaw.

He crunched off a finger with casual ease, not even chewing before swallowing as Gaphit fought to keep the appalled disgust off his face, his smile straining.

His client tossed the hand back into the bag and retied it, putting the bag on the ground for a moment as he fished out a leather pouch from the mishmash chaos that were his upper garments, starting to leisurely count coins, seemingly satisfied with his order.

Then a loud but muffled ringing came from the man, and he let go of the pouch instantly, sending a mess of silver, bronze, and copper crowns clinking on the floor as he fished some strange, glowing necklace that looked to be equal parts machinery and jewelry out of his clothes, taking a short second to stare at it.

Then he blurred into motion, darting back and wrenching the door open hard enough to have it thrown into the wall. Dropping to a crouch just outside his shop front, he jumped up with enough force to dent the floor with a deafening bang, a quickly receding chorus of distant thumps and clangs indicating just how fast he was retreating from the area.

Gaphit stared blankly at the mess on his business's entrance before taking a deep, deep breath to cool his anger.

He was never dealing with this guy's bullshit again.

What the *fuck* was that about?

His eyes wandered to the coins littering his floor. At least he'd paid three times as much as his order actually cost. And he hadn't even taken it.

He could only hope he wouldn't be an unreasonable jackass and come back here with an entitled attitude to demand his money back. He hadn't used combat skills in years, and he doubted he could even pin down the speedy bastard for long enough to rip him in twain.

With a tired sigh, he got to cleaning up the mess.

She idly observed the gaudy open building composed of glass and bronze latticework, two colorful Carmeran flags proudly sitting above its gargantuan main entrance.

Then she made her way forth, still just . . . watching, firelight eyes darting from spot to spot from behind her gas mask's confines at a frantic pace.

She couldn't remember much from before, but some token, barely caring part of her still wished to observe and mull over all she saw just in case some random scene would trigger some scraped-out memory to be dug out from the mess left behind.

Maybe that rotund man smiling down at his prissy daughter would make her remember some scene from her childhood. Maybe the main teleporting station of the upper capital would allow her mind to recall how she even ended up in the Dungeon in the first place. Was she born there, or did she come through here? Was she some merchant's daughter, or just some morbidly curious tourist? A child worker or a gutter rat?

But the structure didn't have that . . . haunting, uneasy flicker of familiarity. She doubted she'd achieve anything here besides satisfying some of her curiosity about the outside world.

Tempted as she was to explore the upper city, see all the things she'd heard whispered about it, from the moving clockwork sculptures of Lakerci that dotted all the major squares, to the airships that casually swam through *clean,* open air, to the taste of untainted meat and vegetables, she couldn't quite muster the will to survey the surface more than she already had by coming here.

Every step farther from the Dungeon felt like another step into a place she simply did not belong in. The air was too thin. Her mask filter was barely even picking anything up. The people were well-fed, well cared for, and with such colorful clothes and welcoming demeanors that she paradoxically felt unwelcome.

She stood out like a sore, mangled thumb. And she wouldn't care about that normally, but the more people stared at her, the more uneasy she became. Just instincts. She'd rather go hang out with Ghoul and Mirena. She'd seen enough.

A rather lousy way to celebrate, but Ghoul *usually* knew best, and this had been his suggestion. A shitty one, for once.

She continued into the station, eager to return to what she knew, to the safety of omnipresent danger, craning her neck to take everything in.

Two hundred feet tall, more than a thousand feet on each of its four sides. It was difficult to even consider it a building rather than just four gargantuan metal-and-glass walls with a latticework domed roof thrown on top.

She passed through the dozen guards peppering each entrance, staring at the sunny insides of the building. Too many holes.

Fire up here would be so dull, when bathed in all this sunlight.

Too much light. Too much glass.

All around, all above. It would be so satisfying to just . . .

She imagined the scene, eyes turning into hazy orbs of flame as her mind wandered far away, hands sitting still at her sides as she stared through the roof into a blue sky.

A large explosion, a shock wave that would shatter all the glass. A thousand thousand little fragments of glittering crystal, reflecting the lights of the midday sun like a shattered kaleidoscope, their beauty tempered, refined, by the simple fact that they would only last a few moments before they'd break themselves upon the unforgiving ground. All the more precious for how quick that moment of perfect beauty would pass.

She imagined a thousand thousand little shards of sharp crystal break themselves upon the ground in one final explosion of beauty, their innards and limbs flying every which way as they broke themselves upon something they could never best.

As the daydream faded, she sighed, turning her gaze level with the people around her.

She continued, a couple people occasionally turning to stare at her pitch-black garments and the enchantments covering them as she took in her surroundings.

Entire roads seemed to veer off their paths to curve into the open building, those who tread them being separated and given tickets by various blocky little buildings speckled throughout the massive station, corralled around by station workers. And whether they rode upon a wagon, a lizard, a horse, or simply walked their way to the teleportation pads, there were only a few hiccups in the flow of movement.

It was chaotic, yet oddly organized.

Seats were peppered everywhere for travelers who didn't come with a wagon or a caravan, and a few wandering shopkeepers covered in trinkets and minor Dungeon artifacts roamed through the crowds, trying to entice the upper-city civilians into getting some worthless bauble.

She collided shoulders with people multiple times, but she continued, uncaring, eyes following the crowds, the signs, the random little bits of human interaction all around her that were so close yet paradoxically so far away from her grasp.

Up here in the light, it was all too easy to notice all the differences, the colors.

Corfids with their bright-colored plumes of feathers dotting their heads and forearms. Corvids with their raven-black feathers and pitch-black eyes, reminiscent of the birds they had a connection to. There was the occasional slave following their master, either a humanoid or a goblin, vast throngs of regular humans, and for a moment, she thought she even spotted a lizardman awkwardly ambling through the crowd before she lost his red-scaled head in the chaos.

And in the distance, these paths, crowds, and vehicles all eventually converged on certain points at the other end of the cubic building: the entrances to the teleporting pads, most placed on the ground floor, with a few smaller ones placed on a second level made of metal.

She'd gone to the Factory with a portal many times, but never anywhere else, usually just using the Great Tower and the cable lifts to go up and around the floors. She wondered how teleportation would differ in sensation from a portal.

Curiosity drove her forth, mechanically following the crowds in a fugue state as she continued looking at a thousand and one tiny little social interactions happening all around her, until she came face-to-face with a middle-aged woman after a lengthy wait in a crowded queue.

"Dungeon. Third Floor," she uttered after a lengthy, awkward pause as her brain caught up to where she was and what she was doing, twitchy fingers digging into her pocket to grab her coin pouch, only for the middle-aged woman to give her a confused look before speaking, her words muted and indistinct, as if underwater.

Oh, right.

She lifted a finger and activated the speaker system with a tiny spark of mana, flinching slightly at the utter cacophony of sound that suddenly flooded into her mask from her surroundings. She hadn't realized just how loud the teleport stations were until now.

She wondered how long it would take to make the only sound in the station be the crackling of fire.

"—ould you repeat that, dear?" the woman repeated. And so she did, her mask turning her voice into a tinny hiss rather than a mumbled series of indistinct sounds.

She quickly paid the absurd fee and grabbed a hold of her ticket. A strangely resilient piece of paper.

"Now, just look for a teleport pad with a plate that says 'DF3' over the entrance. They'll check your belongings to make sure you don't have anything that could overtax the mana batteries, like dimensional storage items, and you'll be back in no time," the woman said, and she nodded before walking off, opting not to think too much on the "back in no time" comment. It *was* pretty obvious she was a Dungeon resident.

She eventually came to a stop, slowly swiveling her head around to try and locate the teleport pad with . . . what was it, a "DF3" sign hanging over it?

There was a "DF1," a "DF1-A," and almost a dozen other variations of that labeling pattern, but she'd almost walked across the entire station before she finally found the one she was told to go to.

It was, unsurprisingly, empty, both inside and outside. She walked through where the queue would be if there was one, past the singular guard staring at the ceiling, and headed straight to an extremely bored-looking man who was basically lying across his chair, idly flipping through a book while sitting next to a bunch of magical devices on his absurdly long metal desk.

They looked expensive.

But then again, so did everything up here, by comparison.

She was getting rather impatient, so instead of talking, she walked up and simply kicked the metal separating them, getting a startled squawk from the man on the chair, his book flying out of his hands as he jumped, comically fumbling with the spinning book to stop it from hitting the floor before managing to stabilize it. He clutched it to his chest in relief before shooting her a venomous glare.

A small smile of amusement stretched across what remained of her lips.

That was fun.

Some remnant of her humanity idly noted he was cute, and the smile disappeared at the surge of bitterness that followed that thought.

"Item check," she simply said as she put her ticket down on his desk. The man huffed as he gently put the book on an unused corner of the table, moving until he was directly across from her to quickly check and pocket the ticket, smoothing down his well-used green uniform right after as if to salvage some sense of professionalism.

"Right, just put everything you have on top of here. I can activate an illusion if you don't want someone to peek at your belongings, but it costs two silvers. Then I'll just check them over with some craftsman's goggles, do a body check, and you'll be free to go. Please remember that dimensional storage items tend to cause unexpected problems during teleportation, many of which could easily prove lethal to even the most powerful of mages, so please do not withhold such items on your person," he said, his voice gradually switching to a mechanical monologue as he continued.

She simply nodded as she lifted her right leg and unsheathed the mage dagger from her calf to reveal a bronze textured handle that led up to a seven-inch-long silver blade covered with inert red runes. She threw it on the desk before doing the same with her coin pouch.

The man stared at her with an unamused air about him.

"The mask and necklace too."

"No," she said firmly, flexing her fingers at her side.

His brow furrowed in annoyance for a moment, then he just sighed before reaching behind him to bring out some absurd-looking goggles, almost as large as his head and with twelve different lenses sitting on spinning mechanical arms.

That thing was basically covered with a dozen different enchantments, and for a moment, she could only stare with a blank sense of disbelief at how someone had managed to even make that thing without it melting or imploding from the mana load.

"Fine, just sit still so I can look at them at least," he replied, swiftly tying the goggles onto his head and flipping down a set of lenses to observe her, one of his fingers touching some odd switches on the side of his head.

Less than a second later, he let out a sudden yelp as he jerked back and yanked the device off, one hand fumbling for a spot to put the device down while the other frantically rubbed at his eyes.

"Holy . . . what the fuck is your level?" he hissed out, finally managing to find some empty spot on his desk to let the goggles down.

She simply blinked at him, her mind slowly realizing someone had somehow made goggles with [Mana Sight] and gave them to a teleport station employee. Were these things common up here? That was akin to a minor artifact in the Dungeon.

"Okay, check is canceled. I'm pretty sure I burned my cornea, and you're the only passenger anyway, so feel free to die if you have dimensional items you haven't told me about. So just . . . go. I'll turn the lever once the doors close." He made a vague shooing motion before he fumbled back for his chair with that arm, his other hand still rubbing at his eyes while hissing in pain, occasionally lifting his hand to blink rapidly at his desk, struggling to focus on anything.

She simply observed him for a couple seconds, finding the sight oddly amusing, until she got bored and grabbed her dagger, sliding it back into its sheath and turning toward the teleport pad, a rather plain, massive circular room at the end of a short, enclosed corridor.

Behind her, masked behind the idle chatter between the security guard and the station employee, a set of hurried steps approached, and she turned her head around to casually check, mana gathering at her fingertips just in case.

She grew much more tense when she realized the approaching pair were looking right at her, jogging to catch up, almost two dozen feet behind her.

She quite appreciated the Perception points now, even if they were usually a pain in the ass outside of fights.

Body and core tense, she came to a stop, turning to stare at the two men behind the one-way glass of her mask. Two brown-haired men with features she didn't care to even note, mediocre physiques, and wearing two identical sets of vests and slacks.

Her [Mana Perception] was not so low that she didn't note how suspiciously empty they were of mana. Either masking it through some hidden item, consciously suppressing it, or useless thugs dressed in better clothes than they deserved. The chance of two random people looking for her while being this magically weak was too low for this to not look suspicious. Some attempt to put her at ease before striking, maybe?

Suspicious man number one smiled at her as he and his companion slowed to a fast walk, a fake smile just a tad too tense for her not to notice.

"Hello, miss. Are you—"

He stopped himself when she took a step back as he took one forward, the air swiftly growing hotter around her while her fingers eagerly curled and uncurled, a giddy feeling coiling at her gut, forcibly suppressed.

"Don't get too close. What do you want?" she hissed out of the mask, eyes narrowed to a glare as her eyes frenetically danced around her environment, checking for traps, suspicious people, and details out of place, always keeping the duo at the edge of her vision.

The way the security guard seemed more concerned with scrutinizing her rather than the other two was worrying. The way his foot shifted toward her showed he was getting ready to spring to action, as if already certain of whom he would side with.

Definitely bribed. The guy with the goggles just looked confused and unsure while still rubbing at his eyes. He was likely unrelated.

A couple people in the distant crowd stared at them, likely out of curiosity, nobody who drew attention besides a man in artificially dirtied and rumpled clothes who was doing a bad job of pretending he was just looking for his pad.

Four versus one wasn't a terrible situation to be in, especially considering how much leverage she had in the way of multiple thousands of innocent people all around her. Assuming they cared about collateral damage, or knew what she could do.

The men looked a bit awkward for a moment, glancing at each other in a way that gave away some sort of long-term familiarity.

Good at teamwork—not good.

The man who took the lead in the conversation turned back to her, hands placatingly spread open at his sides.

"We're here to offer a lucrative job for the adventurer who goes by the name Holocaust. Would that happen to be you, miss?" he asked, seemingly more out of courtesy than being genuinely uncertain.

"How did you know I would be here? Or who I am?" she demanded instead of answering the useless question, fingers slowly stiffening.

"Our employer didn't disclose that, miss. We know you've made a name for yourself in the Dungeon, so our employer wished to buy your services. We're just here to offer you the job, the details of which we can't easily discuss in public, and the reward of which will be whatever price or favor you set, within relative reason," the man explained.

She took a short moment to think about her reply.

" . . . Why not my team and just me? Could've contacted us through the guild. I also don't work with people who refuse simple questions. Tell me how they found me, or I'm leaving," she dryly said, the tinny hiss of her voice rendering the men to become visibly indecisive as she felt her patience fray. She hated speaking, and she hated when people beat around the bush and meandered in their speaking.

After a moment of seemingly psyching himself up, the first man shrugged, not convincing her in the slightest with his awkward smile.

"Fine, feel free to go. Rather unfortunate that you'll never know who you were, or where your family is. But since you won't cooperate, we can't do much more. It ain't no skin off our employer's back. Make sure to have fun scraping bits of Ghoul off the wall back at your quaint little hideout," he said, so casually, that for a moment, she simply stood stock-still in shock, her brain struggling to comprehend what he'd just said.

"My—My *what?*" she hissed, fire wreathing her uncovered arms and gloved hands as she stomped forward, the man in front of her suddenly far more nervous than before as he hurriedly backtracked to the left, his hip coming up to scrape against the table full of gadgets. Her nostrils flared as a phantom burning settled in her chest—the familiar heat of anger.

She didn't *have* a family. They didn't exist. She didn't have a family, and if she did, she'd fucking vaporize them in an instant.

No. Fuck that. She didn't care about that part anymore.

"What the fuck did you just say about Ghoul? Where is he?" she snarled, a throaty, mechanical rumble filtering out of her gas mask as her eyes glowed through the darkened glass like two soulless suns. The fire spread throughout her body in an instant, wreathing her in angry twirls of heat and plasma as the men hurriedly backed away, the first man sending a desperate glance to—

The security guard?

Just as she turned her eyes to glance at him, a tide of drowsiness and exhaustion suddenly slammed through her mind and body, making her stumble and her flames flicker, her [Mental Resistance] straining under the foreign spell as her legs wobbled, vision momentarily blurring as her eyes closed on their own before being wrenched open through sheer will.

She flared her mana, hoping the straining of her circuits would help her struggle to stay awake as her [Mental Resistance] slowly started to crumble. Her mind whirled in confusion at the suddenness of everything. The two men had backed off entirely to melt into the confused crowd behind them in the span of a single sluggish blink.

She stumbled in a circle, eyes searching for a man who wasn't there anymore, her breaths speeding up as panic, glee and fury setting in in equal measures. She refused to be caught. She refused to be chained again. She refused to let this chance for release slip between her fingers.

The crowds melted into swathes of black coats and faceless heads. The gadgets at the table twisted, their limbs ending in scalpels and rune seals, her blood running thick with sedatives that weren't there. A half-blind man stumbled away in panic, and she didn't hesitate to throw an [Ignite] spell at his clothes, his agonized screeching filling her ears as chaos erupted from the crowd.

The security guard was nowhere to be found, heavily armed entrance guards rushing at her through the parting swathes of kindling.

Her hand flew to the necklace at her throat, a manic smile splitting her face in half, a frozen, gaping rictus that none could yet see. A surge of unfathomable glee flooded her entire being, pure euphoria at the thought, at the confrontation, shivers of pleasure keeping her awake as a stuttered, wheezing giggle escaped her throat, her mind growing fuzzy.

Why was she angry or scared? None of them could touch her. None of them could chain her.

It'd been so long since she could just *let go*.

It'd been so long since she had so many people to burn.

So many little embers that would break themselves upon her in one final explosion of beauty, their innards and limbs flying in every which way as they broke themselves upon something they could never best.

Her thumb pressed the button on the necklace before clutching it in a fist that glowed white blue split by orange cracks, melting it, vaporizing the metal, and dismantling the enchantments in the blink of an eye.

The guards continued moving toward her, encircling her slowly, so *slowly*.

Her head pounded with agony, struggling to put her to sleep.

The metal around her started glowing, screeching, and screaming in protest as the temperature jumped from neutral to the insides of an inferno, turning to luminescent slag that quickly lost cohesion as her core dumped every ounce of mana she had into her body, the air wavering and wriggling all around her from the overpowering heat, bending her sight.

Her feet dug into the molten metal. A raging sun boiled her insides, scorched her heart black, filled her vision with dancing wisps of blue-orange flame, twirling and dancing for her, a mesmerizing sight that blurred as the spell fought to make her submit.

She crushed her mana in an infernal fist, her pupils dilating into two black circles surrounded by a flaming sclera.

A guard threw a metal spear with a deafening crack, and she idly watched as it turned to slag mere feet from her before uselessly splattering against her stomach.

Her clothes writhed before bursting into flames and evaporating; her mask cracked and constricted, the enchantments unable to protect her belongings as they turned to toxic vapors, melting off her face and shoulders and hips.

Through the chaos, she felt another familiar surge of mana from somewhere within the crowd, and she spun, blue flame escaping from the bottom of her foot to propel her twist, barely managing to keep herself upright through the dizziness. Her head lolled limply to the side as she nailed her gaze upon the bribed security guard, her shoulders quivering from excitement before going slack once more.

She only caught a glimpse of the man, his expression determined and composed, uncaring as to what was about to happen. Or simply unaware of it.

Of course they didn't know. Even with this display, nobody knew how much she'd grown from being the little runt who destroyed Tillenhall. Nobody knew how fire *begged* for her to control it, to let it rage and devour; how it had a mind and soul of its own that screamed at her to help it cover everything in sight.

Before another one of his sleep spells could hit her, she felt the skin at the corners of her mouth split open, her cheek muscles tearing and spasming as her gaping smile fought to represent the pure ecstasy she felt, the world turning into nothing but scorching euphoria as she poured every single bit of mana she had into a single spell.

A single moment of hesitation.

"[Raging Conflagration]."

A single phrase, reverently whispered through a flame-scarred throat, and Carmera watched her earn her name.

CHAPTER 24

When the wolf finally felt its mind slip away from the clutches of oblivion back into the usual fugue of pseudoconsciousness it had obtained by having its [Restful Awareness] jump to level fifteen, the bone-deep, pulsing pain radiating off the back of its neck was the first sensation to greet it.

The first *thought* was the question of what the difference between being knocked out and being asleep was, for the skill to only activate *now* instead of earlier.

It brushed aside the System's updates, quickly attempting to fix itself with manual haste. It snapped its spine back into place with a meaty pop, regenerated the cut and damaged nerves in moments, slid intervertebral discs back into place, and all damage was forcibly reverted in a matter of a couple minutes of focus.

Torn muscles in its neck, burst eardrums, and six shallow but gaping holes followed, thankfully not bleeding still, as the wolf quickly ran a mental check on its body for anything else requiring immediate attention. It saw it had a torn open nostril, lingering blood loss, and minor bits of frayed bone tissue that had lost a bit of structural strength, but those were all things it saw no reason to waste its mental capacity on for the immediate moment.

Frankly, it was immensely lucky it had only become paralyzed instead of outright killing itself. That was not its best moment.

As it waited, the wolf idly wiggled its antennae and forced its fur to ruffle to get at least a muted sense of its surroundings, shaking off the half-dried bits of slime covering it from snout to tail, the events that had led to its precarious situation slowly filtering back to its mind.

It mentally blanked, however, when its fur and cerci hairs tried to undulate under the human's limb on its back, its antennae very vaguely giving it the impression that the human was lying . . . basically on top of the wolf.

While the insect's drying corpse was just a few hand widths from its snout.

As it slowly recanted the events before it had panicked and almost accidentally killed itself, it quickly pieced together what had likely happened, despite how difficult it was to believe.

The human had somehow dropped down a distance several times her height and saved it, judging by the mild scent of charred decay in the air. A turn of events it was not at all expecting but was very thankful for.

While [Pack Hunter] was a skill which allowed it and the human to share a deep and accurate feeling of where they were and what direction they were focusing on during moments of perceived danger, it hadn't exactly been of sound mind while fighting for its life to consider that she might manage to fight through her injuries to come to its aid.

That thought brought the wolf full circle, back to the simpler facts of the events that had led them to this position.

It had almost died, and would be insect food by now if it wasn't for the human.

And the only thing it could *really* blame was its reluctance to use its own abilities to their fullest extent. The reluctance to having its form changed too far from what it had known, to veer outside of its comfort zone, of "blending in" as just another dog.

As if blending in even mattered. It didn't *need* to blend in; the attempt was simply a thin comfort blanket so it wouldn't feel as alone, pretending to be part of a larger collective of similar beings so it wouldn't have to learn what being different from everything else meant, how such a thing would be perceived by the humans.

For all it knew, it could grow a second head, and the humans wouldn't even care. But a paranoid caution had kept it clinging to covertness. It was a simple subconscious thought that had kept it . . . not stagnant, but not growing as much as it could be.

It felt . . .

Stupid.

It hadn't been improving itself as much as it could because of *feelings,* because the notion of changing its body too much was somehow uncomfortable. As if comfort mattered more than being alive. Just thinking it aloud made it feel even dumber.

It waited for a few minutes in silence, both mental and physical, waiting for everything important to finish before changing from manual change to conceptual.

A quick fix of its more minor injuries was applied; it would start as soon as the wolf was done changing itself, a process which could take a lot longer than usual this time around. Because for once, it truly wasn't going to hold back whatsoever.

The process of remembering and inspecting the human arm structure didn't take much time at all. It was extremely simple in comparison to other things it had messed with before. What took time was trying to understand how the wolf would have to change that structure to fit into its biology.

For starters, the wolf was missing a *lot* of the human musculature needed to move their arms that way. From their pectorals to the way their trapezius helped elevate or lower their shoulders, to the various muscle connections and the ways those muscle groups weaved around each other to function, many of which the wolf did not even have.

The wolf had to make *some* sacrifices to do all this. Its chest and rib cage were far too narrow to support that musculature properly, so the first order of business was expanding its ribs to the sides and adding more stretchy bone mass to offset the larger area coverage. Then it had to fiddle around with its tendons and muscles just a bit to make sure nothing would catch or strain from the changed base its bones provided.

It felt like the process took a *really* long time, but in this half-dreaming state, it didn't know if that was true in the outside world. What it did know was that this was all going to cost a *lot* of essence—essence it hadn't been replenishing for what felt like one to two weeks.

Its meat storage had depleted by almost one-fifth already. It was mildly worrying, but the wolf reminded itself it had to be *alive* to hunt in the first place, and returned to its task.

After another while of fiddling with the placement of various things, adding and removing bits and pieces, and a hundred other tiny details, it had finished changing its rib cage, as well as restructuring the musculature of its back. It also added a small set of collarbones—a bone its own biology didn't have—whose main function was to greatly assist in keeping its shoulders on the sides of its body instead of on the front.

Next were the bones and joints of its forelegs. Joints were mostly what gave the humans the incredible range of movement they had. Some closed and opened like hinges, such as their knees and elbows; others were more versatile and sacrificed a bit of power for incredible range of movement, a change the wolf was more than happy to apply.

But before it did that, it had to stop and consider how these changes would *affect* said movement. Now, its forelegs were made for forward movement, the elbows naturally tilting outward and sliding back along the sides of its rib cage with each bound, making it so the wolf benefitted from having its forelegs' paws close to each other as it ran. With its widened rib cage, that sort of running would be impossible with its current legs, as its elbows would just slam into its own ribs all the time.

But even if it changed its forelegs to resemble human arms, its movement would still have to change a bit. Humans' arm structure was vastly different, and vastly larger than its own, with almost double the muscle mass to assist them in their more varied movements.

Trying to imagine itself with a set of roughly humanoid forelegs was a bit difficult, but it could sort of visualize it, and thus where it would have to make some very obvious changes. For starters, their palms were far too long and flat, so the wolf shrunk them a little, shortened the metacarpal bones, and added a bunch of its own paw padding at the bottom, just to make them better for running than manipulating things.

Then it removed the thumb, seeing as it would only get in the way when doing anything that *wasn't* fiddling with human devices, and looked at the fingers.

Again, too long. They'd just slap against the ground with every step and slow the wolf down, so it left from the knuckle to the first joint of each finger, and severed the two final ones, copying the tapering structure of the final joint to graft its nails at the end before adding rough toe pads at the bottom again. Not thin enough to bruise its fingers whenever it ran, but not thick enough to prevent the wolf from bending them inward at a sharp angle.

After a bit of fiddling with its mental design, adjusting proportions, tendon thickness, and considering the pros and cons of everything it was doing, trying to mentally simulate movements it would be doing and checking for issues, it ended up with a . . .

Surprisingly solid version of a vaguely humanoid set of forelegs. Besides the additional muscles on it and the different proportions, it didn't even look *that* much different from its old legs.

It could bend its fingers enough to rake its nails—or claws, rather— through whatever it wished, at whatever angle it wished. It could move to the sides, and even reach its own *backside* with a bit of stretching. Its gait would have to change a little bit with how its forelegs' upper arm was twice as long now, and the forearm was shorter. Its elbows would probably have to flare out to its sides a lot to not make its trot awkward, but that was perfectly fine.

Another minor change was that human arms were a bit *too* muscular, so the wolf focused on making the muscles wiry but incredibly tough and strong to offset that problem. Too much top weight didn't feel right, and adding all that muscle, bone, and fur on its upper body to accommodate its changes was already making it feel like a problem.

It would take some getting used to, and the process of such drastic change would likely be *very* awkward, but the wolf applied the change and turned to other matters: the empty space it had created in its chest cavity by enlarging its rib cage.

Frankly, it didn't need to put much thought into it. It just enlarged its lungs to fill the space up. A good little bonus to its stamina.

Next, its antennae. Immeasurably useful thus far. And very awkwardly placed. Having to move its entire head and neck just to get a better feel of its surroundings was not the greatest idea it'd had thus far, even if it had served the wolf well.

It stuck a small ring of antennae around each of its front and back paws' wrists, about six inches long—enough to easily brush the floor when it wished them to. Then it quickly ran the nerves through its limbs up to its brain. And to prevent information overload . . .

As difficult as it could be, the wolf decided to work with what it already had and build off from that. It knew chronic pain changed the way the spinal cord, nerves, and brain would process unpleasant stimuli. It was how pain tolerance worked. So for the first time, it tried to mess around with its own brain, just a little bit, to see if it could set up some sort of mental block for the antennae, to prevent being overwhelmed.

In short, it took the nerve endings connected to its antennae and looked into how its brain processed that information.

And it understood absolutely nothing. Everything was a mess of tiny electric signals, proteins, fats, odd tissues, and it was altogether just . . .

Too complicated. It was feeling overwhelmed and confused from just glancing at it all.

It could *vaguely* understand the basics of its own mind, but messing with it was *way* out of its abilities at the moment. And maybe ever. A tad disappointing, but the wolf didn't dwell on it.

Deciding to go for something simpler, it removed all the antennae from its snout to offset the chance of its mind buckling under the strain of sensations, and put its whiskers back into place, allowing its mind to quickly cannibalize the antennae and their nerves.

A quick mental evaluation revealed that its antennae-related changes would only take a dozen or so hours, which was a very sharp difference from before, where they'd taken the wolf around . . . a couple days or so?

Something to keep track of.

Another issue it had idly thought of fixing during the long hours of dragging was that the wolf tended to have issues falling asleep when it had nothing else to do and wished to speed the changes along. After a certain point, its body just refused, too full of energy to even consider sleeping, something that had become a far larger issue when it had reached level seven on Endurance.

The thing that mainly induced sleep was the pineal gland, a little gland at the center of its brain that produced a chemical called *melatonin*, which would make the mind sleepy and drowsy. Usually a *call* to sleep, rather than the thing *prompting* or sustaining sleep. Still, it was as good of an assist as any, so the wolf made a tiny gland to make melatonin in its abdomen. It led the created melatonin into a small sac surrounded by a thin film of muscle the wolf could contract to squeeze the fluid out into its bloodstream. Less efficient than directly excreting it into the brain, but the wolf wasn't going to be messing around with its skull anytime soon.

Establishing a mental connection to the muscles around its new chemical sacs was something it would probably have to do manually. Its body didn't quite recognize that those muscles were there, so the wolf would just . . . go and tug them about, try and make its own body properly feel and realize that those little muscles were there and could be pulled.

Unwilling to leave it for later, the wolf swapped to manual and did exactly that, trying to get its body to feel the new muscles in its stomach and how to pull them to squeeze current and future sacs easily. After a couple minutes, it felt like it could do it while awake, so it changed back to conceptual change.

With its chest, back, shoulders, forelegs, antennae, and another sac of chemicals on the way, it focused on the finer details.

Its fur was too thin, too weak. The wolf thickened and toughened its hide until it was as coarse as sand, as tough to cut as layered leather. It would definitely be a little *too* warm, but it didn't feel like there would be an issue of overheating.

Next, its new fingers had too much fur around the nails, so it got rid of the fur at the tips and removed the hair follicles to make sure nothing would grow on its fingertips to really bring out the length of its nails. It turned to its gums and peeled them back, as low as they could go, and encased its teeth in tight vises of hardened bone instead of its weak gums.

That relatively simple change almost doubled their length. Its canines were a little longer than half the length of the human's fingers. A sizable upgrade.

So much of the height of its teeth had been buried in its gums, it was a little frustrating to think it'd only decided to do this *now*. It was also a little disappointing that two-thirds of its teeth were too flat to really cut through something unless the wolf tilted its mouth to use their edges, as they were mostly crushers and such. Thankfully, it could still feel from the skill that being able to change its nails and teeth was not too far-off a possibility. It was already getting ideas for how to change them.

Beyond that, however, as it looked at its body and added a bit more vascularity to its muscles to keep them properly fueled, it had to pause to consider other options, its mind struggling to come up with new ideas.

But it didn't really wish to stop now. It had gone into this with the thought of removing all inhibition, and besides its forelegs and upper body, it didn't feel like it had changed enough. Maybe once it was a little stronger, its bones would be bending from the pull of its muscles, but that wasn't really a problem yet, and neither were most of the tiny issues it could spot. Fixing them would only bring about more problems for the most part.

Still, with a bit of creativity, it located a few problems—and plausible solutions to them as well.

For starters, it was far too top-heavy. Its muscle mass on the upper half of its body had almost doubled from its changes, despite its attempts to downsize the muscles by making them tougher and smaller. Its balance would just be completely off.

One way to change that was the simple solution of weighing its bottom half down as well.

Without elaboration, it sounded like it was just creating another problem. Why weigh itself down just to get a little bit more balance? But the more the wolf considered it, the more it felt like it would only be a boon.

When it'd charged the insect, its strength hadn't been the issue. Its legs hadn't offered much help; the thing that had slammed into its enemy was just the wolf's body, and the impact had been mostly dictated by a mixture of the wolf's weight and its speed. And its weight right now was *really* light. Even if the wolf had gone incredibly fast into the charge, there was just not enough bulk to throw the insect back with enough force to prevent retaliation. That was what had made its charge so ineffective.

It had really good strength for its size, but it didn't have the weight to properly ground itself and *use* that strength in fights.

Maybe it would become a little slower with all the added bulk, which was a mild concern, but as its muscles grew tougher and stronger with every passing day, and its body adjusted, it didn't feel like it would ever come across the problem where it was *too* heavy to move itself at the speeds it wanted to, unless it tried to make itself an absolute *giant* of a canine. Giant as in, twice as tall as a human at shoulder height. Just . . . *massive.* Then it could imagine that such immense weight would become very hard to push around.

But until and if it got to that point, weight would only give it an advantage in fights.

And a disadvantage when trying to move across the human nest, considering how unstable and rickety much of the terrain was . . .

The wolf was starting to feel like everything was a trade-off, and it didn't much like that possible realization. But when thinking about what really mattered, it felt like the weight would be worth it in the short-term. Maybe when it got outside and had to traverse the long swathe of pits and drops that was the human nest, it would change itself back to something lighter.

The added bulk itself was not mere fat. After much time and visualization, it added a few more minor but strong muscles to assist with maneuvering its hind legs, abdominal muscles somewhat similar to humanoids to help its abdomen curl, and added a whole host of musculature and tendons to its back and tail. *After* deciding to double its length.

The tail was there for balance and communication anyway, so adding weight onto its tail just made sense. Being able to actually grab things with it was another bonus. And being able to actually grab it with its mouth was another. No more spinning in circles!

Beyond that, however, it was part of the solution to another problem—that problem being the human. Carrying her around was getting really frustrating, and now that they were in some sort of structure, the wolf assumed the trip would only get more annoying for the both of them. Stairs, debris, random things which would catch on her coverings that hadn't been there in the mossy, rusty pipe. The slowly dwindling supply of meat in the wolf's storage. Maybe they'd even have to jump some gaps if they were unfortunate enough.

So the wolf was just going to carry her on its back for the sake of comfort, convenience, and speed.

It would use its new and far more dexterous tail to hold on to her legs to make sure they didn't hit everything all the time, and then design a rather cumbersome carrier made of bone on its back for her. While the idea was rather silly, the wolf was too annoyed by constantly pulling her along to consider any other alternative.

So its lower body was weighed down by a somewhat prehensile tail and more muscles after an indeterminate amount of time, and with its mind exhausted, the wolf set to the last thing it wished to create: the carrier itself.

And then it remembered the strange, sticky, veiny slime of the insect, and almost woke up from its slumber just to smack its own head into the dusty floor for being so damn hasty. It didn't need a carrier. It just had to copy whatever that insect had done on its back and use it to carry the human. Obviously.

How convenient.

Discarding any thoughts of bone-made carriers for its human packmate, it created another skin sac full of modified blood for the human on its leg, and finally turned to the System to see its progress.

You have progressed on your Path.
[Hound of the Keeper] Level 16 → Level 17

-Available Attribute Points: 1
-Attributes:
Strength (+0)
Speed (+1)
Dexterity (+0)
Endurance (+7)
Perception (+1)
Resolve (+1)
Intelligence (+5)
Soul (+1)

Without much thought, the wolf put the point into Strength, one of the only two attributes that still had a big zero next to it. Perhaps in the hope it would offset the additional muscle mass and help it not feel bogged down by it.

Strength (+1)

[Poison Resistance] has Leveled Up. Level 12 → Level 13
[Echoes of Oblivion] has Leveled Up. Level 3 → Level 4

[Soul Perception] has Leveled Up. Level 2 → Level 3
[Mana Manipulation] has Leveled Up. Level 6 → Level 7
[Sonic Blast] has Leveled Up. Level 1 → Level 3
[Tremor Sense] has Leveled Up. Level 2 → Level 3

-Acquired Traits:
Enduring has progressed to Struggler.
Struggler (2/5): You have felt the chill of death many times and survived.
You are tougher.

The wolf proverbially stared at the trait for a few moments with a mixture of satisfaction and realization. It finally knew what those numbers next to the traits actually meant. Some kind of level progression, albeit obviously different. It still wished the trait would explain *how* much tougher its body was, though.

With nothing else to do for now, it sat and rested for a couple hours, finding that even though [Devourer] and the symbols had both retreated, it could still *think* during its sleep. It was muddled, slow, and hazy, as if the wolf were dizzy and had trouble using its brain, but basic thoughts were still rather easy to form.

Most of those thoughts tended to wander to how nice it felt to have something warm and alive next to itself without that being a cause of immense concern. A few of them lingered on how unfortunate it was that its eyes were done changing, and it couldn't even see all the infinite shades of new colors because of the pitch-black void around them.

Eventually, however, it thought of how flesh tended to degrade over time, and shook itself awake, carefully wiggling away from the human's grip to stand on its own feet.

They felt awkward. *Moving* felt awkward. Like everything was just a bit off-center, a bit too long or large. Comparing its size to the human made it abundantly clear that the wolf was growing bigger at an almost alarming rate, and it could only assume that sleeping for an unknown amount of time had made that growth all the more apparent compared to *before* it had knocked itself out. It was the size of a normal dog by now, if a bit more muscled. There wasn't even a hint of malnutrition on its body, judging by the image it was getting from the vibrations.

It could only assume that this feeling of awkwardness would increase tenfold when the changes to its forelegs and body finished in a few dozen hours.

Oh, it could actually *feel* flesh growing under its skin if it focused.

Leaving that observation aside with a shiver of discomfort, it tapped a foot while rubbing its half-digested snout antennae on the floor to get a better picture of what it was looking for, then trotted to the decaying insect's scattered limbs.

Eating them was . . .

Absolutely disgusting. It had eaten half-digested, half-melted, and half-rotten scraps of meat that were more appetizing than the absurdly bitter and salty slime that made up the insect's insides. Its hard exoskeleton was an absolute pain to swallow, forcing the wolf to very slowly chip away hard pieces so nothing would gouge out its throat when swallowed, so the wolf got to *enjoy* the disgusting, tongue-burning flavor for as long as possible.

At least the texture of the slimy, stretchy, oversize veins covering the insides of the bottom section of each foot was surprisingly enjoyable.

Six limbs later, it was debating whether it should go to sleep just to deactivate all of its taste buds before continuing with the body.

But it *really* wanted to know what it could get from the damned thing, and it was in no mood to hunt down another one to understand how to get that sticky slime for itself. The venom, whatever it was, would be a nice addition as well.

With a low, slow grumble of misery, it got to work on the tear-shaped body, biting into its flank and ripping open a hole to its squishy insides.

Eating the whole thing took *hours*.

Not just because of its surprisingly hard-to-swallow exoskeleton nor because of the horrible flavor, but because the wolf simply hadn't considered that biting off things at random might not be the best idea. So it had been forced to go into self-repair mode when it had bitten into and swallowed a venom sac through its scratched-up throat which had paralyzed it up to its eyes, having to manually move its diaphragm up and down *while* it figured out how to make its body flush the venom out.

That venom was some *extremely* potent stuff, considering it'd easily worked through its Struggler trait and Endurance. Thankfully, it could actually scoop out tiny bits of the venom from its bloodstream and hold them in place to observe what they were made up of. It was an extremely complicated mixture of specific enzymes, proteins, carbohydrates, a cocktail of molecules specifically designed to mess with nerve signals, and a half-dozen other things.

Then it had to figure out how to make its body wipe it out by having its liver metabolize and burn said mixture, make its brain's receptors respond less to it, and carefully nudge its immune system into attacking that very specific mixture of things the moment it detected them. Viciously.

While manually pumping its diaphragm to keep moving oxygen into its brain.

It came out of the experience with a relative immunity to being paralyzed by that specific venom, and a pounding, agonizing headache which felt like something was repeatedly slamming a human-size boulder into its brain.

When the [Devourer] skill activated, it didn't even bother to look at what it had learned, brushing it aside and settling in for a very, very lengthy sleep during which it turned off [Restful Awareness] for the first time.

When it woke up an indeterminate amount of time later, it was to a relatively mild migraine, at least compared to what it had before, and a human hand carefully playing with its ears.

It grumbled, stretching its legs out with a gaping yawn.

"Hey, buddy," the human whispered, a volume that the wolf greatly appreciated. It chuffed in acknowledgement before dragging itself upright to finish eating the flame-charred insect. Just a bit of its main body left and a couple organs, and then it could change itself again and get moving.

Well, that was rude. She'd been hoping for the beast to start talking to her. The exhausted fuzz in her mind demanded socialization, however, so she continued speaking to the beast.

"I know you likely don't understand me, and you've been out for a long time, but I'm kind of really hungry," she murmured, hearing the crunching and wet snap of its jaws. "Yeah, you greedy goblin. Keep eating," she complained quietly, half-jokingly. "I really have to teach you Carmeran. And my name. And [Haste], so you stop giving me bruises every time you want a boost," she mused, her fingers idly brushing at the warmth left behind on the stone, where the beast had been asleep.

She missed that warmth.

Dragging herself all the way back to it was such a pain. Even finding the beast again was a pain in the ass, having to find it based on nothing but the faint sound of its breathing. And then it got up and walked away an hour later. So rude.

"And some manners, probably," she breathed out, oddly relaxed despite feeling like she was half-freezing to death. It was relatively warm down here, but with all this moisture in the air, it didn't feel like it.

Then again, it could be a side effect of a million tiny different things that could be wrong with her.

"You know, you're really interesting. I could feel your body sort of . . . twisting and bulging under the fur, just a bit. Pretty weird. It's a real problem for me, personally, 'cuz I don't know how to refer to you. You're shaped like a dog, but you're growing way too fast, you're probably smarter than the average citizen, and your body just . . . writhes and undulates, slowly, in its sleep. So you're some kind of beast or monster, but you're the nicest damn monster I've ever heard of. Even if you have your moments of being an asshole or eating my teammates," she slowly continued, unsure and, at this point, uncaring of if the beast was hearing her.

It gave her one of its chuffs in reply before digging into the spider again.

"You're gross. Eating spiders. And my arm." She let out a short, raspy giggle before lifting her hand to massage her forehead as the humor faded.

"Why am I laughing at that?" she questioned before mentally shrugging.

Why *not* laugh at that? She didn't exactly have much in the way of stress relief down here, and the high of victory over the eight-legged horror had already faded.

In fact, she'd almost had a rage-induced aneurysm when she'd opened her System screen.

She quickly brought it up again.

-Species: Humanoid
-Race: Elf
-Name: Embreeil
-Path: [Infuser] Level 13

-Available Attribute Points: 1
-Base Attributes:
Strength (+0)
Speed (+0)
Dexterity (+0)
Endurance (+3)
Perception (+2)
Resolve (+1)
Intelligence (+4)
Soul (+2)

-Racial Skills: [Attuned], [Quick Learner]
-Acquired Skills:
[Magic Resistance – Level 5]
[Mental Resistance – Level 6]
[Poison Resistance – Level 9]

[Pain Resistance - Level 19]
[Illumina - Level 8]
[Sparkburst - Level 17]
[Haste - Level 15]
[Mana Perception - Level 20]
[Mana Manipulation - Level 19]
[Mana Tank - Level 5]
[Mana Conduit - Level 7]
[Tough Skin - Level 1]
[Infection Resistance - Level 2]
[Disease Resistance - Level 2]
[Telemantic Construct - Level 7]
[Mana Touch - Level 1]
[Iron Stomach – Level 1]
[Soul Perception – Level 1]

-Acquired Traits:

Kindhearted (1/3): You have shown yourself capable of both sympathy and empathy, and have backed up your emotions with actions that you believe were moral. Gain +1 in Soul and Resolve when helping sentient beings as long as you do not assist them with committing actions you find immoral.

Vampiric (2/2): You have sustained yourself on nothing but blood for many days and have taken many steps toward the path of vampirism. Blood is extremely palatable, sustains you as well as any food, severely hastens your natural healing and stamina recovery, and drinking the blood of others gives you a temporary boost to all Attributes. Healing, stamina recovery, and the duration and strength of the Attribute boost depends on the amount of blood you have consumed and its quality.

Enduring (1/5): You have felt the chill of death multiple times and survived. You are slightly tougher.

She let a low hiss of frustration escape her lips as she read the Vampiric trait over and over again. Because of course she got that *now*. Of course she couldn't have gotten that any sooner so she'd already be able to walk by now. No, that would be too kind of the universe.

She wasn't even a vampire yet. She didn't know what the process to becoming one was, but if it was going to give her the Vampiric trait, at least MAKE HER ONE?!

Stupid System.

At least she got [Mana Touch]. She wasn't *completely* blind anymore, at least for a couple feet, and for the relatively low cost of tossing mana out into the open air. Although some part of her felt like she should be jumping for joy right now, she just . . . It was infuriating.

The Vampiric trait just felt like a Band-Aid at best.

"I feel like this thing is made to mock me, you know?" she murmured. "Never does what I want it to. Never gives me what I want it to. Never gives me something useful *when* I want it to. Is that just me, buddy? 'Buddy' sounds weird," she murmured, her head limply lolling side to side as she continued her ramblings. "I should give you a name until you can give yourself one. *If* you want a name—I don't know how smart beasts do things. But naming you makes me feel like I'm declaring you as my pet, which would be dumb, you know?"

The beast took a short moment to chuff back at her, and she felt a smile tug at her lips. She could *almost* delude herself into thinking they were having a genuine conversation.

"I know, right? You could probably kill me twenty different ways. Naming you like you're my abomination monster dog . . . sounds like some of that patented Elven arrogance." She shifted a bit to straighten her back, wishing she still had that face covering.

"I actually saved you. That was pretty . . . cool," she murmured, her fingers coming up to slowly trace the gaping holes of her eye sockets.

Surprisingly, they didn't feel as tender as before.

"What's the score, buddy? Ten for you, one for me . . . ? Just gotta . . ." She paused to muffle a yawn, her fingers moving down to trace along her pulse and jugular. "Save you nine more times, and we'll be even," she finished.

A short, mutual silence followed, the beast continuing to crunch away at the spider.

"If we ever make it out of here . . . I'm going to do so many things," she softly breathed out, feeling tears come out of her abused tear ducts as she gave the empty void a watery smile full of hope. Not that she was sure of *why* she was crying, but her emotions were all over the place lately.

Her sockets didn't hurt anymore from the salt, at least.

"Or at least try. I'll find Katherine. I'll find some way to see, then join an adventuring team. A real one. A good one. I'll buy a telepathy spellbook to speak to you, teach you Carmeran. Could probably teach you how to read and write as well. You're certainly smarter than I was as a kid. You could do it. You could show me your evil lair full of human bones and spooky bats, and I'll show you that little cube apartment I bought for myself." She imagined it, her smile widening.

"Actually, it's probably been sold or broken into by now. I'm probably considered dead. Wonder what happened to my stuff. Woe is me, I lost my notebook and singular change of clothes," she deadpanned, feeling her nostrils flare in amusement. Her mirth faded quickly, a strange clarity filling her mind.

The beast paused for a moment, giving her a tired and oddly . . . light grumble-bark-howl kind of sound. As if it kind of understood her mirth, even if not its source and reasoning. Or maybe she was ascribing humanoid patterns of behavior to something monstrous just so she'd feel like she could understand it a bit more. Regardless, it was nice.

The crunching and shearing sounds continued, and she just snorted at the absurdity of what she was doing.

The beast snorted back at her.

"Getting sassy, aren't we?" She clicked her tongue in mock disapproval, her smile widening into a grin as her chest shook with mirth for a short moment.

In reply, the beast trotted closer, a dusty paw coming to brush against her mouth and making her sputter and cough as she accidentally inhaled a healthy mouthful of dust. It grumbled at her, a light, chiding sort of sound, then pawed at her cheek, where the face covering she had would be.

She spent a few more moments violently coughing to the side, then groaned as she flattened her back to the floor once more.

"Food?" she tried, hoping to teach it how to speak instead of pawing at her mouth with its dirty paws every time it wanted to feed her. Then she repeated it a couple times as the beast got increasingly annoyed with her, until finally, it mimicked her instead of pawing at her face.

"Fhwoood," it growl-howled, and she let out a soft laugh, lifting her hand to pet along its head and ears, something that the beast surprisingly welcomed as it tilted its head around to show her where it wanted scratches.

She had trouble *not* thinking of it as a dog sometimes, especially when it did things like this.

"Good job, buddy. Food," she murmured, then let up on her petting, covering her eyes with her hand and opening her mouth.

Compared to before, the blood felt utterly *divine*.

After biting off the skin sac and settling down for a quick nap with its snout nestled into the hollow of the human's throat, it prepared itself for some quick changes.

The first odd thing about the insect was that it had a very odd name.

Roof-Tumor.

That . . . didn't make any sense. At all. It wasn't a tumor, and the insect didn't seem particularly attached to heights when it was trying to get to the human.

Maybe that's just what the humans called it? So . . . did the symbols use the human's names for everything? Why and how . . . ?

Regardless, the biology of the insect was both extremely simple and extremely complicated. It used some absurdly overcomplicated system of liquid pressures to move its limbs, which even a single puncture could easily jeopardize.

It was, frankly, stupid.

It was just a bad system, so it completely ignored it. Its chitin carapace was an interesting idea, being fairly stretchy while being about as hard as regular bone, but the wolf couldn't find anywhere to put that to use, so it also ignored it for the moment.

At the end, it only cared about the sticky slime veins and the venom.

It quickly put its paralyzing venom sacs into its own abdomen and connected them to two chitinous, black fangs that it created on the underside of its jaw, right at the end. They were fairly mobile, even if they lacked much of the supportive structure the insect had, so the wolf could easily just close its mouth and press its snout into something, then use the fangs to paralyze them. They weren't even visible unless the wolf tilted its head up, so it didn't have any compunctions about adding them immediately.

The dosage would have to be a bit delicate because the venom was *absurdly* potent, but if it was planning on eating whatever it was trying to paralyze, it didn't really matter.

The second point of interest was the veins. The slime was simply a unique sort of mucus produced by the insect. It was naturally *extremely* sticky and really easy for the body to produce, but the way it became so rigid and why it seemed to almost actively fight against the wolf's movements back then was because the mucus responded to the pulses of electricity that came from the veins. Almost like a muscle contracting.

That electricity was what made the mucus so tough and difficult to struggle against. The molecular bonds changed when electrically stimulated and fought any changes to their structure based on the electrical signals given by the veins. If someone tried to stretch the slime in any direction, it would actively try to pull itself back to what the veins were telling it was its neutral position, fighting against whatever they restrained without any active effort on the insect's part. There were specific signals of varying intensity that could direct the mucus as well, like urging it to move in one direction or another.

It was utterly ingenious.

The veins themselves were just as interesting, even if they weren't *actually* veins. It was just more convenient to think of them as such. They were actually supercompressed networks of stretchy material made up of intertwining layers of insulative fat, stretchy tendon tissue, and nerves, which would get filled and covered with a unique mucus. Using that mucus, the insect would send electrical signals to the nerves to direct them the way it wanted and fill the smaller, branching veins to expand outward or contract inward.

The outside mucus would stick to something, then through the veins, more of it would be secreted and directed until it could basically cover whatever it wanted to. Afterward, through the same electrical signals, it could basically just soften the inside layers of the mucus that didn't have filth stuck on them and suck it back in, while the outer layer would harden and disconnect, being left behind on whatever surface or animal they'd stuck themselves to, to prevent the insides of the insect from being clogged with trash.

Its application was also surprisingly easy. The wolf just had to make a sort of . . . flat, fleshy pocket across its backside filled with the veins and the insect's mucus membranes along the walls, then make a thin slit across its back where the veins would come out of. Then connect the nerves to the odd, oversized tubes, and figure out how to control them.

It was delightfully simple to copy and apply. The wolf made the [Devourer] skill spend a bit more essence on nutrition for the mucus production and the extra material it would be fueling, both in terms of muscles and weird snot-veins, but it was more than worth it.

It then had the idea of climbing straight up walls like the insect had. If it could support both its own and the human's weight . . . it could just climb up shafts and vents until it got to the surface.

So it added two smaller pockets—sheaths, really—on the front of both its hind and forelegs; above the wrist on its forelegs, and just above its paws on its hind ones.

It was positively giddy about *walking up walls*.

How *amazing* would that be? Just being impervious to gravity? Maybe it could even stick itself to some of those metal boxes the humans used to move around and see what it was like to hang over thousands of feet of cables and walkways without any worry of slipping off.

Its tail thumped almost painfully against the floor, and it heard the human make some short yipping sounds at the sound.

And now, the wolf had a small dilemma to deal with.

On one paw, it really wanted to get going.

On the other, it really wanted to sit and wait for all the changes to happen, and then acclimate itself to them before rushing out into the unknown. It didn't particularly want to try fighting anything when it could still be trying to figure out how to walk properly.

It took a long time to come to a decision, but it eventually did. Rushing out without thinking would likely not end well.

It shook itself awake a bit, feeling the human's left hand caressing and squeezing along its right paw and toe pads, her right shoulder being slightly occupied by the wolf's chest and head.

Then it grumbled at her.

It wanted to practice human speech.

"You certainly had a nice dream, huh, buddy?" she murmured, her voice light, and the wolf noted that she was asking something. It wasn't sure what, so it just started trying to mimic her words.

Even with minimal assistance from [Logotexnia], it did pretty well, in its opinion.

"Uuu ssseertuhuunweee . . ." it started, the sound more of a mangled, low howl than anything, and focused a bit more on the skill, using it to twist the sound waves into what it was trying to mimic.

"Aad ei naiiisss dhuream, haah, buuhhhryy?" it finished proudly, then poked her in the side lightly.

The human did her odd yipping sound again, a bit subdued.

"That still sounds *so* creepy . . . you abominable little goober," she sighed, and before the wolf could try and mimic that, she grabbed its paw and thumped it against her own sternum. "Emhreeil. Emhreeil," she repeated. The wolf curiously tilted its head, its ear twitching against the human's cheek.

Was she trying to tell it that was how "human" was said, or trying to explain the sound that referred to her specifically? Regardless, it copied her.

"Eeemmmmrrreeeee-eel," it started, then grumbled. It didn't sound right. So it tried again and again while the human pet its head approvingly, until it figured out that it was making the last sound too far apart from the rest.

"Eemreee-eel," it finished, then let out a short, victorious howl. A very low-volume one—it didn't want to attract anything else to them right now.

"Good job, buddy," the human said, the sound a bit stuttered through her happy yipping, before, for some reason, repeating the sound and thumping its paw against her chest before letting it go.

Seeing the pattern, it did the same.

"Eeeemree-eel," it said, then awkwardly patted her collarbone with its paw.

The wolf could basically *smell* the human's happiness. And if it couldn't, the almost violent petting and frantic repetition of "Good job!" whatever that meant, was a good indicator of how joyous she was at teaching it her human-specific sound.

Or at least, that's what the wolf assumed it was. It knew humans had specific sounds for each other, as it had observed them using *dozens* of greetings or pay-attention-to-me sounds that always made only *one* specific human turn around to communicate with them, and "Emree-eel" sounded like one of those.

Then, with the same odd method of paw touching and dragging, the wolf learned how to say "arm," "hand," "head," "chest," "stomach," and "haste," as well as what those sounds correlated to.

It was a very . . . relaxing way to spend a couple hours.

And although the young canine instinct to want to play with her was fairly strong, it wasn't sure of *how* to do it. When it would observe the dogs of the human nest, it was always like a . . . mock fight of sorts. It had never had a mock fight with anyone before. And the human was weak and squishy and injured.

Well, if it could get her out of this place and return her to the human nest to heal, it could find her later and try. It had her scent memorized and baked into its brain by now.

Eventually, it settled down, half on top of her, for a good, extremely long nap, squeezing the melatonin sac in its stomach dry, and starting to feel extremely drowsy and sleepy within just moments.

If anything came toward them, the wolf could wake itself up in an instant with a shot of adrenaline, anyways.

As the beast quickly fell asleep, she had trouble staying still. The temptation to keep petting it was nigh irresistible. Despite the terrible situation, she was almost . . . *genuinely* happy. It was so easy to get lost in the pleasant parts of her predicament, and she did exactly that.

It was just . . . *fun* to teach it how to speak. And it learned so *quickly*. And when it wasn't speaking like a creepy demon from the depths of the dark, it was just . . . !

Cute.

It was goddamn adorable. She loved this thing.

So what if it was a predator that had definitely debated tearing her throat out a couple times on the staircase? They'd been strangers then. Now . . .

The way it nestled its head under her jaw made her smile like an idiot.

Sure, the mental high she got from drinking its blood probably helped with the odd giddiness she felt, but even that thought just made her smile more. This "beast" was giving her its *own* blood just to keep her alive.

She'd thought so for a while now, but it only really sank in at this moment. It was probably some kind of shape-shifter, considering it was never injured or anemic after feeding her. But *still,* the gesture just made her heart swell with warmth. It could bite through iron and crash through two stories before fighting some giant spider and be up and walking around just a day later, but it still decided she was worth going through all this trouble to keep her alive, despite the fact it didn't *need* her.

She couldn't really think of anyone in her life who would care enough to do something like that. She wouldn't even care enough to do that for *herself,* with how much self-loathing she'd grown to nestle near her heart in recent times.

But this thing did.

Unable to help herself, she gently started running her fingers up and down its foreleg, slowly being lulled to sleep by its breaths.

Waiting for the changes while awake would have taken a couple days.

Waiting for the changes while constantly forcing itself back to sleep shortened that time period to just over . . . maybe forty hours?

Despite being woken up a few times by both the human for her meals and the uncomfortable sensation of its own flesh moving and growing under its skin, it usually managed to fall asleep soon after. It mostly spent its sleeping hours tugging its new muscles around to form the mental connection so it could easily feel and contract them when it woke up. Although that did have the side effect of making the human curiously grope at the muscles that seemed to move of their volition, as if it was a puzzle she couldn't quite figure out.

And now, it simply lay on top of the human's shoulder, experimentally flexing its forelegs' right paw. It was so strange to be able to move its fingers. Being able to wiggle its fangs under its jaw and secrete liquid venom from them was equally odd.

It wriggled off the sleeping human and raised itself up. The first note of interest was the extremely odd sensation of its shoulder rotating so wildly, and its wrist doing much the same. The additional muscles were a close second.

The extra weight was, thankfully, not terribly noticeable. It could only feel it if it was looking for the difference. The thing that was *extremely* noticeable, however, was its tail.

It experimentally curled it into a loose spiral shape, then unwound it and pressed it hard against the ground. It curled its hind legs and hopped off the ground to test the strength of the tail, its forelegs keeping its upper half supported. It was . . . adequate. It could hold up its bottom half with a bit of trembling and effort.

It flared the antennae on its legs as it hopped down, finding this method of feeling the vibrations a lot more convenient, and a lot more accurate and long-reaching as well. The impacts of its legs hitting the ground worked a lot better to make it *feel* what was happening by having the entire limb itself perceive the shocks. And having almost double the antennae between its four limbs than before, it could feel things quite a lot farther.

Just experimentally, it trotted around the empty space for a bit. Its first few steps were almost like learning how to walk again, its elbows tilting too early and at completely different spots than it was used to, making its body tip almost at random as it fumbled for balance. The distance between its legs being a *lot* wider than before didn't exactly help.

After a couple minutes of hurriedly walking in circles, however, it got the hang of it. The wider stance of its new legs could easily be adjusted by having its wrists closer together and its elbows flare out to the side more, just like it had visualized earlier. It wasn't that much different from what it was used to, this way.

Within half an hour, it was effortlessly running around the room, its paws wreathed in silence to not wake up the human. It tested its newfound four directional capabilities by running forward then trying to lunge to the side, running forward then swiping at shoulder height, even by leaping at imaginary enemies to hook its nails—or claws, rather—into their backsides.

It was so *easy*. It should have done this *so* much sooner.

Then came the hard part.

Trying to figure out how to control the veins and the slime was an absolute *chore*. It took *hours* of constantly forcing the veins through the open slit at its back, and even then, trying to keep the slime, or specialized mucus, solid enough to stick to the veins while moving each tiny individual nerve to spread and flare them out was extremely difficult. Holding a position was easy by comparison, but it still took almost a third of the wolf's focus just to keep them stiff enough to, say, hold the human in place.

It should have put that attribute point into Intelligence.

And the odd sensation of having a slowly expanding network of veiny, mucus-filled tentacles wiggling into the open air out of its back, was . . .

Really, really, really weird.

Regardless, what seemed like uncountable hours later, it felt confident enough with the veins to do what it wanted to, and with its heart beating furiously in excitement, the wolf walked to the wall under the rectangular holes full of glass, putting its forelegs against it.

Tiny pulses of electricity shot out of the numb nerves in the veins, and within seconds, a small network of wriggling, foul-smelling tubes covered in slime was creeping over its paws to stick to the wall. It curled its hind legs in and slammed them onto the wall, putting all of its weight onto its forelegs, carefully keeping the slime just liquid enough to be sticky and just solid enough to support its weight.

After a short moment of disbelief at the fact that it hadn't fallen down on its back yet, the realization slowly crept unto reality.

It was sitting on a wall.

Vertically.

It quickly wreathed its head in darkness and let out a deafening victory howl only it could hear, its doubly long tail slapping the rock floor below.

Wagging its tail with this length felt strange and off-key, but it ignored it in favor of being giddy at the ability to just stick to walls if it wanted to.

It repeated its actions with its hind legs, the load on its front paws quickly halving, and then with a gait which felt equivalent to the pace of a snail, it started crawling up the wall.

At some point, it reached the metal flooring above and had to turn and crawl across the wall on its side, but it was still so much fun, it couldn't even bother feeling annoyed at the obstruction. The practice was great for its speed, too. Every step went from taking a couple minutes to hovering around sixty seconds, then thirty.

Just as an experiment, it tried to quickly detach, and completely stopped the signals from the nerves to the mucus. The slime took a second or two to actually loosen up, but then, the wolf's body simply fell down with a startled yelp before hitting the floor with a harmless but loud *thump*, the liquid slime coating its legs quickly having lost all cohesion along with the veins.

After a moment of observing the effect, it tried to quickly retract the veins into its legs with a few short signals, only using the mucus on the inside to deflate and sucker them back in. It was a . . . twitchy, mildly disturbing, but very quick affair, only taking a couple seconds to have them back in place in their little flesh pockets, though this method did waste the *vast* majority of the mucus it had produced by not taking the time to retract it with the veins. Mucus which was now coating all of its paws.

Not that it minded. It was absolutely ecstatic.

It simply rolled over and shot to its feet, and unable to contain its excitement, activated [Bloodrush] and started speeding in wide circles, tongue hanging out of the side of its mouth. Making sudden turns was so *easy* now*!*

It just had to throw a paw to the side, hook its nails into the stone at almost full cutting capacity, and let the pull of its momentum swing its body in the direction the wolf wanted it to before resuming its run.

It didn't stop there, trying various maneuvers and acrobatics, like leaping at the walls at an angle, then using its forelegs to spin its lower body above its head and kick at the wall with hind legs to shoot itself at an imaginary enemy. This freedom of movement felt *amazing.*

The human let out a loud, questioning sound, and the wolf just used its [Logotexnia] skill to send a *very* specifically directed grumble-howl of elation, making sure the sound wouldn't bounce around too much and draw attention to them, before resuming its practice.

It jumped at iron pillars, using the dexterity of its forelegs to spin its body and absorb the impact, before using its hind legs to jump at imaginary enemies at an angle. It tried using its tail like a whip, which surprisingly worked, judging by the strong impact it felt through its feet and the bruise on its tail tip. It tried using its tail to help it execute rolls that would help lessen the impact of a sheer drop. It used all of its instinctual and biological knowledge to strain its body and fully explore everything it could do.

By the end of it, even its seven points in Endurance couldn't keep up, and the wolf was happily panting as it dragged itself back to the human, its muscular tail—twice as long as its own body now—limply dragging on the ground.

Despite its tired state, it wanted to do nothing more than start making its way back to the surface, but it refrained, taking a quick nap to rejuvenate itself before waking up, stretching, and turning to the girl.

It poked the human's side lightly with its knuckles.

"Hhaaannnnd," it growled, and the human's reply came out in a sigh.

"Sure."

A limp-wristed hand was presented to the wolf, accidentally bopping it on the nose before the human readjusted it.

"Sorry."

With its teeth blunted, it tried to figure out how it was going to do this.

Eventually, it simply stood parallel to the human on her left side and took her wrist in its mouth. Then, as slowly as it could manage, it lowered its body and tilted on its side before swiftly rolling onto her torso, its back against her chest.

She made a strange *oof* sound, idly adjusting her wrist between its teeth.

"Uh . . . what are you doing?" she whispered the question, and the wolf simply grumbled through her wrist in a chiding manner, a sort of *be patient* sound. It took a few seconds, but the pocket on its back swiftly inflated before the first bits of the veins started creeping out.

This position was really awkward. It was only its flattened back and rib cage that kept it from tilting to the sides constantly.

Maybe it could do this by lying next to her next time?

Even weirder was the sensation of having to feel along the human to conform to her shape and wrap her up. The sensory abilities of the veins were like . . . a very, very numb tendril. Not that great.

Regardless, within a minute or so, the veins and the mucus/slime/*whatever* had covered the front of the confused human's chest before finally inching toward her stomach and the torn parts of her coverings at the shoulders, prompting a weird exclamation of surprise from her when they touched her skin.

Judging by the strength of her clothes, it could probably roll her over onto its back now.

It turned a paw to press against the ground on their left, and started to rock its body side to side, getting ready to turn itself over and finally start making progress.

With a final heave to the right, pushing away with its left forepaw on the ground for added momentum, it managed to swing itself over onto its side as the human yelped, going rigid against its back. Then it curled its right paw into its side, knuckles grinding against stone. With a growl of effort, it lifted them both upright, stumbling and staggering for a moment as its tail quickly curled around the human's knees to stop her legs from flopping around everywhere.

Bones had to set to heal, and having them sliding and hitting everything in their path wouldn't help one bit.

With the human secured to its back, the wolf adjusted her a bit so her head would be hanging off the right side of its neck and her left hand over the left side, just for balance's sake, before swiftly expanding the veins to grip onto her sides and hips for added stability.

Then it took a few experimental steps, the human's breaths growing deeper as she was jostled around yet kept in place.

It was . . . pretty heavy, in all honesty. Mostly on its already trembling tail. The human's navel was at its tailbone, as the wolf was still pretty . . . normal sized. So it was supporting almost half of her body weight with the tail. A tall order.

Compared to dragging her entire body weight by its teeth, however, as well as fighting the friction of her clothes against wet rust and moss, this was about half as hard.

Next time it napped, it would add a little sheath of sticky veins on the upper side of its tail, or try to find ways to make it a bit stronger, but for the moment, it started trotting to the rusty door on the other side of the room, releasing the human's wrist with a light, playful grumble.

Her hand immediately jerked up to feel along the mucus and veins. A sharp gasp escaped her.

Unlike the reaction it was expecting, which was something along the lines of confusion or appreciation, a sudden surge of fear entered its nostrils, with the human as its source, prompting it to stop walking and nudge the top of her head with its snout where it hung by its neck, a vaguely questioning sound escaping its throat.

"A wolf," the human breathed out, still rubbing one of the veins in her hands as if . . . *impressed?* Impressed and scared?

Humans still didn't make sense.

"You're a *wolf*," she croaked out, her tone strangely heavy.

"Wooohhf," it mimicked, and the human went silent for a moment, the scent of fear quickly retreating. Her head thumped against its shoulder as if in defeat.

"Of course you're a *fucking* wolf. Shape-shifting canine. Can cut through iron. Way too strong and resilient for its size. How did I not—How did it take me *this* long to realize? How did it take seeing you literally *steal* another being's body part for me to figure it out?" she breathed out, her body going completely limp against its back.

Then, she got oddly spirited as it continued blankly staring at her, unbeknownst to her.

"Well, no, I know how. You're way too smart and friendly and cute, if you ignore all those times you were about to rip my throat out back at the staircase. And then there's the whole *supposed to be fucking extinct* thing—and aren't you supposed to be like, psychotically aggressive and constantly hungry? How did you even get down here? I mean, it doesn't matter to me that you're a legendary predatory monster, but what the *actual fuck* is—I'm just talking to myself at this point, aren't I?" The human groaned out miserably, letting out an odd, frustrated sob into its shoulder, and the wolf . . .

Honestly, it had no idea what the human was going on about, so it just turned back toward the rusty door and kept walking as the human continued making rapid noises at it, going from heated whispers to rapid hissing to wildly gesticulating with her hand as if trying to point at a . . . vague . . . something?

But she was blind. What was she even . . .

Whatever.

Its human made even less sense than her kin, it felt like.

At least the door crumpled like wet paper from their combined weight as they made their way out into the tunnels again.

CHAPTER 25

[Mana Touch] was a pretty curious skill, from the little bits of use she'd given it while being carted around. It was a rather "toggleable" type more than a usable one, meaning that as long as she didn't manually turn it off, she could feel her own mana all the time like a tactile sensation.

Which, unfortunately, meant she could also *feel* every tiny bit of flesh and sinew and veins and *everything* inside her body. Constantly.

[Mana Tank] was a terrible combination with [Mana Touch].

It was immensely disturbing, so she'd decided to just turn [Mana Touch] off whenever she wished to practice or *not* feel the slimy sensation of her intestines wriggling in her stomach like lazy worms.

The skill was also interesting because of how mana itself functioned.

Mana itself *could* go through walls, should its wielder demand it. It was a bit of a Resolve type of issue—willpower, in other words.

Willpower wasn't tangible nor measurable, nor even a resource or an energy. It was purely mental, and thus, different for everyone. It was a very uncertain thing to say "I have enough willpower to do this" without trying first. It was simply arrogant of a mage to say "I can make my spell do this" without having attempted it first.

Most people didn't mess around with Resolve too much.

It was, after all, the only attribute which mentally affected its wielders, and most people were very hesitant about mental changes to themselves from the notoriously unpredictable System. People could get stuck on ideas that were false, or become so heavily invested in a belief or ideology that it was impossible to break away from it, even when presented with factual evidence or rational arguments.

It was one of the reasons that most highly ranked religious officials had such high Resolve. Unwavering faith required unwavering willpower to not be swayed by other gods or corruption or . . . something like that.

In contrast, most regular folk would rather keep their minds relatively malleable. Even mages, who were the biggest benefactors of Resolve points, were instructed to only put a maximum of three to five into the attribute. After all, if one's mind became too stuck up on ideas and the like, learning became difficult. Or at least, so it was said.

Others disputed and disagreed with that, as was the ever-evolving nature of social debate, but regardless, the general consensus of the population's perception when it came to Resolve was "don't touch it too much unless necessary," at least from what she had observed.

So, she'd never planned on putting more than a single point in the damn thing.

But.

[Mana Touch] was her only real means of perceiving her surroundings.

So when she realized she could only force her mana to move through the floor or walls for about a couple inches, she let out a heavy sigh, opened the System, and dumped her banked-up point into Resolve, despite the intense desire to put it into Soul.

As useful as it would be to have a bigger soul, and thus a bigger rate of mana regeneration, she was more interested in either Endurance or being able to use her mana more efficiently. And considering her current companion, she felt . . . not safe, but safe enough to try and do something stupid.

Adding a point to Resolve was surprisingly fruitful, almost doubling how much her mana could penetrate the walls—about eight inches instead of three to five. The mental battle of sending out her mana with the intent to pierce was not intense, but it wasn't easy either.

Maybe if she had finer control, she could just summon a cluster of mana into a wall and feel that way, but her range of both controlling and feeling the energy was . . . very good for her level, but nothing extraordinary.

The tactile sensation of moving through objects was likely exactly what ghosts felt, she mused, as she used her limply hanging hand to feel along the floor and a little bit *through* it. It was so *odd.*

Mostly out of boredom, she turned her palm to face the direction the wolf—*the fucking wolf. She still couldn't get over that. Just HOW*—was moving in, just to test her range. Feeling *through* things wasn't as important as feeling things in general.

A few pulses of directed mana and . . .

If she had eyes, they'd be considerably widened right now.

While her normal ability to sense through mana would have been restricted to *maybe* ten feet—with the assistance of a high-powered [Haste] at that—[Mana Touch] helped her feel at a much larger distance. For twenty or so feet, a pulse of mana would give her a *very* accurate feeling of her surroundings before the sensation faded.

In fact, it was so accurate, she could probably draw the rectangular tunnel they were in like a capture crystal in her mind—minus the colors—down to the texture of the pipes nailed to the ceiling above them.

Of course, this long-range perception didn't extend at all to *controlling* the mana at any respectable range, but . . . but she could *see.* Her natural mana regeneration was already good. Combined with [Mana Tank] and [Mana Conduit], seeing semipermanently for at least like . . . ten feet, wouldn't cost *any* mana.

Hope blossomed in her chest like a withered, crumpled flower finally feeling the sun and its first drops of water. She smiled.

When she got out of here, she'd have a *chance.*

They continued their silent trek through the darkness for another long, uneventful hour before Emhreeil decided to just get used to feeling every muscle fiber in her body pass through phantom fingers, turning on [Mana Touch] once more and starting the mana exercises she'd learned.

Her mild motion sickness, coupled with the sensation, did make her dry heave and retch a couple times, making her companion stop and nose her head. But she powered through it, nuzzling the wolf's snout back with the side of her head before going back to training.

Having spent another hour without feeling anything but the light wobbling of her body in its slimy bonds, she realized that the sensation would take a *long* time to feel less . . . utterly revolting and skin-crawlingly uncomfortable.

At least she knew *exactly* what the condition of her body and bones was.

The long and short of it was that she was actually starting to have a rather gaunt figure, and her bones were healing at a frankly ludicrous speed.

She supposed drinking *fucking wolf's blood* would do that.

The cracks were growing infinitesimally smaller by the *hour.* Rather than a couple months, she expected she'd be able to walk in a couple days, or a week at most. Even though her left leg was healing wrong, the bone fragments just a bit misaligned and likely to end up with her having a semipermanent limp, she was just overjoyed.

Her future seemed less and less uncertain by the second. She could *see*, sort of. She would be able to walk, and she'd have mana capacity and regeneration that people would kill their mothers for. Her debts were wiped out, along with her tormentors. And her legs were healing. Sure, she'd have to buy a slave to . . . to drink blood from them to keep the Vampiric trait up until she could find a vampire to turn her. And . . . and she had a *heavy* dislike of the practice, but she'd be able to heal that way.

And in the hypothetical scenario that she was unable to find a vampire to turn her, she could always just . . . *work*. Adventurer, mercenary, seamstress, or factory worker, *anything*, and live, save up, fix herself up. She'd just release the slave back into society as a free man—

Her mind provided her with the image of her, one armed, weak and alone, starving, trying to get her slave to just willingly give her his blood in an inn room.

Her chest tightened as her throat went dry. The padding of the wolf's feet turned to the slapping of flesh on flesh. The filth tugging her hair down turned to thin, calloused fingers in her hair. The veins turned to ropes. The wolf's fur turned to rough sheets. The world grew distant. She choked on air, her hand tightening on the wolf's fur.

"Say something," she rasped out, gasped out through lungs which felt like black holes that would never get enough oxygen, realizing she was having another one of those—those episodes.

The wolf suddenly stopped, twisting its head around to nose at her face with a faint whine, and she desperately nuzzled back, dragging her fingers through its fur with all her strength, the sandpaper-like texture helping her ground herself as she crushed the remnants of her nose into its neck, her breaths uneven and her shoulders quivering with a sob she refused to let out, gritting her teeth with spite and hatred.

She wasn't *weak*. She wasn't going to let her stupid brain win. She was in a desolate, godforsaken tunnel in the depths of the Dungeon, with a wolf and nothing else around them. She wasn't going to let her mind convince her otherwise.

Her grip tightened, and she forcefully turned the wolf's head, her forehead rubbing up against the side of its neck as she gasped in air, feeling the real world return to her piece by piece, the freezing nose of her companion brushing against her right shoulder, confused grumbles and little whines of concern letting her know exactly what her companion was thinking.

It took a minute or two, but eventually, her grip loosened, her body slowly relaxing, her mind settling down as the void inside her lungs filled with air.

It took another minute or two for her breaths to return to some semblance of pace, and she sighed, her fingers brushing the left side of the wolf's neck as they rubbed their heads together. Like animals. No masks, no judgement. Just two animals trying to survive together. In that moment, that was all they were.

She found she rather liked the simplicity of it. Some animalistic, primal part of her recognized this to somehow be a bigger expression of trust and care than even the tightest hug, and she let a small smile form on her face.

"Thank you, buddy. I'll return the favors one day. I swear. I owe you so much," she whispered, and the wolf, likely realizing she was no longer on the verge of having one of those shell shock–like episodes, chuffed, gave her shoulder a single lick, and turned around to continue its trot as if nothing ever happened.

She appreciated that a lot more than she expected she would, yet her mind still wandered back to her previous statement. *Release them back into society as a free man.*

Yeah, she doubted she could handle that. She'd just get a female slave.

Maybe.

People probably sold fresh . . . *anything* blood *somewhere* in this fucked-up place, right? There was no way that wasn't a thing. Alchemist guild?

She sighed and sank back into her slimy bonds, deciding to turn the overthinking part of her brain off for the moment. She'd cross that bridge when she got to it.

The structure they were in was quite simple, starting out.

The room they'd been in was some sort of half-empty storage area. Right outside was a large rectangular room full of odd machines with empty canisters mounted atop them, with a dizzying mess of wires and fine bits of machinery going into the ground and splayed out all over the floor like the spilled innards of a corpse.

Having sensed nothing in the way of upward mobility but a few too-tight vents in the middle of the ceiling, the wolf was faced with two options. Moving back up that endless pipe they'd arrived through—an even more exhausting journey considering it would be *upward* this time, the wolf was bulkier, and they wouldn't fit into the pipe with the human on its back, so they'd go back to dragging.

Or just going down the long rectangular tunnel nestled at the corner of the room behind a dozen gutted machines, and hoping it would lead to freedom.

It chose to take its chances with the tunnel.

It was, frankly, an almost relaxing trek, besides the human's odd bout of paranoid fear. Though it could relate, considering she was blind. It too had had one such episode when it was . . . significantly smaller and had gotten some strange-smelling liquid in its eyes. It couldn't see for an entire day. Every little noise had made its heart leap up to its throat.

But regardless of that little hiccup, things were nice, silent, and boring. Despite being an hour and a half into it and not yet sensing any end to the tunnel, it didn't even feel the need to speed up all that much, deciding to conserve energy for what could be another nigh-endless journey.

To its right were some metal rails embedded into the stone, taking up about a fourth of the tunnel's width, and to its left and above were a bunch of small, rusted pipes stuck to and throughout the stone. Eight feet tall and twelve feet wide, it was quite spacious.

At some point, mostly due to boredom, it considered why and how that "Roof-Tumor" insect had ended up down there. Perhaps fallen down through the pipe? Or it'd willingly chosen that area as some kind of nesting spot due to how remote it was? Maybe they should have checked around for eggs . . .

Its conclusion was that it didn't matter. The wolf was just thinking for the sake of thinking, at that point. *Not* thinking of anything just drew attention to the gnawing hunger in its soul, which it could mostly ignore, provided it had a distraction. The human's petting was a good one, for example.

After stopping for a bit and sitting on its stomach and chest for a short recovery nap, it continued, occasionally growling "Haste" at the human to speed things up a bit without exhausting itself, until finally, it sensed a change in the vibrations after a particularly hard slap of its paw into the floor.

It might have stumbled a bit from the confusion of being bombarded with information, but the human's yelp brought it back to the real world quick enough for it to hurriedly straighten itself as it parsed through what it felt.

About a hundred and fifty feet away, the tunnel ended in two giant metal doors, behind which opened up a larger area it couldn't feel any details about.

Finally, a change.

Its pace redoubled into a jog of sorts, and the human, obviously feeling the sudden rush due to her attachment to its back, raised her hand up to rub along its head and ears again. It was *very* pleasant, so the wolf tilted its head up and around for her to properly give it the pets it wanted, seeing as it didn't need its head to be stable to navigate.

"Found an exit, buddy?" she whispered a question, and the wolf chuffed in acknowledgement, more out of habit at this point than as a genuine answer to a question it couldn't yet understand.

A hundred and fifty feet turned to fifty, and the wolf felt the pungent miasma of dried oil and stale, dusty air wafting through the gaps in the closed doors. A stench which would become far worse, it assumed, when it broke through, considering there wasn't any wind down here and it could *still* smell it from this far.

It was actually kind of mind-numbing . . .

With a sense of distaste, it trotted up the last few feet to the doors, occasionally stomping a paw without breaking pace just to get a better feeling of the room beyond.

It was massive.

Considering the things humans built, it wasn't sure why it was even surprised anymore.

Despite being right next to the doors and stomping down with its paw, utilizing their combined weight so much that it felt a light bruise forming on its paw pad, it couldn't reach or feel the other end of the room.

From its perspective, the doors just opened up to a vast abyss of empty air looming over a floor riddled with complex networks of pipes, cables, and inner valve systems. The surface of said floor was peppered with bits of debris, rotting tools, and giant pyramid-shaped machines which tapered up to large pipes that reached up to what it assumed was a ceiling it could only barely feel the outline of before that, too, faded.

That, and the pyramid-like parts of the machines all felt strangely hollow. Likely gutted like the ones from before, though in a less messy manner. It was curious, but it didn't know anything about human machinery beyond some vague, surface-level labeling, so it refrained from making assumptions or dwelling on it.

Instead, it focused on something much more important, which was getting *through* the doors.

They were *really* thick, maybe eight inches, heavy, and their insides were a complicated mess of fine machine work which seemed to be some sort of locking mechanism. Either side had been dug into the wall itself, so just brute-force charging it wouldn't do anything but bruise its shoulders. The strangest thing, however, was that whatever metal they'd been created from seemed impervious to rust and had that faint, barely present tingle of mana.

It scrutinized the length of its nails. About an inch long. If the locking mechanism was sufficiently damaged . . . it *should* be able to just push them open, right?

For the first time in about two hours, it lay flat on its chest and stomach, and started slowly retracting the slime and veins, making sure not to waste any of it by being hasty.

The human shivered.

"This is *so* disgusting," she murmured, wriggling a little before settling down again. "Then again, I've been drinking wolf's blood and pissing myself for days, so I feel like I should be past the point of giving a crap. What do you think?" she asked lightly.

The wolf just chuffed, clicking its chitinous fangs together, barely audible to even itself. Having new limbs still felt so strange. That, and the clicking was oddly satisfying. Almost amusing, actually.

Clickclickclick.

"True words of wisdom, oh wizened wolf," the human sighed out in an odd tone. Sort of tired, but also light and . . . it couldn't quite tell.

A minute or two later, the wolf slowly loosened its tail from where it was curled around the human's knees, snaking it off to the side, before slowly shuffling the human off its back toward the left after the veins packed themselves back into their sheath.

Readjusting to the feeling of its mucus veins becoming part of its innards again, it shook itself, hoping the outer bits of slime would dry and peel off quickly. It didn't like the feeling of its fur being so *sticky*. Also, it thought it could feel a tiny pebble in its flesh sheath, which was annoying.

Shaking off the mild discomfort, it walked up to the wall and got up on its hind legs, its forelegs positioned over the lock. Thankfully, the lock was just at four feet tall—exactly at the right height for the wolf to begin its arduous but boring task.

It hooked its claws and angled one paw's fingers to the left while the other angled to the right.

And then it got to scratching.

Despite feeling no resistance when cutting through the iron, the deafening screech of rent metal made it flinch and flatten its ears, having grown used to the quiet mumblings of its human and the soft pattering of its paws.

But what really made it freeze in place was the sudden burst of sparks that flared out across its vision.

It stood shock-still as their light faded, leaving it in complete darkness once more. But to its unadjusted eyes, the imprint of their light danced and writhed, a hundred subtle shades of color it had never seen before just suddenly . . . there. It knew, conceptually, that some things were supposed to be a certain color. Many different ones it simply couldn't imagine or conceive of, but were in its head regardless, occupying space as labels to throw on things.

Until now, that was all they were. The blood it saw might *seem* brown yellow to its canine eyes, but it knew it was, from the perspective of whatever source its knowledge came from, labeled with the color descriptor "red."

It *knew* that, but it had never *seen* other colors. So when in those sparks, it saw *orange* and a familiar yellow with a billion tiny little shades in between which made the sparks so mind-numbingly beautiful, it could only freeze as its mind engraved the sight to memory.

It covered one of its nails with silent darkness just to be rid of the noise, and slowly scratched the iron, eyes glued to the door. Nothing.

It gave a second scratch, a far more aggressive one, mildly paranoid that it had somehow messed up and wouldn't see the sparks again. To its immense relief and joy, they did appear, just like the first time, sudden, violent little bursts of immeasurable beauty. Speed seemed to be the key.

And these . . . these were just two colors of the wide spectrum that human eyes could see.

What would it be like when it got to the surface? Would it even see the same world as before?

It quickly sheathed its paws in soundless darkness and started frantically scratching, putting rents into the iron in one direction, and then shaving pieces off by scratching in the opposite one, making a jagged hole into the middle of the doors, bit by bit.

It paused when it felt a very faint rush of mana wash over itself and the door, and it twitched an ear, noting that the human had a hand extended toward it.

Whatever she was doing was harmless, so it just got back to scratching a giant hole into the door, five shavings of iron at a time, slowly but surely making a small pile around its hind paws, eyes firmly glued to the near constant stream of sparks.

It was just so *pretty*.

So pretty that it actually forgot what it was doing sometimes, randomly scratching at the door just to watch the sparks.

By the time it started scratching off bits of the finer machinery inside the door, its shoulders were starting to grow sore. So rather than open the door and continue with tired legs, it walked back to the human, moved to her left side, then threw a paw over her waist and plopped its head down on her shoulder, shuffling into her side to get comfortable.

The human sighed out some of her human sounds and moved her elbow up to tilt her forearm backward, just to rub along the back of its nape.

It was much more comforting than the wolf would have assumed. Especially considering it didn't know what it was being comforted from. Maybe some subconscious fear it hadn't worked out? Regardless, it fell asleep fairly quickly with a small squeeze of the "sleep sac," as it had deigned to call it from now on.

Perhaps its streak of creativity hadn't yet ended, because in that short nap, it decided to add a little chitinous fang at the tip of its tail, covered in hair-like chitin to make it blend in a little better when curled in. Then it made a second venom gland near the tip of its tail. It was extremely small, maybe only able to produce about three to five drops on demand whenever it had to inject something, but that didn't particularly matter. Every drop of that venom could probably paralyze most of a human's body, never mind anything smaller.

Another minor change was thickening its skull a tiny bit, just as a precaution more than anything.

Then it got up again with a jaw-popping yawn and a back-popping stretch with a tiny growl of satisfaction. After poking the human awake despite her feeble protests, it walked back to the door, swept aside the pile of metal shavings, and hopped up to place its paws on the shredded mess before getting to work on making it an even bigger mess. Despite cloaking its entire fingers in darkness, the constant clicking and popping of the complex machinery being shredded to even finer but disconnected bits was annoyingly loud.

That was without mentioning the sound they made as they added to the small pile. The sparks definitely helped soften the auditory irritation, though. Distracting and wondrous as they were, they were also a great motivator for the wolf to push forward and get to see light again.

Just to figure out what other colors it could now perceive beyond orange.

It wondered what blood really looked like in the light. Was red as pretty as sparks?

The dizzying network of gears, ranging from eye-squintingly tiny to the size of the wolf's paw, was quickly destroyed in just a minute or two. Two opposing metal rods surrounded by a spinning circular framework of metal were next, and the wolf took a moment to pause and shake its paws, feeling the dozen tiny cuts covering each.

They *itched* more than hurt. Annoying.

A light punch to the more intact parts of the door let the wolf feel the innards a bit better, as well as sending a cascade of tinkling bits of metal to join the small, second pile at its feet. The doors certainly *felt* looser.

With a tilt of its head, it turned and put its left shoulder to the door, unsure but *fairly* positive that the exit was no longer locked.

It sunk its claws into the stone just for good measure, activated [Bloodrush], and started pushing, its hind legs shaking from the effort, feeling the stone around its nails crack a little as it put all it had into pushing forward.

For a single, long second, nothing happened. And then, something in the door snapped with a tiny jerk, and the doors began to move. It wasn't smooth, the hinges sticky with dried, dust-crusted grease only making things harder, but it made progress.

About three inches, in fact. Just enough for a tiny gap to appear in the doors, prompting a wave of stench to slam into its nostrils in an almost physical sensation. It only had a single moment of tension to sneeze, continuing to push through, before something in the door got stuck on a half-shredded, bent gear.

With a growl of frustration, it snorted in a vain attempt to get the mind-numbing stench of oils and gasses out of its nostrils, then hopped up again and frantically scratched at the shredded locking mechanism before dropping down and bracing its shoulder to the right door as quickly as it could before [Bloodrush] ran out.

Another heave with its shoulder only against one door now and no lock in place, and the metal softly groaned as it began to slide back on sticky hinges, the wolf constantly adjusting its legs to rake its nails through stone for added traction as it growled in effort.

After a few seconds of pushing, a gap just wide enough for itself and the human to pass through was made, and the wolf leaned back with a relieved breath, shaking the bits of shredded metal and gearwork off its fur.

Or rather, tried to. It was all completely stuck into the remnants of the mucus covering its backside.

And the wolf, not wanting sharp bits of metal in and around its innards— as numb and unnecessary as those particular innards were—got to learn very intimately the extent of its flexibility, carefully shaving off bits of sticky fur dotted with iron bits for almost half an hour before it felt comfortable with grabbing the human again.

It had to see if it could somehow circumvent that little issue. Stickiness was never pleasant.

Putting her on its back was as awkward as the first time, with the wolf having to swing the human onto her back, lay on her chest, and then annoyingly turn them both upright, but it managed to fairly quickly bring them both to traveling condition.

"That . . . smells like rotted fuel and stale air. I doubt it's an exit," the human murmured as the wolf walked through the doors, its head swiveling around, not particularly liking the oppressive ambiance of distant, muffled thuds echoing into the room from the vast unknown.

The floor underneath its paws was sticky and grimy, dust mixing with dried oils and grease, barrels of the stuff left lying on the ground at random intervals. As it continued through the darkness, a more complete picture formed in its mind.

If it used its imagination, it could almost fill humans into the image doing . . . human stuff. Using and fiddling with all the machinery, empty carts full of broken glass, stray, rotting wires, and tools strewn about randomly around the colossal pyramid-like machines, each of them about fifteen humans tall and half as wide, with a large pipe on their tip that traveled upward, assumedly up to the top.

The room in general was a strange mixture of busy and empty.

Busy because of the small things littering the—for the most part—sticky floor, but empty due to how easily things were dwarfed by the machines, making everything else, including the wolf, feel small and insignificant. The complex machinery underneath the very floor it was walking on only added to that feeling.

The gridlike arrangement made everything feel too purposeful to have been discarded the way it was, and its curiosity itched for an answer as to why the humans had left this place.

It hoped the answer was a terribly boring one.

Its attention was split between observing its surroundings and the fact it couldn't deny that the deafening silence, only broken by distant echoes of sound, was mildly disturbing.

Thankfully, [Echoes of Oblivion] made stomping around for a better feel absolutely silent, so the nagging paranoia of lurking predators in the darkness waiting for a noise to pounce on was easily circumvented. The veins on its back unfortunately didn't have any mana pathways going through them, so the human was uncovered by the silence, and it didn't particularly want to try pushing the skill in that direction lest it feel that intensely uncomfortable sensation of mana veins being forcefully created again. It could probably do that next time it stopped for a rest, anyway, even if the wolf mentally chastised itself for not thinking of doing that until just now.

Its maximum range of vibration senses seemed to be around a hundred and fifty feet without any boosts from the human—who was a little busy uselessly throwing her mana out into the open air for some reason—and about a hundred if it wasn't stomping down with enough force to jostle the human around. With [Tremor Sense], about another thirty feet were added to its sensory range.

So when it finally felt the wall parallel to the doors they'd gone through, with only vague mental calculations to go with and a hazy visualization in its mind, it estimated the ceiling to be about . . . two hundred feet, and the walls about four hundred feet apart, while the sides were of an unknown width.

Some kind of rectangular room again. Humans sure loved those. Unless this was some kind of hallway, which . . . would make this structure a little bigger than the wolf was comfortable assuming it could be.

As it walked along rows of workbenches, pipes, and various miscellaneous discards, it realized another problem.

"Hhhaaaasstthe," it growl-hissed to the human, who startled before tapping its neck and going back to wasting her mana for some bizarre reason it would probably never understand.

There was no exit it could feel anywhere on the wall, and even its hardest stomps, which made the human yelp and hiss in reprimand, could only barely reach along a few feet on the edge of the ceiling. The human didn't give it a very strong boost this time.

Still, no way out.

But, operating on simple logic, the humans had to get down here *some* way, so it walked up to the wall and decided to follow it, turning to the right.

Fifteen minutes of walking through the same repeating grid of machines, with the only difference being the random stuff thrown about and how many of them there were, it realized how humans would get down here, and let out a long, weary exhale as the vibrations outlined the first irregularity it had felt in the gargantuan wall.

Those moving lifts the humans used.

It was a cubic-shaped platform made of metal, sixty feet wide and seemingly dug into the wall behind a grid of metal bars on the front, likely so the humans would be able to see it come down when it was still operational.

And judging by the way said platform had broken off the rails at two of its corners and was hanging at a tilted angle thirty feet off the floor, it certainly wasn't operational now, even if the human *could* figure out how to start one up.

The wolf slowly sat on its haunches, taking care not to move the human's legs too much as it sat silent in deep thought.

The human's hand petted its head between its ears as she asked it something, likely feeling the sudden change in demeanor. It let out a grumpy grumble in reply, wanting to think in silence. Thankfully, she didn't ask again, just rubbing along the rim of its ears as it lost itself in thought.

It could attempt to just . . . climb up the metal shaft. The walls were rusty, but thick and sturdy. Additionally, the X-shaped interlocking rods of metal evenly spaced along the platform's framework provided the wolf with a good spot to rest. A *scary* spot, but a good one. Stable and wide enough not to have to dig into the wall.

The scary part was the main reason it was hesitating.

The wolf was tough, far tougher than before, but there was absolutely no chance of it surviving a two-hundred-feet drop if something went wrong up there. Maybe *even if* it used the human as a meat cushion.

It could just keep walking and try to find some other exit. Maybe even walk into one of those pyramid machines and crawl up until it got to the top through the pipe.

But it just wanted to get out of here as soon as possible.

It wasn't going to pretend that it was unaffected by the environment. Its mind felt numb from the smell. The distant, rhythmic vibrations traveling through the floor felt disturbingly like the beating of a heart. The pipes and machine work it felt all around them felt like observing the arteries of a comatose titan. The dead silence of the gargantuan room felt unnatural and disquieting, and having such a small radius of sight made its brain always wonder what was *just* beyond its reach, paranoid thoughts wondering if something was always lurking at the edges, staring at them.

Also, *colors*. It wanted to see more of them.

It continued to waver between two choices for almost thirty silent minutes, despite a rising desire to just *pick something* and get on with it. To climb up the shaft, or just go off and try to find some other exit. Both had their risks and their benefits.

Eventually, it decided to first test if it could actually support both its own and the human's weight before picking either.

Walking up to the smooth metal wall to its left, it slowly extended the slime from its upper paws, supporting their weight with its hind legs before jumping up and sticking them to the wall as well, one at a time.

Surprisingly, it could support both of them without too much issue.

Then, it sort of just . . . wiggled from side to side, trying to get a feel for how resilient the slime was; how much more strain it could handle. Turns out, it had been underestimating the mucus quite a bit. It felt like it could carry another half of a human without concern.

After carefully detaching—making sure to waste as little slime as possible—it sat still for another minute, thinking, and then decided to just go with the platform's shaft. It had resting stops. It was basically right next to the wolf, just a hundred or so feet away. And hopefully, it would be very tall, perfect for getting them both to the surface.

It just had to not think about the *very* lethal drop waiting down below if it messed up, but the wolf was rather used to that, living in a place like the human's nest. Every other railing usually had a death drop right beside it.

"Hhaaandh," it growl-hissed to the human, and she gave it her wrist without a word. It gently bit down on it then tilted its jaw down until her hand was on its chest, pressing her palm into it by letting go and trapping it between its bottom jaw and its collarbone. Then it straightened, satisfied that the human was keeping her hand there.

"Chuuheest."

" . . . Chest? Like . . . hold on to it?" the human asked, tightening her hand into its fur.

It let out a low bark-chuff in approval of her understanding its intent. Moving its forelegs with her arm flopping about everywhere was only mildly annoying, but it didn't want any obstructions when it would be having the most tedious climb of its life.

With a light stretch of preparation, it started its trot toward the platform, observing what it had to deal with.

The underside of the platform was a mess of broken steel beams, bent gears, and torn-open metal cables. Rotting fabrics, metals, and some kind of . . . pneumatic pressure system nestled into the platform's underside, almost like the insect's but mechanical, inert and empty of whatever powered it. Under the platform was a cube-shaped hole in the floor for the platform to sink into and be level with the floor, about four or five feet deep and covered with some protruding open pipes that looked like they were meant to slot into the platform when it lowered.

The wall of metal bars on the front of the open platform shaft stopped just twenty feet off the ground, more than ten feet below the platform itself, so the wolf would have to go under the platform, climb up to its tilted edge, then clamber on top of it before it could start the *actual* climb.

It got an idea, pausing to wiggle its fingers against the dusty metal floor. It could give itself fully functional human fingers and just . . . climb using the bars. That would be *so much* faster than using the slime and shimmying up the giant platform shaft. And once it was done, it could just revert the change. Additionally, the bars were *thick.* Just a bit thicker than the human's wrist, gaunt as it may be, and with the room's relatively low humidity, they weren't all that rusty.

It would have to take a nap soon, it seemed.

With a rough plan in mind, it resumed its trot. The iron bars passed above them as the wolf hopped down into the cubic depression in the floor, prompting a surprised yelp from the human and a tightening of her hold. Then, they walked into the thicket made of cables.

The wolf felt the human tense as a stray, inert wire brushed against her back before she threw mana around and relaxed.

Maybe that's what she was doing? Stress relief? Strange.

It largely ignored the wires for the most part, just letting them harmlessly brush against its body, only pausing to sweep aside some which looked like they could tangle the wolf and be a nuisance. It carefully avoided any of the bent, rickety bits of metal supporting the platform, not wanting to disturb them whatsoever.

It was in no mood to be flattened by a few tons of metal.

Considering, however, that the platform was tilted at a thirty-degree downward angle toward the back right corner, and the platform was fairly snug to the bars on the front, it would *have* to brush past those parts to get to the only corner the platform was accessible from.

And it did, carefully punching the floor every once in a while to feel for the weakest parts, making sure to stay away from them, winding a zigzagging path through hanging wires and having to occasionally stop to cut through some tangled mess of cables to progress.

Caution paid its dues despite taking longer, and they arrived at the corner unharmed.

Finding a flat enough surface to stick its paws onto was a bit of a challenge, as the edges of the framework surrounding that platform on three sides were full of holes, rails, and indentations for the platform's up-and-down movement. But a foot-wide section of the massive iron supports was just flat enough for the wolf to begin its ascent, even though its wrists were almost close enough to be touching.

The ascent itself was just *tedious.*

Even when it wasn't all that concerned with preserving as much mucus as possible, it still took around seven seconds for a single step. And to properly progress for that entire step's worth of distance, it had to repeat that process, one by one, across four different legs.

Every foot of distance traversed took around thirty seconds to climb. And it would be *even slower* if the wolf were trying to conserve as much mucus as possible for a longer climb. It would take genuine *ages* to climb up the shaft this way. The Roof-Tumor insect could do each step in just one second, but the wolf didn't have that much experience with the veins yet, and it was not going to test its limits in this place. Climbing the bars was the only real, viable option it had now that it realized just how slow it was.

To deal with the dust, it would be using tiny bursts of [Sonic Blast] to clear things up, both to conserve mucus and give itself a better hold.

Its nose was going to be *so itchy.*

After almost fifteen minutes of slowly inching upward as the human's breathing deepened, likely due to nervousness, it sucked back the slime from around a hind paw and flared the antennae just above the flesh pocket, tapping the cold metal with a sticky paw and letting the organs brush along the clean parts of the metal.

The platform was right above them. It was a spacious fit, around six feet between the bent pieces making up the platform and the human on its back.

Another couple feet of very slowly inching up, and the wolf made its first deviation from the upward path, shimmying diagonally to the side to get on top of one of the horizontal, rectangle-like rods that framed the giant metal X.

It idly wondered what the purpose of that odd design was. Just a repeating pattern of four iron rods with a metal X in the middle, each block about thirty feet tall. It just seemed like a waste of metal. Not that there was any shortage of that in the human nest, but still. Maybe structural support?

And then it remembered that trying to understand humans was nothing but a headache, and focused back on its task, eventually managing to hang on to the left leg of the X and swing its hind legs onto the metal rod supporting it while its forelegs remained on the diagonal rod.

A very arduous couple minutes of shimmying into the wedge where the X and the rod met, and it finally considered it safe enough to try detaching for a rest. However, having the human hanging off its back had its balance so uneven it didn't feel safe detaching even then, sticking its right foreleg to the support rod next to its hind legs as its left remained on the top part of the wedge.

Which had the human precariously hanging over the gap and a thirty-five-feet drop. It hesitated, mentally wondering if it would have enough strength left over in its tired limbs to swing the human into safety, where she *wouldn't* be tugging the wolf toward said drop.

"Hhhaaastte," it growled, the first sounds exchanged between them during the entire climb. She obliged, giving it a sizable boost that made its tired limbs feel as light as a feather.

Not energized, just . . . lighter. It was a strange sensation.

Then it activated [Bloodrush] and quickly retracted the veins into the squishy sheath of flesh on the back of its paw, the slime quickly losing cohesion.

The second its paw detached, the wolf swung it around its chest and under its waist with as much strength as it could muster, using its left hind leg to pull itself back by curling inward and its right foreleg to push down, tilting its back toward the left with all its strength. Then it hooked its left foreleg's nails into the iron and pulled, assisting its back in tilting.

With a low snarl of effort, a lot slower than it would have liked, it swung the human on top of its back properly, her left shoulder smacking into the iron wall along with its own.

It finally retracted all of the veins on its paws, slumping down onto the support rod like a corpse with a faint wheeze as its chest and bottom jaw hit the metal with faint, muffled thumps and a click from where its venom fangs hit the iron.

It didn't even care that its right foreleg's forearm was dangling off the rod. It was tired.

Still, after a minute of catching its breath, the wolf got up and walked along the rod with careful steps until it was certain that even if they fell off, the platform below would catch them, then plopped down again, adjusted its body so the human was leaning against the wall for their combined safety, stuck its left foreleg onto the metal wall just for added security, and promptly went to sleep.

[Restful Awareness]'s high level thankfully allowed it to keep the slime sticky without issue as it dove into [Devourer] after brushing aside the System's updates. It quickly fashioned itself two human hands, complete with thumbs and furless paws for more friction with the metal it was going to be climbing.

These were also changes it wasn't planning on keeping, so it made sure to make the hands as big as shovels, with tendons so thick they might as well be cables, moving its dewclaw from the side of its wrist onto the thumb.

It considered the essence spent on them as an investment more than anything. The more time it wasted in the nest's abandoned innards, the more essence it would lose. Besides, it hadn't really needed to run anywhere so far, and humanoid hands would be far more useful for traversing these unfamiliar environments and grappling with opponents.

And when the wolf got somewhere where it could run and its comfort during walking mattered, it would just turn them back to normal.

As it fell asleep, it impassively read the System's updates before retreating back into its lucid sleep.

[Tough Skin] has Leveled Up. Level 4 → Level 5
[Echoes of Oblivion] has Leveled Up. Level 4 → Level 5
[Tremor Sense] has Leveled Up. Level 3 → Level 4
[Logotexnia] has Leveled Up. Level 4 → Level 5

CHAPTER 26

Thumbs were weird.

Even after tugging them around during its sleep to establish the brain-to-muscle connections, new limbs and appendages still felt odd.

Feeding the human while stuck like this was another challenge, but one it rather enjoyed figuring out a creative solution to. It made the skin sac full of modified blood on its shoulder, created an exposed arterial vein on it to act like a straw, then used the [Logotexnia] skill to growl out a clumsy imitation of the word *food*. After a while of prodding at her lips with it, she begrudgingly opened her mouth, then it just used manual-change mode to tighten the skin sac until it was empty before setting it to be cannibalized by [Devourer] and going back to sleep.

And now, here it was, its left hand still glued onto the wall, opening and closing its right one as the wolf scrutinized it. The tendons were twice as thick compared to before, standing out like cables against the back of its hand, and the beefy muscles it had added would hopefully last a while when climbing.

It detached its left paw from the wall and got to clumsily walking forward, immediately developing an intense dislike of this design. Every step, its palms and fingers would slap the ground, and they wouldn't bend back the other way, so it had to awkwardly tilt its wrists to the side with every step or walk on its knuckles, making its nails harmlessly—but annoyingly—dig into its palm.

After only a few steps, it decided that it was going to get rid of these as soon as possible.

It punched the metal below, feeling the vibrations snake down the connected rods and onto the platform, a mere four-foot drop from their vantage point. It was *mildly* concerned about the stability of said platform, but it doubted their tiny contribution to its immense weight would change anything, so with a little bit of awkwardness, it moved to the wedge on the opposite end of the support rod, to the most stable-feeling connection the platform had, and awkwardly shuffled sideways before tilting its body to the right and jumping off.

The human let out a sudden cry of what it assumed was surprise, her fingers clamping down on its fur, but before they'd even hit the ground, she'd cut herself off, transitioning it into a muffled yelp.

The wolf landed well, despite its back legs momentarily buckling from the human's weight, the dull thud providing the wolf with a great feeling for what was ahead of and around them. Its tail thankfully managed to keep her legs from hitting the iron.

"Maybe warn me next time!?" she whisper-hissed into its neck, flicking its left ear with a finger.

It grumbled and jerked its head to the side, twitching said ear at the same time for a masterful counterstrike, slapping her hand with it.

The human just sighed and slumped back down, grumbling something under her breath before idly starting to pet along its chest fur as it turned its attention to the bars innocently sitting right beside them. Without much preamble, it closed a couple feet of distance, hopped up on its hind legs, and grasped them, removing its hind legs from the platform to awkwardly brace them up against an iron bar, ignoring the human's little exclamation of surprise.

Both actions were, thankfully, effortless.

Well, not effortless, but it could probably climb sixty or so feet before taking a short rest, just for safety's sake. If anything, its legs were the problem, unused to this almost bipedal position of movement and with too small a paw to comfortably rest on any bar.

Still, it got to work, keeping close to the corner, grasping one bar, then pushing up with its other hand and reaching up to grab another, rinse and repeat.

Despite its mindset being oriented toward slow and steady, it still made progress very quickly, counting feet by increments of the X shapes on the side of the platform, each being just about thirty feet. By the time it started feeling rather winded, it had gone up three segments, about ninety feet, so it carefully shuffled its way back onto the support pipes, the three-feet-deep wedge just wide enough for the wolf to comfortably rest.

A short nap, and it repeated the process. The ceiling of the room below eventually reached them, but thankfully, the bars remained, even though its fingers were always squished between them and the metal wall behind.

Beyond that change, its routine continued—climbing, resting, back to climbing.

Again.

And again.

By the fourth time it had repeated this process, it was beginning to wonder if this had been a good idea as it lay panting, listening to the human's words and replying with random, tired grumbles.

They must have gone up almost three hundred feet by now, and it didn't feel any exit within its sensory range.

So, it went to sleep again.

And it got up again, crawled to the bars.

Started climbing again.

Went to sleep, bars, climbing, rest on support rods, repeat, with very little in terms of variety.

From rough estimation, it assumed about one-and-a-half to two days had passed. From rough *feeling*, it felt like it'd been climbing for a *month*. The fear of falling wasn't even enough to get its heart rate to spike anymore. It was just frustrated, hungry to the point where not even thinking of the sparks was enough to fully take its mind off the gnawing emptiness in its soul and stomach, and its only reprieve were the moments after sleep where the human would poke and nudge its snout for a small bout of tired play fighting, her trying to poke the insides of its mouth and the wolf letting out half-hearted growls, trying to fake bite her fingers while she tried to dodge its jaws and poke its gums.

And occasionally scratching at the support rods for some nice sparks to look at.

Those two activities were fun, and distracting.

Which was even more appreciated, considering the wolf could feel the distant thuds slowly getting closer. They made it nervous.

Unwinding its tail from around the human's knees almost felt weird by now with how used to it the wolf had gotten, so it didn't bother letting go of her legs at all anymore. It felt rather comforting.

Letting out a low, long exhale, it forced itself up again before resuming its bihourly ritual, shuffling across the thick metal corner of the framework to grasp the bars and start climbing.

Again.

* * *

As she continued being carried around like a toddler in a backpack, her mind, inevitably, wandered, despite the permanent anxiety of being connected to life by nothing more than slime and the wolf's now humanoid hands.

Living in the Dungeon for two years had taught her many things about its structure, both above, below, and in between, and a surprising amount of small details about each. And in the silence, broken only by their breathing and the light wobbling rattle of metal bars, she couldn't help but run her mind through some of them.

The Dungeon was separated into four floors with their respective underground bits, and the active floors just underneath, which were referred to as "the Factory" just to delineate them from the habitable parts of the Dungeon. Each floor had its own sewer system, and with a mixture of science and magic, handled their trash either through vaporizing it into gasses and smog and pumping them down into the fourth floor, or through a winding network of pipes that ran down the sides of the Dungeon's walls for the things they couldn't deal with, usually factory waste, and sent it through some specific spots to flow down into some processing facilities that would destroy the discard, also on the fourth floor.

So if they went into the sewers, no matter what direction they went, they *should* run into some form of civilization eventually. Down would lead them into the cauldrons, where they burned the trash or sent it through the pipes down into the fourth floor, and hopefully, into some worker who could help her. And going up would lead them to the surface.

The problem was distance. The Dungeon was *colossal.* Ergos was a monstrously gigantic planet, but even so, she didn't doubt that the bottom of the Factory was probably well below the planet's crust. One could fit *several* small countries' worth of people down here and have space for more if they used both the above and underground parts of the Dungeon.

But from what little she knew of the public's perception of the underground sections of each floor, the first floor's was basically clean, while for the other two habitable floors, anything deeper than a couple hundred feet underneath the topmost levels of the sewers and underpipes was considered as little more than a metal catacomb for the dead and those that fed on them. There was a reason besides the somewhat vertical nature of the Dungeon for the only modes of transportation being the Great Tower, platforms, cable lifts, and portals.

Everyone knew that for the second and third floor, the underground sewers were dangerous for some reason. The problem was that she didn't *really* know what that reason was. She knew that the deeper one went into the underground, the more dangerous things became, but nobody could ever give a concrete answer as to why and how exactly, only speaking in vague, almost mystical tones about the perils below, as if they were trying to speak of some stupid fairy tale.

Was it environmental hazards? Monsters? She could only assume so, because her imagination couldn't really come up with other possibilities.

It was the reason that low-level adventurers and mercenaries would delve into the sewers and abandoned depths to raise their level rather than jumping into the supposed meat grinder that was the Factory, so she knew this danger was true to some extent. Coincidentally, that was also why nobody had truly cleared out the underground.

When the entry level to the Factory was at least level fifteen or twenty, people who'd just gained their paths needed *some* way to level up, so the authorities—royal and local—tended to only *trim* the upper parts to reduce dangers to their citizens, but kept whatever bizarre ecosystems existed below relatively intact for an ample source of experience.

That was, after all, exactly what her old team had been doing before her companion rid the world of their existence. They'd never stepped foot into the Factory.

And this climbing reminded her of just how *deep* they'd gone into the third floor's underground.

So this prolonged period of tedious peace? This desolate silence? With every hour that passed, it only made her nervous anticipation rise, every minute only adding to the sense that *something* would threaten them any minute now. A sort of constant, stretching tension that had no release.

Because *nothing* happened.

There were no flying monsters, no giant spiders, nothing. It was just pure silence with slowly approaching, groaning thuds, their breaths, the brain-numbing scent of rotted fuel, and the wobbling of metal as the wolf kept climbing.

Still, her imagination ran wild, boredom and nerves combining into a self-sabotaging mixture that only made her more unnerved. Turns out, one's imagination became quite active when they no longer had eyes to see things.

She turned her attention to the wolf she was attached to after a particularly sickening mental image of a humanoid slug. Her fingers rubbed at the light cuts and bruises on her palm and the sides of her digits, idly remembering how some prissy, sneering noble girl had complained about how their family dog kept biting her playmates too hard while playing, something about lack of socialization.

Maybe she shouldn't be hiding how hard the wolf was biting her during their little play sessions?

What did "lack of socialization" even mean?

Was it only biting her so hard because it hadn't learned boundaries and control? That made sense in her head, but she'd never owned a dog, and this was a wild *wolf*, for gods' sake. For all she knew, wolves might play by ripping limbs off each other because by tomorrow they'd have them all back.

She sighed and started petting its neck, being awarded with a pleased, low grumble for her efforts.

At least she no longer felt sick from being dangled and jangled around as the wolf kept climbing. Not that she could complain; she was *literally* being carried.

A bit after the wolf lost count of the number of X segments they'd gone past, it clambered up to the nearest wedge, squeezed them both into the three-foot surface, and the moment its paws touched down on the rod with a weighty slap, now unhindered by slime, it paused, its ears shooting up straight as its head jerked upward by sheer reflex.

One of the walls above, the one opposite to the bars, was hollow.

It could only feel the very edge of it, but there was some kind of empty space behind one of the walls, just on the edge of its senses. And the wall itself had no support rods on it, just a single, gratelike plate of metal thrown on top of the topmost support rod of the segment below it.

The wall was also . . . wavy, and thin.

Easy to cut through.

It tampered down on its excitement and settled down for another quick nap.

An hour later, it woke itself up with a little shot of adrenaline, shook off the sleepiness, and returned to its familiar routine of climbing.

One segment passed, two, and at the third, the wolf paused, tightened its grip on a metal bar, then used its left hand to punch the vertical support rod by its side, holding its fist against the metal for a bit to get a good picture.

And a good picture it did get.

It wasn't exactly a wall; it was more like a series of interconnected wavy plates that would be sucked into the top of the door by some spinning mechanism connected to two covered operating switches. Just beyond the door was a short but massive corridor sixty feet wide and thirty feet tall entirely made of stone which eventually cut off into a more open area full of pipework.

The corridor itself was covered with some kind of rail systems on both the left and right side for about twenty feet each, with some rusty carts still sitting inert on some of them. In the middle of the corridor was a twenty-foot section that was relatively clear, which transitioned into a metal bridge with a grated bottom full of holes and rickety railings on the side—a bridge that extended over a canal-shaped depression full of pipework and complex machinations below. It traveled over that section for about a hundred feet before the wolf lost feeling.

And below . . .

Below gave it a headache.

Besides the metal supports of the grated bridge and the rail systems, there wasn't a single simple or flat thing down there. Not one. It was a mind-twisting mess of dozens of feet of pipes attached to other pipes covered in rivets, nails, metallic boxes; a set of circular fanlike designs laid on top of one another, nestled into a thicket of fabric and metal and cables, surrounded by coiled rings, covered in spongy stuff, and . . . It was just a mind-twisting headache.

The wolf shook its head and pressed its antennae back into its fur, trying to get rid of that image lest it become dizzy.

It put its hand back onto the metal bars to climb up a few feet, until it was just across the thin wall, then used the slime to shimmy across the edge onto the bottom-right leg of the X-shaped support rods, making its way over to the left leg. With only a couple feet from . . . some notion of safety, it couldn't help but grow excited. It had grown absolutely *sick* of climbing.

Sticking itself onto the thick corner of the support segment, the wolf carefully tested its weight and made sure it could reach, then with a bit of trepidation, it detached a paw . . . hand? Was it a paw or a hand?

Didn't matter, it decided. It retracted the slime, reared its left hand back, and slapped it onto the wavy wall with as much strength as it could spare without straining its slimy support.

It wasn't expecting much in terms of durability, considering the ridiculously thin nature of it, but the wolf hadn't been expecting the wall to be so thoroughly chewed through by rust that a foot-wide circle of it shattered into a mess of thin flakes, shooting rust powder into its face and filling the shaft with the cacophony of every single rusted plate rattling against one another.

It dug its hand out of the hole, turned around, and started coughing and sneezing for a few long seconds, very thankful that it had been keeping its eyes closed for a while now, lest it damage its new, precious eyes.

After snorting out remnants of wet rust powder for another minute, it turned back to the odd wall.

It curled its hand close to its chest then swung it outward, backhanding its forearm through the wall, its thick, coarse fur shielding it against chips and shards of rusty metal as they flew in every direction, feeling through its other three limbs what size a hole it was trying to make.

A second of visualization, and it resumed, punching through the corner of the wall bit by bit, occasionally stopping to scoot upward on the support rod it was hanging from for a better reach.

Almost a minute of uninterrupted ear-grating banging and rattling later, it put a hand through the hole, cupping its hand, and dragged out a small mountain of rust powder and bits of thin metal, carelessly throwing them down into the abyss. It could feel just how ridiculously humid everything beyond the door was by the exposed skin on its palms.

Great, wet fur.

It never liked wet fur.

It rather awkwardly waited a couple seconds for its left paw-hand to stick to the floor before carefully repositioning its body one step at a time, eventually dragging itself and the human through with a bit of readjustment.

Finally on flat, solid ground once more, it stretched out its tired limbs with a small groan of satisfaction, then took a deep, calming breath.

The air was so humid it felt like it was inhaling thin water more than air, but it didn't particularly care, moving away from the hole just a couple feet before plopping down to rest with a sigh, starting to very slowly detach the human from its back.

In fact, the air here was . . . the cleanest it had ever smelled. It didn't even know air *could* be this clean. It was almost cleansing to its lungs.

Then, a faint sound echoed down the corridor from the other end of the bridge. A shuffle, the scrape of metal on metal, a small series of clicks. A faint vibration traveled through the stone below, come and gone before the wolf could even react.

A tense silence filled the room as its eyes instinctively snapped open, and the wolf froze as its gaze was met with the sight of a softly glowing room, a hundred thousand tiny bits of moss splattered through the walls and floor glowing a soft green yellow before a background of gray-black metal.

It was so beautiful it could almost cry, and it might have let itself have that moment of peace if it weren't for the two metallic legs standing in place on the other end of the bridge, only illuminated up to the ankles by the moss below.

For a few seconds, nothing happened, a stare-off between two figures obscured in darkness. The wolf was simply too stunned and confused to consider attempting speech with its . . . adversary?

The figure suddenly started moving forward in a steady, unhurried pace, each thundering step making the bridge's railing rattle, like the clicking of teeth in a shivering jaw. The wolf's slimy fur rose in a bristle, yet it remained silent, focusing on its senses as it hurriedly retracted the veins, lowered its chest to the ground, and tilted to the side, dropping the human on the ground. To her credit, she didn't let out a peep, simply raising a hand and tapping its shoulder before rolling away a little awkwardly.

The boost was so strong that the wolf almost choked in surprise.

It felt the hallway on the other end of the bridge, felt the massive circular staircase just beyond, the hundreds of feet of it submerged underwater. The two winding tunnels to the side of the hallway, snaking upward toward another floor. It felt the source of the thumping—an utterly colossal machine—like a beating heart futilely drafted into a corpse. And just beyond it, an open tunnel with living things inside, hundreds of them, extending into an open, canal-like tunnel full of water.

A way out.

But it also felt the immeasurably complex machinations of the clockwork golem on the bridge—from the strange rock in its chest to the engine surrounding it, and its odd, tapering left arm—a split second before the humanoid machine stopped in place. A massive yellow eye flickered to life on the middle of its face, shining a spotlight straight into its unadjusted eyes, forcing them shut.

Blind once more, but now from light.

Its ears pointed forward, its lips curled into a snarl, and its fur stood on end across its back like slimy spikes. Still, it held the sound in its throat.

The mechanical human, like one of those stone golems down by the waste rivers but infinitely more complex, didn't move.

The light turned off, and the wolf opened its eyes just in time to see the golem's eye turn red through the swimming mess of colors in its sight. It was almost enough for the wolf to freeze again, seeing what *red* really looked like, but a well-honed survival instinct, sharpened through a dozen different brushes with death, crushed that excitement and awe and shoved it into the furthest corners of its mind to be considered later.

It didn't speak. Instead, a deafening, hornlike alarm sounded out of the golem, and with a burst of steam from its back and the clicking of a hundred different mechanical parts, its right arm spouted blades. Then it lowered its torso and began a frenzied sprint across the bridge.

It was unnerving, its movements . . . *wrong* in how simultaneously awkward yet purposeful they were. Its torso was tilted forward, but its two arms remained pointed at the ground, unmoving, and its red eye was still nailed to the wolf. But it was *fast*, even when the very vibrations of its movements felt like they were slogging through a world that was too slow for the wolf to live in.

Without the human, it felt like it would have never been able to match how quick this thing was. Even now, it was certain it could not afford to feel its opponent out. It had to end this fast.

A part of the wolf was scared. An unnatural abomination like the thing running straight at it with a mechanical laser focus, backlit by nothing but its own red eye and the contradicting peaceful lights of the glowing moss, thrice as tall and just as wide, made its animal brain instinctively want to turn tail and run for its life.

A bigger, entirely unreasonable part of it was excited. Its veins thrummed with the beginnings of adrenaline, its heart picked up pace, its entire body shivered as its eyes bulged open, half-blinded by the light but still hungry for use. Its antennae writhed involuntarily in excitement, feeling the air, the vibrations of its *heavy* opponent.

It knew it would gain nothing by killing this thing. But it *wanted* to kill it. It craved action. It had felt what a real fight was like, tasted victory for the first time in ages back then in that trash pit, and now it wanted more, after a lifetime of scraping by with less than nothing.

The golem's feet broke the metal grating, but with unnatural, stumbling grace, it simply weaved them back up through the holes it made, overcompensating its next steps, and repeating the process.

A hundred and fifty feet turned to just fifty in the proverbial blink of an eye, and the wolf finally let out a throaty, rumbling snarl, its entire chest vibrating with the force of it. Its adrenaline sac was squeezed dry in preparation.

A mere second later was when the wolf learned there was such a thing as too much adrenaline.

Its brain almost shut down; higher thought utterly vanished. Every thought process turned into nothing but an urge to move, to run, to fight and kill and shred and do *anything* but *nothing*. Every single fiber of its body *screeched* for action, and almost like a dream, the wolf didn't question what it was even doing as it activated [Bloodrush] and exploded forward with a bark so loud it was almost like a roar, crossing thirty feet of distance in the blink of an eye, the world blurring around it.

The golem didn't pause, lifting its left forearm, and from the tapering tip, a short explosion of blue flame came, far too short to hit the wolf. But the blast of wind that cracked through the air slammed into its shoulder before it could even get to the bridge.

Its right shoulder popped out of its socket with a meaty snapping sound, barely audible over the violent rattling of metal all around them and the blaring alarm.

The wolf didn't even feel it. It simply forced itself into a diagonal roll to conserve momentum, purposefully smashing its right shoulder into the stone as it came out of it to shove it back into place with another pop, simultaneously using its left arm to claw through the stone and launch itself forward.

With its right hand already reared back, it turned its fingers into a diagonal position—the claws touching and forming a rough, flat formation—and thrust forward.

The golem obliged it, doing the same with its own.

Neither dodged.

The golem's bladed fingers slammed into its ribs in a sideways swing, the blades that came out of its fingertips catching on the fur and flesh for a brief millisecond before a flare of mana filled the air, forcing the metal through as if cutting through water before stopping at its fingertips.

The wolf barely felt the blades shred its left lung. It didn't feel pain; it didn't even care. Its mind was full of nothing but frenzied violence.

Its right hand slammed into the side of the golem's plated chest, its claws cutting through without resistance. But its claws were much thinner than its fingers.

It didn't care. It forced its hand through regardless, feeling the joints snap, feeling its skin and flesh be scraped off by the machinery and torn metal up to its knuckles, fur getting cut and caught in the moving abomination's innards.

The golem was moving too fast, was too heavy, and the wolf's arm crumbled into its chest as the golem's charge sent the wolf barreling back, their mutual grasp of each other destroying their balance. They fell over, the twisting snap of the wolf's fingers breaking barely registering as a tingle, its focus directed on how the golem's higher height sent it tumbling over the wolf as their legs tangled into each other's.

Neither let go, but the wolf's speed and the golem's weight landed them just as the wolf wanted: with it on top, and the golem sprawled out on the stone beneath it.

Before the golem's fingers could exit its chest for another thrust, the wolf turned its left hand to a fist and slammed it into the golem's elbow in an uppercut, forcing the blades to get caught between the wolf's ribs as the golem's arm was twisted. The wolf jerked its torso to the left, feeling the vibrations of metallic joints breaking reverberating through its rib cage, using the motion to simultaneously dig its right hand deeper into the golem's chest as it raked its hind legs' claws through the golem's hip and knee, feeling things snap and lose cohesion with immense satisfaction.

The elbow didn't break, unfortunately, and in a flash, the golem reared its hand back, its elbow smashing into the stone, and thrust forward with misaligned blades once more toward the wolf's head.

A tingle of caution entered its thoughtless mind, and its left hand moved to block. The blades pierced through its palm, one tip getting stuck in its bone, and the wolf's fingers snapped down on the golem's hand and wrist like a bear trap, hooking its claws into the metal then blunting them.

The fight, for a few seconds, turned into a mauling.

Its jaws clamped around the golem's face, its right hand shoving itself deeper into its chest. Its bones and tendons scraped against jagged metal while its legs alternated from raking through the golem's hips and knees and vying for purchase in the stone as the golem bucked and twitched in stilted, jerky motions.

The wolf's fangs cut through the eye, jagged bits of metal and glass entering its mouth as it bit down and jerked its head around before cutting through and repeating, a whirlwind of motion and bestial fury in a world that felt like molasses around it, its vision filling with sparks and its ears with the screeching of metal and alarms.

The golem's right arm scraped against stone, changed angles, tried anything to release itself, but the wolf's claws held it in place, pushing away and not letting it stab, ignoring the golem's left hand as it tried to push the wolf away, its hits and pushes doing nothing more than bruising its flesh.

Then a click sounded, and the golem, despite the struggle, managed to put its left hand's tip against the right side of the wolf's ribs.

The wolf felt through vibrations the moving of gas, the clicking of machinery, a surge of mana, and even with the absurd speed it had, its mind didn't make the connection until it was too late to react, too busy with trying to decapitate its opponent.

Just as it was about to attempt to minimize the damage, it felt a strong force fueled by mana suddenly burst into existence beside the golem's arm, tossing the wolf's entire torso sideways and ripping its fingers out of the golem's chest, but also smashing the golem's forearm against its own torso. The device on the golem's arm cracked once more, blue flame leaving the tip and scorching its fur, but the explosion of air, almost point-blank, slammed into the wolf's left forearm instead, whether by pure coincidence or the golem's doing.

A loud crack like the snapping of wood accompanied the feeling of tearing bone and bending muscles. Its hand lost its grip on the golem's, whose bladed fingers violently teared out of the wolf's palms, mutilating both their hands.

The wolf was momentarily thrown to the side by the two explosive interruptions, its shoulder muscles straining and tearing from the sudden impact, so rather than fighting it, it went with the momentum to roll away from the golem, a clumsy motion not at all helped by its barely functioning hands.

It hurriedly righted itself and turned, lowering its chest almost to the floor, snarling through shards of glass, metal, and frothing blood while the golem turned over and punched the floor to throw itself upright, a movement both calculated and clumsy as its left leg failed to move properly.

There was no pause.

The golem and the wolf rushed at each other again.

The golem swung with three mutilated fingers, wide and clumsy and off target, as it rushed forward with jerky, stumbling steps, the wolf taking advantage of its superior speed to duck its head under the swing while turning its snout up to latch onto its wrist. Both its arms wrapped around the golem's right leg—the only functioning one—nestling its right shoulder into the gap between the robotic legs as its tail coiled around the left one. With its momentum, the wolf twisted, yanking the golem forward and up, and lifted with all its strength as it pulled the golem's arm down with its teeth.

The golem's head smashed into the stone with a loud crackling sound before its momentum once again brought them to a roll. The golem swung its functioning leg and arm with surprising strength and speed, swinging the wolf over itself, and before the wolf could react or understand what was happening, a muted click sounded as all three limbs the wolf was holding on to detached, sending it flying four feet into the air and toward the human, who had been throwing mana over both of them the entire time.

The golem's left arm snapped to the wolf in an instant, barely four feet of distance between them, and the wolf only had time to realize what was about to happen before it did.

Another flare of weak mana burst near the golem's arm, trying to redirect its aim, but all it managed to do was shift it from the wolf's chest down to its stomach. A sharp crack filled the air and slammed into its stomach, the inert bones within snapping like toothpicks before the wolf was sent flying, spinning through the air, the golem's limbs discarded as the wolf flailed for something to grab on to while soaring straight toward the rusted wall and its death.

The golem's arm exploded immediately after, and the burst of air against its fur reminded the wolf of the skill it usually used when on the brink of death, the thought cutting through the hazy frenzy in its mind.

It had Speed and the Perception to match, so in the mere moments it took for the wolf to be aligned in a way that wouldn't propel it forward but backward, it had a [Sonic Blast] ready and roiling in its single working lung.

And so, it fired it, tilting its head away at the last second. The explosion stopped its spinning and violently spun it the other way around, its momentum cut completely and utterly. Its right shoulder slammed into the floor, followed by its head, its legs hovering in the air for a moment before its body tilted to the side and they limply fell to the ground alongside its tail.

Its ears filled with an incessant ringing, muffling both the human's cries and the blaring alarm.

As quickly as adrenaline came, it left.

That moment of confusion and disorientation as the wolf lay sprawled out on the ground, trying not to choke on its own blood and somehow force the world to stop spinning, was enough for it to feel the first prickles of pain. And once it acknowledged that pain, a tidal wave followed, so much that even [Pain Resistance] could only do so much for the wolf, the beginning of shock creeping up on its mind, a sensation like frozen panic.

It had to sleep, or it would probably die.

It coughed, trying to clear its throat of the blood—a frothy mixture of air and slimy crimson—it was rapidly swallowing, the shards of glass and metal in its shredded jaws making even more pool in its mouth.

It had to sleep.

As the boosts wore out—its limbs turning to lead, and the world turning dull—it squeezed its melatonin sac. Its body complied easily, leaving the wolf with the blind hope the golem wouldn't find some way to kill it without limbs.

CHAPTER 27

Fuck, fuck, *fuck!*" she cried out over the alarm drilling into her ears as she wriggled and crawled to the wolf, its gargling breaths sending a fresh spear of ice into her chest with every passing second.

The horrific hunk of metal was still trying to crawl to them using its half-destroyed chin, as if it was intending to headbutt them to death, but she didn't give a shit about the damned thing.

She had medical experience, the bare minimum, and her companion sounded like he—or she—had both feet in the grave, ready to slide in. Her fingers scraped against blood-wet stone, and with the last dregs of her mana, she sent a weak pulse toward her companion's head.

She felt more metal, nails, and glass shards in its snout than flesh.

With a grunt and a heave, she grasped onto its shoulder—at rust-powdered, blood-slicked fur—and pulled. It barely moved the wolf. It wasn't much bigger than a medium-size dog, one of the less deformed ones, but it was much heavier and much more limp than she could deal with.

"Fuckfuckfuckfuck," she hissed out in a rush through gritted teeth, finding a less slick part of its fur to pull again, groaning in effort as her hand seemingly refused to hold on, her muscles refusing to contract, weakness permeating her entire body. She could barely clench a fist.

She gave the wolf a mental apology and nudged its head away with her own, putting her lips at the small puddle of blood that had dripped out of its snout, clumsily drinking and lapping at the stone, fully aware of the bubbles of air and spit mixed into the ichor.

Undignified or disgusting, she didn't care; she needed Strength. The more time the wolf spent on its back, the harder it would be to breathe. She was amazed it hadn't choked to death in the minute it'd taken her to crawl toward it.

The boost provided by drinking this blood was about half as mind-numbingly orgasmic as when fed the other odd version of blood the wolf gave her, but it was enough. It *felt* enough.

She put her hand on the wolf's shoulder and pulled, using her right shoulder to dig into the stone for added friction, and after a few seconds of gritting her teeth and hissing out in effort, the wolf *finally* rolled over, stomach first, onto the stone.

And half on her shoulder. She quickly wriggled away and twisted to the left a little, reaching for its snout. She pulled it to the side, pressing the side of its head against the stone instead, and pulled open its shredded jowls, letting the blood exiting its throat with every breath just trickle down onto the floor.

Then she went to reach into its mouth, just to pull out whatever bits she could, and hesitated, a sudden nervousness filling her.

Part of her was mildly terrified. Her mental image of her companion was that of a hyperintelligent wolf who was rational and even kind enough to keep her around for some reason or another. A monster in nothing but categorization. In reality, a rational beast.

So *feeling* her companion suddenly snap into a frenzied monster shredding apart metal like a blender of claws and fur and gnashing teeth, an action much more intimate than even watching it happen, was a shock. It made her realize, once more, just how dangerous the creature she was helping was. It made her realize that maybe it was just keeping that legendary wolfish aggression tamped down to use it on whatever bothered it.

And it once again made her come to the conclusion that she didn't care, as long as its jaws weren't snapping at *her* face.

With a steadying breath, she reached into its mouth, feeling with [Mana Touch] for the sharp bits that might be a pain for the wolf to remove—nails, glass shards, and the like.

Every time her fingers brushed against the wolf's teeth, her heart leapt into her throat, but she continued still, carefully and steadily, ignoring the scrape of metal on stone as the golem slowly crawled toward them. It couldn't do anything anyway, and her companion was more important.

Little tugs of telemancy and her deft, spidery fingers, and within a few minutes, she'd taken out most of the things embedded in its tongue and mouth, only some large pieces left within that she didn't want to take out in fear of them causing more bleeding than the wolf could handle.

Her attention turned to the moss around them, tingling with mana. Her fingers reached for a tiny patch, barely perceptible but in her range, and her nails scraped it out of the stone, holding it in her bloodied hand for a moment.

She knew the basics of the sewers, a necessity to make money.

Where the air was clean and the moss was full of mana—or just glowing, for those without such senses—it was a good spot to harvest alchemy ingredients. She didn't know how it worked or why, as it wasn't her field, but the rough explanation she'd been given was that some types of moss could take in mana and store it.

But she also knew that in emergencies, people used moss as a bandage. It sucked up liquid like nothing else, and despite its filthy surroundings, finding dirty moss was extremely rare. The thing was a natural at cleaning the filth of the dungeon.

At the very least, she knew that this moss was the cleanest thing for miles, and when it dried, it would soak up blood even better, so she gently stuck it into the shredded roof of the wolf's mouth after taking out the last bits of metal and glass that she could find. If it helped, it helped. If it didn't, no harm.

And she kept doing it. She lapped up fallen blood like a dog, scraped moss off the floor, and stuck it on top of the wolf's injuries.

It was tedious, it took ages, but it was *something* to do as her mana slowly recovered. It was the only thing she really *could* do.

Thankfully, a combination of her skills, the Kindhearted trait, and the wolf's blood made her mana recovery utterly ridiculous, so by the time she'd covered the holes on the wolf's chest and mouth, both her mana and the wolf had seemingly recovered.

Its breaths stopped coming out with trickles of frothy blood, and its mutilated torso and hands closed up, the skin knitting back together. Meanwhile, her mana was already trickling back into her body from a full core.

She was still a bit concerned for the wolf, as it had bled almost half a bucket's worth of blood, but she was not expecting it to get up anytime soon, and with her having drank a lot of said blood, she felt like she had more than enough ability and time to deal with the golem that had caused all this.

At least she knew why this place was abandoned, whatever the facility's purpose had been.

She hoped the poor saps who'd once worked here had gotten out before the golems fell under the Dungeon's influence, and if not, that at least their untimely demise had helped people understand why metal golems were illegal in the Dungeon.

The thing was still blaring the alarm, but she barely noticed anymore. Her brain had gotten so used to it that it was basically just background noise at this point.

What she wanted was its core. It was *powerful,* and judging by how it was still active, its core was likely automatically charged by the ambient mana. It explained why it had been sitting here, dormant for however many years, just leeching off the moss's mana to keep functioning.

If she could strip its core out of its metal bonds and just have the core crystal, she could probably sell it for a price that could restore . . . at least *one* of her eyes, with change left over for her to live off of until she found somewhere to work.

Maybe she could even hold on to it and go to a golem maker to make her a personal one, which was an even more appealing idea. Expensive, but *very* appealing, especially considering her likely state once she got out of this place. Even if the fact it had almost killed her companion made her blood boil and made her want to shove her hand on its head and cast [Sparkburst] until it melted to slag.

Actually . . . its core wasn't in its head. Why not do both?

She took a steadying breath and shuffled toward the accursed thing—which was slowly inching toward them by scraping its jaw against the rock—ignoring the crunching, dried-up slime covering her from neck to thigh in favor of reaching the golem.

It wasn't all that difficult. It had made surprising progress by slithering and scraping forward, at least from where it had been sitting on its back twenty feet away just an hour or so ago. She just had to reach forward and melt its head off before attempting to do the same to its chest to get the core out.

Then she realized just what kind of situation this was as she lifted her head to look straight at its mutilated arm with a small pulse of mana, and felt laughter bubble up in her chest, her limbs losing strength.

Two broken, forgotten slaves staring at each other while wriggling on the ground like little worms just to kill each other, while a foot or two away, a *wolf* was just casually napping away life-threatening injuries. It was almost snoring due to all the blood in its throat, in fact.

It was like something out of a satirical theater play. It was utterly ridiculous.

She couldn't help it. She let out an undignified *pffffft,* going limp as she burst out laughing.

"F-Fuck, this—this is—so fucking *stuhhhhhppppiiid . . .*" she trailed off into a wheeze, a wide smile on her face as she laughed her heart out, grinding her forehead into the stone as her stomach convulsed, choking and coughing between bouts of hysterical laughter as she let the mirth of this utter nonsense wash over her.

She could feel her blood rushing to her face as the seconds passed, her weak lungs growing sore while she continued laughing and giggling between gasps and wheezes, her cheeks aching from the wide smile on her face.

By the time the tickling mirth in her lungs retreated, she could barely breathe, her lungs feeling as if they'd been scraped raw with sandpaper.

"Aaah, that—that was great," she sighed out with a little cough, her heart and mood feeling a thousand tons lighter.

Laughing was a very cleansing experience.

But she still didn't forget feeling the golem's bladed fingers slam into her companion's chest, the mana crawling over the metal almost feeling like she was holding its metal fist as it did so. She had barely done anything during that fight to help. Sure, if she stopped to think about it, she may have helped, but in reality, she didn't *feel* like she'd done anything useful.

Her smile vanished, and she extended a hand, clamping down on the back of the golem's neck.

She held the spell, compressing the burst to be as short and violent as possible.

"[Sparkburst]," she breathed out, her tone frigid, and felt the golem try to twist and retract its neck into its shoulders with a hiss of superheated steam as the crackling of sparks momentarily drowned out the blaring alarm.

Patching up a lung was a lot harder than it had first assumed.

Mostly because it couldn't, for the life of it, keep all five of the jagged holes within truly closed. It just didn't have the mental capacity, and the brain damage did not help whatsoever. It hadn't been as close to death as it had thought—thanks to its Endurance, it assumed—but the wolf had still been closer to it than it felt comfortable with, unable to focus and dizzy even within its own skill.

It took almost an entire hour to fix its lung. Fixing the other injuries was easy, so it left those for later besides stopping the bleeding. To fix the brain damage, it simply considered how its brain had been during the last time it took a nap, and made the skill return it to that state. It was expecting some terrible side effects, like memory loss or maybe something in its chemical receptors messing up, but nothing like that happened.

And now that it was sure it wasn't about to die, the wolf forced itself awake, hearing the human *still* shooting off sparks and talking to herself—or the golem—for whatever reason.

It couldn't be *that* hard to fight a golem without limbs, right?

The wolf wasn't entirely healed; not even close. The only things that had really healed were its mind and lung. Its arms were still unusable, and its shoulder muscles were still torn. But for safety's sake, it squeezed its adrenaline sac just a *tiny* bit, mildly wary of it now, and shook itself awake. It forced its eyes open and flared its antennae, using both its senses to drink in the bizarre scene of the human shooting sparks into a wriggling metal torso, angrily hissing at it whenever a burst of steam burned her hand.

It wanted to do nothing more than just lay there and drink in this entirely different world before its eyes, with its *oranges* and *greens,* but it felt like it had been put through a wringer, so it briefly flicked its eyes to their surroundings, getting ready to jump back to sleep.

All around the wolf and its human was an utter mess of black, smoking and deformed little bits of metal tubes, wires, plates—

And *what* was in its mouth?

It moved its tongue, and immediately curled its lips up in distaste, hurriedly trying to unstick the strange, hard, but organic-feeling bits out of its aching wounds, prodding and pushing them off.

Then it paused.

It hadn't experimented much with the [Devourer] skill, but it knew it accepted organic material as food. Things that came from living beings. And this weird, wet, smooth . . . *furlike* thing in its mouth, attached to some sort of . . . dirtlike base, *felt* organic, even if it wasn't alive whatsoever. It felt like that little thing it had seen down next to the burning rivers. Those things *moved,* right? So this was . . . likely kind of alive?

With a bit of trepidation, it used its half-working, mangled tongue to shove the weird material into its throat, and swallowed.

Worst-case scenario, its skill just didn't acknowledge it, and it had to force it out of its stomach by retching. Forcefully.

It turned its attention back to the human and the wriggling torso trying to resist being melted apart, the human aggressively trying to dig into the wound its own fingers had made. After confirming that she, indeed, did not need any help, and that its body still hurt despite the thin layer of skin covering its wounds, it squeezed its sleep sac and quickly returned to its rest.

You have progressed on your Path.
[Hound of the Keeper] Level 17 → Level 18

-Available Attribute Points: 1
-Attributes:
Strength (+1)
Speed (+1)
Dexterity (+0)
Endurance (+7)
Perception (+1)
Resolve (+1)
Intelligence (+5)
Soul (+1)

It was mildly tempted to put the point in Dexterity just to get rid of that zero, but it refrained and put it on the only attribute that had consistently saved its life.

Endurance (+8)

-Acquired Skills:
You have gained the Skill [Maddened Frenzy - Level 1]
[Restful Awareness] has Leveled Up. Level 16 → Level 18
[Pain Resistance] has Leveled Up. Level 19 → Level 21
[Tough Skin] has Leveled Up. Level 5 → Level 7

After another second of waiting, it realized that was it.

Frankly, it had been expecting a little more, considering it had been rather close to death, but it couldn't really complain.

Focusing on its new skill, however, definitely made it *want* to complain. A massive attribute boost to *everything*, in exchange for a complete loss of reason and thought. It didn't even know if it would be dodging or blocking hits in that state; that's all the symbols told it. It assumed it would be much like that adrenaline overdose episode it'd had with the golem, but worse.

Would it even be able to activate the skill without shredding the human to pieces? Likely not.

It sounded like another absolute-last-resort type of skill. Better than nothing, but it would have much preferred something it could use regularly. With a mental sigh, it dismissed the symbols.

Once it moved past the symbols to start fixing itself, however, it was *very* pleasantly surprised to see the skill had actually recognized the thing it'd eaten and had broken it down. Even though it seemed like the dirt had just . . . vanished.

Unfortunately, the skill had only given the wolf some rather . . . surface-level knowledge. It knew what it did and the rough process, but not the specifics. Thankfully, the wolf didn't *need* the specifics. It was apparently a "plant" called Elfin-gold moss.

And it was the single most efficient thing it had ever seen.

Its feeding cycle was incredible. It could somehow absorb mana through the air, then *store* said mana into some complex, unique cells it had, which would use the mana as a power source, mix it with some enzyme, and create a chemical reaction that would produce light within its microscopic leaves, making them glow.

Then that light would in turn power its secondary feeding mechanism, where it would take something called *carbon dioxide* out of the air, do . . . some process it couldn't quite understand with that chemical and its own light, and produce food that way.

It was effectively absorbing water and mana from its surroundings to produce its own food and grow, an infinite energy and food source.

Of course, the wolf immediately considered how to put this on itself. It was a low maintenance way to supplement its essence storage by reducing how much of it the wolf was spending on keeping itself well-fed, instead passively feeding itself by just . . . existing.

Additionally, if it became a part of its body . . . would that mean that it would have access to the mana this moss stored?

It hoped so, even if it didn't have much to spend that mana on.

The easiest and least dangerous way to implement this was to graft the moss onto the bottom half of its body, where it didn't have any of the important organs it needed to keep functioning, so getting rid of its furry armor for glowing moss would be a very acceptable change.

After delivering the human back to her pack and starting to hunt humans and whatever else it could get its claws on, it could just cover up the glow with [Echoes of Oblivion].

Another interesting point was that this moss was practically invincible to a lot of chemicals. It had a sort of . . . immune system of its own. It was more compact and simpler—more of a targeting system, really—but more than effective enough in dealing with anything harmful.

The moss would identify things that were detrimental to itself, and slowly . . . *somehow* program any new mana storage cells it made to react to said chemicals by spending all their energy in obliterating the molecules. It was exchanging energy and food for immunity that way, so at the start, it *could* be overwhelmed, but after a certain point, it could be a practically invincible plant.

Then, this sort of . . . immune system library the plant made would be passed down to its reproductive system and onto its "children," slowly ending up with an entire colony of moss that was immune to a bunch of chemicals from the start.

Actually, that wasn't just interesting.

It slowly realized the actual implication of this, its tail starting to hesitantly wag as it considered what it could actually do if it could learn how to recreate these mana storage cells and that specialized immune system.

They could be programmed to attack specific molecules, which it assumed they did with frightening capability. And they could just . . . passively collect mana, with equally incredible capability.

If it could add these cells to itself—its own flesh and blood and bones, or just its bloodstream alone—how much more mana could it have without doing *anything?* If the genetic information in the moss's individual pieces could be passed down to the wolf, how many of those corrosive chemicals in the burning rivers could it just *casually ignore?*

It didn't have enough information to just throw that moss onto itself, half the specifics outright missing. If it added it to itself right now, it would probably do little more than be a leech for its blood. But the wolf was in a long, giant room full of moss. It had more than enough.

It quickly turned its attention back to fixing itself, wanting to hurry the process along as much as it could, despite its heavily diminished essence storage.

She went limp, body, mind, and core all utterly exhausted, the golem's smoking crystal clutched tight between her burnt fingers.

It had taken her almost two hours of nonstop [Sparkburst] casts, a headache-inducing amount of effort in control, prying away molten bits of metal so she could dig deeper, pushing away the steam bursts, and making sure nothing exploded in her face, but she'd managed it.

Despite her rather shredded gambeson-like shirt, her so-far empty pockets had been left relatively untouched, so she quickly shoved the crystal into her left pocket, pressing the latch down until she heard a click.

And now, she could finally relax without the constant screaming of an alarm digging into her ears.

She went to sleep to the sound of teeth scraping at stone, and smiled.

* * *

The moss thing didn't taste very well.

And it also didn't give much, if any, essence.

Still, this entire area was *covered* in it, so the wolf spent a healthy hour or two simply scraping bits off the walls and eating them. Partly because it really wanted to keep looking at them, in all honesty. It could have stopped after a couple batches.

Curiosity stalled it even more when it trotted over to the human with her single functioning arm, her other one clutched to her chest, and bent down closely to stare at her, at all the million little wondrous shades of color in her . . . everything. Though the yellow-green glow providing the light probably changed the way the colors looked, at least a little.

Her skin color, despite the muck and grime on her face, seemed to be something like . . . a light yellow pink, like a very diluted version of red. Her hair was an odd brown mixed in with a little bit of . . . orange? Red, maybe? Her coverings were a mixture of black-brown filth and light-brown cloth.

There was something in her pocket utterly exuding mana, and it was curious, but it simply didn't care enough to investigate, too invested in noticing all the little colors.

And not just that.

Everything was so much *sharper*.

It felt like it had been looking through a foggy piece of colored glass its entire life and was only now seeing the real world hiding just behind it.

It felt just about ready to swing the human on its back and run to the damn surface, now that it'd felt a likely way out. Instead, it nestled into the human's side and fell asleep. Mostly because its injuries were still in the process of healing, but also to see what it had learned about the moss.

The moss it had consumed was split apart into a thousand different tiny little layers.

It learned of photosynthesis, of how plant cell walls were constructed of layers of long, linear "polymer" microfibers made of something called "cellulose," although it couldn't quite understand what that cellulose thing was.

What it knew was that these cell walls were very strong. These cell walls and their supportive structures were much stronger than animal cell membranes, a bit more rigid and far less stretchy, but they were also mildly incompatible.

It wasn't sure what it could do with these, honestly, so it took a very long moment to think.

The first thing it came up with was to patch up the gaps in its rib cage by creating a plate of cellulose microfibrils right behind the rib bones, something like a mix between fabric and wood, a fairly tightly woven mixture, but just enough so that it would expand with its rib cage and not impede its breathing while also being protective.

In short, a thin plate, but bendy.

Thinking of different scenarios and possible complications was always the most annoying part of the process, and it was no different this time. It considered various movements, how much space it had in its chest, and dozens other little possibilities, but found no reason not to add this, so it did.

Mentally crafting a thick but flexible wall of said microfibrils was an absolute chore. It was like trying to make an anthill by picking up individual grains of dirt. Just making a tiny portion of it was annoying, but thankfully, as soon as it had made that little bit, it told [Devourer] to upsize it, saving it a few hours of pointless frustration.

Keeping it fueled was also a very easy thing to do, as the skill automatically did that because these things were growing out of its own body and were thus attached to it.

It really loved how simple its skill made things. Well, almost simple. Because it still didn't know why it refused to fuel the microtendons in its bones the same way. It was just a strange distinction, and it didn't know why it was happening. So it let it go. What's done is done.

Then, it considered other places to put this . . . almost platelike construct.

Its neck wouldn't work, since its neck was extremely mobile, and what it had made was a little too rigid to *not* impede that.

So it thought about making something similar but more complex. It made thin, compact strips of these microfibrils, braided them around and between each other in a gridlike pattern with some points of fusion, and then mentally bent them around to see how this improvised, inner armor would work.

The answer was *very well.* It was very flexible, and sticking it over its neck muscles, below the skin, was not very difficult.

The wolf grew a little excited as the actual possibilities of this were fully revealed. It was *flexible* armor, under its *skin.* A *third* layer of it. It would have its fur, then its skin, then the braided "plant" armor it had made. Or, stolen, rather.

It wouldn't even have to change anything significant because it could put the armor under or *in* the layer of fat around its body, meaning that its skin would still stick to its body properly. It had gone through almost half of its essence storage since falling down here, however, so it hesitated to just . . . put this little armor design all over its body.

It quickly checked how much every bit of this structure took out of its essence storage . . .

And it was actually *way* more expensive than it thought it would be. Maybe because it was so far distant from its own biology? It wasn't sure, but every six-inch square strip took about as much essence as it took to fix its left arm's injuries and replace all the lost flesh.

In other words, *way* too much.

With a heavy heart, it put the armor only on its vitals. A slightly loose cylinder around its neck, double layered at the bottom to protect its jugular and the arteries there, and the plates it had already put inside its rib cage.

Then, it turned to the rest of the knowledge it had gained.

And the wolf instructed its body on how to make these mana cells, how to deliver them to every bit of itself it could reach. In its skin, its bones, its marrow, its blood supply.

It looked into dozens of incomprehensible bonds of substances and poisons, and took the moss's immune system, integrated it into its own, and told it to use the mana cells to eradicate the poisons it had categorized as harmful only if they exceeded the default levels of them already in its body.

It cannibalized the fur on its abdomen, hips, hind legs, and tail, and replaced it with the moss, fiddling around with its roots to make them a little more organic, to make them *be* a part of its body a little better. It knew the moss would change color overtime because of what it was feeding on, but it didn't care too much. It would be fun to see the moss change its glow from yellow green to blood red.

Making the moss turn off its natural inclination toward reproduction and growth was also surprisingly easy, and without those processes taking up energy, it would only help the wolf even more.

Most of the work, in truth, was done by its skill. The wolf gave directions with as much specification as it could, thought about what it wanted, nudged it along, and [Devourer] did the rest.

With its changes finished, it looked into how much food the moss would be passively producing for it, and was just *slightly* disappointed to see it was about the equivalent of . . . maybe one or *maybe* two rats worth of food?

Considering its daily essence intake for nutrition and growth was about six to seven rats, that wasn't a whole lot, but it was a lot more than a plant like that would be creating for itself if not connected to the wolf. It had, realistically speaking, been expecting maybe half that amount. In fact, that amount could probably go up, assuming the moss was impacted by the environment.

The place it was currently in was probably sucked dry of this "carbon dioxide" thing due to the giant moss colony peppered around the room, so when it went outside, it assumed the moss's output would increase as well.

And even if its caloric output didn't go up when the wolf left this place, it was still a good supplement to its essence storage for doing absolutely *nothing*. The fact that the moss was heavier was a slight negative, but it also helped its balance, considering all the extra material on its upper body.

And it would have pretty lights to stare at whenever it wanted.

As for the mana cells . . .

It was ridiculous. It didn't have any way to quantify or be certain of the numbers except a very *vague* feeling, but the added mana storage was incredible. It felt like it would be gaining multiple times its original mana resources once the changes finalized. Quadruple? Maybe even quintuple? And if the wolf needed even *more* mana, it could just make its body *make more* of these cells, just like that.

It was just . . . it was amazing.

So yes, all in all, it was *extremely* satisfied.

Its sleep was long, relaxing, and triumphant, but eventually, it shook itself awake. Its changes and regenerative processes were only just starting, really, but it wanted to move out, and quickly. It forced itself upright, put the human on its back again after a minute or two of grumbling at each other, and trotted with careful steps across the bridge, eager to get to the surface.

The slowly receding hair on the bottom half of its body made it feel quite a bit lighter, but it didn't let itself be fooled by it, moving carefully and steadily.

The drop was only about twenty feet, but the wolf was still only half healed, so it wasn't in the mood for risks. Its fingers only barely bent, and the tickling sensation of muscles knitting together and new ones being grown made its nerves act up and not respond properly.

Thankfully, nothing of note happened, and the wolf stepped off the grated, rusty iron with a mental exhale of relief, walking to the end of the stone hallway, which quickly opened into a gargantuan, cylindrical room about a hundred and fifty feet wide. The sound of rushing water filled the air with a strange, calming atmosphere.

The walls went up and down way farther than its vibrations could feel, and in the center was a circular staircase, its center pillar a hollow platform surrounded by rusted stairs. Bridges extended out of the stairs at seemingly random intervals, giving off the impression of a winding spiderweb as the wolf craned its head upward to drink in the size of everything.

From somewhere up above, a steady stream of water fell, turning to mist as it continued its fall, breaking and dripping off bridges and support rods and wires, covering everything in filthy-smelling sewer water, the soft lights from below gradually painting the pale mist that descended into a beautiful emerald yellow.

It lowered its head after a couple moments to look at the flooded depths below, its eyes getting lost in the glowing waters, the mushrooms, the moss.

It was all so new and beautiful.

The wolf paused for a moment, a profound sense of peace filling its mind as it stared at the dark shapes, big and small, moving around underneath the glowing water, leaving behind trails of slowly dissipating green-yellow light. Its eyes roamed the walls, covered in moss and buzzing insects that seemed a little too big for comfort. Its ears twitched to follow the relaxing ambience of buzzing and falling water, its nostrils flaring as it inhaled the air, an odd mix of sewer stench and the cleanest air it had ever smelled. The constant, loud thumping only mildly ruined the calm atmosphere, but not enough for the wolf to be unnerved.

And the wolf stood there until it decided to sit, its shoulders slackening, and its eyes turning half lidded, calmly roaming its environment.

There was no reason to rush toward the surface. It had plenty of essence left.

It could . . . it could take a break to enjoy itself, right?

It had earned one, it felt like.

CHAPTER 28

Even though it wanted to test out how these mana cells interacted with itself, the wolf couldn't feel too much of a difference yet, just a vague sense of phantom awareness of more mana in its body that let it know its changes were still happening. And it wasn't going to wait however long the full changes took to show before moving on.

Additionally, as fun and relaxing as it was to just sit and observe the surroundings, a couple hours of doing so had made the whole thing lose some of its charm by sheer volume of time, so the wolf waited until its injuries were well and truly healed, from the broken bones in its abdomen to the flesh on its hands, then forced itself out of its relaxed fugue back into action.

The stairs looping around the walled lift platform were almost decoration at this point, unfortunately, but after barking for a [Haste] boost from the human, it managed to feel out its surroundings fairly well.

Most of the bridges extending out of the staircase led to rooms overlooking the rail system that wound around the inside of the walls, likely for the humans to have easy repair access, while a few led to small batches of machinery covered in levers and buttons connecting to complex mechanical systems that it didn't bother paying attention to.

The general trend, however, was that most of the machinery and pipework within and around the walls seemed to converge on that colossal room where the thumping came from, just about a hundred feet up.

It wasn't quite as large as the room below the platform shaft, but it was a cubic grid of about four hundred feet across with six machines within, only one of which was operational, and next to it, a jagged hole in the stone walls that led out into a square-shaped tunnel half full of water, around and within which little four-legged creatures scurried about. Rodents, most likely.

Hopefully.

There was another exit where the cylindrical room opened up into another wide corridor, about two hundred and fifty feet up, but it couldn't feel where that corridor led to, so it took the more obvious option.

The way up was a long one, not due to distance but because the wolf had to meticulously tap along the rusting metal and feel where the most stable parts were so it could move forward.

The bridge that led to the staircase was easy, but the metal stairs themselves? Not so much. It had to punch the central pillar constantly to know where to put its feet, occasionally using its slime to shuffle across some spots where the stairs had been so rotted through that even mild vibrations made the iron flake apart.

The threat of falling into water was a good motivator for exercising caution, considering the wolf didn't know how to swim, and the human would likely drown if it detached her.

After a mentally exhausting hour of slowly making its way up, it finally climbed the last couple steps and turned to the bridge at its left.

The odd thing about this particular bridge was that it was seemingly *made* to be detached at the press of a button, and it was in a strangely good condition. Inert latches with stray wires at the four connection ports sat idle, waiting for a twitch of electricity to send the entire bridge plummeting.

Why the humans would make something like this, it wasn't sure.

It was thankfully much thicker and more stable than all the other bridges dotted throughout the cylindrical room, with only a little bit of surface rust, so the wolf began to quickly trot across the near-hundred-feet-long bridge, leading straight into another pair of doors.

Up here, the moss was a lot less dense, and combined with the large distances, the light was, at best, just barely enough to see vague outlines from where tiny bits of it clung to the railing. The reflections of light in the misty sewage water as it cascaded were pretty, but not helpful.

So the wolf simply closed its eyes to focus on the vibrations more as it walked up to the doors.

Thankfully, the constant banging was so intense it didn't even need to do anything to get a detailed image of everything within a hundred feet. The metal audibly vibrated with every thundering boom, and it quickly concluded that this pair of doors was the same as the ones below, if a bit smaller.

And rather . . . damaged. All across the metal doors was an absolute mess of thin, shallow cuts, as if a human had picked up a sharp rod and just started hitting them for a few hours. Some were equally spaced, like claw marks, while others were solitary and random, coupled with a couple tiny dents.

It was odd, but the wolf didn't care much. There wasn't anything beyond the door nor around them, so it didn't consider it a threat.

It set the human down and began scratching.

Its hands' palms were once again covered in scratches and metal bits by the time it felt the doors become a little less rigid. It calmly dropped down, swept the metal shavings to the side, and prepared itself for a test push.

Bracing its shoulder against the door, the wolf dug its claws into the metal and pushed.

Nothing. The doors barely moved half an inch.

So it got back to scratching, fully intending to just burrow through the metal if that's what it took to get out of here. Not even ten seconds into its renewed efforts, a sudden rush of mana swept around and past the wolf, all of it moving out the air and being sucked into the door.

It felt the latches of the bridge snapping open a split millisecond before it heard the clicks and activated [Bloodrush]. As the bridge dropped out from underneath its feet, it hooked its left hand's claws into the door, and as [Pack Hunter] immediately activated, it wildly swung its right hand toward the human's, clasping her wrist in an iron vise.

Its ears were filled with the human's scream of terror as her weight swung down, yanking the wolf's form down with a sudden jerk. For a brief moment, it felt like its claws were going to be ripped out of its fingertips by their combined weight, the tendons straining like frayed rope to keep its fingers in that pinched position, trembling with desperate effort. Then her momentum slowed, cut short by her body slamming into the iron wall with a dull metallic thud and a wheeze.

It hurriedly extended its slime over the human's forearm, red throbbing veins flooding over its fur in all four limbs, faster than it had ever done before. As the human's wheezing coughs faded into panting breaths of terror, the scent of it choking the air, the wolf snarled in effort, struggling to focus on how to thicken the slime while also very aware of the possibility they could both die if its fingers gave out. It just didn't have enough strength for this.

It mentally prepared itself to drop the human the moment its confidence in staying alive wavered.

Thankfully, in a mere three seconds, it managed to stick all three of its available limbs to the wall and door, feeling adrenaline pumping through its veins as its heart raced.

It opened its eyes and looked down past the human's hanging form to the giant platform racing down the glowing depths, crushing metal and snapping bridges like toothpicks, the deafening clamor vibrating around the room and through its bones to combine with the constant banging of the machine just beyond the door.

For a few, short moments, it just stood there in shock, drinking in the sight all the way down, until the bridge slammed into the waters below, almost parting them in two as a huge splash jumped up several stories.

It was, unsurprisingly, very nice to look at, even from this far away.

Something *very* large suddenly moved in the waters, angrily swirling around the rapidly descending bridge, until eventually, both faded out of its effective eyesight, turning into vague blurs of black in a lake of glowing yellow green.

The wolf was more thankful than ever that it hadn't gone near the glowing water nor tried to catch any of the things swimming around in it. It mentally added another moment where caution had saved its life.

It quickly turned its head around, scrutinizing its position with both sensation and sight, its antennae writhing incessantly.

In truth, nothing had changed but how comfortable this would be.

Putting the human on its back again was, at most, an annoyance, as it had to awkwardly swing her around, hook her elbow around its right shoulder, and put her back-to-back on the expanding veins in a bit of an awkward diagonal position, but it managed it fairly easily.

Cutting through the door was a lot more frustrating, once that was done. It only had one arm to work with without the risk of falling off, so its speed was halved, and without the proper leverage to actually *push* the doors open, it had to come up with another solution.

And without any other options, it did exactly that.

It didn't think it was possible, but at some point, the wolf had gotten so used to seeing sparks that it actually grew a little sick of them.

By the time it finally saw a flash of light-blue light filter through the hundred thousand cuts and scratches on the door, its right hand was dripping blood down to its forearm, and it was forced to change to its left.

It also had to flatten its ears, as the banging grew so loud that it was actually starting to hurt its ears a little. Another hour passed, and then another, and finally, it had a hole right in the middle of the doors it could put an entire arm through. Judging by the hinges, these doors thankfully only opened inward.

And so, it awkwardly stuck three of its limbs on the right door and put its left forearm through the hole, bracing its hand on the inside by hooking its claws into the left door in a very awkward angle which made its shoulder ache. Then it began pulling back with its left arm and shoulder, simultaneously pushing with its three other limbs on the door it was hanging off of.

Even though it could feel its muscles burning and the snarl in its throat raking against its vocal cords as it pushed and pulled with all of its strength, progress was slow, the right door opening one inch at a time.

The hinges weren't even sticky or rusty.

It simply wasn't strong enough.

The moment a gap wide enough for its hand to go through appeared, it paused. Slowly, carefully, the wolf stuck its right hand in there, hooking its claws into the left door again, and then tilted its body almost sideways, using its arms to pull and its legs to push.

Exhaustion quickly filled its muscles, the straining burn turning into a numb weakness. It waited until it felt like it could no longer continue, then activated [Bloodrush], redoubling its efforts.

At some point, the human started using her weird mana-push technique to help, and after a couple more minutes of struggling, the doors finally widened enough for the wolf to squeeze through—which it did with great relief, fixing its grip on the left door and hopping off the right, planting its back paws firmly against stone with a mental sag of relief.

Its shoulders and the human's awkward position made squeezing through the gap in the doors a bit of a painful process for both of them, especially considering its bleeding paws, but with a final awkward twist to not bang the human's legs onto the metal, it stumbled into the room, finally.

The tide of blue which filled the room with each bang seemed to come from a machine on the back left corner of the massive room, but rather than rushing there, the wolf took a moment to appreciate both the feeling and the *sight* of the room.

Even if it hated the absolutely deafening explosions.

Five gutted machines, each a hundred feet tall and wide, with bits and pieces of plates and pipes and tools scattered across the floor, flanked it on either side like gigantic metal skeletons. The ceiling above was barely taller than the machines, and with the flashes of blue constantly highlighting that sight, it made it feel a lot more claustrophobic than a massive room like this should ever feel, so the wolf quickly trotted across the empty space between them.

Comparing the broken machines to the functional one made the difference even more apparent.

They seemed to be missing pretty much everything that made them function, from the dozen smaller engines within to the finer details of valves and pipes.

The strange thing was that all the removed parts weren't just missing. With every bang, it felt and saw the mess of haphazardly made machinery sitting next to the working machine, the hundreds of tools seemingly pooled together in a twenty-foot area.

The air stank of sewage, fuel, and rot.

Then it felt something strange to its right and paused, backtracking a few feet and peeking around the corner of one of the machines, staring into the empty space between it and the one previous to it.

Another deafening explosion filled the room with blue, and the vibrations confirmed its curious find.

Three human skeletons, picked clean and old enough to likely crumble to dust at the first touch, were arranged in a small pile, their skulls placed on the floor side by side to face the wall in a way that felt distinctly purposeful.

Odd.

It turned around and resumed its walk, not paying much mind to what it had seen, already filtering it out of having any importance in its mind.

The closer it got to the machine that made the explosions, however, the more it hesitated, flinching with each blast. It was just so *loud*. Its antennae were giving it a great look of the tunnel system beyond and all the creatures in them, but it was three hundred feet away from the thing, and it could feel its ears starting to ring already. It felt like it couldn't even hear its own thoughts.

It would probably burst its eardrums to walk past it, and it doubted any boost would make it fast enough to speed away in time to not pop the membrane. Maybe it should have put a bit more thought into how it was going to go about leaving this place.

It lifted a hand to press its ears flat against its head, pressing down with bruising force.

That helped, actually.

The wolf sat down, racking its brains for what it was going to do. It probably couldn't rest with those rhythmic, deafening explosions constantly playing in the back, and thus, not heal. It also couldn't just rush past the machine and fight however many dozens of rodents were just beyond it in the tunnels, and it—

The wolf stiffened, its hand lifting off its head as it struggled to comprehend what it was feeling.

It didn't have the time to.

In the span of a couple seconds, everything on the tunnel just beyond had done some sort of . . . erratic movement, then stopped, falling limp to the floor. It blinked rapidly, the fur under the slime struggling to rise in a bristle.

It didn't know why, but its instincts were screaming danger.

No, not danger. Death.

In the span of a second, the screaming turned into a deafening screech. It felt like it was about to die, the mortal fear of certain death clutching at its mind in a steely vise that froze it in place.

The miasma of terror coming out of the human made it aware that she somehow felt it too.

It was about to activate [Echoes of Oblivion] and try to snap itself into action, find some corner or nook in one of the machines to burrow into and hide, when the object of its fear blurred into sight from around the blue-flashing machine, sliding sideways on a single humanoid foot, its other curled into its chest, its upper body leaning almost parallel to the floor.

Its momentum halted after a few feet, fluidly transitioning into a loose crouch, head forward and arms limp at its sides.

It wasn't sure if it was from shock, but the wolf didn't even bother using its antennae, simply staring at the distant figure, frozen.

The flash of blue faded, and darkness fell.

The silence felt suffocating.

A whisper of air moving, the shuffle of cloth, the lightest of vibrations echoing through the floor into its retracted antennae, before they all suddenly cut off.

Another flash of blue illuminated the figure one long second later, now standing upright just fifty feet away, its metallic head staring at them without eyes, three hornlike protrusions coming out of the top of its head, and three symbols painted in white where its face should be.

The suffocating sensation of imminent death suddenly faded, as if it was never there, and the wolf gasped out a wheezing breath it hadn't realized it had been holding, lowering itself into a pose of submission, tail curled under its legs, making sure to keep its eyes away from the man's metallic head.

Because it *saw* the moving flesh. It saw the skin, the metal, and it distinctly felt the lack of a heartbeat as vague vibrations bounced around in the human's chest cavity.

A biological impossibility. A dead human, walking and running. It was so unnatural it made its skin crawl.

Even if it tried to run, it felt like the creature could kill it in less than a second, so it simply lay flat on the floor, tense and afraid, hoping for mercy, its tail so far between its legs that it was brushing its neck.

It hated doing this.

"Who are you?" the human male asked, and the wolf sincerely hoped its own human would make her own sounds and negotiate for them.

Which she did, thankfully.

Part of her was utterly elated to hear another human again.

Another part of her had emptied its bladder.

"I—uh, Emhreeil. A-Adventurer. Bronze rank," she squeaked out, barely audible over the echoing sounds of the explosions, her voice so croaky she sounded like a dying frog. She winced, a thousand thoughts in her mind swirling like a tornado. She was too scared to send mana his way, lest it be perceived as a threat. She was utterly blind.

"I—please, we need help. We've been stranded down here for—I-I don't know how long—"

"I don't care," he dryly replied, and she just fell silent, unsure of what to even say to that or what to think. Another bang filled the room, and the man spoke again as soon as the sound had faded enough.

"How did you get here? Answer clearly and honestly."

She didn't hesitate, seeing a lifeline.

"We-we were in a trash pit. Something happened, and we fell down the gears, and then it found some pipe down there, and followed it, then u-um, just kept following it, then fell into a room, walked through a tunnel, through s-some kind of-of factory with a bunch of rotted fuel in it, I-I think. And my, uh, companion here climbed up some kind of . . . shaft or-or some vent with me on its back, and then we found a bridge that led to this—this staircase outside, and he took us here. I-I'm—my legs are broken, so it's been carrying me," she stammered out, her voice cracking, her heart pounding at the sudden interrogation, the chance of rescue.

The man was silent. Another explosion in the background, and he spoke.

"You're not lying. Which is weird. How did this . . ." he suddenly trailed off, and she held her breath, every second of silence mounting the tension in her chest.

"It's a wolf," he spoke, his tone still oddly dead and uncaring with just a hint of realization, and she flinched in surprise.

"N-No. I-it's just—just a mutant I found—" she rushed out, and was cut off by another bang.

She didn't say anything after the sound faded, and neither did he. Swallowing a lump that had lodged itself in her throat, she wondered what to say and how to salvage this. There was no way he would believe her; not after he'd said it so confidently, so quickly.

How on Ergos could she possibly convince an adventurer to leave a *wolf* alive? How the hell did he figure it out so quickly? Was he even an adventurer?

Another bang, and as the sound faded, the man's footsteps neared, the voice that filled the room carrying perfectly, like a sentence that was somehow whispered but still carried across an entire room. "I'm curious about something. You are dependent on this creature right now. You know what it is. You're riding on a monster .One that is essentially the *definition* of the word, at least culturally. I don't know how or why it's being like this, or how you got it to like you, but the fact of the matter stays the same. You are on the back of one of the most dangerous monsters that have ever existed. So I can't help but wonder."

Another bang filled the air, and he resumed right after.

"Do you want it dead?" he asked.

"No!" she replied instantly, her lips blurting it out without any forethought, mildly panicked at the thought of her companion getting killed, her fingers tightening on its shoulder.

"Really?" the man asked slowly, somehow making it sound perfectly flat. "What if I put you on my back and carried you to safety? To some clinic? You wouldn't be depending on it anymore. Would you want it dead then?"

She didn't hesitate for a millisecond despite the fact that to her, it almost sounded like an *offer* to take her straight to safety in exchange for its life.

"No."

It was a stupid choice, logically, but she didn't feel like a logical creature right now. She hadn't for a while.

Another bang.

"In the Dungeon, the easiest prey is people. It has killed, and it will do so again. Your choice will have made that happen. Every person this creature kills in the future will be dead because you said no to my following question. So, think. If I were to help you out of here, would you want it dead then, knowing this decision might cost ten lives?"

For once, she hesitated.

She'd become far more jaded and cynical ever since she'd come down to the Dungeon. It was impossible not to. But still, the knowledge that her . . . friend of sorts could be the reason a child's parent would not come home one day, that a parent's child might never return home one night, that someone's lover or wife or husband could end up as nothing more than an added arm to her companion—that made her hesitate.

But what were the chances of that? What were the chances it would kill a gangster who terrorized regular people, some murderer, some rapist, some loan shark, some drug pusher or a slaver or just someone who was already dying from exposure in the Dungeon's dirty streets? Were they equal, by some stretch of the imagination?

Regardless, he was right. This was a monster, and she wouldn't be able to stop it from being one. Her mind wandered back to how it'd torn the golem's face to jagged ribbons of metal and glass and wires, and she gulped, indecisive.

But she also thought about how it had nosed at her face when she was having one of those episodes down there, how it had every reason to kill her and eat her, but hadn't. How it had fed her from its own blood because it wanted to. How it lugged her useless form around for what felt like months. How it gave her a health potion when she was certain she was going to die from either bleeding or infection.

She came to a conclusion. A conclusion that scared her, truth be told.

"No," she breathed out.

Another bang.

The man walked closer, and she felt the wolf tremble underneath her, tensing. Her hand instantly darted to soothingly pet along its neck.

"What about a hundred?"

"I . . . No," she repeated, feeling some part of her wither and die inside her as she realized just how easily that admission had come.

"What about a thousand? Where do you draw the line?" He paused, and she heard the shuffle of clothes. "*Do you* draw a line? What is the point where you look at the monster you care for and decide that enough is enough?"

She took in a deep breath, struggling to push aside her confusion and the desire to just say whatever he wanted her to say in the vain hope of assistance, to just scream in frustration and ask him to fucking *help her or leave* already, instead of giving her this sudden interrogation to deal with.

Would she draw a line?

The version of herself who had walked into the Dungeon for the first time would have drawn the line at ten people, regardless of how much she owed her companion, how incredibly attached she'd gotten to it.

That unrecognizable person who existed only in her memories was much less selfish than the person she was now. Much less desensitized, much less desperate, much less bitter and spiteful and without a single loose screw in her mind.

Were she forced to choose between a thousand strangers and her companion, what would she choose now?

The answer came easily, and no matter what absurd number she added to the tally of lives, it never changed. Five thousand, ten, a hundred, she just . . . couldn't choose them over her companion. Even when she stopped herself and tried to imagine every number and convert them from a faceless statistic into people with unique memories, experiences, and dreams, nothing changed. It budged, it bent, her heart ached, but the answer stayed the same.

Only adding herself or Katherine to the equation made her pause.

And the fact that her mind just refused to attempt choosing one or another told her that's where she drew the line.

"If . . . if it goes for me or K—someone I care about," she whispered truthfully, taking in a deep, shuddering breath as her ears filled with another rhythmic explosion.

Just uttering those words made her chest tight.

When had she become this way? What would her old self think of her? What did she think of herself, right now?

Did it matter?

The man said nothing, breathing steadily.

"So you do not care about the death toll your decision might cause, so long as it doesn't affect you or that person," the man stated, and she resisted the urge to cuss him out, gritting her teeth.

"Yes," she bit out, feeling like she'd just thrown herself down into a hole she'd never crawl out of.

Another explosion.

"What will you do afterward?" the man questioned, and the question sobered her up immediately, a giant blank forming in her mind for a few seconds.

The answer wasn't complex. In fact, it was almost offensively vague, but she didn't want to go into specifics. Not with this man, who could be some fragment of her imagination for all she knew due to how absurd this discussion and his entrance to it had been.

"I . . . live. I just—I want to live around people I care about and who care about me. People who are like me, and just enjoy life with them. Enjoy freedom," she stated, unbothered by how awkward it was to talk to someone while lying face up on top of a wolf.

"Freedom . . ." he almost scoffed. "Freedom is power. And to have power is to be a monster."

The man turned silent until another bang passed. The shuffle of clothes predated a long exhale that sounded almost like a sigh. Something clattered, metal against metal.

"I've made up my mind. I dropped a mana compass on the floor. It's mapped to point you to the safest route possible to the surface. I will give this to you if you answer my questions and do something for me," he stated, and her heart leapt to her throat, ready to agree to pretty much anything. "First, do you know how to guide someone here?"

"No, I-I have no idea. I have a [Mana Touch] skill, but I only got it after we'd arrived at this . . . this place. I was completely blind before then. I'm sure I could . . . I could do it, if you gave me some instructions or-or another compass?" she hopefully offered.

"I won't," he said, confusing her for a moment until she realized he'd meant if she could lead someone here *if she was captured* and forced.

"Second, you have a golem's core in one of your pockets. You can't legally sell or use it after you get out of here. I won't explain why; you'll see once you're outside. I know a bishop in the Six-Eyed Crow's church who will take it off your hands for a good price. Third floor, fourth quadrant, walk down street ninety-three, just past the open square. You will go to them, ask for the bishop. *Only* speak to the bishop. Tell him the password, sell the golem core to him, and give him the compass. The password is the following phrase. I won't repeat it," he said, then paused for a couple seconds as she parsed through what she'd just heard, hurriedly committing the location and instructions to memory.

Another bang, and he resumed.

"Tell him this. *Exactly* this. 'I saw a ghoul on a conveyor belt, and it turned around to smile at me.' Then give him the compass. He'll owe you a favor. A small one. Do with that what you will. Do you understand?" he dryly intoned, and she gulped.

"Yes. Yes, I do. But—how am I going to find this place? I'm blind . . . ?" she asked, confused.

"Not my problem. Figure it out. Repeat the instructions to me. What are you to do in exchange for my assistance?" he pressed on like a drill sergeant, and she gritted her teeth.

"Third floor, fourth quadrant. Down street number ninety-three, past a square, speak to the bishop. Tell him that I saw a ghoul on a conveyor belt, and it turned around to smile at me, then give him the compass."

"Good. I have something I need to take care of. Lead yourselves out, and never come back here again. If you tell anyone about this meeting or this place, I will make you suffer pain you can't even imagine. I might look for you in the future for some similar, simple errands. Goodbye for now."

The sound of something light and metallic sliding across the floor was the only thing she heard besides the faint rustle of cloth.

"W-Wait," she blurted out, and felt a light tingle of that fear enter her mind again, letting her know she had his attention. "Why me? For these— these errands? I'm—"

"A cripple," he cut her off, and she flinched. "Cripples and the downtrodden are those who are the least likely to draw suspicion going into a church, so you and your horrific appearance are convenient for me. And if you ever return to your adventuring career or fix yourself, I'd have a good contact for information on what's happening for both the outside world and the Dungeon. I'll also pay you for the mentioned information if I decide to look for you. So keep your ears peeled, and your mouth shut. Oh, and do not reveal the wolf's existence to anyone. Monsters exist to be hunted. Goodbye," he spoke, quickly and monotonously, and with another rustle of clothes, silence filled the room for all of about three seconds before another explosion made her flinch.

She cautiously sent a pulse of mana out into the room, finding nothing but machinery and broken bits of metal all around both of them, the wolf below her cautiously raising its head. She quickly twisted around to the best of her ability, ignoring its grumble of protest, and snatched the compass, clutching it as hard as she could to her chest.

The mental, directional tug in her mind was so comforting that she couldn't help but let out a strange sob-laugh of relief.

A way out. Finally.

Even as the wolf began detaching her from its back, covering her in yet another fresh layer of slowly crusting slime and depositing her on the cold stone, she just clutched the compass to her chest, taking deep breaths.

She'd have to separate from her new friend soon, but that was fine, even if she never saw it again. Even if she never got to feel that high of drinking its blood again. Even if she would be responsible for every life it took from here on out.

That entire conversation just baffled her. Few parts of it made sense. She was half convinced she was having some kind of fever dream. But as the wolf tried to nudge its head under her shoulder with a grumble, holding its hands over its ears as it tried to sleep, she thought to herself that this all certainly *felt* real.

And it felt good, no matter how conflicted she was about what she'd discovered about herself.

CHAPTER 29

W hat about a thousand? Where do you draw the line? *Do you* draw a line? What is the point where you look at the monster you care for and decide that enough is enough?" Ghoul spoke over the speaker, and for once, her attention broke, her mind finally registering the background noise of his voice.

She paused, feeling anger spark in her chest.

She grabbed the communication tablet lying inert on the table with a short, snappy motion, abandoning the framework she was working on in her moment of frustration.

"Are you interrogating the intruders or *me*, Ghoul?" she hiss-clicked out into the voice port, her wings fluttering in agitation.

After a short moment of no reply, she returned to her makeshift forge, a pale imitation of what they had before Holo's *colossal* fuckup, using three hands to form the runes and the fourth to carelessly throw the comm tablet onto the table before using said hand to stabilize the mana flow.

The fact that he hadn't killed them already was baffling.

What if they had messed around with her power source? Did he have *any* idea how rare it was to find a machine like that just lying around with a mana configurator already inside? It took her *days* of nonstop work, with absolutely *zero* sleep, to convert the crystal into lightning energy, and another week to wire that into her current, measly forge.

She wanted him to kill them already so she could stop fussing over their presence. It was stressing her out. Leave it to Ghoul to turn a simple extermination into a lecture, or whatever the hell he was doing. She wasn't even sure of *who*—

Her mind idly worked through the backlog of information it had cataloged but not processed, and she turned stiff for a brief moment.

She snatched the comm tablet with her two top arms, sticking her mask right next to the voice port.

"Did you say *wolf?* Are . . . " she trailed off, processing the rest of the conversation.

There was a *wolf* in the Dungeon, just a couple hundred feet from her forge and their measly excuse of a new hideout. He could be mistaken, but he was the most perceptive person she'd ever met. There was no way.

There was a wolf nearby.

A wolf that could, with one careless swing of its paw, *break* her power source beyond repair.

"I swear to every god in the cosmos if that creature breaks my forge, I am smuggling myself out of this island and going to the Xhilatni jungles to live in a tree," she ground out, hoping that despite her stunted vocal abilities, her rather emotionless delivery would convey how irate she was right now.

"If . . . if it goes for me or K—someone I care about," a croaky voice replied through the comm tablet, and her chitinous fingers shook, her mandibles clicking and grinding together.

She turned it off and tossed it to the corner of the table, a lot harder than she'd intended. For once, she was thankful of how weak she was, because if it had broken, she would have lost her mind.

She took a deep breath, trying to focus back on her work, but the moment she returned to the enchantment framework, her mind wandered, sticking to that woman's words like glue, refusing to leave her alone.

And working on enchantments with a wandering, furious mind was either a gateway to losing a limb or destroying the materials one was trying to enchant.

Her hands fell on the table with clicks that hung onto the silent room uncomfortably long, and she bowed her head, white hair falling forward to block the sight of the damp, cramped room around her, her shoulders slackening as her breaths deepened.

The sight of her hair only made more resentment and fury boil up in her throat. Her mind always screamed at her that the color was wrong, that it should be different, but it never told her *what* the right color was supposed to be.

Her eyes flicked down to the floor, littered with bits and pieces of machinery and crystal dust.

Unreasonable as the emotion was, she hated that woman.

Because she couldn't help but project herself onto her, years ago, saying much the same thing without knowing what that would really mean.

And here she'd been for the past week and a half, working herself to death to avoid having to confront the things she'd seen, been complicit in, to avoid going through that moral crisis always waiting just around the corner.

Where did she draw the line?

She didn't know anymore because she constantly had to reassess everything, lest she be forced to leave behind the only family she'd ever known to shield her conscience.

When a flaming demon in a gas mask and a creature covered in boiling gore broke her out of Tillenhall, she'd been ready to do and agree to anything, everything, merely a shivering, mad husk of a human being in a body that wasn't hers.

It took a long time and countless days of struggle and agony to stop hooking her chitinous fingers into every nook and cranny of her exoskeleton, trying to peel away the insectoid armor and find the human body she *knew* was hiding somewhere in there, trying to rip off her second pair of arms because they *shouldn't be there*.

It took years for her mind to start resembling some rough notion of sanity. It took years of being a worthless burden for her to finally start participating and being more than simple deadweight. At some point, Ghoul had asked her the same question he'd asked the intruder, and she'd answered in a very similar way, watching with mild distaste as he ate someone's leg.

And yet now, every time she looked at Holocaust's face, still lying in that pod *she herself* had created, her mind flashed back to the day everything went to shit, and she had to ask herself that same damn question a hundred times a day without an answer.

Where did she draw the line?

It was one thing to *say* she drew the line at Holo trying to kill Ghoul, and only there.

It was another thing to walk through hell itself, through a tornado of flames, with orange rods of latticework metal slowly sagging down from the sky like the web of a spider closing down on its prey; over piles of charred corpses, molten glass raining down on her back.

It was another thing to check a newspaper and read the casualty report, go through the thirteen hundred names of the dead, and the two thousand injured.

It was another thing to watch the Guard flood the Dungeon and beat submission onto innocents to appease the upper city, for they could not find the terrorist who attacked the teleport station. To watch the country be brought to the utter brink of a civil war.

It was another thing to watch the world turn against them. To have to leave everything behind and crawl into the sewers like rats because everyone, both from the Dungeon and above, wanted their heads on pikes. After all, there were only three pyrokinetics in Carmera who could wreak such destruction, and two of them lived in the upper city. The person who did it was obvious.

And she didn't know if she could just ignore the actions of her friends anymore.

There was less to be conflicted about when the extent of moral questioning she had to do was "Where is Ghoul getting these body parts from," and "I should probably be more concerned about how happy Holocaust is to be burning anything that can scream."

In a way, Ghoul's question had been prophetic.

She couldn't just ignore how many times the age of the deceased was in the single digits, how their bodies crunched and crumbled beneath her feet as she looked for her friend in the fire, how all those innocents were burnt to a crisp for no seeming reason.

She could just imagine their horrific screams of agony as their flesh was rent off their bones, and it made her sick.

They still didn't know what had happened, as Holo was comatose.

Had she just decided she wanted to hear some screaming that day? Was she attacked? Did she just want to "let out some steam"?

She was torn between leaving, unable to deal with the guilt of what Holocaust had done, the consequences of their actions that could lead to *thousands more* people dead, and reinforcing the answer she'd given Ghoul all those years ago. That she would only draw the line if Holocaust tried to kill him.

Her emotions were going haywire.

She knew she shouldn't even be hesitating. Her friends were a genocidal sadist who would happily burn the entire planet just to watch the fire roar into the sky, and a ruthless, remorseless, intelligent ghoul who had no idea what the word *guilt* even was besides a dictionary definition of it.

Logically, morally, she shouldn't even be here with them. She should have walked away the moment she realized what Holo had done.

But she just couldn't.

It was Holo who would act like a heater for her whenever she was cold or needed some physical comfort, offering some dry commentary that would make her mandibles try and twitch into some imitation of a smile. It was Holo who helped her practice and work with mana, who taught her the basics, who taught her how to read again. It was Holo who commissioned the mask she was wearing right now, one which allowed her to look into a mirror without breaking her fists on it, a present for her "freedom day."

It was Ghoul who would pry her clawing fingers off her chitin plates whenever she was trying to peel them off. It was Ghoul who taught her how to calm herself down during a manic episode, how to stop herself from succumbing to the intense urge to harm herself, to crack her shell and find the human within. It was Ghoul who taught her how to fight, how to think for herself, how to regain independence and confidence, how to find something that clicked with her.

And when she'd found it, it was him who would spend days running around trying to find books and information and spellbooks to support her. Him who would show her how she could apply her talents out into the real world, in the Dungeon, in a fight. It was him who brought her out of her cocoon and allowed her to help them with the things she made.

It was those moments and another million smaller ones that all made her love them with all her heart, like family.

But guilt was tearing her heart in two.

She had to speak to Ghoul. Honestly, and openly.

Not these underhanded questions through a fucking *comm tablet* while he was interrogating someone who had somehow busted into her power room.

With a long, long sigh, she rubbed her two top hands on her mask, tracing the edges of the white rubberlike material perfectly shaped into an imitation of a human nose, mouth, and jawline, pressing into the space just below her eyes and extending to wrap around her neck.

And with her bottom two arms, she reached for the comm tablet once again, clicking the button with a childish scribble of a skeletal head on it.

Holo's work.

After a couple of seconds, Ghoul accepted, and she simply stood in silence, listening to him give out instructions to the intruder and give some barely believable excuse as to why he was giving her a task to complete.

Cold, cynical, remorseless—she could call Ghoul a lot of things, but she couldn't call him cruel. Especially considering that task was meant to be given to someone else he knew.

Her mandibles tilted into a rough *V* shape under her mask, an automatic response that was the closest she could get to a smile. Her mask gave a slight, polite smile, the enchantment as off-kilter as usual. Still, it was better than nothing.

She waited until the background explosions had faded before speaking.

"Sorry for being snappy. When you have time, could we . . . just sit and talk?" she asked, her trilling, clicking voice still unable to properly convey much emotion. Deep and mechanical, almost, with a vague hint of femininity.

Maybe she could imbue some voice enchantment into her mask. It would probably help with the surge of sickness she felt when hearing the inflectionless clicking rhythm her insectoid throat made.

"Sure. I'll clean up the other tunnels from whatever's getting close so you can work in peace, make sure our new informants leave, and then I'll come by," he replied easily, and she breathed out a slow, deep breath.

She appreciated how unflappable he was.

She supposed that someone who had basically raised two borderline insane freaks like Holocaust and herself after breaking them both out of Tillenhall had simply gotten used to having nerves of steel.

She still remembered when she'd tried to stab an electric rod into Ghoul's skull during an episode of hers, and Holo had sat with her afterward and listed off the times she'd tried to hurt him while freaking out over one thing or another, as if that was supposed to relieve her from her guilt.

Her mood lifted just from the memory alone. The way Holo had been trying to comfort her but failing so miserably in her execution was actually rather funny in hindsight.

. . . Gods damn it, what was there to talk about?

She knew she'd never leave them. Holo and Ghoul could both tell her they would kill her, and she'd just tilt her head away to give them better access to lop her head off. They'd saved her from a fate worse than death, and she owed them more than just her life. She owed them her very sense of self.

She didn't need to talk to Ghoul to come to a decision. She had to talk to him to figure out a way to cope with the heartrending guilt. She could probably take it.

Losing them *wasn't* something she could take.

"It's . . . thank you. I think my line . . . is still the same. Just . . . never mind. We'll talk when you're here, face-to-face. I'll go back to making those grenades."

"Alright. Be there in a couple hours at most, Mirena. Oh, and if you ever need help with something—"

"You'll try to help if I let you know; I know. Thank you, Ghoul."

He gave off an acknowledging hum, and the comm tablet's light flicked off.

She let out a sigh through the mask's nose and got back to work under the uncaring glare of half a dozen light crystals.

CHAPTER 30

Sleeping became infinitely easier after the wolf managed to fall asleep for a short minute and mess with its cochlea to turn off its hearing.

The constant vibrations and [Restful Awareness] helped a lot with putting it at ease, because there was a constant reminder that there was nothing walking or alive within three hundred feet.

That human was so absurdly strong that the wolf was starting to reconsider how easy it would be to hunt humans for food. There *had* to be a reason they were the dominant species in their own nest, right? It couldn't just be numbers.

Something to consider when it got out of here, because truth be told, it was utterly terrified of that man, and the thought of being as far away from him as possible only spurred the wolf toward escape with more urgency.

But it had to rest, fix its hands, and mess around with its new mana cells for a bit first. Just until the human was sufficiently far away and unlikely to come back to kill them for accidentally tailing him.

That time of rest also gave the wolf a lot of time to think about and theorize changes to itself, most of which were put on the mental back burner for later, with the exception of a few small ones, like putting a thin film of cartilage at the entrance of its ears to stop its eardrums from bursting by the machine when it walked past it. Then it checked its moss-fur changes, which would still take about two more days to finish, much to its disappointment.

That left it with a body that was half furless because it hadn't considered to check how much time those changes would make, so it quickly put fur back on its body and nudged the [Devourer] skill into naturally letting its fur fall out when the moss emerged and grew from underneath.

After it had finished checking itself and applying the changes, it mentally prepared for the likely arduous task of figuring out how its mana cells would work.

It was wrong once more, and it couldn't be more thankful. It was actually very easy.

The wolf could *feel* the mana in its body if it focused, a faint sensation of *something* being there, and all it had to do was focus on its mana veins and try to sort of visualize them *sucking in* the mana instead of pushing it out, like they were used to.

That took three minutes of intense effort, but it figured out how to do it. Its mana veins couldn't pull mana from the air, no matter how hard it tried, but the mana cells? Not only were they *made* to store mana from their ambient surroundings, but it seemed like for one reason or another, it was converted to be the *wolf's* mana. So taking it felt as natural as breathing.

It wasn't exactly sure of how it could tell, but it could. The human had different mana to itself, and the air did too. So did the moss in the rooms below. But the cells could somehow convert that. Maybe it just wasn't smart enough to understand the absurd complexities of the mana cells, but no matter how much it scrutinized one, it just couldn't quite tell *how* it did it.

Half an hour of messing around with its new cells later, it got a light mental prod by the symbols. With a sense of groggy confusion, it turned aside [Devourer] and let them spread out over its mind's eye.

-Acquired Skills:
You have gained the Skill [Mana Conversion - Level 1]

A mental prod at the skill gave the wolf a vague understanding of taking mana and converting it to be its own, more felt and conceptualized than with actual images.

It paused and reached for the mana veins in its throat.

And with as much focus as it could muster, it *pulled.*

It was like trying to suck in sentient slime through a thin straw which kept constantly trying to return to the greater world and pulling itself away. But it *could* feel that foreign mana, interact with it, try and exert control over it. It didn't know how, why, or what changed, but it could.

And as the wolf held on, keeping the foreign energy in its throat and trying to suck it into its mana heart, something quickly changed, the mana somehow becoming less . . . thick, easier to move. The skill was doing *something*, but it wasn't sure what.

Shortly after the energy began moving through the mana veins in its throat and through its physical flesh, it came into contact with its mana cells. Within seconds, the mana was sucked in, and the wolf *felt* it become its own, the cells almost buzzing with energy.

It hurriedly sucked it out of the cells and into its mana heart through its phantom veins, allowing them to continue the process, watching in wonder as a steady stream of mana trickled into its phantom heart.

A stream which stopped within mere seconds, as that same heart was completely full of mana already, pooling it in its veins instead.

Without much thought, it activated a full-body [Echoes of Oblivion] just to burn some energy, and was almost snapped out of its rest as the sensational equivalent of a billion worms crawling through its flesh into the open air repeated itself, the mana veins quickly moving through every tiny bit of extra and added flesh. It had forgotten it hadn't activated the skill on a lot of its body for a while.

It couldn't help the way its body twitched and curled in discomfort, but it managed, just barely, not to wake up.

And then it was over, its body wreathed in pitch black.

The way the mana veins interacted with the mucus in its back was especially interesting. It was like they just . . . melted together into an incoherent, easily changeable blanket.

The wolf kept the skill running to burn mana, and continued practicing how to suck in the energy through the air, trying to make the difficult process something it could do on a whim while doing other things, such as fighting. If it somehow ran out of mana completely, it wanted to be able to use this to quickly recover *something*.

It was honestly not nearly as excited as it should have been for something this monumental. [Echoes of Oblivion] was a very cheap skill to use, mana-wise, and the only skill it could actually pour any substantial amount of mana into was [Sonic Blast], which was more of a suicide attack than something it could genuinely use in a fight.

It considered the possibility of pouring all of its energy into a single blast, adding on the mana it had stored in its body, then keeping the skill in place while the wolf sucked in mana through the air and continued to pump it into the blast.

The ball of air and sound probably wouldn't even leave its throat before detonating and turning its body into a messy pile of gore. It had already been difficult holding it all compressed when it had one-fifth the mana capacity, back when it'd fought the Roof-Tumor.

So yes, it wasn't particularly excited about potentially quintupling both its mana capacity *and* regeneration. Useful to have just in case, but that was about it, really. It was more excited about realizing that practicing while it slept was something it should have been doing a lot more of, considering how many levels it'd gotten from just one nap. Its mind felt a lot less well-rested in comparison to its body by the end of it, but it was worth it.

[Restful Awareness] had gone up to level nineteen from eighteen, [Mana Perception] and [Mana Manipulation] had each gone up a level, to level twelve and level eleven. [Echoes of Oblivion] went to level seven, which simply made it feel a bit more fluid and faster to use, and its new skill had gone up to level two by the time its body decided it had to get up after doing the same thing for hours in its lucid dreamlike fugue.

It fixed its cochlea to turn its hearing back on, and after squeezing a bit of adrenaline out of its stomach sac, it opened its eyes to a familiar room, its head still half wedged beneath the human's shoulder for protection from the noise.

After a short moment of wondering why everything looked strange, it remembered it had [Echoes of Oblivion] still running and quickly cut it off, confirming for one final time there was nothing alive for hundreds of feet.

Wow. Its lower body was absurdly itchy. Growing moss was painless, but still annoying.

The human, unfortunately, did not have the luxury of being able to control her body, so she'd been awake the entire time, and it showed. Even the way she moved her mana felt sluggish and tired, half aware. Like someone half-heartedly stirring liquid.

The only difference that made to the wolf as it quickly laid on her front and attached her to its back was that she provided not even the faintest grumble of disapproval, sighing out a "Finally!" sound in a relieved sort of tone.

After rolling over onto its feet, it began moving toward the machine in a hurried trot.

"I'm getting motion sickness . . ." the human groaned in complaint. It chuffed in acknowledgement, speeding up its pace. It too wanted to get out as soon as possible.

"Oh, you—you cheeky *shit*. I bet you understand me, and you've just been fucking with me the entire time," she gritted out with a strained, odd voice, lightly flicking its ear.

It ignored her this time, only flicking its ear back at her to smack said hand in revenge, simply continuing to move across the room, mildly flinching with every explosion as it felt the human hiss and try to maneuver her arm to cover both her ears, to little success. It paused for a moment, its trot slowing, and extended a couple of the larger mucus veins to her head.

The human jerked her neck inward as if to hide it between her shoulders with a yelp, and the wolf grumbled, knowing full well that her eardrums would *definitely* burst if it just walked her past the machine.

Much to its annoyance, though, the human was squirming and trying to brush away the veins. It grumbled and wrapped them around her tucked-in neck like a collar before snaking smaller ones up to her ears and enclosing them, making sure the mucus wouldn't melt too deep into her ear canal. It wasn't sure if that would do anything to her fragile human biology, but it would definitely be annoying. As was the human, with her constant gagging and squirming.

"This is ssoooo fuuuucking *gross*." She paused for a dry heave. "F-Fuck, this is so *weird*. And you've fed me blood through a vein straw. I should probably stop talking to myself, actually. Can you just . . . grumble at me at least, so I can pretend we're talking? Not sure that I'd hear it, but I can feel it through your back," the human slowly rambled, almost sleepily, gesticulating randomly with her arm.

The wolf ignored her, passing one, two, three machines, and then turning to the left, clumsily stepping over tools and climbing up the makeshift ramp of rubble that led to the jagged hole in the wall.

Part of it was curious and wanted to look at the machine—what was making that massive bang, where exactly that light was coming from—but another bigger part of it was fairly sure it had felt an exit in the form of one of the humans' smoke-spewing pipes at the very edge of its sensory range. It had been boosted by the human, and it was brief, but the wolf roughly remembered where it was. And was thus *very* invested in leaving as soon as possible to get there.

As it stepped out of the room and into a pitch-black, twenty-foot-tall and wide tunnel, its nose was assaulted with the familiar miasma of sewer filth and rotting corpses. It paused, realizing all those odd lumps on the floor were the rats it had been feeling before the human came along. And they were all dead, perfectly intact, besides the dozens of various flies and insects slowly eating them. About half of them were on the other side of the tunnel, and thus, about ten feet of sewer water away, sprawled out on the stone walkways flanking the waters.

It turned its head to the right, deeper down the tunnel, seeing some of those odd, glowing acid flies all busy melting a rodent the size of the human's head.

Greed and hunger warred with impatience.

The victor was clear in seconds.

It reached down, bit a rodent, shook off a bunch of the insects, flies, and various other weird crawling creatures that infested it to the best of its ability, and using its rather large teeth and its left hand, held onto the rodent, biting off large chunks of it at a time, brackish blood dripping down its chest.

The human jerked on its back, swatting at the air, and it twisted its head to the best of its ability, feeling how she was trying to mash her forehead into the back of its neck.

After a short moment of incomprehension, it realized the problem. Insects and open, fleshy holes. Not a great combination for the living. Or the dead. So the wolf extended two mucus veins to cover her eyes, making a squishy, slimy blindfold.

The human let out a strange grunt before gritting out a "Thanks" sound, and the wolf returned to its snacking.

Eating with human hands was *so much* easier. It could just hold on to the thing with one hand, twist it around however it wanted, and bite off chunks. Not having to waste half its eating time maneuvering or holding down its food against the floor was *so nice*. And it had to deal with much less dirt and waste on its already filthy food.

Maybe it should add a pair of long, thin, human hands, try to find someplace comfortable to tuck them into, keep them out of the way until it had to use them. It would be nice to be able to fiddle with human devices and hold on to its food like this once it changed its hands back into paws. Grappling with things in a fight would also be easier.

Another idea for the back burner.

Eating all the rodents in the tunnel would take way too long, so for once, despite its greed, the wolf darted to the ones that seemed the least bloated or chewed through, scarfing them down with impressive speed, feeling that soul-deep hunger be ever so slightly sated.

After the tenth of the fifty or so rodents it could feel, the wolf decided it was already wasting too much time, and reluctantly turned away from its free meal to quickly move down the tunnel.

Just a hundred or so feet down the square passage, it split into three different paths. To the right was an open door which led down to some kind of room that transitioned into a tunnel which gently curved around and under the sewer floods. In the middle, the tunnel simply continued, with no seeming end in sight. And to the left, just across the door, the tunnel split.

The possible exit to this place it had felt was somewhere to its left, so it quickly half ran to a rusty little bridge curving over the sewer waters below, the only "safe" way of crossing the sewer stream.

It was rusty beyond belief, but as the wolf tapped its knuckles against its base, it felt both thick and sturdy, so it quickly clambered up the two steps and made its way across.

"Wait, nonono! Wrong way! Turn around!" the human said in a hurried voice as she curled her body to the left to point behind them, her voice barely audible over the explosion's echoes and trickling waters. The wolf stopped in the middle of the bridge to briefly check its surroundings for threats.

Nothing. It wasn't sure why the human was getting worked up, but it didn't care at the moment.

Her protests to turn around grew ever more annoying as the wolf continued down the tunnels, trying to use her hand to grab its snout and turn its head around, tugging and pointing back with urgency.

But there was *nothing* behind them.

Frankly, she was starting to piss it off. But maybe she was hallucinating, so the wolf tried to be a little more patient than usual, only letting off warning growls and grumbles in reply to her constant pestering.

Until she grabbed onto its ear and tried to yank its head around.

It stopped in its tracks, a sharp snarl rumbling out of its chest, tensing in warning. Even if she couldn't hear the snarl, she would damn sure *feel it.*

The human's hand jerked back, a faint scent of fear in the air, quickly retreating. She mumbled something, sounding defeated, and *finally* seemed to give up, going limp against its back.

It curled its lips back down to cover its teeth and pushed forward, consciously deciding to forget about her annoying paranoia episode, or whatever that was.

The tunnel continued for a while, eventually starting to curve upward, the flat stone beneath its hands changing to carved steps. The rushing rivers and trash they carried raced past them as they quickly made their way up to the strange room it had felt.

It had quite a few encounters with stray packs of rodents, but they were barely worthy of note. It just had to wait until they were close and then sweep them aside into the water to be carried away by the stream. And if they were on the opposite side of the tunnel to its right, they would do it by themselves, throwing themselves into the water without thought.

The tunnel curved right after a couple hundred feet and started to slowly flatten, the slick stone turning flat once more. There were various random tunnels and doors along the way there, all leading to rooms seemingly designed to just . . . exist, empty and without purpose besides *maybe* being useful for taking shortcuts through the immense amount of stone around them, rather than following the tunnels. It didn't go into any of them.

It paused to punch the floor hard enough to wince, all of its antennae writhing against the floor. Its head shot up, ears rigidly pointing upward.

How did it not notice *that* before . . . ?

It activated [Echoes of Oblivion], making the human stiffen on its back, and lowered its chest, cautiously stalking forward, driven by both curiosity and confusion.

The door it was looking for was about a hundred and twenty feet ahead.

The strange, very vaguely humanoid creature hanging from the ceiling was about eighty feet away from both of them. So the wolf stalked forward, ears and antennae all focused on the ceiling and the thing clinging to it.

The closer it got, the clearer the image the vibrations gave it, and the more confused the wolf got.

It *was* a human. Its organs and limbs were roughly placed the same, just of different proportions, but the biggest giveaway was that it *was* wearing human coverings around one shoulder and its crotch, shredded and torn and little more than rags, but still there.

It was just . . .

Not quite right.

Its limbs and fingers were ridiculously long. Its arms were about as long as its entire body from toes to head. Its foot bones were squished together at the start and flared out unevenly the farther they got from the ankle, and its toes were multiple times as beefy and long as a normal human's. Its tendons were so thick that the wolf wondered how it was possible for this thing to *not* be a giant ball of muscle, and was in fact, somehow, absolutely *skeletal*.

Though considering it lived in a sewer without much food, that made sense in a way.

The distance closed, and the wolf very cautiously punched the stone, wary of drawing its attention but hungry to see more details about the oddity it'd stumbled upon.

Every few feet of distance drew more bizarre details to the wolf's attention.

Its ears were *huge*. Its face was disturbingly elongated and flat with a gigantic crooked mouth. Its eyes were just straight-up missing. The skin felt . . . very wrinkly and aged, like an elder human's, but not quite attached anywhere, loose around its form, and oddly thick. Its hair was there, matted, wild, and heavy, hanging down a foot off its perch.

Its teeth were pointed and jagged, with just a couple crusher teeth still remaining near its jaw. Said jawbone was also very malformed, half of it seemingly lumpy and twice as thick as its other side, and it tapered down to an almost sharp point. Its neck was a bit too long.

In fact, its spine was strange in general. It was more formed for an animal than a human, the face pointed forward rather than downward, and it was ridiculously thick, almost a third of its body's width.

The closer the wolf got, the more it noticed all the big and small parts of this *thing* that were wrong. And the more it felt its instincts push back against its desire to move forward.

It didn't feel like when that metal-headed dead human rushed to them.

This was a more subtle, nagging sensation, like it was getting close to something dangerous rather than pure death, even if it had no idea how its instincts decided that this creature was a genuine threat.

But it trusted them, so with the utmost caution, it stalked underneath it, ready to activate [Bloodrush] and make a run for it if something happened.

And something did happen, in the form of a rodent on the other side of the tunnel finding some kind of cockroach and charging it with one of its usual shrill screeches.

The wolf became statue still, its attention splitting between curiously feeling the bizarre way the humanoid creature hung onto the ceiling pipes to quickly and near silently shuffle across the ceiling, and the bridge just ahead of it that would take it to the other side of the tunnel.

It slowly and carefully moved toward the bridge, making sure it didn't kick some random trash in its path and draw attention, and doing its best to observe the scene going on at the other side of the tunnel, just ten feet away.

As it crossed the bridge and stepped off onto stone again, it turned its full attention to the humanlike creature, slowing its pace, too damn curious to leave just yet.

The rat was preoccupied with shredding the cockroach to bits, and the wolf felt the humanoid move itself to be hanging over it, positioning itself into an . . . almost ball-like shape.

A strange, barely audible whistling sound suddenly came out of the creature's lips, a soft sound that undulated with varying tones, almost like a soothing song.

It actually sounded quite nice.

It didn't seem to bother the rat nor have any real effect on it, but the humanoid tilted its head around in strange, erratic ways for a few short seconds, as if trying to catch some sound with its ears.

The wolf was really curious as to how this thing hunted, stopping entirely despite the door it had been looking for the entire time being just a couple dozen feet away. It was no less tense than before, ready to bolt and barrel through the rusty door should the need arise, but for the moment, it was stationary, all its attention focused on the extremely careful way the humanoid seemed to unfurl itself.

Its back legs' toes had hooked around the ceiling pipes, and the creature slowly let go with its arms, curling them into its chest as its torso hung down and its legs unfurled, ten feet of elongated, skeletal humanlike physique hanging over the rodent in the tunnel, the humanoid's size almost making the space feel cramped.

It slowly extended one of its ridiculously long arms to hover over the rodent chewing through the cockroach, and the wolf quickly calculated the distance, realizing what was going to happen.

Or so it thought.

It was expecting the creature to grasp onto the rat and calmly crush it to death before eating.

Instead, the lethargic humanoid's hand darted down to pluck the rat off the floor, and in the blink of an eye, brought the shrieking rodent to its mouth, headfirst, crushing half of it to paste and ripping off the other half with such speed that the sound of violently tearing flesh and fur filled the tunnel.

Enough for the human to hear it.

The wolf barely had a millisecond to realize what she was about to do when she extended her hand out of the shadows in the creature's direction, and by then, it was too late, a surge of mana filling the tunnel.

All three inhabitants of the tunnel froze.

The wolf simply sat still, hoping to go unnoticed. The humanoid creature stopped chewing and started tilting its head in strange ways. And the human was so unimaginably terrified that the wolf could feel her heartbeat thump into its rib cage through the mucus and fur, her horror so immense it choked out the scent of the sewer around them.

The human buried her face deeper into its fur, thankfully, muting her deep, terrified breaths in the inky mist of nothingness that veiled them.

A long, tense moment stretched in the silent tunnel as the wolf waited with bated breath.

And much to its immense relief, the creature seemed to lose interest in the mana surge after a couple seconds, returning back to its gored meal.

It tensely resumed its pace, hurried but careful, and as the creature was slowly left behind, the wolf felt it curl back up against the ceiling, idly hanging there. The distance made it breathe a little easier, and then it finally came up to the door it was looking for.

Getting through without making a racket and triggering the creature behind them into action was an exercise in patience.

It had to glue its side and left arm to the door's rusty hinges and carefully cut through the door's lock with precise cuts to make sure nothing fell on the floor, then hurriedly open the damn thing in the most awkward position it had ever been forced in.

And with that done, it dropped back on all fours and turned to the cubic staircase just before it.

It took half an hour of careful steps, occasionally clinging to the wall, and constantly checking that the creature behind them hadn't moved, but eventually, the wolf finally walked the last few rusty steps and turned to the right, its claws sinking through the grated metal floor beneath as it entered the room it had been looking for.

The smell was *horrific*. It was an absurdly potent miasma of chemicals, death, and human waste, all mixing together into something that burned its nostrils with each breath. It could *taste* the air. It had been able to smell this from down the tunnel, but it hadn't expected it to be so much *worse* just from climbing up a staircase and going through a door.

It growled in annoyance and yanked its claws out of the floor before blunting them, then deactivated [Echoes of Oblivion] and opened its eyes to observe the softly glowing room, bits of moss clinging to the smooth stone support pillars and the walls.

It was a simple circular room, about four hundred feet wide and a bit over a hundred feet tall, half of which was full of churning sewer waters. There were various pipes and holes along the walls, tilted upward and downward, throwing trash and waste into the muck, and a modest but mercifully sturdy metal bridge cut the room into two equal parts.

There were three gigantic metal doors at around the water's level, ones it knew from experience were meant to open to allow waste to rush through to the canals. Considering how the room wasn't filled to the brim with waste and water, they were still functional.

Beyond the door on the other side and a bit to the left, buried into the wall, was one of those pipes the humans used to pump smoke and such out of their factories, a particularly large one. And these usually pumped the smoke out into the open air. Which meant a clear exit out of here.

It tapped its knuckles on the bridge a few times, but it felt more than solid enough to carry them both without much issue. It was grated, but the metal was only rusted on the surface, and the grate was thick.

It hesitated to walk on the metal due to how difficult it was to properly feel the wider vibrations around it when it was touching such a bouncy material, but one quick glance around the semi-illuminated room convinced it there was nothing really around for it to be wary of.

So with great joy, it picked up speed, half running across the bridge, catching glimpses of the churning waters below through the railing on the side, occasionally glancing down to see the oddly disgusting and simultaneously beautiful sight of trash being consumed by softly glowing little grains of *something*. It looked like the glowing moss in color, but it was just . . . liquid.

The water's height was rather close to the bridge itself, about ten feet, so maybe if it wasn't saddled with the human, it might have been able to hop onto a stone pillar and dip its fingertips into the water to better observe the tiny motes of light.

The trickling of water was also oddly calming, and all in all, it felt like the depths of the human nest were almost congratulating it on finding a way out.

Shortly after thinking that, however, something changed.

As it continued its quick trot across the bridge, a light tingling sensation, something it couldn't quite place, started bothering it. It was like the brush of *something* against its mind, a faint huff of air at the back of its neck from something that shouldn't be there, like there was something watching it.

Its trot slowed, and the wolf lifted its head above the railing, craning its head around the room and even glancing behind it, all of its antennae writhing against the metal below its feet.

There was movement in the water all around the room, either from pipes adding more to the little pool of filth or just random bits being moved around by the almost circular current, but beyond that? Nothing.

It turned around, mentally dismissing the sensation, and resumed its walk, pointing its snout down to watch the pretty water.

A dark shape moved into the corner of its line of sight, barely visible through the murky, glowing depths. The wolf barely had the time to process that the shape seemed to be *changing* as it moved, before it twisted.

It didn't have any time to react beyond stiffening in surprise.

A green-black blur as thick as the human burst out of the waters and slammed into the side of the bridge with a sharp crack, the bent railing smashing into the wolf's side as the entire portion of bridge they were standing on detached with a metallic screech.

It spun through the air, its eyes barely catching a glimpse of crumpled metal hitting the water and a blurry mass sinking back into the murk, and then its chest slammed into the water, and it was wreathed in chemicals and filth in an instant, sinking.

The human struggled and choked on its back as the wolf tried to tightly close its eyes and nostrils to prevent the burning chemicals from entering its body, wildly swinging with its hands to try and reorient itself, to breach the surface, the human nothing but deadweight on its back.

It hurriedly detached her without any regard for conserving its mucus, for both their sake, and used [Pack Hunter]'s awareness to grab on to her arm and tug her up for a brief moment as the churning waters almost turned her upside down.

It wasn't sure if she could make it to the surface or even stay there, but it didn't have a second to even think about that when it was certain that something was in the water and wanted them in its stomach.

That impact had knocked the breath out of its lungs, so despite its body's Endurance allowing it to hold its breath for ages at this point, there *was* no breath to hold. It had to get up to the surface.

Its hands and paws pushed and brushed aside mucous filth, human waste, rotten fabrics, and who knew what else as it poured all of its strength into catapulting itself up, the thick waters making it feel twice as heavy as usual, human weight combined.

The worst part was suddenly being stripped of all its senses. It couldn't hear much of anything. Its eyes had to stay shut. Its nose would smell nothing but the acrid stench of chemicals. And its antennae—

As it breached the surface, finally, gasping in a giant breath and whipping its head around, it focused on its antennae as it treaded its hands through the water to stay afloat. The sensations were muted at best, and far too generally directed, but it *could* feel two sensations, a beating tempo of movements that disturbed the water far more than anything else.

The human, still underwater, struggling to get up with one arm only.

And something far larger quickly speeding toward her.

The wolf didn't have much time to make a decision before circumstance made its decision for it. It *could* just swim away, claw up the wall and go on to escape. A somewhat guaranteed path to survival.

And survival was all it had known until now. It hadn't known companionship; it hadn't known play. It hadn't known the feeling of a heart beating in sync with its own as they rested, the feeling of having a pack, however bizarre and small it might be. And the wolf enjoyed all of those things, didn't think it would ever gain them back if it lost them.

So . . . in truth, it *couldn't* just swim away.

It took a deep breath, allowing the mana cells to deal with any chemical poisons it might suck into its throat, and dove back into the murk.

The enemy was faster, but the wolf was closer.

It kicked and clawed at the water with its palms cupped like small shovels, and within just a few hurried pumps of its arms, it reached the human, who desperately extended a hand toward the wolf. It grasped her hand and yanked her up, using its strength to almost launch her over its head, as close to the surface as it could get her.

There was no way to know with any true accuracy where the enemy was, neither in direction nor distance. All it knew was that it was getting closer.

And thus, it was unprepared for the battering ram that slammed past the human, throwing her upward and away, a split second before it hit the wolf.

It curled its arms around its head as it activated [Bloodrush] and felt a steel vise made of teeth crush its torso, its organs pulling at its insides as its momentum went from zero to a hundred in an instant.

[Bloodrush] and its natural defenses prevented the massive teeth from puncturing more than one or two inches along its shoulders and waist, but the wolf couldn't focus on that when the pressure on its ribs was trying to force its breath out between gritted teeth, its collarbones fraying and bending dangerously as its shoulders tried to crush together from the overwhelming power.

It could barely move its arms, its forearms locked around its head by barbed teeth, but it did so anyway, ripping through and tearing its flesh open to reach for whatever it could, raking claws through its captor's maw and teeth with cramped movements, feeling the pressure of the waters increase with every passing second as it was dragged to the depths.

And then it was released with a wild jerk of its captor a short moment before something thin slammed into its chest in a diagonal, cracking the fibers of its rib cage into a frayed mess and forcing out a burst of air bubbles out of its snout.

Its back hit the floor, a squishy mess of trash and congealed filth.

It forced its way through the pain and confusion, the crushing pressure, twisting its body to set its limbs against the floor and kick up, trying to rise to the surface in a wild scramble, unable to fight back against its enemy whatsoever when in its own element.

The wolf barely made it three feet before something whipped through the water, and it was only due to knowing how that motion felt in vibrational senses that it managed to duck its head, the creature's appendage slamming into its left shoulder with a familiar pop which reverberated through its entire body a short moment before its snout and right shoulder smashed into the floor again, the cracking of its bone fibers almost audible.

It didn't take a human's intelligence for it to realize what its adversary was doing. It knew that the wolf needed air, and it knew the wolf could rake through its mouth if it tried biting onto it, so it'd decided to simply keep the wolf down until it choked to death.

Instincts had never failed the wolf thus far, so it listened to them once more. It punched its shoulder back into place and twisted around, hooking its claws into the floor. Squishy trash and congealed slime parted for its fingers until they hooked into stone. Curling its abdomen, it did the same with its back paws.

And with its chest brushing against the bottom, it began to run across the floor, hooking its claws with a precise, instinctual tempo of blunting them for grip and traction and sharpening them for release, almost zigzagging across the water.

It felt the vibrations of its enemy circling just above, waiting for the wolf to start trying to rise for air, and used this time to continue moving across the floor, dodging piles of trash and keeping to flat ground. It felt the human breach the surface of the water, swimming away from both the wolf and the creature with clumsy, one-armed paddling.

The wolf finally reached the support pillar it was looking for—a thick rod made of rock—and stopped paying attention to the human, reassured that she'd be fine as long as the wolf figured out a way to kill this thing.

It wasted no time, pushing off the floor and scrambling up the pillar.

The vibrations of its enemy grew frantic and stronger, likely realizing what it was doing.

But they also let the wolf know the rough direction of the creature, so it twisted around the pillar, waited for the vibrations to change direction a little, and continued changing its positioning, always keeping the pillar between itself and the aquatic predator, spinning around in frantic circles as it tried to breach the surface.

And then the vibrations grew too close, too wide, and it was only that faint prickle of danger in the back of its mind that made it instinctively flatten its body to the pillar and wrench its upper body to the side, feeling the water churn and flatten its fur as the creature's jaws snapped shut an inch from its fur with an audible snap.

The chase resumed, the creature circling in random patterns to try to grab on to the wolf. When that didn't work after its third attempt—which came even closer than the other two—it seemed to give up, instead going in a wide circle and slamming its tail into the pillar itself.

The impact was so strong, the wolf almost lost its grip from surprise, the entire pillar seemingly jumping by the force, the sound audible even through the water and the cartilage blocking its hearing to some extent. And as it resumed its mad scramble for air, it felt the cracks in the stone as it climbed past them.

Thankfully, it didn't do that again, the creature instead resuming its incessant, looping chase around the pillar, almost coiling around it as it blindly followed the wolf. Those brushes against the pillar gave the wolf a very vague image of what it was even fighting, and the image didn't give it much confidence in winning, by sheer dint of size alone.

Some kind of triangular head with a sharp bony point at the end, two almost humanlike short arms, and a long, *long* tapering body with a massive, vertically flat tail. It was almost thirty feet long from snout to tail, and the wolf had no idea how to kill it besides latching onto its head and scraping its brains out. Assuming it had a brain.

It finally broke out of the muck and gasped for air as it continued to scramble up the pillar, the vibrations in the water growing even more muted, and so it opened its eyes, despite the water entering them absolutely *burning* the outer protective layer.

And they did open—to a chorus of red lights flashing in and out of existence along the ceiling of the room, turning the green room yellow and back to green, a distant blaring horn filling the wolf with immense relief.

It had seen this before, and been swept away by it as well.

All it had to do was last long enough for the waters to drain into the canals and sweep away the creature.

Which was easier said than done, because the moment that realization and plan formed in its mind, the sound of bursting water and a prickle on the back of its mind made it once again throw its body to the side, trying to dodge whatever attack its adversary had thrown at it, simultaneously twisting its neck to try and get a visual on the creature.

What it saw instead was a black-green pointed snout as large as a human's entire body snap down on its tail.

In an instant, the wolf threw a hand down to try and cut its tail off at the base, but it was just a fraction of a second too slow. The creature violently jerked in a wide arc, assisted by its weight, and the wolf felt its fingers stretch and the joints snap as its nails were torn out of the stone, the vertebrae in its tail snapping apart from the wolf's weight as it swung in a wide arc.

It flew through the air with speed it had never felt before, feeling its side and shoulder smack into the water, making its body bounce off and violently spin for a brief moment before it hit the water again and tumbled through into the muck.

For a few seconds, it just kicked and writhed, disoriented beyond belief, unable to tell up from down as its brain bounced around in its skull. By the time it breached the surface to cough out the burning water in its throat and gasp in a breath, it saw the creature's dark form racing toward it through the glowing waters, closing the distance at a frantic pace.

Out of the corner of its eye, it saw the walls of the room curve toward it, and the wolf quickly turned around, coming face-to-face with the massive metal doors behind. It practically threw itself toward them, pawing at the water with all its strength, and set its hands onto the metal, hooking its claws and catapulting itself out of the water.

As its claws raked through as it scrambled up, a small shower of sparks hit its chest, something it was going to ignore as it twisted around to catch a glimpse of its pursuer. But a strange *fwoom* sound, accompanied by a sudden flash of orange light, made it jerk its head down, watching in surprise as flame suddenly raced out from its chest, covering its limbs in the span of a single shocked second.

A frenzied sense of panic clutched its heart in a vise as the fire flashed up to its snout in an instant, and the wolf yowled as agony burnt through its snout, hurriedly closing its eyes before twisting on the metal and diving down to the waters once more.

It felt the air crack past its mangled tail as its assailant's own tail smashed into the metal with a thundering clang, a strike it avoided by pure luck as it dove headfirst into the waters, the fire petering out of its fur in an instant.

Without any time to waste, it tried to grab on to the metal and continue the chase, continue to buy time, but its position was too awkward, its body and its surroundings too chaotic, its mind too panicked.

It only managed to clumsily hook two claws into the metal before it felt the creature's pointed snout rushing toward it.

With a jerky, uncontrolled movement, it threw its body deeper down with so much force it felt the muscles in its arms tear, twisting its chest to the side. The sharp point of its adversary's snout scraped against its ribs and cut a shallow rend through its side before it slammed into the metal behind the wolf.

And it finally saw an opportunity.

The wolf's arms grabbed onto the thing's snout, claws hooking into leath-erlike skin and steellike bone, and it hung on as the odd, snakelike creature started throwing its body in random directions, spasming and twisting in its attempts to buck it off.

It squeezed as much of its adrenaline sac as it dared to, feeling strength and vigor flood back into its body.

The water and trash tugged at the wolf like hooks sinking into its body and yanking it away with every sudden movement, its back paws struggling to find their way back to the beast's snout and carve through anything as its bottom half was simply swung around like a rag doll.

It had no idea where it was or what was happening; it simply held on, held its breath, and did its best to rake its back claws through its enemy's snout without losing its grip, clenching its snout as tight as it could to keep its breath in.

And then the beast's course suddenly grew straight and rigid, speeding through the waters straight down.

The pressure on its body grew to a familiar, all-encompassing crushing strength, and the wolf let go of its grip on the underside of the beast's jaw to hook its left hand's claws into the top of the thing's snout, allowing the pull of the water to drag its body down the length of its enemy's head, until it was at what it would consider to be the head's base. Then it blunted its claws and hooked its right hand ones at where its neck should be, roughly.

Unfortunately, the skin was so thick around the braincase and neck that the wolf could barely reach actual flesh, or at least that's what it felt from the few remaining antennae that hadn't snapped off yet.

The snakelike creature twisted away from its straight-down trajectory, doing so with an extremely tight turn which gave the wolf another heavy dose of motion sickness, and then it sped upward.

The wolf didn't waste the opportunity, using its hand to desperately cut through the odd skin around the creature's neck, shredding it with fast, frenzied rakes of its claws, hanging on with its left arm. [Bloodrush] faded, strength and toughness leaving its body.

And then the water's pressure vanished, and its eyes snapped open to a room full of burning water, the green glow seemingly gone entirely, replaced by a lake of fire extending out below them.

Its adversary leaned forward, giving the wolf a very panic-inducing look of the flame flashing up the thing's tail and straight toward it, and in that moment of distraction, unsure of what its opponent was even doing, it had no time nor any way to react when it snapped its entire body back like a whip.

A coiled mass of incredible weight and blinding speed slammed the wolf into stone, who let out a short, wheezy puff as its breath was forced out of its lungs, feeling the bone fibers in its rib cage snap and tear open like frayed rope. Its heart skipped a beat, then two, and as they began their descent back into the waters, the wolf was wreathed in flames.

It breathed in as best as it could through the mind-searing agony as its heart resumed beating, [Pain Resistance] being the only thing keeping it from succumbing to shock.

Its mind's last observation before it activated [Maddened Frenzy] was that the doors of the canals were finally opening.

And then it felt power. Pure ecstasy.

Fur turned to strings of marble, muscles to steel cables. The world slowed down as if in a hazy dream. Its senses exploded, feeling every inch of the waters and the tunnels beyond for hundreds of feet, the meat bag squirming under the water in the distance, the prey beneath its paws.

In the corner of its mind, it felt a million chains snap like strings, and it was finally free.

Free of inhibition, caution, sanity, and thought.

[Devourer] roared for blood and carnage, and the wolf roared with it, a snarling bark turned to rumbling thunder.

Its jaws stretched open as far as they could go and further, almost flattening on its prey's head, its jowls and muscles tearing, the jawbone dislocating, and as they fell, the wolf bit down between the eyes of its food, its canines hooking into its skull in a perfect grip, the scorching of the flames against its eyes and lips little more than a pleasant tingle.

With four limbs free, it didn't hesitate a millisecond.

Its claws dug into the thing's eyes, its tail wrapped around its throat, and it began clawing its outer armor to ribbons, barely noticing the change when they crashed back into the water.

It continued snarling out its air, jerking its head from side to side, opening the wound further, every frenzied rake of its claws crisscrossing with the next. And in the bloody whirlwind they caused as its prey bucked and twisted underwater, the doors opened, the current sweeping them away.

It didn't stop, the world spinning, flickering, from wild rushes of liquid to mists of liquid flame, feeling concrete slam into its back as its prey and itself tumbled down the flaming tunnel, carving off the creature's armor one little piece at a time, its feeble struggles simply making it more excited.

The grip it had on its skull fractured and broke between its teeth, the sharp points gouging out the flesh on the inside of its snout.

That unexpected snap almost managed to separate them, but the wolf hurriedly shoved two fingers into its prey's vacant right eye socket, making them tumble around each other for only a short few moments before the wolf forced itself back onto the creature's head, resuming its near relentless mauling as they crashed in and out of the flaming wave.

The wolf shoved the top part of its snout through its prey's left eye socket, biting through the thick bones and skin for a grip, then continued shredding its neck to ribbons with its left hand, forcing its right one through the eye socket, looking for its brain with uncaring, rapid thrusts, its back paws scraping through the skin on the thing's backside.

Its food tried to twist in every which way and direction, desperate to put the wolf in its jaws, even only grasp a single limb, to no avail. The wolf was too fast, too strong, too small.

Its right knuckles broke, the fingers flattening against its palm as it jammed its hand as deep as it could go into the spasming, roaring pile of meat's head, the socket just a bit too small to fit its wrist.

Its shoulder slammed into the bottom of the down-tilting tunnel, its elbows crushed beneath the weight of its food. Its body was torched and quenched repeatedly as they struggled for purchase, for domination, within a flaming tide of chemicals. It lasted an instant to the wolf, and an entire minute of near free-fall to the world.

It finally cut through the armor on the thing's neck, feeling the soft flesh beneath, and it flattened its fingers, thrusting them into the soft flesh and arteries below. It couldn't taste nor smell the blood, but it could feel the furious pump of its veins as they parted around its hand.

Its prey curled into a rough ball, its clawed, webbed feet trying to reach up to its neck to dig out the wolf's hand. Its rumbling roars were replaced with choked gurgles as the wolf breached into its neck, wiggling its claws and grasping onto the base of the thing's tongue, shredding it to a squishy mass of mutilated muscle. Savage glee raked through its body with a pleasant shiver, its charred fur spiking on its back; whatever wasn't melted together.

The tunnel tightened, the space for the fire to bloom lessened as the wolf continued to try and saw through the thing's neck. And then, without warning, they were falling, spinning in the air.

It didn't care where they were or where they would land.

It kept biting, scratching, bucking, and twisting on its prey's neck, trying to shove its clawed fingers into its brain, into its throat, tearing its flesh open one rake at a time. Seconds passed in what felt like minutes as a waterfall of liquid fire dumped them into the gargantuan canal below.

The frothing waters embraced their flaming forms once more, and they slammed through them to the bottom. Its prey landed chest first, several dozen bones snapping beneath the wolf's paws, and the wolf used the sudden impact to saw another inch through the thing's neck before the waters swept them out into the open air again, into the flames.

Their twirling mess of a fight continued, tumbling down the canal in a desperate brawl that grew more lethargic by the second as its prey slowly bled out from the giant hole in its neck.

The wolf's body was smashed into rock and lead more times than it could count, each impact sending jolts through its abused organs as the world spun and fractured around them, but the wolf felt nothing—wanted nothing but to kill its prey.

Something solid slammed into its prey's body, the impact sending them into an even more chaotic tumble that turned the wolf's lower body off its prey's back and onto its snout. As its prey saw an opportunity, it snapped its head to the side, its serrated teeth and steely jaws snapping onto the wolf's stomach, life entering the exhausted beast at the prospect of a chance to fight back.

The canal bent, a gentle curve, but with their momentum, they crashed onto the tilted sides like tumbling boulders. Without a single instance of rest, its prey bit down with every ounce of strength, its teeth only barely managing to dig an inch into the wolf's stonelike body as its shattered arms clawed at the stone, their bodies once more wreathed in flames as they met open air.

The prey tilted its head up as far as it could go, its tail pushing on the ground to lift its entrapped body ten feet into the air, and the wolf used its hold on the prey's flesh to readjust its claws to hold onto its skull, moving its jaws to bite around its food's eye socket with a rumbling, furious snarl.

A crack of thunder roiled out of its throat and exploded straight inside its prey's skull.

Through a single, half-functioning eye, it watched in mindless fury as a spray of gore and brain matter misted out into the open air from its other eye socket, the explosion backblasting into its own throat and rupturing a lung in the process as the air slammed through its body despite the wolf's attempt to twist its head around, an instinctual movement it didn't care to know the origins of.

The roof of its food's mouth burst, the explosion of air impacting the wolf's stomach and ripping its body out from the clutches of the creature's teeth in a spray of blood. The wolf tilted its body to the best of its ability, landing on its paws and rolling on the floor to dissipate the impact, its smoking form still flickering with errant bits of fire.

And then it was left without an enemy, but it had to cut, to rip, to tear and kill and devour and dominate something, *anything*.

It charged at its prey's twitching corpse before it even hit the ground and began clawing out pieces, shoveling them into its mouth or flinging them around the canal as it bit off chunks, barely pausing to breathe through the frothing blood in its throat as it sank into a feeding frenzy.

Even so, every one of its senses scanned for something alive to kill and hunt and break beneath its paws.

In the desolate silence of the human nest's fourth floor, however, there was nothing to kill, so the wolf continued its eating binge until [Maddened Frenzy] faded, and it collapsed in an instant as the boost disappeared, its mutilated, charred snout nestled deep into its prey's throat, the towering machinery all around them poised like gravestones spearing into the smog.

As its mind faded into unconsciousness, it idly noted that despite feeling like so much had changed about itself, the familiar sight of the open canals and the meaningless machinery of the abandoned floor remained the same, a grim welcome back to where its life began, the empty quiet of the fourth floor's canals a familiar background to its rest.

CHAPTER 31

She didn't have the time to process it, but as she dove beneath the burning surface of whatever the hell she was swimming in, she couldn't help but replay the moment in her mind.

Feeling her companion snap back like a whip, stop just as suddenly, and then just . . .

Vanish in the middle of falling.

She couldn't feel it, no matter how much she focused.

Was it dead? Just like that?

Was she next?

Eventually, her air began to run out, and so she surfaced, [Telemantic Construct] propelling her up, just long enough for a single gasp of air before she used it to push herself down just as the searing lick of flames against her skin was felt.

She then heard the faint groan of machinery through the sound of rushing waters and the deafening siren, through the mucus protecting the inside of her ears from the chemicals.

The water around her suddenly began pulling at her, and as she hurriedly threw mana into her surroundings, she felt the metal doors brush just a foot away from her shoulder, and she was catapulted forward, flanked by trash and the wispy plasma of fire lurking just above her.

She didn't fight the current; she just curled up into the best approximation of a ball she could make and allowed herself to race down, down, down.

Sometimes, her shoulders would break into the air, and fire would flash over her torn, gambeson-like shirt, and she'd throw herself just a bit deeper under the wave with [Telemantic Construct], holding her breath to the best of her abilities.

The tunnel wasn't steep. There was very little, if any, curving. It was deep enough for her to not slam herself into something solid.

Yet it was no smooth ride.

Bits and debris constantly slammed into her, nothing too big but sometimes heavy enough to bruise. Figuring out what direction was right and left, up and down, became nigh futile for the vast majority of her fall. She had to take a breath, she knew that, but even as her lungs tightened, she also knew that surfacing into the open air for a breath was a massive risk.

She was on the brink of panic by the time she managed to find an opportunity to do it, when she knew the height of the water, the height of the tunnel, where the fire was, and everything else she needed to know through a burst of mana.

But she was too disoriented.

Fire licked at the left side of her throat for a single long second as she rotated to the side instead of going down before she fixed her casting and threw herself below.

The burn was agonizing. It felt like a million ants were chewing a hole through her throat.

Half a minute felt like half a day of constant struggle for her orientation, for safety from the flames above, for her mental stamina.

And then the tunnel shrunk, the waters pushed forward with even more speed, and from one moment to the next, she was tumbling through the air, feeling a wild, violent spray of water hit her back, the tunnel cutting off without warning.

Fire flashed over her limbs for two long seconds, and she felt the skin of her left arm writhe from the heat, the rest of her adequately protected by remnants of her companion's slime. She didn't bother flailing, nor panicking. She'd already been face-to-face with death. She simply stayed in her roughly curled position, and the churning waters embraced her once more.

For a moment, as she peacefully drifted down the strangely still waters—exhausted, frustrated, on the edge of despair—she was tempted to just continue to sink. To just let the water in. To just give up.

Then the waters she'd been in for so long mixed with something hotter, warmer, and she writhed in agony with a burbling cry, feeling something hotter than fire eating through her skin. A wild series of mana constructs propelled her out into the open air, meeting soft foam instead of flame, but the water continued to boil her alive, a pain worse than any fire.

Through the slime in her ears and the self-loathing whisper in her mind telling her to dive back down, she heard voices, human ones, yelling and hollering somewhere to her right, and without a second thought, she paddled through a sea of foam and churning, bubbling chemicals, wild bursts of mana along her torso and aching legs making her cut through the waters like a fish, a panicked, spinning, boiling fish who was spitting foam out of its mouth as it tried not to waste its breath with screaming.

Their voices grew closer, more aggressive, but she didn't care, nor was she capable of comprehending words at the moment, gasping for breath and trying to wrestle her own body under control to properly paddle to safety. Wild bursts of mana continued to propel her, making her tumble through the water, straight toward the voices, until eventually, her right shoulder impacted stone with bruising force, her body crumpling upon chem-slick stairs.

She twisted, clawing up with agonized gasps, wriggling like a worm, her body twitching and spasming without her input, every scrape of her greaves against the stairs accompanied by pulsing, white-hot shards of agony.

The voices continued, growing more and more heated.

Soft, hurried footsteps rushed toward her.

Two gloved hands, small, like a child's, grasped onto her hand and pulled with a growling grunt before one of them let go of her gaunt wrist, fisting into her shredded shirt's nape and pulling her onto dry, flat ground.

As she lay there, hyperventilating and spasming, two small hands brushed aside her melting hair, and two gloved fingers jammed into her lips, pulling her mouth open.

The familiar pungent taste of a healing potion on her tongue ceased any attempts she was about to make to pull away, and she greedily clamped down on the vial with her teeth, gulping as fast as she could. The searing chemical claws flaying her skin retreated just enough for her world to be more than agony and noise.

Then something slammed into her cheek, whipping her head to the other side, and the vial's top broke into her mouth, the rest of it clattering away onto the stone. The distant noises turned into the distinct sounds of a heated argument as the side of her head rested against cold, smooth stone, dazed.

"The hell are you wastin' healing potions on dead meat for, huh!?" a voice above her hollered. The sound of a meaty thud accompanied a yipped croak and the sound of fabric hitting stone.

She spit out the broken top, coughing weakly as she tried to regain her bearings. A pulse of mana from her hand provided an image that made no sense.

A guard loomed to her right, hunched over, his hand fisted in a cowering goblin's hair as she lay sprawled out on the ground, a club held in a tight grip on his other hand.

A stone walkway that transitioned into stairs, most of which were under the waters. The usable part was just fifteen feet wide, flanking the pool of chemicals at her back, ending just twenty feet to her right.

And just to her left, an extremely irate man in a worker's uniform was arguing with another guard, something about a curfew, their body language on the brink of violence.

Then the man's head turned, and she *felt* his teeth grit, his brows furrow.

"Don't you touch my property, you jumped-up, rat-fucking maggot!" he screamed, his spittle flying through her mana, taking a step toward the guard to her right.

The other guard didn't waste a single moment to swing his club at the man with a sharp crack at his ribs, and as violence erupted, it wasn't so much a fight as it was a beatdown.

She rasped out wheezy breaths, still twitching and shuddering in agony, bits of foaming spit trickling out onto the stone below her half-melted, chewed-through lips. The healing potion's merciful numbness receded, and she let out a strangled gurgle of agony as she felt the regeneration fade, the chemicals continuing to chew through her skin, melting her alive.

The uncaring steps of the second guard rushed past her to join the first, and as she wheezed and twitched on the floor, the man's yells turned to coughing, to agonized wheezing, then to silence one meaty thud at a time as he was beaten into the floor.

One of the guards spit out loud, and she didn't dare use her mana on them, trying to stay as silent and motionless as she could manage, gritting her teeth into dust as [Pain Resistance] leveled up, allowing her another moment of evading their attention.

"Tsk, the people on this floor are ridiculous. Nobody fucking listens. On the second, at least they know their fucking place. Nothing but disgusting fucking gutter rats down here," a gruff voice said—the one who'd kicked her.

Another meaty thud, without reaction.

"I'm with you, but I . . . think you killed the guy. This is kind of bad, isn't it?" the second guard asked, a more hesitant, ratty voice.

"Eh, not really. Nobody will care about a random dude disappearing." The gruff voice snorted. "Go strip the goblin for me while I toss this guy into the sump, will you? I'm taking dibs on first round."

"Let me go first *one* goddamn time. I don't wanna shove my dick in a used hole," the second guard complained as he walked back toward the goblin.

Her nerves continued misfiring like fried wires, feeling like a blender made of a million blades was scraping her flesh off. She could do nothing but force a hissed, wet croak between gritted teeth, feeling foaming spittle exit her mouth as her abdomen and chest convulsed.

She wanted to laugh.

No, she wanted to fucking cackle.

All her hopes of rescue amounted to this.

The man walked past her, and she let out a small burst of mana, feeling the way the goblin seemed to realize her fate, crawling back, her head snapping around for an escape that wasn't there.

Her skin flashed between searing heat and spine-chilling cold, and she could do nothing but feel a shard of glass be ground to dust between her teeth as she clenched her jaw.

"Then use the back once I'm done. Unless you wanna fight me on it?" the first guard replied rhetorically, and she suppressed the bubbling laughter, the nausea, the bile rising up her throat, the rage.

An audible, rough heave of effort, and something splashed into the sump.

The man didn't wake up as the hissing waters drew him to their depths, and never would.

Just like that.

She sent out light pulses of mana again, as inconspicuously as she could, feeling with phantom fingers as the second guard—a skinny, gaunt man—used a knife to cut through the goblin's clothes as he held her down by the throat, growling threats at her whenever the poor thing wriggled too much.

It felt like she was holding his hand as he cut through the goblin's belt.

If she let her mind wander, searching for an escape, she could almost feel his hands turning to steel, the goblin's hair turning into wolven fur, holding hydraulic claws within her mana as they slammed into the wolf's chest.

A friend that might not even be alive anymore.

The first, bulky guard walked past her, and she felt him give her a side-glance before continuing, entirely uncaring, crouching by the stripped goblin.

The chemicals seared her nose and clawed at her throat with every breath, lit her neck on fire with every pulse of her blood, slowly gouged out her flesh as she lay on the ground.

She was dying, within and without.

A memory came to her—one of comfort, of how it felt to drink the wolf's blood. That feeling of invincibility, of the world being vivid and clear despite her lack of sight. The warmth of power raising goose bumps on her skin, soothing the weakness within her as it flooded her gaunt limbs. The sensation of feeling every single strand of her clothes brush against her skin, hearing her heartbeat, feeling the rush of blood move within her. That comforting certainty that she could bend an iron pipe with her grip alone.

Blood.

Blood, that taste of copper and life.

She needed blood.

A fistful of mana washed over the ongoing scene just a few feet to her right.

She felt the position of their weapons, the strength of their builds, the stability of their positions. She felt how the thinner man turned around and crouched down on his haunches to stare out into the frothing sump; how the stout, taller man tried to maneuver the goblin into position, his pants around his knees.

A choked series of convulsions wracked through her chest as she fought to keep the hysterical laughter down.

She wanted to be rescued. She'd expected it when she swam toward civilization. Another strike of naivete; a subconscious thought that people, out of the goodness of their heart, would help. That was just like her. Always naive. Always expecting better of people for no reason.

There was no rescue, and there was no one to help her. Nobody human.

Not when she'd lain crying face down in an inn bed, rope marks around her wrists. Not when crushed beneath gnawing teeth and fur. Not in the tunnels. And most certainly, not now. Because there was no one but herself to rely on anymore.

The wolf was gone.

So she would save herself. She'd take what she needed from those who couldn't stop her.

The croaking cries of the goblin heightened while she wriggled and twisted under the increasingly irate guard as Emhreeil's mana faded from the air.

Her twitching fingers curled into a fist, her fingernails digging into her hand.

Blood dripped onto the stone from crescent cuts in her palm as she drew her arm in, pressing her knuckles into the floor, and began pushing down, lifting her uncooperative body, utterly confident that nobody was glancing her way, any sound her shuffling made being drowned out by the hissing waters and the struggle just teen feet away.

Constructs of mana, turned to physical force, braced around her legs.

Every drop of mana inside her body was converted into power for a single cast of [Haste].

The world turned to acrid glue.

She felt every fiber of muscle. Every tear, every tiny injury. Every contraction. The complex mechanisms of bone and flesh and tendon as she flexed her ankles, fighting to balance her body as she dragged herself upright. The way the shards of bone in her legs, half healed and connected with fragile tissue, flexed and ground precariously as she stabilized.

Her head limply hung from a neck without strength, chin to collarbone.

A small surge of mana left her fist, washing over the scene to her right. A sickening scene; one that almost symbolically embodied exactly what her experience in the Dungeon had been like so far.

The goblin was giving the guard hell, at least, bucking and twisting constantly despite his bruising grip, his snarled threats. His heartbeat was so loud, his frustration pumping more blood into the vein on his forehead than the one in his dick.

It was a sickening scene.

But it was also fucking hilarious to her, for some reason she couldn't understand.

A broken, mangled imitation of a laugh finally left her bleeding lips, turned into a hysterical rasping cackle as her lips curled into a face-splitting smile filled with rapidly clicking teeth, her jaw twitching and gnashing as her muscles fought the searing poison.

The guards jerked in surprise, tried to turn.

Much too slowly.

From an eyeless visage, she glared with hatred, dashing forward in an instant, her fingers unwinding. It was clumsy—her right leg buckled with a random spasm, forcing her to slam her knee into the rock and use it like it was her ankle to continue her momentum—but her aim was true.

With [Mana Touch] giving her an accurate feeling of everything around her, it was hard to miss.

Her cupped hand slammed into the guard's ear, his head half turned toward her.

A [Sparkburst] burst through his eardrum and popped his head like a melon, a wild mass of sparks, smoking brain matter, misty blood, bits of bone, and viscera flying through the air in all directions.

For her audience, it happened in less than the blink of an eye. For her, it was a process. A process of feeling the sparks annihilate his eardrum, gather in his cranium, turn his brain to mush, and blow through the skull with a million little explosions that vaporized or separated everything in their path into fine bits.

She "watched" in slow motion, felt every tiny piece and blood drop flow through her phantom fingers; every tiny piece of gore and blood that splashed onto her face and arm an intimate understanding of what she'd just done.

She thought she'd feel some kind of revulsion, disgust, guilt.

All she felt as her hand dashed down to grab his club with superhuman speed, was catharsis.

She felt the man's body ripple from the force, from his neck to his legs, the explosive power and the smack of her palm sending him tumbling off the goblin before the first drop of blood had hit the stone.

As she used her left leg and [Telemantic Construct] to forcefully halt her momentum before she tumbled over the goblin and the corpse, her fingers clutched around the base of a metal club, she turned with all her strength, all the added Speed, feeling individual muscle fibers tear from the violent motion, and whipped her arm around to the left in a wide swing, spinning on her right knee.

The second guard, still half crouched, awkwardly half turned toward where she was a moment ago with wide green eyes, one hand fumbling for his club, had no time to react.

The moment the club left her hand, she shot a short, explosive burst of [Telemantic Construct] outward from her palm to add to its momentum, using the last shred of the mana in her core. She hadn't aimed at all. She didn't know where she was even throwing it, her fingers numb and barely functional. All she had was an intimate feeling of where everything around her was.

It was a perfect throw.

It didn't slam into his face as much as it slammed *through* from the side.

The handguard cracked through his eye socket, and the club landed across his eyes with a guttural snap and a popping sound, blood and viscera bursting into the open air, the club embedded into his face for a solid inch, his face caved-in like paper.

His head whipped back violently as the club's momentum carried it out of his face and into the sump, and with her balance lost, they both tumbled to the ground, slaves to gravity and momentum.

She tried to catch herself with a hand, but it crumbled with barely any resistance, her stomach convulsing with choked giggles. Her right shoulder hit the stone, then her chest, and the left side of her face followed.

For a moment, she stayed there, trying to fight through the agony, wheezing giggles being forced out of her convulsing body as she tried to stop the laughter and breathe, put some air into her abused lungs. Her attention turned to the cut belt next to her foot, the singular healing potion still sitting in a fabric sheath, and with a weak burst of mana, it tumbled next to her waist.

Lethargically, she wrapped spasming fingers around the frayed, cut end of the belt and dragged it above her head. She grabbed onto the vial's sheath and clamped her teeth around the top, throwing the belt aside and quickly uncorking the vial with her shivering jaw clamped tight around the wood, spitting it out and shoving the vial's top back between her teeth.

For a moment, she simply held the bottle in place, hatred and adrenaline funneling out of her system for a brief moment.

It was the simple act of drinking something that wasn't the wolf's blood.

Her giggles mixed in with an ugly sob, some vague spark of hope in the back of her mind being the only thing that prevented her from crumpling to the ground and staying there to wail her eyes out.

With stuttering breaths and choked, coughing sounds that could barely be identified as any sort of sound of amusement, much less laughter, she tightened her jaw, ground her bloodied fist onto the ground, and lurched to the right, over the stump of her right arm, rolling onto her back.

As the slimy, thick taste of a hundred different things washed over her tongue and down her throat, she simply tried to keep it all down, one gulp at a time, fighting through the nausea in her stomach, through the pain and the hysterical laughter trying to bubble out of her throat again.

The temperature slowly fixed itself with every gulp, no longer flashing between ice cold and flame hot, new skin and scar tissue growing under her sloughing skin, like a snake shedding its hide. Strange shocks of electricity, nerves misfiring—it all faded.

She still heard two heartbeats that weren't her own.

As the morbid amusement of the situation faded, the vial ran out, so she turned her head to spit it out onto the ground and swallowed, her chest heaving with deep, wheezy breaths.

Breaths that dragged out endlessly, each inhale and exhale feeling like it was drawn out for ages.

Outside of action, high Perception seemed more like an annoyance. A maddening annoyance.

Or at least, something she had no idea how to reduce.

The world still felt like moving through half-dried glue. She wanted to rip her clothes off and peel off her skin because it was scarred and didn't move right against her muscle fibers and the scant amounts of fat she could feel on her body. She could feel the tiny motes of poison sinking into her lungs with every breath, clinging to the tissue within. Every tiny imperfection was laid bare and felt, judged by her own mind.

She brushed it all aside, once again swinging herself onto her front, torn muscles and melted skin finally repaired, the agony halved to a constant, throbbing pain.

With a growling grunt, she forced her knees below her belly, forcing [Telemantic Construct] to form two braces around her half-broken legs once more, feeling her core slowly drain what she had deemed as her reserve mana with every passing second.

She pushed down with her fist and used the momentum of her torso to swing herself up, staggering in place. Without using her Speed bonus, every motion felt like moving through sludge. The world was just too slow.

But it wasn't like she could balance herself by going faster, so she endured for a few seconds, fixing her center of balance to the best of her ability, focusing on the man dying just a few feet away.

She felt no remorse as she stumbled atop him and unsheathed his knife.

She felt no disgust as she cut a clean incision into the side of his neck, right against his fading pulse, and held his bloody hair in her clenched fist as she drank, and drank, and drank. The taste was so much more vivid, the sensation of the slimy liquid running down her throat so much more soothing.

She felt no shame as she stripped her melted, torched, torn rags off her body. Shed what felt like a thousand days of suffering and companionship off her frame. Removed the metal cages around her legs and clothed herself in the underclothes of the man she'd just killed, in the audience of a single horrified goblin frozen in fear at the edge of the platform just a foot away from the sump, as far as she could retreat.

As the [Haste] boost faded and the world returned to normalcy, she took a deep breath, feeling the energy and strength that had infused her limbs.

It was pathetic, compared to a single mouthful of the wolf's blood.

But the wolf was gone. Maybe dead, maybe not. Even if that thought felt like nothing but a coping mechanism, it was the one shred of hope she refused to let go of.

She'd search every corner of this oversize hellhole before she gave up.

A light pulse of mana drew her attention to the still-warm corpse of the burlier guard. She picked up the compass and the golem core off the ground, shoving them into her new pants' pockets—golem core to her left hip, and magic compass in the left knee's pocket. She sheathed her new knife—seven inches of well-forged steel—on her new belt.

She leaned back on her knees, fully aware of the precarious way her half-healed leg bones strained as she shifted her weight, letting her head hang backward, staring up at nothing.

The ambient scent of rot, death, and chemicals filled the air, thick enough to taste, to feel against her nostrils. The sound of roaring, rushing liquids continued, one tunnel spewing one thing, while another spewed something different. An alarm turned off.

She was exhausted. Mentally, emotionally, physically.

She felt numb as she forced herself upright, staggering and gritting her teeth through the pain racing up and down her legs. The healing potions hadn't healed them enough to put all that much stress on them.

With her mana regeneration, she could employ a semipermanent brace of mana, so she did. Casting [Mana Conduit] as soon as it was off its cooldown period was as automatic as breathing by now. Two perfect tubes conformed to her legs and flattened her pants against her gaunt limbs.

She shuffled over to the second guard and lowered herself down, straddling his midriff as she turned off the constructs. Hacked open one wrist, drank, then did the same with the other, a thin trail of crimson running down her throat from the side of her mouth and onto her chest and ribs, staining her new shirt.

She sucked everything she could get out of the cooling corpse, then turned to leave, bracing her legs for the painful process of getting up, palm on her left knee.

And she paused, turning her head a little to the side by sheer habit, sending a weak pulse of mana out toward the goblin. Shivering in fear, cold, trying her absolute best to limit her breathing, pretend she didn't exist, hide from her. Wearing nothing but two worn rags around her feet and two grimy little gloves.

She once would have called people who did the things she'd done here monsters. And it was an assessment she couldn't refute.

Even if she was a monster, however, that didn't mean she had to be a monster about it, did it?

She carefully peeled off the guard's jacket, an exhausting, frustrating endeavor that took her several minutes. It took several more to use the knife to scrape off the badges and insignia, cutting off pieces of reinforced cloth or messing up a sewing job by scraping the tip in X shapes continuously.

Putting the jacket on herself, one armed, was much less frustrating than she had thought it would be. Removing the shirt from the burly guard's corpse was much easier than the jacket.

She only held the oversize shirt in her hand for a moment, phantom fingers feeling the fibers, the crust of blood on the collar.

Without turning, she balled it up as best as she could, tossed it at the goblin's feet, and turned around, staggering down the pathway.

She didn't know where she was going, and she didn't put much thought into it. The poison in the air felt like it was choking her through the regeneration, through the remnants of the healing potion in her body.

Stone turned to metal stairs; metal stairs to empty walkways within silent hallways, free of poison.

It still ate away at her, regardless. She didn't know how she felt it, but she did. It was a sense of wrongness in her lungs that traveled up to her head.

Her mana lessened with each step, so she turned off the constructs, her pace slowing further in exchange for sight. She went up a cubic staircase that she could barely climb without falling, then she heard the faint sound of small, muffled footsteps rapidly getting closer.

She sent a pulse of mana behind her, bracing herself against the wall with a fist, feeling dizzy, like her head was stuffed full of cotton.

The goblin girl padded behind her, clad in the oversize, bloody shirt, wearing it like a dress, before stopping some six odd feet away.

She didn't have the energy to question why she was following her, so she didn't, instead pushing off the wall and continuing to stagger meaninglessly through the metal hallways.

Minutes passed in what felt like seconds, a vague, dizzy fugue of activity.

A slight tug at her jacket forced some notion of awareness back into her mind, and she stopped, half stumbling in place as she sent a weak blast of mana around her.

The goblin was holding on to the empty sleeve with her left hand, the right pointing down a corridor she was about to walk past, jabbing at the air insistently while simultaneously looking tense enough to bolt at the slightest hint of aggression.

She just turned and followed wherever the goblin led her to.

It gibbered at her, shaking her awake whenever she'd start keeling over from exhaustion, barely perceptible bursts of mana giving her enough of a mental picture to avoid stumbling into anything.

Her mind wandered off to topics unrelated—hopes and dreams, comforting and discomforting memories. Like a snapshot between each one, she'd realize she was in a completely different place than before, but she could hardly care.

Then she walked through another door, exhausted, and felt the metal and stone walls give way for cobbled stone beneath her new boots, an open expanse around her she could not feel. Without the goblin hanging on to her sleeve anymore, she continued blindly into the Dungeon, easily recognizing the third floor's decrepit depths.

She'd likely landed in some waste processing facility. She hoped the wolf had as well.

Before long, the fog in her mind grew too much, noises and voices muddling and sticking together like glue, melting into an incomprehensible mess. Her legs buckled, and she only made the barest effort to not land face-first on the ground, the gibbering croaks of the goblin growing frantic, pulling and tugging at her.

A hazy memory of her curled up on her bed with Katherine awkwardly sitting by her side as she taught her how to read surfaced, and she replayed it in full, a little smile pulling at her lips. It might have lasted an hour or a minute, but as the memory faded, she felt hands, human ones, turn her over onto her back; arms hooking under her frame and carrying her away, hushed voices in her ears.

She was too tired to know if she was in a dream or reality anymore.

She brought up the System screen, almost an afterthought, brushing aside the level-ups and updates in favor of simply *seeing* something rather than feeling it.

And stared in exhausted, mute amusement at the empty space where Kindhearted used to be, her head lolling around in time with the people's movements.

-Species: Humanoid
-Race: Elf
-Name: Embreeil
-Path: [Infuser] Level 17

-Available Attribute Points: 4
-Base Attributes:

Strength (+0)
Speed (+0)
Dexterity (+0)
Endurance (+3)
Perception (+2)
Resolve (+2)
Intelligence (+4)
Soul (+2)

-Racial Skills: [Attuned], [Quick Learner]
-Acquired Skills:
[Magic Resistance - Level 5]
[Mental Resistance - Level 6]
[Poison Resistance - Level 13]
[Pain Resistance - Level 24]
[Illumina - Level 8]
[Sparkburst - Level 19]
[Haste - Level 20]
[Mana Perception - Level 23]
[Mana Manipulation - Level 25]
[Mana Tank - Level 8]
[Mana Conduit - Level 8]
[Mana Touch] - Level 10]
[Tough Skin - Level 7]
[Infection Resistance - Level 4]
[Disease Resistance - Level 2]
[Telemantic Construct - Level 15]
[Iron Stomach – Level 1]
[Soul Perception – Level 1]

-Acquired Traits:
Vampiric (2/2): You have sustained yourself on nothing but blood for many days and have taken many steps toward the path of vampirism. Blood is extremely palatable, sustains you as well as any food, severely hastens your natural healing and stamina recovery, and drinking the blood of others gives you a temporary boost to all Attributes. Healing, stamina recovery, and the duration and strength of the Attribute boost depends on the amount of blood you have consumed and its quality.

Enduring (1/5): You have felt the chill of death multiple times and survived. You are slightly tougher.

She fell asleep dreaming of wrinkled hands tugging off her clothes, whispers of sound, and the scent of medicine and herbs all around her as the letters faded from her mind.

ABOUT THE AUTHOR

SomeoneToForget is a LitRPG author whose debut series, Fleabag, was originally released on Royal Road. He writes to inspire in his readers the childish glee and wonder he has always felt upon discovering and immersing himself in new stories, and hopes his own stories will not soon be forgotten.